T0372968

A
LETTER
FROM THE
LONESOME
SHORE

By Sylvie Cathrall

The Sunken Archive
A Letter to the Luminous Deep
A Letter from the Lonesome Shore

SYLVIE CATHRALL

A LETTER FROM THE LONESOME SHORE

orbit-books.co.uk

ORBIT

First published in Great Britain in 2025 by Orbit

1 3 5 7 9 10 8 6 4 2

Copyright © 2025 by Sylvie Cathrall

The moral right of the author has been asserted.

Illustrations by Raxenne Maniquiz

A CIP catalogue record for this book
is available from the British Library.

Hardback ISBN 978-0-356-52374-3
C format ISBN 978-0-356-52373-6

Typeset in Granjon by M Rules
Printed and bound in Great Britain by Clays Ltd, Elcograf S.p.A.

Papers used by Orbit are from well-managed forests
and other responsible sources.

MIX
Paper | Supporting
responsible forestry
FSC
www.fsc.org   FSC® C104740

Orbit
An imprint of
Little, Brown Book Group
Carmelite House
50 Victoria Embankment
London EC4Y 0DZ

An Hachette UK Company
www.hachette.co.uk

orbit-books.co.uk

To J., again, for braving the abyss and bringing me back ashore.

*(I hope everyone else reading this dedication
will choose to interpret it literally.)*

Prologue

DRAFT BRIEFING FOR THE CREW OF THE *PERSPICACITY*, JOINTLY AUTHORED BY SOPHY CIDNORGHE AND VYERIN CLEL, YEAR 1003

To our future crewmates,

It is our pleasure to welcome you aboard the *Perspicacity*! The purpose of this briefing is to provide some context for our mission, which is quite unlike any other. What we aim to accomplish may well be impossible. Without colleagues like you, it certainly would be unthinkable! Consequently, we – Sophy Cidnorghe and Captain Vyerin Clel, that is – could not be more thrilled and grateful to have you with us.

(I don't imagine anyone will believe for a moment that *I* had a hand in writing the above paragraph. Especially with that final sentence as it is. – V.)

(Are you *not* grateful for their participation, Vy? We've been trying to secure our crew for the better part of a year! – S.)

(I am grateful, but certainly not thrilled. I've grown quite accustomed to peace and quiet aboard my vessel. But I suppose I can endure the company. For Henerey's sake. – V.)

Surely you must wonder who we are and why we decided to embark upon an independent expedition without official support from any Campus! (Considering the sensitive nature of said expedition, however, we do request that you refrain from sharing the contents of this briefing.)

Sophy Cidnorghe is an unaffiliated cartographer and former Scholar of Wayfinding from Boundless Campus. In Year 1002, Sophy participated in the first fully staffed survey of the ocean's depths: more commonly known as the "Ridge expedition". Sophy and her colleagues – Scholars Eliniea Hayve Forghe (now Cidnorghe, as you'll see on our ship's roster), Ylaret Tamseln, Irye Rux, Vincenebras, and, eventually, Tevn Winiver Mawr – encountered mysteries in the abyss that were never fully revealed to the Scholarly public at large. After contending with eerie underwater sounds and massive sea creatures, the Ridge researchers made the oddest discovery of all: a ruined Antepelagic passageway, deep in the ocean, that led to a luminous chamber inhabited by the sort of sea-woman one might find in a Fantasy. This sea-woman, apparently acquainted with Scholar Mawr, alleged that she could help the assembled researchers "escape" to someplace – but then promptly transformed into *sound* before her claims could be investigated thoroughly. Upon returning to their research station, the crew realised their entire mission had been orchestrated by Chancellor Orelith Rawsel for the purpose of finding that very sea-woman – for reasons he would not explain. In protest of Rawsel's deception, the entire crew resigned from their positions as Scholars!

(On second thought, perhaps it would be more prudent to omit those Ridge details entirely. Our crew doesn't really need to read all that old history, do they? – S.)

(Even if they did, I suspect they wouldn't believe it. – V.)

(I hardly believe it myself! – S.)

Co-leading this expedition at the helm of the *Perspicacity* is Captain Vyerin Clel, one of the finest Navigators living and working today. *The Intertidal Campus Current* once described him as "the wittiest man on the water". In Year 1000, he received the esteemed "Medal of Magnanimity" for his tireless generosity of spirit.

(Sophy. Wherever did you find that immensely questionable biography of me? – V.)

(I asked your very own husband to supply me with one! – S.)

(As I feared. For the record, that line from the *Current* was penned by Reiv himself, as part of our wedding announcement. He also awarded me the medal as a birthday present. It's nothing more than a sentimental piece of nonsense. *Please* replace with something more reasonable, such as the following: "Vyerin Clel is a husband, father, and brother. He also knows his way around a boat or two." – V.)

(I suppose that "sentimental piece of nonsense" is the selfsame pin you've worn upon your cap for as long as I've known you? – S.)

Our friendship developed, rather unexpectedly, in the aftermath of a great tragedy. Well over a year ago, the historic underwater home known as the Deep House was destroyed by what was generally understood to be a rogue sea-quake. At the time, we feared the calamity claimed the lives of our respective siblings – E. Cidnosin and Henerey Clel.

(Vy, do you reckon I described the familial situation clearly enough? It's awfully awkward to explain. Every time I try to tell the story to a new acquaintance, they end up misunderstanding and assuming you and I are also siblings, somehow. – S.)

(You have, of late, spent far more time with me than with your own brother ... – V.)

After studying the letters Henerey and E. exchanged (yes, old-fashioned *letters* – as our siblings vanished just before Automated Post technology became so widely available last year!), we made an astonishing discovery. E. and Henerey did not simply vanish in a random accident. In actuality, they boarded a depth-craft that Henerey borrowed from his research colleagues, and, we believe, travelled to someplace else entirely. (More on that in a moment!)

Consequently, they may well still be alive.

(Ought I to mention that they were in love? – S.)

(I reckon that goes without saying. – V.)

3

E. had been vexed for tides about a strange object – which she called "the Structure" – that appeared out of nowhere in the Deep House's undergarden. With Henerey's assistance, E. determined that the Structure was, in fact, ancient Antepelagic technology, presumably lost to the waves a thousand years ago when the doomed cities of the Upward Archipelago plummeted from the heavens. But what was this Structure's purpose?

Thanks to the unlikely involvement of Scholar Jeime Alestarre, E. was able to form a hypothesis. It seems the Structure's emergence near the Deep House was no coincidence. E. and Sophy's mother, Amiele Cidnosin, constructed their family home in that specific location precisely because she believed such an object would appear there one day – a conclusion she based on the prognostications of a secret society known as the Fleet. According to the Fleet, the Structure was an example of an "Entry": a doorway created by the inhabitants of some hidden civilisation to transport people from our world into a refuge of sorts. The Fleet's teachings also spoke of "Envoys": peculiar, powerful beings sent to guide us to the Entries (like the sea-woman Sophy and her colleagues found at the Ridge). Before the dissolution of their society, the Fleet spent their days predicting the potential appearances of Entries like the Structure and . . . writing poems about them, apparently. Doesn't it all sound rather unbelievable?

Well, E. was rather open to the concept of unbelievable occurrences – as she'd recently survived one herself. Her letters to Henerey revealed how the Structure conveyed E. to an island in a sea unlike any she'd seen before. She returned home with waterlogged sketches in her pockets as proof and the perplexing nature of her travel weighing heavily upon her mind. E. no doubt believed that investigating the Structure via depth-craft was essential to understanding her curious voyage and her mother's interest in the "other world". We suspect – and, above, all, hope – E. might be there now, in Henerey's company.

That is why we shall set off in the *Perspicacity* in a few days' time. We intend to use the Fleet's coordinates to locate another Entry, through which we will travel to find Henerey and E. You will be joined aboard by the finest colleagues you could imagine: Sophy's genius wife, Niea; the enigmatic Jeime herself; and esteemed alumni of the Ridge expedition Tevn, Irye, and Vincenebras. (Sophy's brother Arvist may also be there.)

You are not expected to follow us into parts unknown, of course. We only require your assistance up until the very moment when we step (or swim, or whatever verb proves most applicable) through an Entry in search of our siblings. It is also our sincerest hope that you will not waste time telling us how reckless our plan seems. Trust us – we are well aware.

But, after all we've endured, we simply must try.

(O, Vy, why don't we abandon this entire draft? I'm afraid there is no way of encapsulating everything we've experienced together without the summary sounding contrived or nonsensical (or both). – S.)

(Agreed. Why don't we ask your "esteemed" friend Vincenebras to pen some anodyne alternative? – V.)

(Don't say such things, even in jest. He *will* know. He is probably putting pen to paper as we speak, though he knows not why. – S.)

Chapter 1

EXCERPT FROM THE JOURNAL OF HENEREY CLEL, YEAR 1002

To any Scholars of the future who may read this,

Today, I'm afraid I discovered that I am the sort of person who reacts to unprecedented adventure in the same way your average Frangible Jellyfish responds to the most incremental change in water temperature. That is to say – by nearly perishing with all due haste.

What an awfully bleak way of beginning these notes! I brought only my scientific journal with me, and I hate to sully it with anxious ramblings of a personal nature. If I thought I might encounter a purveyor of fine stationery in the fathomless depths, I would toss the whole book overboard and start afresh. I daren't even cross out the preceding sentences, because it is so very quiet aboard our vessel, and, as I tend to scribble with great vigour, E. will certainly hear me, and I don't wish to trouble her more than I already—

Shall we leave those gloomy lines as they are, then, and begin once more?

I believe it has now been a short while since my dear E. and I reunited at her majestic Deep House and set off on our expedition. I say "I believe" because the hands of my pocket-watch still spin about with jaunty irregularity, and, besides, I do not feel confident in my ability to track the hours accurately at present. Because I am, I'm sorry to say, a bit of a mess – an emotional shipwreck – a weak-limbed limpet!

Perhaps I am also too self-critical. I described myself using those very words (weak-limbed limpet, etc.) just a moment ago, and E. immediately offered a firm rebuttal. I agree; such phrases are neither kind nor fair! Yet I cannot help but think back to the previous iterations of Henerey Clel – the young boy, paging through books of Fantasies and dreaming of extraordinary experiences – the young man, doing much the same – and feel the weight of my past selves' shame as they realise I have commenced the most noteworthy venture of my life (and of our generation?) in such a pitiable fashion.

You see, E. and I did not quite *intend* to find ourselves lost in some inscrutable sea. For my part, I came to the Deep House today for the primary purpose of visiting the correspondent who has lately grown so dear to me. My spirits soared as we navigated my borrowed depth-craft to that vexing Structure in the coral reef that comprises E.'s garden. I'm afraid my own giddiness rather prevented me from fully considering all potential outcomes of our little sojourn.

Naturally, the most unlikely outcome was precisely what awaited us.

Moments after we docked onto the Structure – just as I was considering whether I could risk glancing fondly at her again – we were suddenly plunged into absolute darkness. Though the interior lights in the depth-craft activated quickly, all I could see outside was impenetrable murk. No luminous fish, no shadowy deep-sea whales, not even a solitary bubble. I had imagined such scenes before, when I yearned to take part in the Ridge expedition, but I had never experienced the all-encompassing depths myself. As my eyes adjusted, the depth-craft continued to shrink around me. I became convinced I was pressed into a glass slide in some sublime scientist's microscope. I could feel only the confining motion of those hungry, heavy seas – well, that and an intense rocking sensation that would not cease.

"What is the cause of that infernal shaking?" I asked at last, surprising myself with my ferocity. Never have I sounded so much like my brother! I tried pulling my eyes from the portholes to anchor myself to E.'s face. Under the grim silver lights, she looked resolute and metallic, like some sculpture of an esteemed Scholar from centuries past.

"I fear you are the one shaking, not the depth-craft." Her frown alarmed me. "What is the matter?"

I responded by promptly losing my ability to breathe. My head spun. I gasped like a beached Forbearing Shark. I tried desperately to focus, but I could not stop panting and heaving. Shapes and colours swam about me.

I remember hearing the ghost of E.'s voice politely asking if she could help me sit. I nodded a vague assent. I felt the faintest touch of her hands on my shoulders (which, in retrospect, I regret that I barely had the ability to appreciate at the time) as I collapsed into the navigator's chair.

"You will be all right, Henerey," said E., seemingly from afar.

"Do you – what is – am—" I sputtered (or some fragments of that nature – I cannot recall the exact phrasing).

"I promise you shall survive this. I believe you are suffering from an attack of the nerves, and they only linger for a few moments. For a count of one hundred, let's say." Her voice bobbed like a buoy, and I tried to let my mind swim for it.

"May I count it for you?" she continued. "And would you kindly hold on to this for me as I do?"

I heard a click and felt a cold chain of shells and pearls drop into my palm. A distant part of my brain remembered that E. was wearing a necklace with a nautilus design on the pendant. I ran my fingers along the carved nautilus, the pointed spires of the shells, and the smooth curves of the pearl beads, and let the current of my terror carry me as far as it could.

To my surprise, I began to return to myself as E.'s gentle voice counted to twenty, then fifty, then eighty. The pressure on my chest somehow vanished. After she reached a hundred, I felt exhausted, but otherwise recovered. Still, I could hardly look at my companion. I also had no desire to see that horrible void of the ocean again, so I focused on the floor of the depth-craft (which desperately needed sweeping).

"I am terribly sorry," I said. "I don't quite understand what just happened. How did we reach these depths so swiftly?"

"I believe we've *travelled*."

At last, I found myself sensible enough to detect the perfectly understandable tremor in E.'s tone. I couldn't help but infuse my next statements with reassuring cheer.

"Well, that certainly explains why we no longer appear to be in your garden. So the Structure does indeed possess powers of transportation, as we hypothesised. But does that explain what came over me just now? Was it some kind of protective – I don't know, curse, or something of the sort, created by the Entry? Like in *The Vengeance of the Thermocline*?"

To my surprise, E. unfolded the supplementary navigator's chair from its hidden panel in the ceiling and sat right by my side. When I dared to look at her, I observed such genuine sympathy in her eyes. It was the visual representation, I would say, of the kindness expressed so openly in her every letter.

"I have experienced many such attacks in my life," she said. "All occurred under quite ordinary circumstances. I am not surprised in the least that one could be triggered by what we just experienced."

"But I felt like I was dying!" I coughed politely to distract from the unpleasant way in which my voice cracked at the end of this exclamation. "Could a mere attack of the nerves truly affect me so?"

"I fear many use the phrase 'attack of the nerves' to refer to any moment of anxiety. In actuality, it describes a particular physiological experience that I would not wish upon anyone – especially not you."

Previously, I would indeed glibly say that I had experienced such an attack as an overdramatic way of describing a burst of intense worry – such as what occurs when one goes to examine a tank full of Good-Humoured Shrimp, only to find that one's research assistant accidentally placed a Ravenous Grouper amidst the innocent crustaceans! I did not, however, confess this to E., as I was far too preoccupied with the stimulating challenge of relearning how to catch my breath.

How much worse would I have felt were E. not with me? I could not bear to think of her experiencing anything similar, either. Had she truly survived "many" of these attacks? Who – if anyone – spoke gently to her and helped her through that terror when she did? (If only it could have been me!)

"It would appear," I said, pleased to hear my voice growing stronger, "that Chancellor Rawsel was wise to exclude me from the Ridge expedition. I suspect I may have a most unforeseen aversion to deep water. But how are you faring, E.? Did you not say in one of your letters that depth-crafts make you claustrophobic? If so, you are certainly managing it admirably."

"Fortunately, this is the most spacious depth-craft I've had the pleasure of boarding," E. replied. "And – well, it's rather curious. I found that my desire to help you through your distress temporarily eclipsed any anxieties I might have experienced myself."

"I am happy to be of service." (And I did truly mean that!)

"To be clear, I am now appropriately alarmed," she continued. "To calm myself, I am doing my best to think of my sister and her colleagues down at the Ridge, and how they live and work and joke and care for each other in such an environment without a second thought. Because we can't see anything out there, I'd like to imagine that we will float past Sophy and Niea in their diving suits at any moment."

In response, I tapped the navigation system, hoping the depth-craft would reveal something of the landscape outside (or, perhaps, E.'s dauntless sister come to rescue us). Instead, a sharp warning chime indicated that the lamentably outdated equipment could not recognise any topography.

"My dear E.," I said, slowly, "would you agree that we have, perhaps, found ourselves in rather more adventurous circumstances than we anticipated?"

She nodded. "I don't know what I thought would happen after we, well, entered the Entry. Henerey, I can barely brave a single day outside my home, and now I'm adrift with you in an unknown ocean. Whatever was I thinking? I can't apologise enough for forcing you into such a nightmare."

"A nightmare? Isn't that going a bit too far? Now that the attack of the nerves is behind me, I'm having a marvellous time." I attempted the most comforting smile I could muster – which, in truth, is not particularly difficult when gazing at her. "Besides, do recall that this is not the first mysterious journey you've survived. Why, you're the more seasoned adventurer of the two of us!"

"Isn't *that* going a bit too far?" Her focus shifted from me (alas) to the ocean outside. "But I do find our present situation most peculiar. We are, evidently, still underwater. I assumed that if the Structure were to carry us anywhere, it would have to be . . . there."

Her dramatic emphasis on the last word was unnecessary, as I knew exactly where E. imagined we would end up. "There" was an island on a luminous and lonesome sea, where E. had travelled – by some art or technology unknown to us – and she'd told none but me of her journey.

"We may yet be nearby." I gestured towards the portholes without looking at them. "During your previous adventure, you were only returned to the Deep House after you spent some time ashore. Perhaps we need only pass a few pleasant hours on that island to be sent home."

Ever the optimist, I took the opportunity to give the automatic navigation panel one more go. With the system continuing to resist, my initial technique for locating the island simply involved steering at random as we sat in companionable silence.

After a short spell, E. offered to relieve me from my duties at the helm. I think she fears I am still weak from the attack, and she is not incorrect! That is how I have come to enjoy this brief respite and write about my experiences. I cannot guess what might happen next, but I hope we will soon find what we seek. If the mysterious creators of the Structure were skilled enough to construct a device that could carry people across vast distances, why did they not design it to deposit said passengers in the correct location?

As I write, I've thrice now heard E. inhale as if to speak, but no words followed. I wonder if I should encourage her. Would that be appropriate? We have only enjoyed a short time in each other's physical presence, and I am not sure what rules of conversational behaviour apply to our interactions. Yet we always communicated most comfortably in our letters. (We even spoke of love, though I certainly lack the courage to broach that topic face to face!)

Surely I should not say anything. Surely it would sound patronising – and perhaps unsettling – if I were to cut in, but—

"E.," I said in a near-whisper after several moments (approximately accounted) passed, "what are you thinking?"

She glanced away from the helm to meet my gaze. How sharply green her eyes are – like the scales of a Permissive Wrasse when the surface light catches them – but that is not quite the point, is it?

"I am beginning to worry, just a little, about being away from the Deep House."

How wonderful that I can already recognise her unsubtle use of understatement!

"We'll be back in no time, I'm sure," I said, "and, depending on the hour and your willingness, I might have no choice but to stay for dinner."

"We won't enjoy much of a meal, I'm afraid, if everything flooded because I neglected to properly check the systems before we departed."

"Do you mean the systems regulated by that funny panel near the airlock door? If so, perhaps it will reassure you to know that I distinctly remember seeing you push a great many buttons there."

Then E. smiled, truly, and I remembered how remarkable it is that we are here, not as correspondents, but simply as two people existing in

13

the same place – enigmatic though that place may be. For a moment, I felt dizzy again. It was not another attack of nerves, but rather a beautifully swirling light-headedness that seemed more electrifying than alarming.

"That does reassure me," she said. "Still, I predict it won't be long until I am overcome by a state of panic that renders me most unbecoming."

"Impossible!" I exclaimed before I realised what I was saying.

"I assure you that it is not merely possible, but also highly likely."

"That is not exactly what I meant," I muttered, wishing one could cross out embarrassing statements in life as in letters. O, but luck is on my side at last! Before she could ask any clarifying questions about what exactly I found impossible, the enormous head of some unknown beast (a Refined Oarfish? No, they could never brave such depths!) slammed into the frontmost porthole of our depth-craft. The ocean possesses such perfect timing!

AUTOMATED POST MISSIVE FROM "L." TO "THIRTIETH SECOND", YEAR 1005

Dear "Thirtieth Second", or whatever your true name happens to be,

I thought I would open this letter by declaring my victory. Instead, it seems we have reached a rather frustrating impasse. While that is most perturbing, and will set back my progress significantly, I must congratulate you nonetheless.

When I agreed to take tea in your study, it was only for the purpose of stealing that box of documents you keep so naively in plain view atop your crystal cabinet (or, at least, that rectangular structure described as a "cabinet" in my world). That was why I suddenly asked you to check if a bird had struck the window – for I had set a wind-up automaton of mine to flap against the glass at that precise moment. My intricate creation lured you away, leaving

14

me to my machinations. To guarantee my success, I forced myself to wear an uncharacteristically elegant cape with what should be an illegal number of ruffles, all of which were perfect for secreting what I sought to obtain from you. After we said our farewells and that funny machine (should I call it a "Structure", an "Entry", or a "Sculpted Saviour"? They are all the same thing, aren't they? Whyever are those three distinct terms used interchangeably? I do wish someone would standardise the nomenclature post-haste) transported me home, I felt almost disappointed that you proved such an easy target.

Thank you – and curse you too, of course – for proving me wrong.

For I have now deduced that when you stepped to my right, offering what I assume is the equivalent of a plate of fruit pastries in your civilisation – which I happily accepted, smug as I was with your secret archive newly in my possession – you chose that precise moment to slip your dainty hand across the brim of my hat, which sat stately and proud on the back of my chair, and procure the following objects: a microscopic shorthand copy of the log from the *Perspicacity*, a needle-sized scroll of blueprints and research notes, and a memory-recorder from a most singular Automated Post machine. Have I made any errors in my suppositions? No need to answer – I know I have not. I rarely make errors, which is why I am astonished by how wrong I was to assume you are merely an innocent from the bottom of the sea. Or wherever your city actually is. My employer once attempted to explain the broader cosmology to me, but I have no interest in the nature of the universe or anything beyond my immediate perception. The work I do involves only what I can see, touch, and take.

That is all to say that I do not know much about you, Scholar "Thirtieth", nor, for that matter, the world you inhabit. At present, my task is simple – acquire, for said employer, all documents relating to a particular incident of historic import and the Cidnosin family's involvement therein.

Do I care about the Cidnosin family's involvement in anything, historic or otherwise? Not personally, I suppose. By sheer coincidence, I did happen to know something of them before this commission. In my previous career as a Courier, I operated a mail-boat, and I remember becoming particularly frustrated by the unreasonable number of letters E. Cidnosin began receiving on a near-daily basis during the year 1002. Then Automated Post took off like the tide, and the Deep House was destroyed, and Courier work became sparse. To keep myself in spending money and ships, I decided to try my luck in the controversial field that many Boundless Campus Scholars describe in hushed whispers as "Document Acquisition". (Are such questionable activities present on the other Campuses, I wonder, or is the drive to succeed by any means necessary specific to my own home? Don't bother answering. I am well aware that *you* wouldn't understand a thing about our Campuses.) It was not the first time I considered such a profession. In fact, as a little girl, I—

Look at me, rambling on about unrelated personal matters as if I were one of those Cidnosins myself! Let me simply say that from the moment I adopted my striking Acquisition Alias (which is critical, if you wish to be taken seriously) and began rifling through other people's possessions with glee, I knew I had hit upon my calling. After all, I spent years modelling discretion while delivering letters – I cannot deny the secret pleasure I take in being able to read them at last! Because of the rather precarious (and not undeserved) reputation of my new profession, the number of Scholars who will deign to utilise my services is somewhat limited. But I do get by, so here we are.

To return to my original point – let us now consider the unique situation in which we find ourselves. At present, each of us holds precisely the documents that the other needs. Under the circumstances, may I propose a begrudging business arrangement?

I will return the documents I stole from you (after I make copies of them) if you promise to do the same. I would not want either of us to renege before every paper returns to its rightful place. The pages I've included for you, extracted from the diary of one Scholar Henerey Clel, are both proof of threat and of good faith.

I hope you will not keep me waiting. Perhaps you, too, serve an employer who yearns to have your files back in their possession. I await your correspondence eagerly.

As sincerely as I can manage,

L.

AUTOMATED POST MISSIVE FROM THE THIRTIETH SECOND SCHOLAR TO "L.", YEAR 1005

Dear "L.",

Hello there! Would you believe that this is the very first time I ever replied to a letter from a stranger? Until recently, I was not acquainted with anyone besides my Scholarly colleagues – and we exclusively communicate with each other in person (or through rather testy comments in our daily records). As a result, I was delighted to see your note appear on the fascinating "Automated Post" device that my new friend Scholar Sophy Cidnorghe left behind for me, but it took me some time to formulate a response.

You see, I fear you misunderstood the entire situation. At the same time, I find your misunderstandings fascinating!

I have no "employer" in the way you suggest. What an old-fashioned concept. Imagine being compensated for information! No, I work in service of a greater cultural imperative, which necessitates excellent record-keeping in every aspect of our lives. It is for this reason I am most disappointed that you would *steal* the documents created by certain members of the Cidnosin and Clel families during their time with us. Before formally adding those papers to our archives, I needed to set them in new waterproof bindings, convert dates from our own calendrical system to correspond with your world's, and attach any relevant addenda (such as assorted drafts from my own records that I blush to read now), which is why the files were temporarily unprotected in my quarters in the first place.

At any rate, when we met, I invited you to tea because I thought you seemed like a friendly person (and because it is still rare that a stranger like you visits our city). When I noticed your attempts to deceive me (there are no "birds" here, incidentally), my heart sank. I should have confronted you in the moment, but I am not adept at navigating such altercations. Instead, I did what seemed right at the time – I took something of yours. It was my hope that you would notice what you'd lost, realise the hurt you caused me, and return my things with appropriate contrition!

(Considering that you specialise in stealing information, I do wonder why you kept your own valuable documents hidden behind a most obvious flap on your hat?)

I wish to have my documents returned. That much is true. Still, though it goes against my nature – which is generally quite optimistic to a fault – I'm sad to say, my dear "friend", that I do not especially trust you.

Consequently, would you be so kind as to send me something of mine to start us off?

Otherwise, I shall simply set myself to the onerous but perfectly manageable task of recreating all my missing documents – Henerey Clel's journal entries, E. Cidnosin's unsent notes to her sister, even that fateful, final letter written during the very climax of these proceedings – from recollection alone. I do have an excellent memory. If possible, I would prefer not to waste it on a task like this. I simply have too many other things to do!

Dutifully yours,

The Thirtieth Second Scholar (or 30.ii, as we might write it shorthand here)

AUTOMATED POST MISSIVE FROM "L." TO THE THIRTIETH SECOND SCHOLAR, YEAR 1005

Dear "30.ii" (what manner of name is that?),

How clever of you to pretend this is all coincidence, and to write in such a sweetly ingenuous way! ("This is the very first time I ever replied to a letter from a stranger"? Spare me, please. Who would believe that anyone other than a literal newborn has never received such a letter before? Correspondence is the centrepoint of society!)

I assume you exaggerate the strength of your own memory. Yet there is something about you – and your correspondence – that intrigues me. (How frustrating.) It's been a slow few tides in the world of document acquisition, and I find myself in need of entertainment. While I have not entirely bought into your bluff, let us go ahead and pretend otherwise. After all, I've heard stranger things about your city and your Scholarly colleagues from *my* new friend, Niea Cidnorghe. I shall acquiesce to your demands because it would be simply impossible for me to remember the contents of the documents that you lifted so elegantly from me. Even if I could, my employer is a stickler for originals.

Give me a few tides (or however you measure time in your world – I understand there's some kind of bizarre temporal discrepancy) to make my copies of the Cidnosin Papers, and I shall send them back with the expectation that you will return the favour immediately.

With haste,

L.

AUTOMATED POST MISSIVE FROM THE THIRTIETH SECOND SCHOLAR TO "L.", YEAR 1005

Dear L. (however do your colleagues know how to classify you when your name is but a single letter?),

It is no bluff to say that I am immensely patient!

As you make your copies of what you have dramatically termed the Cidnosin Papers, I do hope you enjoy reading them.

I also hope you will not judge me too harshly when you do.

30.ii

Chapter 2

DRAFT RECORD BY THE THIRTIETH SECOND SCHOLAR, 1002

By my Oaths as a Scholar, I pledge to record every observation from today's expedition and swear I will document all I experienced.

Normally, I write "nothing" in my daily records because I have seen nothing, and it would be inaccurate to say anything else. Yet today is different. A successful crossing occurred at last!

I am tempted to mention that I, the Thirtieth Second Scholar, have long dreamed of becoming the first among us to shepherd Imperilled people to safety. Because I am dedicated to concision and precision (and because I know the watchful eyes of the Fifteenth First Scholar will review what I write), however, I shall resist the urge to discuss my dreams and accomplishments at length!

As I do every day, I took the Mechanical Beast *Ieneros* to patrol the infinite seas that border our refuge. I stood within the very head of my dear Beast, gazing through the window of its vast right eye as is my custom. After several hours of watching the waters (which my Oaths require me to say, truthfully, proved as onerous as ever), my vigilance was rewarded.

For I spotted a small craft, designed in a much less intricate fashion than a Mechanical Beast – its shape nothing more than a simple sphere!

I wonder now if recording my emotional response to this sight would be irrelevant, or whether I must note it for correctness' sake. I shall err on the side of caution and omit it to reduce the number of hours I must spend listening to the Fifteenth First Scholar's criticisms. (Of course, I say "criticisms" most respectfully, for I know there is no greater gift a First Scholar can give a Second Scholar than critique . . . and there is no greater giver of such gifts than the Fifteenth First Scholar.)

I attempted to direct *Ieneros* to the craft, but I fear the grace of my movements was somewhat reduced. In fact, without even trying, I managed to bring the Beast so close that its head crashed against the porthole of the other vessel!

Assuming that Imperilled people might not be familiar with Mechanical Beasts, I opened one of the speaking-tubes that project like tusks from *Ieneros*' mouth and announced myself as protocol demands.

"Be not afraid, wanderers. I am the Thirtieth Second Scholar, and I shall bear you to safety. Do you possess a speaking-tube of your own?"

Though neither the eye of *Ieneros* nor the vessel's porthole were completely transparent, I could see through both windows well enough to notice the urgency with which the strangers placed their hands over their ears.

"Apologies," I whispered through the tube after they recovered from my initial cacophony. "Is this volume more suitable?"

I should note that I will refer to the Scholars by their proper names from this point forth – since I am writing this record after completing my mission, and I think that will lend the most accuracy to the narrative.

At that point, then, the person whom I would come to call Scholar Clel nodded to confirm that my message had been received. The other, whom I now know as Scholar Cidnosin, was warier.

"Be not afraid," I said again, after determining that such a phrase seemed appropriate to repeat while rescuing those escaping the perils of our forsaken former home.

As little else could be communicated at this juncture, I managed to draw *Ieneros* back and attach its frontmost claw to their vessel – though I am obligated to record that it took me more than seven tries accomplish this feat. Thus, with the strangers' craft propelled in front of me by *Ieneros'* might, I continued my usual route back home.

I must also note that I noticed, as we departed, what looked very much like the flash of a tail fin in the depths ahead. Because I have no definitive proof that the Illogical Ones were present, I hope I may record this observation without risking any contamination of our records with their magical nonsense.

While *Ieneros* made its unhurried journey, I continued to watch the pair of strangers through their porthole. I wondered at the nature of their relationship – or, rather, I considered such a triviality only after pondering how they managed to escape their world when all others have failed.

Given their unusual manner of dress, I could not determine their precise fields of study based upon appearances alone. I did notice that they both seemed ill at ease, which is perfectly understandable. I do not know how long they spent drifting through the sea before I found them.

They had one major interaction of note. I record it here only because of my Oaths. Scholar Clel, whom at the time I titled "The Elegant One" due to his excellent posture and confident bearing, seemed troubled by a trinket that he clutched within a tight fist. Occasionally, he would open his hand slightly, glance at the object, and then hide it away before turning back to smile reassuringly at Scholar Cidnosin.

I presume I may spare myself from logging each individual instance of the afore-described action and simply say that this continued far longer than it should have.

23

Scholar Cidnosin, whom I called "The Thoughtful One" because of her slow, calculated movements, appeared to notice his behaviour as well. In fact, each of them kept attempting to peek at the other in an astonishingly conspicuous fashion.

If I may say so, I think they make a fine pair, and I do believe that is an objective statement, Fifteenth First Scholar! Presumably they must be truly and deeply bonded, like all the heart-sworn lovers in the Frivolous Tales from the days before our exile?

Of course, I only read those tales in my juvenile years, and I foreswore such frippery forever when I gained more significant responsibilities with which to occupy my time. Yet because I have never seen such a relationship in reality, I am fascinated.

Then Scholar Cidnosin started to speak to Scholar Clel, but I heard none of it! I could do nothing but make educated guesses about their conversation based on my extensive literary knowledge of how people from the Imperilled world might behave.

"What is troubling you, my beloved?" Scholar Cidnosin (may have) said.

"O, it is nothing," Scholar Clel (possibly) said, waving his hands dramatically. "I simply must confess that in a moment of weakness, I stole this necklace from you. I required a physical object to remind me that you are real, because you are lovelier than dreams. Can you ever forgive me?"

"There is nothing to forgive," she (likely) replied. "For I too once stole a necklace of yours for the same reason. Are we not so alike?"

"You astound me, my resplendent one. I shall return it to you henceforth so you may wear it again, though these jewels could never outshine you."

At last, Scholar Clel wiped the necklace with the cloth of his fine jacket and pressed it into her hand.

They stood in silence (or so I presume) for a few moments before Scholar Cidnosin raised the jewels to her neck, trying valiantly to make the hooks meet. Thrice did Scholar Clel open his mouth wordlessly before turning away, frowning.

Scholar Cidnosin eventually uttered something wretchedly inaudible (perhaps "I require your assistance – most *desperately*"?).

Then, with the precision of a Botanist handling a delicate plant, Scholar Clel locked the necklace with one swift gesture and removed his hand immediately. Both stared into opposite corners of the vessel, but they seem relatively pleased with themselves.

I have now read back everything I drafted, and I am horrified.

What irrational impulse overtook me as I wrote the preceding paragraphs? Am I no less juvenile than I ever was? Do the Frivolous Tales still possess a hold over me? O, I shall have to rewrite this entire record, or the Fifteenth First Scholar will never let me put stylus to crystal again!

Besides, no evidence suggests that they are romantically involved. Though perhaps it is relevant to mention that when they settled into the Visitors' Quarters, they requested separate (but adjacent – adjacent!) bedchambers . . .

What is it about these two strangers that sparks my curiosity and imagination so?

Now, that is the end of that. It is time to abandon this mess and write anew. It also occurs to me that the Fifteenth First Scholar might find my preamble about spotting the strangers and communicating with them somewhat irrelevant as well. I shall stop writing now and request her guidance.

(And if I find myself tempted to imagine more ridiculous dialogues in the future, I shall force myself to picture Frivolous conversations involving the Fifteenth First Scholar and the Sixth First Scholar instead. How distressing!)

OFFICIAL RECORD BY THE THIRTIETH SECOND SCHOLAR, WRITTEN UNDER THE SUPERVISION OF THE FIFTEENTH FIRST SCHOLAR, 1002

By my Oaths as a Scholar, I pledge to record every relevant observation and pertinent detail about what I experienced after rescuing two Imperilled people from the endless seas.

Upon spying an unknown vessel in the distance, I provided towing assistance in accordance with established rescue protocol. The additional burden of the strangers' vessel decreased *Ieneros'* speed by approximately 50 per cent, but it was not long until I returned to the city with my unusual cargo. The Twenty-Ninth Second Scholar happened to be on duty in the docking area, so it was to him I ran before the newcomers debarked.

"Have you brought me a new vessel as a gift? What a wonderful surprise," said the Twenty-Ninth Second Scholar by way of greeting. "Though my Oaths require me to mention that your design lacks the eighty essential features of a suitable craft. How anomalous!"

"It is not my own creation, but a gift to us all!" I said in an especially calm and collected manner. "Twenty-Ninth! I saved two of the Imperilled!"

To my delight, the Visitors chose this very moment to prove their existence to the Twenty-Ninth Second Scholar. Scholar Clel clambered out of the hatch first, aided by a walking stick with a most unnecessary sculpture of some unidentifiable fish atop it. Scholar Cidnosin crept out afterwards. As she stood on the dock some paces behind Scholar Clel, Scholar Cidnosin's left foot kept tapping with surprising speed.

"I presume you are the people who brought us here?" said Scholar Clel – or, at least, that is what the Twenty-Ninth Second Scholar and I deduced after puzzling over his dialect and tone for a few moments.

"Why, you speak our language," said the Twenty-Ninth Second

Scholar. "We suspected your world would have developed many different tongues by now. Are you simply peculiar?"

"I am both peculiar and a trained Scholar," Scholar Clel replied. "And when I heard you – well, whichever one of you shouted from that fascinating depth-craft – speaking in Archaic – well, what we call 'Archaic Scholar' – I figured I should try that first."

"It was I who spoke to you," I confirmed. "I am thrilled we can communicate!"

The Twenty-Ninth Second Scholar and I immediately provided our Classification Particulars and asked the Visitors to do the same. They introduced themselves as a man titled "Henerey Clel" and a woman titled "E. Cidnosin". (Technically, Scholar Clel spoke for them both, and I requested the spellings of their titles for the purposes of my record. O, and I suppose I ought to furnish brief physical descriptions of our Visitors, to ensure my colleagues are able to recognise them with ease. Scholar Cidnosin is in possession of the most severely creased forehead I ever saw on someone so young, as well as a pale pink complexion, red hair arranged in a messy equivalent of The Thirty-Fourth Efficient Style, and garb somewhat similar to drab sleep-clothes that no self-respecting Scholar would wear in public. Scholar Clel, for his part, displays an illogically cheerful smile that does not quite reach his eyes at present, along with a warm brown complexion; black hair and a beard combed gracefully into what resembles The Sixty-Eighth Intrepid Style; and clothing that is Unclassifiable, but exceedingly elegant.)

(The Fifteenth First Scholar interrupted my writing to remind me that all our colleagues will be perfectly capable of recognising the Visitors – considering that they are, notably, the only two strangers ever to visit us. Her astuteness astonishes me! Please ignore the preceding parenthetical. And this one, I suppose.)

"Do you speak so-called Archaic Scholar as well, Scholar Cidnosin?" asked the Twenty-Ninth Second Scholar.

"I prefer reading to speaking," Scholar Cidnosin murmured, "and that is also the case in my own language."

"Now, pardon me," said Scholar Clel, "but I fear my companion and I know absolutely nothing about where we are. Could you enlighten us?"

"You are in the outer docks of the city of shelter, the safest place in this vast cosmos, and we are the very people who—" I began.

"I am sure one of our First Scholars will provide you with a much more appropriate explanation," said the Twenty-Ninth Second Scholar. Because he once told me that interruptions are the cruellest form of slight, I knew in an instant that the Twenty-Ninth Second Scholar had cut me off intentionally as a silent advisory to remember our Oaths.

"Undoubtedly!" I agreed. "There will be time enough for questions. We only just rescued you, after all. Shall I show you to the Visitors' Quarters, while the Twenty-Ninth Second Scholar breaks the news to our colleagues?"

"I have a more reasonable suggestion, Thirtieth Second Scholar," said the Twenty-Ninth Second Scholar. "You must go to our colleagues instead, and I will play host for the Visitors. That is most prudent."

I, of course, could not argue with that. I departed to engage in conversation with my Scholarly superiors and was therefore no longer required by my Oaths to record my experiences. I shall end this record here (and hope it is satisfactory at last).

UNSENT LETTER FROM E. CIDNOSIN TO SOPHY CIDNOSIN, 1002

Dear Sophy,

You will likely read this letter well after I write it. I hope our current separation will be no longer than the periods we typically spend apart while you are occupied with your Scholarly duties.

Though it feels like I have not written to you in an age, this is, in truth, the second letter I've composed for you within the span of a day. Once you return from the Ridge – and your own glorious adventure, trying to analyse that mysterious door! – you will no doubt immediately read the letter I left on the table in the parlour. (I wanted to leave you some manner of cake, as well, but I feared it might spoil.) Because that letter explains everything already, I will not waste space recapitulating the purpose of the somewhat accidental journey upon which Henerey and I embarked.

Still, I must reiterate my afore-expressed apologies for the impulsiveness of said journey. But if you are reading this letter, I must have returned, and will no doubt shortly explain why I simply had to understand this Structure that might illuminate our mother's secret life. I deeply regret not telling you everything I learned from Jeime – how Mother believed most passionately in another world that she herself would never live to see. I cannot wait until I am home and we can puzzle everything out together!

In my heart, I rather pitifully hoped to find Mother waiting for me when I passed through the Entry. She was not, of course, but I do feel a little closer to her when I am here.

Shall I take a moment to tell you what I mean by "here"?

Well, to start, I am in a room that is not mine, and that is jarring enough. Everything unsettles me. The air lacks the dampness of the Deep House, the gossamer fabric covering the furnishings makes my flesh prickle, and there is not a window in sight. I may be moments away from falling apart.

Perhaps I ought to mention that this room is one among many in a vast inn of sorts, which is itself but a single complex within an enormous underwater city protected by an immeasurable, glimmering fortress! I have no way of knowing our exact depth or location, but I'd wager we are just as deep as you and your colleagues at the Ridge. Oddly, that's the only aspect of my current circumstances that comforts me. I suspect I feel more at home in this improbable sunken city – which is, in a way, a collection of especially deep Deep Houses – than I would if I were to travel abovewater to the Atoll, for example.

(I had to stop writing for a moment. I could not remember if I locked the door and needed to ascertain that all was well.)

The people who reside here seem delighted and shocked by our sudden appearance. They rescued us from the seemingly endless depths, but the experience involved more misadventure than I would have preferred. When Henerey and I left the Deep House, we found ourselves afloat in an unfamiliar sea. As if that were not already terrifying, a veritable leviathan collided into our depth-craft soon afterwards! We would have panicked to the point of near-death, I think, had we not immediately recognised that it was not a living creature but a kind of machine – an automaton on a much vaster scale than your cetacean companions at the Ridge.

The automaton appeared carved or cast in the shape of an imaginary composite creature. I observed a broad, seal-like tail, a curved belly like a whale's, and a sea-serpent's head, with the latter looking the most like something of legend. (So curious was this design that I simply had to draw it! I apologise for the shakiness of my shading, caused by both the movements of the depth-craft and my own anxiety. Why, I even ended up omitting the creature's tusks because my hand was trembling too violently.) The scales bedecking the head resembled pearlescent gemstones – filmy, but not flimsy, and the clang the creature made when striking us was something to be heard!

We were then subjected to another hideously loud noise, which quickly diminished into the sound of a muffled voice projecting through the water. Afterwards, we

I apologise for losing my place and leaving that sentence incomplete; I fear I am not describing this with my usual enthusiasm. I cannot recall what I wanted to tell you next. My Brain troubles me once again. I feel very tired, and I keep forgetting what I have and haven't done. I went to check the door again, despite having already done so several times, and I remain unconvinced that I am safe. How am I to feel safe anywhere that is not the Deep House? I shall abandon this letter shortly and start over when I can.

I do miss you, dear sister. But I take comfort in the knowledge that you will remain in your own depths for the foreseeable future and currently have no knowledge of what has transpired. I may already be back by the time you notice I am gone!

With my love and apologies,

E.

NOTE PASSED BETWEEN HENEREY CLEL AND E. CIDNOSIN, 1002

Dearest E.,

I am writing you a note instead of knocking to come in & say good night, because I do not want you to worry about unlocking your door once more! I promise it is completely unopenable. In fact, if you find yourself overcome by the urge to check the lock again, perhaps you might look to this note as a physical artifact & remember that we tackled this together?

I know it was a mere (though excellent) coincidence that I happened to be in the hall to spy you opening and shutting the door moments ago. Do know that you can come & find me if you need ANYTHING; I am a light sleeper who is not prone to any manner of crossness when awakened (unlike a certain brother of mine). – H.

P.S. You were my saviour today. I shall never forget it.

*

Dearest H.,

Clever as always! Thank you for your understanding. I hoped you would not see me in a state like that until—

Well, I suppose I hoped you never would.

It is not something I am inclined to share with others, especially not someone upon whom I wish to make a favourable impression.

You are my saviour now. Perhaps that is how we will navigate this perplexing world – by saving each other in alternating sequence. – E.

Though your kind reply delighted me, do remember that I wrote my note to keep you company – & here you are, sliding it back to me under the door with an annotation of your own! Please, won't you hold on to it this time? & I hope it will continue to remind you that it would be impossible for me to have a more favourable impression of you. & I welcome the opportunity to help you through anything, as you've helped me. Running out of room; apologies! Sleep well & I shall see you tomorrow – isn't that splendid? – H.

Chapter 3

UNSENT LETTER FROM E. CIDNOSIN TO SOPHY CIDNOSIN, 1002

Dear Sophy,

I apologise for the distracted tone of my previous note! Surely it comes as no surprise that I am struggling with the experience of being in a new place – a place that is not simply unknown to me, but also to you, to Arvist, to Father, to just about everyone except Mother's odd compatriots (and even they never stepped foot here themselves!).

Last night, as you may have gleaned, I engaged in a rather embarrassing battle with my Brain when it could not accept that my door was secured. I can imagine what Dr Lyelle would say – that I should be patient with myself, because such a response is understandable under the circumstances. Do you remember that awful time, a few years ago, when I experienced episodes of sleepwalking and woke to find myself checking the airlock door? I would always feel overwhelmed by the greatest sense of dread, imagining something horrible lurking outside. At any rate, I would not have slept a wink last night without Henerey's generous assistance.

I must confess, Sophy, that I live in fear of ruining this fragile bond between me and Henerey. He is the ideal partner for an unexpected adventure, and I do not deserve him whatsoever. When I woke this morning, I heard him stirring in the room next to mine. It is a strange thing to reside within relative proximity to someone you care about – to know he is existing behind that wall, perhaps marvelling at the unusual glow of the bed sheets, brushing his hair and adjusting his beard, and no doubt feeling disappointed that he did not pack any of his naturalist's equipment (or fashionable garments suitable for adventuring).

Fearing (and, above all else, hoping) he would soon knock on my door, I re-dressed myself in the humble clothes I wore yesterday, attempted to untangle myself from my hair, and sat on the bed in embarrassing anticipation. Soon enough, I heard the door next to mine shut ever so gently, followed by a quick and quiet knock.

I tried not to open the door immediately. I did, at least, wait one moment.

When I finally gave in, I encountered a thoroughly transformed Henerey Clel.

Somehow, he had already acquired the local fashion after but a single night. Like the few Scholars we saw yesterday, he was dressed in a loose-fitting, pearl-coloured chemise, covered by a long overcoat that iridesced in abyssal purples and blues – rather like the water outside the city, I suppose. He had tied his hair back with a matching blue ribbon and completed his outfit with the simple side-bag he carried yesterday.

I must admit he was a rather lovely sight.

We both began to say "Good morning!" at the same time, realised our odd synchronicity about halfway through "good", and then stopped simultaneously to let the other speak. Henerey laughed loudly and looked up to the right as he did, his eyes half closed. He tends to make this expression when he is abashedly pleased, and I feel very privileged that I am beginning to recognise it.

"If anyone could locate a tailor during the early hours of the morning in an unfamiliar world, Henerey Clel, it would be you." I gestured to his finery.

"Did you not notice?" he said as his gossamer sleeves flew about.

"Underneath the bed, there's a — well, I suppose the equivalent of a well-stocked closet. I couldn't help myself."

"How marvellous! But how does everything fit you so perfectly?"

"That is the most remarkable thing of all!" He swung out his sleeve, revealing a tiny ribbon sewn into gathers near the hem.

"These designers are visionaries," he continued. "The clothing is completely adjustable. Such a practical approach, yet it never occurred to anyone back home."

"I am most impressed. You are off to seek out these visionaries, then?"

He paused, playing with that ribbon on his sleeve.

"Actually," Henerey said, "I thought I might seek our hosts, find some food, and, ah, bring it back here. To have breakfast with you. Because I thought perhaps you — that is to say — given your usual habits at the Deep House, I wondered if you would prefer—"

"You needn't worry. I accept that I must leave this corridor eventually if we are to go home," I said, but his kindness touched me. "Still, if you truly don't mind seeing to the food, I would be grateful to avoid strangers for a little longer."

"Then I will return shortly. I do wonder what they eat here — I hope it isn't phosphorescent! But wouldn't it be fascinating if it were?"

I waved him off and returned to my room, surprised by the jolt of relief I experienced upon closing the door again. As much as it unsettled me last night, I do feel somewhat more comfortable inside this unfamiliar room than out of it.

In Henerey's absence, I resolved to search for this supposed wardrobe, and ultimately located a glowing panel on the left side of the bedframe. When I pressed it, a melody of scratches and squeaks played as a drawer emerged — presenting a treasure chest of diaphanous clothing. None of it was my style, you know, but Henerey is such a sartorial fellow! I felt a rather inexplicable desire to impress him.

So on went the least dramatic item in the drawer — a magenta dress with half-length sleeves that fluttered around my arms in a most

35

ethereal fashion. It lacked the decorative embroidery one might see in your Scholarly Regalia, for example, but it did feature a pleasant border of silver pentagons stitched around the collar. Henerey was correct about the unique nature of these garments: secreted ties, buttons, and fabric panels allowed me to make myself as comfortable as I pleased. (Perhaps I would wear something other than shapeless house-dresses if ethereal gowns were made in such a way by our own Fashioners!)

Thus attired, I scrutinised myself in the room's small looking glass, a delicate thing seemingly crafted from seven round mirrors soldered together. The length of my hair continued to prove a nuisance, by the way. After nearly shattering the crystalline combs supplied in my room, I managed to twist those troublesome tresses into a braid. With my hair up and my bright gown on, I looked quite unlike myself – I wish you could have seen me! Still, the transformation was not entirely satisfactory. I had hoped I might take on a more compelling and powerful aspect, as if I were the heroine of an Antepelagic Fantasy of old, rising to face unprecedented circumstances! Instead, my familiarly anxious eyes regarded me wanly. I abandoned the mirror in time for Henerey's return.

"E., might I ask a clarifying question?" he asked as I opened the door. He had acquired a large sparkling bag that he bore upon his back as if it were nothing. "O! What a sublime dress. That colour and your hair, and the embroidery—" He shook his head. "Earlier, were you implying that going out and about would be less troubling if you did not have to worry about other people?"

"I suppose I was," I said, hoping desperately that I was not blushing (or, if I was, that the colour of my blushes would suit me as much as magenta apparently did).

"In that case, would you care to accompany me someplace? We will not encounter a single soul, I assure you."

Intrigued and anxious, I followed him down the hall. Though we passed countless rooms, I did not hear anything to suggest the presence of fellow guests. Perhaps everyone remained asleep – or perhaps the rooms, constructed from unknown materials, were soundproof enough to prevent unwanted noises from reaching the corridor.

After a short while, we came upon a round door made of dizzyingly green stone, which Henerey opened by pulling a triangular latch from beneath a translucent panel. Moments later, I found myself standing before the most incredible garden I ever saw – here, in the very depths of the ocean!

We emerged in a great glass dome of a building, with a ceiling stretching so far above my head that I could barely see its topmost curves. I heard running water, Sophy, and it was the strangest thing – not the slow sounds of the waves, but a constant chuckling. There was a fountain before us, a ceaseless whalespout that trickled into six channels set into the earth. More wondrous still were the trees! Tall, ancient things, like I'd only read about in Antepelagic texts, with pale bark; thin, pink leaves; and fin-shaped blossoms prone to dropping at the slightest provocation and spiralling around us. There was a host of other plants, too, that I could barely begin to recognise. They were certainly not kelp!

Perhaps I should have felt anxious in this unfamiliar, public place, but there were no people to be seen, and the sun was warm and inviting, and—

Then I remembered, once again, that we are under the sea.

"The sunlight," I whispered. "Is it an illusion? Or was the very door to this garden another Entry? One that carried us to a place beyond imagination?"

"That Thirtieth Second Scholar said this conservatory is illuminated by some kind of bioluminescence, like practically everything here," Henerey said. "I thought you might enjoy it."

"I have never seen its equal. Have you? Is this what your home on the Atoll is like?"

"There are several botanical gardens on Atoll Campus, right in the centre of everything. A precious few of their plants sprouted centuries ago from seeds that survived the Dive. But palms are our only trees, and none are so vibrant as this." He gestured to a circular bench in the distance, which sat before a small cascade rippling down an incline of glistering white tiles. "Shall we?"

The view from the bench revealed a hidden avenue of further plants and ponds that continued for fathoms ahead. We sat together, and Henerey produced from his bag two diamond-shaped boxes containing a splendid rainbow of fruits that filled me with relative dread. While I am technically capable of consuming food I did not make myself – I certainly will not decline when Seliara brings over something delicious, and I did take tea with you during our stay in the dormitories – there is a difference between an occasional pie or tea and a full meal crafted by complete strangers, even if their intent is presumably good. A fresh wave of panic overcame me as I took a few delicate bites. What if the fruits contained a natural toxin to which our hosts had developed an immunity over the years? What if it killed us both, purely by unfortunate accident, and that kind young Scholar was cruelly punished for serving these meals to us? And these unfortunate occurrences would be my fault, after all, because—

If Henerey noticed how close I came to having my own attack of the nerves, he was kind enough not to judge. (In case you were wondering, the fruits proved both non-toxic and surprisingly flavourless. What I wouldn't give for a shaker of spirulina!)

"How are you feeling, my dear?" he asked, tapering off slightly on the term of endearment – another trait of his that I feel lucky to know rather well now. "If this becomes a bit much, we can always go back."

"I am perfectly calm at present, considering that it's just the two of us." I decided to say nothing of my food-based obsessions. "But why are we so wonderfully alone?"

"Yes, I suppose I acted rather mysteriously in my excitement," he said. "There are no other people here – or, I should say, in this part of the city. Except the Thirtieth Second Scholar, whom we met yesterday, and who seems to float about the place to ensure our needs are met. Apparently, this entire complex was designed as a sanctuary for visitors like us. These Scholars live and work elsewhere."

"And there are truly no others like us?"

"It seems, remarkably, that you and I are the first people to travel here."

"Henerey," I said, my voice growing faint, "I don't suppose they won't know how to send us back?"

Rather desperately and automatically, I reached out and took his hand. It was very generous of him to indulge me by not letting go!

"The Thirtieth Second Scholar says we will meet with some manner of council later today. No doubt they will answer all our questions. I believe they decided to let us rest beforehand, because they feared we were too tired for practical conversation."

"How surprisingly civil. I don't suppose you are accustomed to that level of thoughtfulness from your department?"

"That is an understatement," Henerey muttered.

"Surely you must enjoy your freedom as best you can before we go home!" I hoped that by speaking those words with such cheer I might lift my own spirits, too. "In the meantime, would you like to take a closer look at some of these plants? And I daresay there appeared to be an odd fish or two in those water features."

"E.," he said, his hand grasping mine all the tighter, "you are truly magnificent."

I disagree, but I certainly appreciated him saying it!

When we returned to our quarters afterwards, a scroll had been placed on the wall at a point equidistant from our respective doors. It instructed us to meet with the Scholars in the evening. Henerey offered, once again, to converse with them on his own, but I have resolved to accompany him, even if the thought of being in a room with others makes me feel as sick as usual. If that is what it takes for us to get home, so be it!

Really, now that we are about to speak with the Scholars, I fear writing this letter to you was foolish. Perhaps they will have an Entry available for our immediate use, and you will see me before long! But I did want to document all that's happened, and I enjoy

39

pretending to tell you about it. How our circumstances have changed now that I am the one writing with news from my adventures!

(Will a long letter about *your* adventures await me at the Deep House? O, I can't wait to read it!)

Hoping to see you very soon,

E.

OFFICIAL RECORD OF THE HISTORIC "COUNCIL OF THE VISITORS" BY THE THIRTIETH SECOND SCHOLAR, 1002

By my Oaths as a Scholar, I, the Thirtieth Second Scholar, attest to the accuracy of the following council record, which summarises the first official meeting between the Body of Scholars and the Imperilled Visitors, Scholar Clel and Scholar Cidnosin.

As determined in a previous evaluation of the Thirtieth Second Scholar's work, I, the Fifteenth First Scholar, will review these notes before they are preserved in our Compendium. – 15.i

We gathered on this day to speak with the Imperilled and discover the secrets of their successful escape. The Second through Twenty-Third First Scholars stood in a half-circle around the First through Fortieth Second Scholars. As a sign of respect, we offered each Visitor a comfortable chair – the very seats traditionally occupied by the Primary and Secondary speakers. (Perhaps it is for the best that only two strangers appeared. What would we have done with four or five? Constructed more chairs?)

I can ignore the parenthetical above, but not the few sentences that follow – all of which verge on impertinent irrelevance. Going forward, I shall style any such sentences as "Personal Notes" and will encourage the Thirtieth Second Scholar to avoid such commentary in the future. – 15.i

[Personal Note: Though it may not be within the purview of my

40

Scholarly duties to say so **(it is not)**, I do wish we could have conducted this meeting in a less intimidating fashion. I know every Scholar is eager to observe the strangers! Yet Scholar Cidnosin spent the entire period clutching her hands so tightly I feared she would injure herself.]

The Sixth First Scholar began the proceedings by quoting some celebrated Scholars' commentaries that seemed relevant to the situation. I do not need to waste time recording those details **(indeed, you do not)** since such hallowed words are known to all of us. Instead, I shall make some brief notes about the Visitors themselves **(you need not do that, either, but I will let your remarks remain)**.

Throughout the meeting, Scholar Clel appeared physically engaged in the conversation. His eyes moved thoughtfully, paying respectful attention to whoever was speaking, and he nodded with such enthusiasm at the oddest of times that I assume his gestures must be somewhat automatic. In contrast, Scholar Cidnosin stared straight ahead, not meeting anyone's eyes, and often looked towards the door as if she were planning to flee.

After an amount of time that I hope is not necessary to quantify **(thankfully, you are correct)**, the Sixth First Scholar invited the pair to speak, which seemed a fitting point for me to start recording the conversation.

"Centuries ago, our people designed the Sculpted Saviours to rescue you from peril, but the fates of our creations have long been unknown to us," intoned the Sixth First Scholar. "Would you tell us how you managed to discover one?"

I suspected Scholar Clel would be the first to speak, and he was – though he did look to Scholar Cidnosin first. She nodded her approval before returning to the task of biting her lip most ferociously.

"I assume you are referring to what we have been calling Entries? Are those the same as your, er, Sculpted Saviours?" How flustered he seemed by that perfectly straightforward phrase!

"Colleagues, wouldn't it be wisest for us to respect our Visitors by using the terms and phrases they find most familiar?" asked the

41

Fifteenth First Scholar – though I rather suspect she intended that as an instruction, not a question. **(Well done.)**

"Please, Scholar Clel," she continued. "Continue to call them 'Entries', and we shall do the same."

"Well, I'm afraid they remain largely a mystery to us. E. and I travelled here by chance when one such structure – we called it The Structure, as a matter of fact – appeared in the garden outside her home. But might I digress? I find myself rather concerned about this peril to which you've alluded. In our research, we read—"

The Sixth First Scholar shook his head. "You are safe from all danger now, young fellow, and that is what matters. You shall face no peril here – that is, unless you are tasked with the proofing of the Fifth First Scholar's historiographies."

Everyone except for Scholar Cidnosin laughed properly. While Scholar Clel did join in, his contribution to the chorus of chuckles was short and abrupt.

"Still," he said once our merriment concluded, "I don't suppose—"

"We are simply desperate to know which one bore you here!" continued the Sixth First Scholar. "My personal favourite was the Woebegone Triangle, of course. Did it seem to be in good operating condition?"

"Did the luminescence still work?" cut in the Seventh First Scholar, her eyes alight.

"We do also wish to know," said the Sixth First Scholar begrudgingly, "if the luminescence still works."

"It does," replied Scholar Cidnosin tremulously.

"In our research, we read a poem with some sinister allusions to an awaiting predator, and I wondered if that might relate to this peril you describe?" persisted Scholar Clel.

Shall I record that this seemingly incomprehensible statement caused every First Scholar in the room to fall into an unsteady silence, punctuated by occasional sighs? **(You may record it, but I urge you to forget the matter entirely. Remember the Burdens that I and my fellow First Scholars bear.)**

42

"Wherever did you read such a thing?" asked the Sixth First Scholar.

"In, you know, the poetry," said Scholar Clel. "The poems you sent into the mind of a Scholar some years ago, which detail the nature of the Entries? Starting with: 'A Luminous Circumference – Melodious – to Spy . . .'"

Scholar Clel may well have continued reciting this poem in its entirety, but my Oaths mandate that I explain why he did not. You see, many First Scholars began murmuring disapprovingly after but a few lines – as is only reasonable – and Scholar Clel's voice quickly trailed off.

He paused to examine each of us, seeking recognition, but I do not think it is a breach of my Oaths to say that none of us knew what he was talking about.

"Poetry?" said the Seventh First Scholar with perceptible disdain. "That does not sound like us. Yet I wonder if *they*—"

"Now, now," called the Ninth Second Scholar. "Is it not true that our ancestors wrote the finest poetry in the earliest days of the Upward Archipelago? Perhaps Scholar Clel uncovered some ancient works."

"I am quite sure that is not the case," replied Scholar Clel. "We were under the impression that – I suppose it sounds rather nonsensical when I say it out loud, but at any rate – your Scholars created a vision that inspired one of our Scholars to compose poetry, and then a different Scholar – one of my personal favourites, incidentally, whom I recommend most heartily – at any rate, again, he founded a Society known as the Fleet—"

"You are correct, Scholar Clel. That does sound nonsensical," said the Second First Scholar, nodding at her fellow Firsts. "We cannot provide any clarification, as we are unfamiliar with the events in question. To compensate for our lack of knowledge, we will answer any other questions you may have."

"Well, I suppose I ought to have led with this." Scholar Clel gave Scholar Cidnosin a wan smile. "Scholar Cidnosin and I would very much like to arrange our trip home. Our families will worry if we do not return soon. Is there an Entry we may use when the time comes for us to depart?"

A hush fell over all the Scholars – the second hush of the meeting **[Personal Note:** which is quite the feat for us].

"What a foolish idea!" scoffed the Fifth First Scholar, just as the Sixth First Scholar said, "That is impossible." They exchanged glances that indicated some manner of unspoken conversational duel. Moments later, the Fifth First Scholar emerged as the victor.

"Our creations help people escape," he said, emphasising the scornful consonants of the *sc* sound so harshly that I feared he might start coughing. "Why would we use one to send you back into danger?"

"That is hardly the most important point," said the Sixth First Scholar. "We left the Entries in your world a thousand years ago. It is our curse that we cannot locate or repair them from within our refuge. We may only wait to see if escapees arrive, as you have. I do very much hope that more Imperilled people will follow your excellent example."

"More might follow us," said Scholar Clel, "if E. and I return home and speak with our fellows. Could you not build a new Entry here?"

The Sixth First Scholar blinked at each First in succession. Scholar Clel and Scholar Cidnosin, of course, could not interpret this established signal.

"Our Body of Scholars must discuss this matter further," concluded the Sixth First Scholar. "We shall call a symposium that will take place in the days to come."

"The days to come?" repeated Scholar Clel weakly.

"If you have further questions," drawled the Sixth First Scholar, "you may submit them later as a numbered list."

"Ah!" exclaimed Scholar Clel. "I do, in fact, have such a list in my possession! Just, er, ignore the parentheticals, would you?"

Scholar Clel produced a scrap of paper from his sleeve pocket and passed it to the Sixth First Scholar, who eyed it with grim surprise.

"How unexpected. Well, we shall respond in a timely fashion. I call this council to a close."

44

Scholar Clel opened his mouth as though to speak again, but the Sixth First Scholar's conversational assertiveness knows no bounds. (**I will allow that comment to stand, as it is fair enough.**)

"Please, Scholar Clel," said the Sixth First Scholar, struggling to sound sincerely cheerful and reassuring. (**Regrettably, that is also fair enough.**) "Do try to rest and enjoy our hospitality. Remember – all your troubles have come to an end!"

Because the Sixth First Scholar officially brought the meeting to a close, I ought to conclude my record as well. When I felt the urge to run after the strangers and speak with them, I resisted the temptation and focused on completing my notes instead. (**At least you are learning.**)

LIST OF QUESTIONS SUBMITTED BY HENEREY CLEL TO THE BODY OF SCHOLARS, 1002

1   How can we travel home? (You simply must insist on an answer to this one, Clel! Harness that tenacity you display when pursuing a wayward crab that does not wish to be observed!)

(All other matters are comparatively trivial when matched against #1, yet I shall enumerate them below nonetheless.)

2   Where is this city located? That is to say – we have seen some sources refer to this place as "another world". Are we somewhere within our own oceans, or have we been carried to a different Planet entirely?

3   How (and, most importantly, *why*) did you use the Structure to take E. to the island? Where is said island in relation to our present location? What more can you tell us about that place?

4   We understand you are the survivors of the Dive, but is it true that you – your ancestors, I suppose – abandoned your civilisation

45

on the Upward Archipelago because of some danger? What is the nature of that danger, and does it threaten us still?

(If I address the issues above, I will allow myself the pleasure of asking the far more trivial question below.)

5   Your depth-crafts – are they fancifully artistic, or are they made to resemble real creatures, extant or extinct? Do species like those inhabit these waters? ~~What must I do to see one?~~

(Perhaps that is too many questions for a single meeting. Knowing me, I shall barely have the strength to address one or two!

No, I must find the courage to speak up – for her sake, if not mine.)

EXCERPT FROM THE JOURNAL OF HENEREY CLEL, 1002

I feel too pathetic to address this entry to any hypothetical future Scholars. I do not deserve even their distant scrutiny! As if my embarrassing episode aboard the depth-craft were not enough, I have now failed E. once more because of my inability to hold ground in a conversation.

Here I am, again, beginning my diary entries (still crammed into the poor journal that normally holds scientific observations) in the most desultory fashion! Fortunately, there are far more important facts to establish before we reach the issue of my incompetence, as I have not written since yesterday. I shall summarise below:

Item 1. We are currently residing within what appears to be a completely self-sufficient underwater city. Its size, population, formal name, and extended history are currently unknown. I can say, though, that there are noticeable architectural similarities between this city and what visual representations survive of Antepelagic buildings. (That seems reasonable, considering that our research suggested this place

46

was created long ago to offer an escape from our post-Dive world. But how did they create it, and why? How could even the brilliant minds of our ancestors accomplish such a feat?)

Outside of cultivated spaces, like a most impressive garden, there are no plants or animals. We are protected from the ocean by an enormous dome made from a material that cannot be glass, because how could it support the immense water pressure? Our finest depth-crafts and the Spheres would barely withstand a year of continuous exposure to the depths before breaking apart!

Item 2. Our hosts possess technology beyond our greatest imaginings, and yet seem just as caught up in strict Scholarly customs as my own colleagues. These Scholars refer to themselves numerically instead of by their proper names, which gave me the chills at first – I believe this may mirror how Chancellor Rawsel thinks of the members of my Department. (No doubt he considers me the least significant figure of all!) When I inquired about this numerical nomenclature, however, the Thirtieth Second Scholar informed me that each individual's mind is likened to a title in a library. They classify themselves to ensure that each Scholar's personal knowledge is catalogued appropriately. Admittedly, I do rather like the sound of that!

Item 3. We may be trapped here for the foreseeable future – and all due to my previously mentioned incompetence, which shall be the focus of this entry henceforth.

Earlier this evening, E. and I braved a meeting during which I assumed our hosts might answer our questions and reveal more about the world in which we've found ourselves. I did prepare – I wrote a list of my most critical questions, annotating it with some encouraging notes to myself. (O, how I wish I had made a fair copy! I could use that encouragement now!) In the end, I did nothing but babble and blather. I hardly had the chance to ask anything, and I curse, as usual, my interpersonal ineptitude.

I said as much to E. as we exited. Because she is the very epitome of loveliness, she recognised my distress and suggested we rest for a moment before letting the glowing pathway lead us back to the Visitors' Quarters.

I suppose that is another note I ought to make about this city. It is laid out on a network of footpaths, each illuminated by transparent shell-shaped votives set with jaggedly gorgeous crystals. The paths are coded by colour and labelled with textured signs for those who cannot perceive the differences between certain hues (and some of them, I confess, are quite easy to confuse). Though I have not yet proven it, I am quite sure each pathway sounds differently when you step upon it, with the cobbles and crystals ringing in unique harmonies.

While the city does not exactly feature any natural surroundings, because the Scholars apparently constructed everything within the limits of the dome, some topographical variety still exists. The "land" itself is structured in a gradual bowl shape, with a slight dip between two vaguely higher ridges. The Visitors' Quarters and this council chamber are in the lower basin, and I can only just glimpse the ridges above me. They are dotted with small octagonal buildings and countless interlocking patterns of the aforementioned paths, which spurred me onto this digression in the first place.

I do not know where every pathway leads, but the pale blue roads connect the Visitors' Quarters to other parts of the city. It was near such a path that E. and I sat – on a thoughtfully placed bench of the same curvilinear form as we saw in the garden – to gather our thoughts.

"I wonder why they are leaving at staggered intervals," E. said as a few more Scholars skittered off. "I have not seen the ones they call First Scholars depart. Perhaps they stayed behind to whisper about us?"

"No matter how I try, I cannot match your visual memory! How have you already learned which are the leaders? I was too nervous to pay much attention to anyone's faces."

"I was only able to make such observations because you kindly led the conversation for the both of us."

"Yes, I must apologise for that," I said, not daring to meet her eyes. "I wanted to take control, and be friendly yet firm, and ask everything on our minds. As it happened, I simply could not. Again, I cannot apologise enough for failing you."

"In what way was the failing yours? They offered you no opportunity to speak! Giving them your list of questions was brilliant, though. I could have applauded when you swung that scrap of paper from your sleeve with such a flourish."

"If only they would read it," I replied mournfully. "If these Scholars are anything like my colleagues in the Department of Classification, full seasons could pass before they give us any answers – unless either of us develops an uncharacteristic sense of aggression and starts making demands! If only my brother were here."

"Well, seeing as neither of us are straight-talking sea captains, I imagine we shall simply have to make our own plans."

I watched as E. drifted away into a thoughtful look with which I have grown fondly familiar. At first glance, some might assume that her expression is simply a distant one, but I can tell by the slight curl in her lower lip and the swift movements of her eyes that she is thinking something complex and crafty, and it is (if I may) a most beautiful thing to observe.

"We need not wait for the Scholars to answer our questions," E. continued. "Despite all we thought we knew about the Structure, the Fleet, and so forth, there is clearly more we do not understand. Consequently, we must see what we can learn in secret. Did you notice how greatly your mention of poetry disturbed the Scholars?"

"It did not strike me at the time," I said, honestly – which was remarkable for me, really. With anyone else, I would have pretended to know exactly what they were talking about. That never feels necessary with her. "I was frustrated when they claimed ignorance of 'A Luminous Circumference'. Was I incorrect in my recollection? Had we not concluded that the Fleet believed in some danger – metaphorically represented as a predator in the poem?"

"That was my understanding. Darbeni's anonymous friend wrote the poem after experiencing a vision of the 'Better World', as Darbeni called it. The 'luminous circumference' referred to the Entry. The 'predator' was the danger we can avoid by retreating *through* the Entry to the very place we are visiting at present. But whoever gave the poet an impression of this place if not these Scholars themselves?"

"Perhaps there are other people? Other societies within this eerie sea? I did hear that rather disdainful Scholar mention a mysterious *they*. Might this relate to the 'Envoys' the Fleet also sought?" I could not help but sigh. "O, we do indeed have more questions than I could possibly contain in one list."

"Our first step, then, is to see if there is a library we may patronise – or sneak into, as the case may be."

I gazed at her in awe. "Really, E., you are full of surprises!"

"I am simply adapting to the circumstances!" Her voice quavered, but there was a smile upon her face. "We ought to ask someone – perhaps the Thirtieth Second Scholar—"

So enraptured was I, watching her speak, that I felt shaken when she stopped abruptly and took my hand.

"This is truly an impressive view, don't you think?" E. now spoke in a loud, bright manner that was entirely unlike her. "I never could have imagined such a unique layout for a city."

Looking over her shoulder, I noticed what she had seen already – the last group of Scholars heading in the general direction of our present location.

"It is unique," I said just as loudly and brightly, feeling strangely thrilled by our shared charade. "In fact, when I see these coloured roads and space-markings before me, I am rather reminded of the layout of several boxed games."

"Are you fond of games?" asked E. with such excitement that I wondered if she had forgotten we were engaging in a pretend discussion to avoid suspicion. "You never mentioned that in your letters."

"I suppose it never came up! I apologise."

"I only meant it's rather lovely that I may still learn new things about you. That makes me feel – well, at any rate, it is rather lovely, as I said," she concluded.

I did not know how to articulate the feelings this gave me. Instead, I merely asked, "Have you heard of The Tidepools Divine? That is my favourite of all, and I suspect you might also enjoy it."

"I'm afraid I know little of contemporary offerings, as I have long been bereft of a proper opponent. How does that game of yours work?"

"I warn you, I have bored Vyerin to tears with my explanations in the past."

"But I am decidedly not your brother."

Decidedly not, indeed!

I then became so caught up in describing the rules that it took me an embarrassingly long time to notice that the Scholars had passed us by.

"That was an impressive performance," I said, "though you needn't pretend any longer."

"There was no pretending involved," E. said, so suddenly and swiftly that she took us both by surprise. Thankfully, she immediately glanced away to conceal a blush, which also prevented her from glimpsing the undoubtedly ridiculous grin that formed automatically upon my face in response!

When our respective levels of self-consciousness stabilised, we decided that I would see E. back to the Visitors' Quarters, and then seek out the Thirtieth Second Scholar. That part of the plan, at least, proved remarkably easy to accomplish. After returning E. to her room (most reluctantly), I wandered the halls of the Visitors' Quarters until I encountered our new acquaintance, who seemed all too delighted to offer us a tour of their "auxiliary library" the next morning. I also learned it was well past what is considered a reasonable bedtime in this world, so I settled in to make these notes about the day.

Now that my writing is complete, I wonder whether it would be appropriate to knock on E.'s door and say good night. Obviously, our situation is a challenging one, but I cannot deny how wonderful it is that E. is here – here, with me, in the same place, after we spent such a long time getting to know each other in markedly separate locations! When I happened upon her in her hour of need last night, I felt secretly elated. Would she seek out my help again if we did not coincidentally wander into the hallway at the same moment?

I almost wish – but no, I shall not risk overdoing things in my ardour, and I must prepare myself for tomorrow's subterfuge!

Chapter 4

OFFICIAL RECORD BY THE THIRTIETH SECOND SCHOLAR, 1002

By my Oaths as a Scholar, I swear that the following account documents everything of significance that occurred on my third day of observing Scholar Clel and Scholar Cidnosin. (The Fifteenth First Scholar generously informed me that I should not, under such historic circumstances, spend so much time editing and composing drafts of these reports. Instead, everything I write should be "factual from start to finish" and "free from any flights of fancy". I note this for reference, because I am asked to record everything accurately, and I presume that includes the circumstances under which a report was written. As the Fifteenth First Scholar only has the time to annotate my council records, I must self-criticise in her stead!)

Last night, Scholar Clel came to me to request library access. How marvellous that such commitment to research exists in both our cultures. Here they are, in a place utterly new to them, and what they want most of all is to study!

Accordingly, I gave Scholar Clel directions to the auxiliary Visitors' Library, and invited him and Scholar Cidnosin to arrive at whatever time suited them best. (It took a mere three hours of rigorous debate to convince the Fifteenth First Scholar that awaiting the Visitors at the library was a productive use of my morning.) I had already read through thirty scrolls by the time I spotted the pair climbing the spiral staircase.

My introductory tour was unfortunately truncated – we visited only five archival chambers, toured a mere three-fifths of the collections on every level, and climbed an unimpressive two hundred stairs while crossing four of the ten Ascension Arches! When I apologised for not offering a more comprehensive experience, their disappointment was so intense that it looked like they could hardly breathe! They soon recovered, however, and praised the quality of my tour (with compliments I was too demure to accept, in accordance with Scholarly humility).

"You've shown us many wonders, and we are grateful," said Scholar Clel. "Out of curiosity, are there any sections we are not permitted to view? As a Scholar myself, I hold the rules of academic secrecy in the highest regard."

So passionate was he about preserving Scholarly secrecy that Scholar Clel's hands shook slightly! What paragons these two are.

"A remarkably sensitive question! We have no such rules in this library, as it was built for Visitors. Considering that said Visitors have been absent until now, we have not organised these shelves in a few centuries. If you find anything that seems out of place, simply let me know!"

"You will be staying here?" asked Scholar Cidnosin. "We don't wish to be a burden."

"It is no burden whatsoever. Of late, it has been my duty to patrol the perimeter of the city in search of the Imperilled. Now that you are here, my responsibilities have changed completely. I suppose I am still tasked with checking for Visitors once a day, but that is no longer the all-consuming task it once was." I gestured to the chair near the entrance that I had commandeered earlier. "I shall settle in over there."

For the rest of the day, I occupied that chair, occasionally glancing over my shoulder in hopes of spying Scholar Clel or Scholar Cidnosin. I did not, however, see them again, and I stopped myself from seeking them out until I grew hungry enough to suspect the Visitors might feel the same.

I found them in the corner, talking in the faintest and most reverent of whispers. As I mentioned previously, their respect for Scholarly spaces is truly admirable.

"I wondered if you might like something to eat," I said. "It is well past midnight. Shall I fetch us a feast?"

"It is past midnight?" asked Scholar Cidnosin with some horror. At the same time, Scholar Clel said, with equal horror, "You would eat in a library?"

"Yes, it is! And yes, of course! That's the beauty of using a reader. When you view a scroll or pyramidal or manuscript in such a way, there's no risk of making a mess."

I showed the two marvelling Scholars how to set up a reader and its projector, and how to wind the crank to cast the words of a scroll in gorgeous colours on the wall, or to rotate a pyramidal book to reveal its inlays. By this point, it had grown still later, and I offered to escort the Scholars back to their quarters.

"I don't suppose we could visit again tomorrow?" asked Scholar Clel before we parted ways.

"Of course!" I said with a smile. "O – but I do have a meeting to attend in the morning."

"In the unlikely event that we awaken fairly early," said Scholar Clel, "might we return on our own?"

"Certainly you may! I simply thought you might prefer company."

"O, we do always prefer company," murmured Scholar Cidnosin.

Out of devotion to my Oaths, I took a moment to observe the Visitors as they departed. I feel it is necessary to document the extremely pertinent fact that they were indeed walking arm in arm.

NOTE FROM HENEREY CLEL TO E. CIDNOSIN, 1002

Good morning, my dear E.,

I'm sad to say that I slept very little and have now reached the point at which lying in bed failing to sleep seems a worse fate than any other. I intend to creep away to the library and see what else I might discover before our gentle guard joins us.

It is unfortunate that we found little but esoteric histories yesterday, and that these Scholars' naming conventions make it difficult to identify the period in which any single item was written. (Surely the Fifteenth First Scholar mentioned in a scroll from centuries past is not the same as the one we met in the council, but how could I tell otherwise when they do not have more individualised titles?) Odder still is that puzzling map you discovered, which depicts the city alone amidst a fanciful sea of stars. Is that a metaphorical representation, or something more informative? (And, if the latter, what does it *mean*?)

At any rate, I would be most honoured if you joined me once again today. If you do not wish to walk about unaccompanied (which is perfectly understandable), I shall plan on returning around "two spirals past circle" (see, I am learning how clocks work here!) to see if you are ready. I hope you are sleeping peacefully, dreaming of something other than an infinite number of scrolls spinning in a hideous dance as their mocking mouths laugh at our inability to discover their secrets (which is simply an example of a nightmare one might have, naturally, and not the specific one that troubled me in the few moments I did sleep—)

Yours as always,

H.

UNSENT LETTER FROM E. CIDNOSIN TO SOPHY CIDNOSIN, 1002

Dear Sophy,

I avoided writing you a letter yesterday because I felt too ashamed. As you are no doubt aware, I have not returned home. Perhaps as you sit in the Deep House – already fretting over me – you might wonder why I thought it would be easy to come back in the first place.

Well, because I had travelled to and from that island, I assumed this route would be much the same. It never occurred to me that the highly advanced society responsible for such wonders as the Structure would not have one of their own readily available. Those were grand and unfortunate assumptions, I'll grant you that, and I am now suffering the consequences. It gladdens me, to some extent, that you are not able to rebuke me for my foolishness.

(I am doing plenty of that on my own, thank you.)

The Scholars are still "processing" the list of questions Henerey shared with them the day before yesterday. Henerey says our new acquaintances are much like Scholars anywhere in terms of eccentricity and temperament, but the Campus lifestyle – whether in our world or another – is all new to *me*! Despite our hosts' persistent reluctance to communicate more openly, however, we have not lost ourselves to despair. We have a project, and though it forces us to behave uncharacteristically, it also grants me some hope.

Our first step has been to fully inventory the library. We began yesterday, finding little of use. (I did uncover a book of ornamental motifs from before the Dive, Sophy – yes, a manuscript over a thousand years old, full of the most beautiful forms you ever saw! Can you believe it? I hardly dared breathe while standing in its general proximity!) We planned to continue our efforts this morning. When I arose, Henerey had set off already. Though he had kindly offered to retrieve me later, I decided to surprise him.

Here is the true surprise of our situation, Sophy – somehow, against all odds, I've found myself in an extraordinarily vast place with very few people about. The Scholars keep to themselves in their own part of the city. There are no crowds, no loud voices, no interactions with strangers to haunt me for hours on end. (Except during our meetings with the Scholars, of course, which I hope will be mercifully few.) Now, you know there is more that troubles my Brain than the mere presence of people, but I am also growing accustomed to the spaces and locations here, and their perceived perils dwindle by the day. The hallways outside of our quarters, which previously seemed impossibly intimidating, now rather remind me of the corridors of the Deep House. When I cannot sleep, I occasionally wander the halls just as I would at home. The prospect of encountering Henerey on such a wander, as I did by chance during our first night here, motivates me to continue my midnight strolls as much as is reasonable.

I will admit, however, that the rest of the city remains rather imposing. This morning, as I stepped out of the Visitors' Quarters and onto the glowing path, I felt all those familiar symptoms again – the rising sense of foreboding, the quickening of my breath, the bewildering array of horrifying images and scenarios manifesting in my Brain. For a moment, I became convinced that the note I read earlier was not written by Henerey, but must be a forgery by someone plotting to lead me away from the safety of our quarters and into this exposed location. I told myself that I should have checked his handwriting more thoroughly and cursed my negligence! I then concluded, with horror, that this unknown villain had harmed Henerey in some way. And I was to blame, too, for not being more meticulous! If I had only read the note a few times more, I might have saved his very life before it was too late . . .

Thus my train of grim thoughts continued.

I have many tricks and tools at my disposal, Sophy, but sometimes it is difficult to provide adequate treatment for oneself when overwhelmed with one's worst nightmares. I simply had to wait for my mental misfortunes to subside. To hasten that process along, I congratulated myself on being able to generate such frighteningly impossible scenarios at a moment's notice. (Perhaps I should become a writer of terrifying tales one day!) Then I forced myself to focus on my surroundings, which is a particularly interesting coping mechanism to deploy in a relatively unknown world. While there is no feigned "daylight" in the exterior areas of the city as in the garden, the surface of the dome does shift its colours slightly over time. I took a moment to observe the particular shades of pink, and imagined such hues recolouring the chaos of my mind into a peaceful monochrome.

Though I felt too panicked to continue walking, I told myself that the only way to disprove my thoughts completely would be to see Henerey alive and well at the library. The building glowed vibrantly from the inside, drawing me in like the lure of a Vapid Anglerfish. He was not near the doorway when I entered – nor was the Thirtieth Second Scholar perched anywhere – so I hurried forth to reassure myself of my dear companion's continued existence.

I found him in one of the library's rotundas, sitting within a swirling circle of crystal that functioned rather like a private room. Hundreds of these exist throughout the library, demonstrating the same empty excess present everywhere in the Visitors' part of the city. There is something heartbreaking about it – or there might be, if that emptiness were not suitable for me personally.

At least Henerey and I are doing our best to put these vacant monuments to good use. When I entered the crystal circle, I saw that Henerey had stacked its shelves with books and scrolls and covered a table with papers – or, I should say, what these Scholars describe as "papers". While the ancient Antepelagic books and scrolls feature traditional plant-based paper as we understand it, the Scholars prefer thin, beaten sheets of crystal that can be marked upon with a stylus made from more malleable stone. (Do you remember when Father took us to that tidepool cove just off the Atoll and showed us how to sketch on rocks with the abandoned spines of pencil-urchins?)

59

Henerey's desk was buried beneath various shapes and sizes of these funny glimmering papers, upon which he had scribbled creatures entirely unknown to me. One resembled a dolphin, but with an oddly disproportionate head, and another looked like a squid, but made up entirely of repeated rectangles. The best of them was a small crab, though its claws and legs were drawn so stiffly and firmly that it seemed armed with needles instead.

As Henerey was intent on his work, I tapped the wall before speaking to avoid startling him.

"You're industrious today," I said. (I did not think it appropriate to tell Henerey how wonderful it was that he had not been slain by the mysterious assailant conjured by my intrusive thoughts.) "What are all these creatures?"

"O! Hello!" he almost shouted, immediately rising from his chair to give me a charming little bow – and knocking most of the drawings to the floor, creating a terrific clattering of crystal. We both flinched at the sound, and I couldn't help but smile at what a jumpy, well-matched pair we are.

"Apologies!" he said, bending down to collect the papers. I joined him on the floor, seeking out a far-flung sketch of what might have been a turtle – if a turtle consisted of nothing but triangles and hexagons. This particular sketch featured an intriguing annotation that mentioned players, cards and forfeits.

"You are making a game?" I asked.

"You flatter me! I am merely replicating a game," Henerey answered. "I spent much of the morning reading through some remarkably dull scrolls. I thought I ought to give my weary brain a creative respite."

With charming formality, he pulled out a chair for me – which I rather embarrassedly accepted – and spread the cards on the desk. He had made a pair of matching game-boards on larger sheets, each filled with vague representations of what I supposed might be smaller creatures that typically live within a tidepool – either that or renderings of unfortunate Bacteria living on the other side of someone's shoe!

"Is it the one you mentioned before?" I asked. "The Tidepools Divine?"

He beamed at me. "Precisely! I'm touched you remembered."

"I pay close attention to everything you say."

"You have no idea how much that means to me." He laughed in a coughing way. "That is, I mean, because I am accustomed to lecturing at Apprentice Scholars who do not care a whit about what I tell them. Shall I show you how it works? Well, I suppose I can't, because I haven't finished all the cards yet. I'm ashamed to say that sketching is an onerous task for me. But I wanted to do my best for you."

Most of the time, Sophy, I feel Henerey is the charmer between the two of us, and I a mere hanger-on who fawns over his every word. After spending this unprecedented amount of time with him, however, I have come to realise he possesses a sweet vulnerability that he barely endeavours to hide. It gives me a sense of fondness I dare not describe further.

Also, because I am awed by his exceptional skills in every other capacity, there is something rather equalising about learning that Scholar Henerey Clel simply cannot draw.

I picked up his stylus and a blank card. "I am happy to assist. Would you describe one of these creatures to me?"

Henerey nodded with astounding rapidity.

"I can imagine no greater honour." He immediately extended his arm and pushed his other cards out of sight. "You must think my attempts entirely crude. I have never been able to get beyond the basics of illustration, which is why I was so entranced when you sent me that captivating sketch of your Elongated Fish."

I seized the sketch of the turtle and examined it closely. "I think your Academic training did you a disservice. I imagine you were taught that all drawing is made up of basic shapes, which is not incorrect, but the true artistry only begins when you use those shapes as a foundation for something extraordinary." I began sketching the turtle's shell, head, and flippers, introducing some dynamism by curving the limbs – as though the creature were paddling to the surface. Based on the description in the annotation, I also gave the turtle a rather unscientific expression of imperious disapproval. (While the final version of the drawing is now in Henerey's possession, I shall include the first draft at the end of this letter for your future enjoyment!)

In this moment, I felt incredibly aware of Henerey watching me. Struck by some unbelievable impulse, I even moved my neck to one side to give him a better view of the sketch.

"You have a true gift, E. I don't imagine that anyone at any Campus can draw as you do."

"It is the product of years of practice, that is all," I said, thankful that I had the pattern of the turtle's shell to occupy me so Henerey could not see my blush.

"As you draw, perhaps I can share my one true success of the morning's research. This scroll—"

It was at this moment that our artistic interlude was interrupted by what sounded like a sob.

We both flinched – again – and turned around to see our new acquaintance, the Thirtieth Second Scholar, standing at the entrance to the crystal circle and wiping away a tear.

"Apologies," murmured the Scholar, straightening their face into a smile. "It is touching to see the two of you together. Fond regard can make me extremely emotional, but that is, well, not the custom here. That is, it is no longer customary to be extremely emotional nor overly fond of others. Sentimentality distracts from our rules and regulations, and such distraction could be the ruin of us all, as they say. But there is something so quaintly charming about fondness, isn't there? Why, the other day – by which I obviously mean several *years* ago, when I still had time for the Frivolous Tales – I was reading *The Dawn and the Doldrums*, and the metaphysical romance—"

I would have happily listened to this speech in its entirety, as I too have read the Antepelagic epic in question, but the young Scholar possesses a remarkable talent for self-censorship.

"Apologies," the Thirtieth Second Scholar repeated. "Digression is a failing of character that I am working diligently to remedy."

Henerey and I shared a guilty glance, no doubt thinking of our own similar tendencies.

"I often find that exploring something unrelated is the best way to discover the truth about a difficult problem," said Henerey gallantly.

The Thirtieth Second Scholar nodded, eyes wide. "How revolutionary! I don't suppose you'd be able to say that to the Fifteenth First Scholar, would you? When I last submitted my notes to her, she – well, I do not wish to disturb you. I merely wanted to bid you good morning before my meeting."

"That was very thoughtful," Henerey replied. "Before you go, might I ask – is there any chance that my list of questions might be addressed at your meeting?"

"O!" the Thirtieth Second Scholar exclaimed. "That discussion has been postponed indefinitely. We have many epistemological debates scheduled at present, you see, and we are still trying to find—" Then they glanced frantically at a conical device on the wall that I had not quite registered as a timepiece. "I am terribly late! Enjoy the library, Scholars!"

The Thirtieth Second Scholar walked out of the library with a little skip that made me smile, despite the grimness of the news we'd just heard.

"I have never met any self-professed Scholar who seems so genuinely earnest," Henerey said after the Thirtieth Second Scholar was well out of earshot.

"My sister would no doubt protest," and I know you will, dear sister, "but the keenness of the Thirtieth Second Scholar rather reminds me of a younger Sophy."

"Really?" he asked. "I shall take your word for it!"

63

"Now, did you say you had something to show me? I could use some cheering after hearing that our fate depends upon the rapid resolution of epistemological debates."

"I feel much the same." Then Henerey began expertly setting up a scroll on one of the projecting devices that the Thirtieth Second Scholar showed us the night before. "These things are exceptional," he said. "You press just here to bring up some convenient reading lights. Where was I? Ah, yes – allow me to introduce *A Wayfinding Guide for the Newly Rescued*, Scroll One."

"Then we are not, in the end, examining classified materials, but rather reviewing the instructional guide our hosts should have given us from the beginning?" I tried to say this casually, but I was most relieved that I would not have to worry about breaking esoteric deep-sea laws after all.

"Indeed! And I can't say I'm not a little relieved." Henerey smiled and stepped out of the way to let me inspect the projection more clearly. "Why don't you read this paragraph, and then we can discuss it?"

"But why would I? Haven't we already established such a wonderful precedent of you reading to me?"

I haven't the slightest idea why I said such a thing aloud, but say it I did!

"If you like!" He moved back to the scroll and cleared his throat perhaps far more times than was biologically necessary. "'As you are now among the saved, we may reveal the secret nature of your rescue, and hope you will see many more of your Imperilled kin enter as you have. Our City sits within a constellation of passageways created by the Sculpted Saviours, which number in the hundreds' – the hundreds, E.!"

"So if we were to leave, we would be practically swimming in Entries – or Saviours – whatever you'd like to call them. Did you notice anything like my Structure in the water when we arrived?"

"I remember nothing useful about the circumstances of our

arrival, I'm afraid," he said in a quiet voice that made me chastise myself for bringing it up. "Still, the Entries must be like doorways. If we entered through a door on our side, we must have emerged through the door on this one, metaphorically speaking."

"By your logic, then, any such door can bear us home."

"Precisely!" he said. "But finding them may prove difficult. As you might recall, the ocean surrounding us is rather unnavigable. On our own, we could float forever without encountering what we seek. That is why I had no choice but to develop a rather unfortunate idea."

"Any idea that restores me to the Deep House cannot be unfortunate."

"It may be if it involves gently deceiving a well-intentioned person whom I shall not name," he said gloomily. After glancing around, Henerey leaned close to me in a manner that was surely motivated only by the need for secrecy.

"I propose we ask our good friend the Thirtieth Second Scholar to take us on one of those scheduled rounds about the city. For sightseeing purposes. While aboard, we surreptitiously note the location of one or two other Entries for future reference. Then, if the Scholars persist in refusing to help us, we will be better equipped to handle things on our own." He paused and frowned – not at me, precisely, but rather the situation. "That all sounds hasty and a little overdramatic when I say it out loud. We are not being held against our will, nor treated cruelly. Still, E., if there is a choice between carrying out clandestine research and being openly assertive with our hosts, I'm afraid I am the sort of person who is fatally inclined to choose the former. Am I overreacting?"

I could tell he was not pleased to be plotting in this way, and it unsettled me as well. Equally unsettling, however, was the thought that if we did not act, we might remain here for tides – or longer – as the debates raged on.

"As a well-established expert in overreacting, I imagine I am a good judge of it," I said. "Your plan is not unreasonable. You are not, after all, proposing we flee right now and take our chances in the ocean. This is merely a precautionary measure, to ensure we have the knowledge that could help us escape. If it comes to that."

"A wise judgement indeed. In any case, we are undoubtedly going against the wishes of our hosts, and I know the notion of breaking the rules troubles you just as much as it does me."

"To be fair, my Brain often makes me believe I have committed an unpardonable offence every time I neglect to check something at least fifteen times."

I could not believe I said that aloud, so casually, to another person. Whatever would he think of me? I did not wish to lie to Henerey about the extent of my condition, but I also did not intend to frighten him with unwarranted honesty.

"With that in mind, I suppose this is no worse," I continued. "I assume we should ask the Thirtieth Second Scholar about this outing as soon as possible. But would the other Scholars allow us both to leave with a single chaperone?"

"I had not considered that. Perhaps it would draw less suspicion if only one of us embarked on this initial surveying trip. Do not worry – I am happy to take care of it."

"Is 'happy' really the most accurate word?" I asked, observing him closely.

"There are far more fitting adjectives. But there is no need for you to worry." Henerey forced a winsome grin, which was charming even in its artifice. "After all, perhaps I'll obtain a sense of peace from the abyssal darkness this time around!"

I could discern all too easily that Henerey was trying his best to seem relaxed – but no one knows more than I do about the tricks we play to conceal our anxieties. For example, his hand was hovering just above the table, with his fingers flexed upwards to stop them from shaking. Seeing someone as courageous as Henerey act this way made me want to shield him from the depths at any cost. After all, it is my general impression that I am far better equipped to survive intense physical and mental stress. I do it every day, in fact.

"I shall go," I said.

"Decidedly not!"

"It is but a short journey. I am not at the Deep House, and that is fundamentally terrifying on its own. With that in mind, does it truly matter whether I am terrified in the city, or aboard a creature-shaped depth-craft?"

Henerey squeezed my hand in the most tragically desperate, affectionate manner. "I can hardly bear the thought of you facing this by yourself," he said slowly, "but such terror, E., overcomes me when I consider boarding a depth-craft again. The more I recall how I felt in that moment, the more I feel afraid now – not just of the water, but of the fear itself, if that makes any sense."

"I know precisely what you mean. While sometimes it's necessary, in my case, to face my fears by exposing myself to them, there are also times when we can best care for ourselves by avoiding that which terrifies us most. Of the two of us, I am less frightened of a short voyage in a depth-craft. I do, you know, live in an underwater house."

"How could I ever forget?" he laughed. "And I yearn to be back there with you, E."

Though my heart jumped for a moment at that statement, I reminded myself that he must have meant "back there with you" in the literal, practical sense. After all, he had left some of his things there, like his old daybook, and would need to retrieve them eventually.

"Then it is settled," I said. "We have a plan, and we – specifically you – worked very persistently to develop it. Until the Thirtieth Second Scholar returns, why don't you rest? I have a great deal of drawing to do."

And draw I did! O, Sophy, I know this may sound ridiculous, but spending the next few hours with Henerey, bringing his visions of these undersea creatures to life (with the artistic quality they deserve), was a gift like no other. I can hardly describe the experience of being with him. You know better than anyone that I have not much in the way of friends. Even my relationship with Seliara is based on nothing more than our shared childhood history and fondness for baked goods. When I remember that Henerey is not merely my clever, creative friend who completely memorised every card from his favourite boxed game, but that there is more to our connection – in this terrifying, thrilling way that I can still scarcely believe, especially since we've not overtly discussed the nature of our relationship outside our letters – well, it is overwhelming, to say the least, but I am immensely grateful for it.

It makes me recall your earlier letters from the Ridge and how much you enjoyed your breakfast conversations with Niea. You understand completely, don't you? Henerey and I had many engaging discussions in written form, but in person, it's all the more exhilarating.

I seem to have lost my original point, whatever it was, but please note that the Thirtieth Second Scholar did return, we proposed our plan, and they agreed (with an enthusiasm that pained us) to meet with me the next day for this purpose. My infiltration begins! Perhaps I shall try my best to act like you, for added confidence? (I did just attempt that bold Adventurer Sophy expression of yours in my looking glass, but I fear I looked rather more insipid than intrepid.)

Your strange reflection,

E.

ANNOTATED SKETCH BY E. CIDNOSIN, 1002

"Upon displeasing the Pontifical Turtle, the Player must Forfeit three cards from their Tidepool."

Chapter 5

OFFICIAL RECORD BY THE THIRTIETH SECOND SCHOLAR, 1002

By my Oaths as a Scholar, I give my word that this is an accurate record of my recent experiences – as accurate as any recording of such experiences could be, that is.

I promised to bring Scholar Cidnosin on my circuit around the city today, since she sought to learn more about our surroundings. I do admire Scholar Cidnosin's inquisitiveness, and that was the argument I made to the Fifteenth First Scholar when she expressed concerns about this journey. (Perhaps she was right to express them. In retrospect, I do feel a little wretched for convincing her otherwise – but there is little use in dwelling upon that!)

This morning, I arrived at Scholar Cidnosin's quarters and beat upon her door. A few moments passed, yet no response came. Most peculiar indeed! I decided to try Scholar Clel's door instead, hoping he might provide a clue to her whereabouts.

He, too, took his time to answer my knock. I was about to lose all hope when the door opened at last, revealing a most objectively weary man. (I can cite the bleariness of his eyes as proof, Fifteenth First Scholar!)

"Good morning, Scholar Clel," I said. "I am here to collect Scholar Cidnosin. I don't suppose you've seen her?"

He blinked several times before responding.

"Ah, good morning. If that is what it is. I do apologise, Scholar, but I believe you had arranged to meet E. some four hours from now?"

I nodded. "Precisely! I am right on schedule."

"I am afraid there may be," he said, his speech still slow, "a cultural misunderstanding at play. When we agree upon a time to meet in our society, nobody is expected to arrive until that precise hour occurs. While I am prone to earliness myself, I do believe you've set a record."

"What a revelation!" I said. "I shall inform the Body of Scholars immediately. At any rate, do you know where Scholar Cidnosin is?"

Scholar Clel glanced over his shoulder into the darkened room behind him, which I found most curious.

"She is – that is, I *suspect* she is asleep. In her own quarters, of course, which is exactly where she should be, under the circumstances. Why don't you return in half an hour to give her some time to prepare?"

I nodded, still delighted by my new cultural discovery. (Imagine making plans to meet without being expected to arrive several hours early. How efficient the Imperilled people are!) I took my leave of him and retreated to the garden, where I rested on a bench and counted every moment until exactly half an hour's worth passed. (As I did, I reflected upon Scholar Clel's odd manner and felt tempted to consider his behaviour and Scholar Cidnosin's apparent absence from her room in the context of an exceptionally Frivolous epic I once read – but no, I did not allow myself to be led astray!) When I returned to the Visitors' Quarters, Scholar Cidnosin awaited me in the corridor.

She remained quiet as we reached my dear old *Ieneros*. The silence continued as I charted our course and we set off, passing smoothly through the dome into the ocean. I tried to engage Scholar Cidnosin in conversation, naturally. She would always nod politely and murmur a few words, but the discussion never continued. I had to remind myself that she requested to go on this journey with me, for there was no evidence that she was enjoying it!

71

Still, I did my best to provide narration. "We've just exited the city and passed the Visitors' Quarters, which you'll recognise through the dome over there," I said. "O, I should explain: one can see through the barrier from the outside, but not from the inside. Now, to your left, down in the lowest basin of the city, is something new to you – our Artificial Ocean, a recreational spot we created."

At this, she stirred. "Like the garden in the Visitors' Quarters, but in the form of a beach? I should like to see that."

"When we return, I shall give you directions." I paused for a moment and observed Scholar Cidnosin struggling with her hair, which had gotten caught in the safety belt I insisted she wear. Before I could assist her, she tugged the wayward lock and lost a few strands with a painful rip.

"My hair is such a bother," she said with sudden ferocity. "This style is rather impractical when I must actually go out and do things."

"Is that unusual for you?" I asked.

"Under ordinary circumstances, I very rarely leave my house."

"We are a little alike, in that way. I may only leave the city for my patrols," I mused. "Sometimes I dream of seeing your world, though I know it is Imperilled and we are forbidden from going there."

"You speak of these mysterious perils so frequently," said Scholar Cidnosin. Thinking of my Oaths, I grew nervous, and wondered what she would say next! "I suppose you can't tell me more about them?"

"You are correct!"

"I assumed as much," she said vacantly. As her distress made me feel rather miserable, I racked my brain for another way of providing comfort that would not provoke a disapproving lecture from the Fifteenth First Scholar.

"Perhaps I can aid you with something else," I said. "I often trim my own hair, and that of other Second Scholars. Would you like me to help with yours?"

"You mean, cut it off?"

"Only if you wish. I could do it right now with my archivist's knife."

"Why would an archivist possess a knife? That is not a common practice in our society."

I hope my colleagues will be pleased to know that I did consider my answer to this question carefully. I soon decided I could perfectly well acknowledge the existence of our archives without letting slip any of the secrets contained within. (After all, thanks to the First Scholars' Burden, I hardly know any of those secrets myself!)

"We store our records underwater, beneath the city," I explained. "The vessels in which our documents reside are prone to barnacles and other such nuisances."

"O, I do know all about that! You won't believe how many barnacles I've had to scrape off the Deep House – my home," Scholar Cidnosin said. "I appreciate your offer. These days, I worry my wealth of hair will be my downfall. I imagine it will get caught in some kind of machinery, or else someone with nefarious intent will grab me by it."

"We have little in the way of complex machinery here, and I assure you that nefarious intent is strictly forbidden among our company!"

"O, that matters little. I tend to spend my days considering scenarios that are unlikely to happen."

"That does not sound exceptionally beneficial to you," I said, because my Oaths forbid me from saying things that are incorrect. "Wouldn't you rather be productive – or enjoy yourself – or, better yet, enjoy the unmatchable thrills of ceaseless productivity – than waste time focusing on illogical thoughts?"

"Certainly I would, if I could." Scholar Cidnosin smiled. "But it is my lot in life to determine how to overcome illogical thoughts. And perhaps cutting my hair might help with these specific worries. Shall we?"

"Just like that?"

"Only if it's really no trouble."

"No trouble at all." I allowed *Ieneros* to steer itself and reached to my belt for the knife, which I turned into scissors-like blades with a flip of my wrist. "How about just above your shoulders?"

"Why not?" Scholar Cidnosin squeezed her eyes shut as I trimmed away. "How far have we gone in our trip around the city?"

"About halfway," I said, which, conveniently, also described my progress on the hair-cutting front. "The location where I found the two of you is just behind us now. I doubt you would recognise it, though, since there is not much to see besides water out here in the—well, in this part of the ocean. O, I am finished, by the way. You may open your eyes."

Scholar Cidnosin reached up to brush against what remained of her hair.

"I cannot believe you did that so quickly," she remarked. "I haven't worn my hair short since I was a little girl."

"Take a look, if you like," I said, directing her to a reflective panel in *Ieneros'* jaw that I often use as a looking glass. As I busied myself with sweeping the evidence of the haircut into *Ieneros'* incinerating engine, I snuck a look at her pleased expression – which pleased me in turn.

"That is immensely fine work," Scholar Cidnosin said. "Now, back to the matter at hand. I was interested in seeing other Entries. Are they yet to come?"

"O, you won't see those," I replied. "That's why my colleagues overwhelmed you with questions about the condition of the Entries at the council meeting, as you'll recall."

"Yes, but did we not pass through an equivalent structure on this side when we travelled here?"

"I understand your confusion. It is not quite like that. The Entries produce a kind of projective force that will throw you, so to speak, through a metaphorical passageway to a particular location. And it only works in one direction, because if not," I laughed, "I may have succumbed to the temptation of visiting your Imperilled world long ago!"

I suspected that Scholar Cidnosin would be pleased by this news – after all, what pleasure compares to that of expanding your knowledge? – but instead she looked disheartened.

"I should have realised that," she mumbled.

"The Fifteenth First Scholar says there is no greater joy than that of correcting your mistaken assumptions," I said. "I am fortunate to share that joy with you!"

"What is your family like, Thirtieth Second Scholar?" she asked suddenly, saying my title for the first time.

"Do you mean family in the archaic sense?" I replied. "That is obsolete. But I do feel rather close to my adjacent Scholars – the Twenty-Ninth and the Thirty-First Second Scholars."

"Are they like your siblings?"

"Well, not in the biological sense. We do not share the same parents. But we were born around the same time, and we completed our studies together as we slowly came of age."

"How would you feel if you were never able to see them again?"

I pondered this for a moment. While such hypothetical thinking is rather unproductive, I must document the conversation as it was said.

"Under what circumstances would this occur? It would be impossible for me to go anyplace in the city where they could not find me."

"Imagine you were going to our world, then."

"But that is forbidden. I was only jesting."

"Is it forbidden to imagine a scenario in which you might do such a thing?"

Sometimes, there is something incredibly intense and direct about Scholar Cidnosin that rather startles me!

"I suppose there is nothing wrong with imagining it from a literary perspective, pretending I am some ancient Scholar from before the Dive writing an epic about a family torn apart. O! In that case, I imagine I could hardly bear it. In particular, I'd be miserably bored without Twenty-Ninth. How I would mourn his absence!"

"That's why Henerey and I simply must leave," she said. "Because our families may be mourning already – perhaps they believe we are dead. Is there nothing you can do to convince the council to help us?"

"Well, they do not need to worry about you dying," I said. "How old-fashioned. We put a stop to that long ago."

To my regret, this statement of a plain fact seemed to confuse her more than anything else.

"What exactly do you mean by that?"

I prepared myself to deliver a lengthy and reasonable explanation that would be safe for Scholar Cidnosin to hear, but, as it happened, I noticed a subtle shift in the water at that very moment. The colours were changing from the beautiful hues of darkness to something paler, more glimmering, and undoubtedly unsettling.

Then, to my horror, I regret to record that I definitively encountered an Illogical One for the very first time in my life.

At this point, as my Oaths demand, I must stop writing to avoid tainting the accuracy of our records.

EXCERPT FROM THE JOURNAL OF HENEREY CLEL, 1002

Today I strolled through the city's majestic indoor garden and pondered the nature of journaling. When I began keeping a diary in my daybook during my voyage on the *Sagacity*, I hoped that chronicling my thoughts would help me document important developments and process my emotions – about rays and romance alike. Surely I should have even more to record under the present circumstances.

Instead, several days have passed and I've written next to nothing. That is not to say that I have observed nothing of note – on the contrary! Yet I am fortunate enough to have another person with whom to share these observations, and I take advantage of this on an amazingly regular basis.

She was not here today, which is why I attempted to distract myself by seeing what wonders I might discover in the garden. Though E. wretchedly outpaces me in artistic accomplishments, I challenged myself to sketch any living thing of my choice on a page torn from this very book. (I discarded said page shortly afterwards. Nothing I draw deserves to be preserved for posterity.)

This proved a difficult exercise, because I have never found myself in an ecosystem with so little animal life. Even when I was confined, for the most part, to our Laboratory Anchorage at Boundless Campus, things were not entirely lifeless – practically everyone had an aquarium or two bubbling away in their office, and there were seabirds that could be tempted down from the skies by simply daring to stand on a balcony with some manner of delicacy in one's hand. (I know our food is unhealthy for these scavengers, but I have no regrets whatsoever about that day when a great Effervescent Auk swooped over my head and seized my entire lunch! What a pleasure to inspect its plumage patterns so closely – and to think that such a miraculous experience came only at the cost of going hungry for the afternoon.)

That is all to say that I might feel more inclined to study nature if I had nature to study. What I ended up sketching in the garden was one of the peculiar fish, which are utterly primeval and unlike anything I've ever seen alive. They are hulking, sublime things, longer than my arm and covered all over with the most dreadful spiky fins that I recognise from the fossil record. Perhaps I shall conduct a more thorough examination of them tomorrow. I hope I might have some company on that occasion!

As I may have mentioned several times already, I am alone today. Brave E. is off on a journey that may ultimately help us return home. I miss her intensely and am moping about in a manner that my brother (and most other reasonable souls) might consider somewhat pitiful. But can I be blamed, considering everything that happened recently – especially yesterday evening?

I must confess that what I am about to write next I dread to put to paper. It feels too precious to be captured in such a way. As I do not know what may eventually befall us, however, I am convinced that a record is necessary. (And, as an additional comfort for myself while I endure the aforementioned missing and moping, I welcome the opportunity to relive these recent memories.)

Let us begin with practicalities, shall we? I suppose I have not yet mentioned my present lodgings – how forgetful of me! That may be because I can hardly describe my room with the vocabulary one employs at home. Firstly, the walls have no portholes or windows of any kind. A series of small openings runs across the very top of the wall, created by thin struts that I hope are far stronger than they appear. To make up for the lack of windows, the ceiling itself is transparent – which poses no issue because there is no sun to awaken us. The carpet and bedclothes glow merrily in purple and gold when I enter. The fibres used to create these textiles must also feature bioluminescence (that somehow remains after said fibres are harvested and processed). Simply astonishing. I always tell myself that I shall have to examine them more closely, but I never do.

At any rate, yesterday evening (if that means anything at all, considering that there is little visible distinction between day and night) we retired early to our rooms. I had already spent a most joyous day with E., but I am nothing if not greedy – I wanted to keep speaking with her, to see her brilliantly sketching those creatures as I described them, or simply sit with her and do nothing at all. Yet I knew she must prepare for her ordeal the next morning, and I did not want to overtax her, since she volunteered to spare me from the embarrassingly spontaneous claustrophobia I developed.

I collapsed on my bed, briefly observed the textiles (described previously), and eventually turned off my lamps (shell-like shapes that hover like clouds throughout the room – one must wave one's hands to operate them). On my first night here, I worried that the luminescence of the textiles would keep me awake, but they dim as soon as I settle down. Is it Antepelagic magic, like from a Fantasy, or simply the result of some fantastic technology that I do not yet understand?

I dozed comfortably for an unknown amount of time until I felt myself pulled from sleep by a quiet but steady series of knocks. How beautifully rhythmic! I stumbled to the door (wearily marvelling *Isn't it astounding that knocking seems to be a cultural practice that transcends—*) and was surprised to see E. before me.

She looked rather frantic, and I suppose I should have said something like "How may I help you?" or "What is the matter?" but instead, like a fool, I uttered in a sleep-hazy mumble:

"I am delighted to see you, my dear."

(For indeed I was!)

"I am sorry to disturb you," E. began, but I made some weary noises of objection that I cannot quite recall. "May I please speak with you?"

Shaking my head to awaken myself, I ushered her in. She paused just inside the door, quivering like a fish's quick gills.

"I told myself I would not wake you unless it was urgent."

"You may always wake me under any circumstances. What is the matter?" Now fully awake, I managed to help her settle on the corner of the bed.

"It may be due to my nerves about the journey tomorrow, or simply a general consequence of our situation as a whole, but I am truly struggling tonight," she said. E. wouldn't look at me, and her hands moved constantly, tapping her knees with agitated strokes. I have never seen her like this before – which is perhaps not surprising, because we have, by this point, spent only about a tide in each other's company.

"Is it the door again?" I asked.

"That is but a part of it. Sometimes – o, I daren't speak of it. I cannot fall asleep when my mind is like this, and I see such awful things in my brain, and I lie there alone utterly terrified, as though any second I am about to die and cause trouble for everyone." Suddenly, E. stood up.

"Again, I apologise," she said, pacing towards the door. "I should not have told you any of this. I shouldn't have come at all!"

My first instinct, as she made to depart, was to take her hand, to stand in her way, to stop her – but I did not want to frighten her more, and any of those actions would be a little out of character for me, anyway.

Instead, I simply stood and said, "My dear E., you are under no obligation to leave – in fact, I would very much prefer if you didn't."

She turned back to me, her eyes vast and unblinking and wild.

79

"You needn't keep this to yourself," I said in a rush. "You did not leave me when I suffered on the depth-craft, did you? There is absolutely nothing you could do that will frighten me, or make me any less fond of you. Please, won't you stay?" I took a breath, allowing my sense of decorum to catch up with me. "That is – consider the possibility of staying. If you would like."

I must have said something right in my ramblings, because stay she did.

As usual, I can hardly record these private moments without acknowledging the possibility that someone may well read them. In many ways, you omnipotent readers of the future, I am at your mercy. I cannot control whether you decide to intrude upon my dear and intimate memories. It occurs to me, however, that I could limit your reach by inventing some fanciful scene instead of writing the truth. What choice would you have but to believe me?

O, fear not. I am simply teasing you. After all, I have no need to waste my time crafting falsehoods for the sake of hypothetical Scholars who may or may not analyse my journal in years to come. With that in mind, I will not say that she fell into my arms and wept and let me truly care for her as I long to do, because that would be a rather silly thing to expect from us, wouldn't it?

She did, however, return to the bed, and I sat on one of the triangular floor cushions (they also glow, incidentally) as she told me of her experiences with similar night-time troubles even within the comfortable confines of the Deep House. I won't record those details – they are not mine to tell.

As our discussion continued, and the hour grew later, I noticed how truly exhausted she was. I could not help but wonder how many nights she'd spent in a similar state. It did not come as a surprise when her eyelids started fluttering closed mid-sentence. Then, not long after, this woman whom I have come to cherish more than anything happened to fall asleep – in my very bed!

You can imagine the state of immense panic this created for me.

I suspect most people might be alarmed to find themselves accidentally asleep in someone else's company, and it was paramount for me to ensure that E. would not feel she was in a vulnerable position. At the same time, I desperately did not wish to interrupt what was undoubtedly well-needed rest.

I sat silently, stilled by indecision, not allowing myself to look at her – though I can imagine, if I dare, that she would have looked incredibly peaceful, and what a beautiful sight it would be to see her free from the troubles that would not stop tormenting her—

At any rate, I suppose it is not a surprise that after wrestling with my feelings for several moments and wondering whether I was obligated to wake her, I resolved the issue by dashing to the door as quietly as possible.

Unfortunately, my agitation affected my attempt at stealth, for I heard E. stirring behind me as soon as the door opened the slightest sliver.

"Where are you going?" she asked in a quiet, almost lazy tone that made my heart surge.

"Please don't worry! You were sleeping, and I did not want to disturb you, and I thought you might be troubled if you knew I were here, observing you, so I thought I would go out and have a rest in one of those nice chairs in the corridor," I babbled, holding up my hands as if I had been caught prying into someone's research files.

E. arose with a speed that alarmed me. "I'm terribly, terribly sorry," she said wearily. "I will go immediately."

"O, there is no problem whatsoever!" I whispered. "Perhaps this bed is more suitable to pleasant dreams than yours; it would explain much."

"What must you think of me? How could I be so inconsiderate?"

"E.," I said, opening the door further so she would not feel trapped, "are you troubled because you are uncomfortable being here with me, or because you don't wish to cause offence?"

"The latter," she confirmed, her eyes wide in the dim light from the hallway outside.

(That was the answer I hoped for, but hearing it was still the most pleasant surprise!)

"Then can you trust me when I say nothing would make me happier than knowing you can rest at last? With your journey tomorrow, you need sleep at any cost! I urged you to stay earlier; I would not ask you to leave now."

She took in a heavy, shaking breath and then gave me a crescent of a smile that could have cured me of every past ill.

"Then you should not leave either," she said in a spectre of a voice.

I reacted to this as any gentleman would – by closing the door, seizing one of the coverings from the bed, and rolling myself onto the floor on the furthest side of the room.

"If you are absolutely sure, then I shall," I said. "The bed is yours. Have you seen what happens to the textiles yet? You must have some in your room as well, but perhaps the colours are different. At any rate, they are simply astonishing."

"You truly don't mind?" E. said. "At the very least, I should be the one to sleep down there."

"It is too late!" I cried as I cocooned myself within my blanket. "I am already fast asleep and quite comfortable. Please try to rest, won't you?"

I could say no more than that. I felt too exhilarated and terrified! We settled into our respective sleeping spaces, and the luminescence began to dim again in that comfortable way.

I did not sleep much myself – so consumed was I with the fear of what would happen in the morning. I suspected E. might be behaving unusually because she was deprived of sleep, and I worried she would panic upon finding herself in this unfamiliar place. By the time the Thirtieth Second Scholar arrived – far ahead of schedule – I was grateful for the interruption.

And E. heard us speaking at the door, anyway, so I do not know what she thought when she awakened, and we took leave of each other so hurriedly afterwards. Now E. has not yet returned, and the hour grows later, and I am alone in my room – this room in which we both slept for a few brief hours – and I cannot unravel my thoughts.

The truth is that I have little experience with the practices and niceties of being in a formal relationship. My knowledge of Natural History is of no use here, as the majority of living creatures other than ourselves build relationships to pursue pleasure and procreation: neither of which are especially desirable to me. As if my lack of expertise in these matters were not enough, I also do not want to unnerve her by making any bold proclamations of affection.

My last confession, the worst of all, is this: I fear I am more concerned about these comparatively trivial matters of the heart than the prospect of being trapped in this underwater world. It is not staying here that terrifies me the most – it is the thought that E. might soon see how the correspondent who seemed charming on paper is just an anxious, sad fellow who forgot even to bid her good night.

It is later still and my fears grow further. I shall put this down and perhaps take to pacing the corridors in a decidedly calm fashion!

Chapter 6

UNSENT LETTER FROM E. CIDNOSIN TO SOPHY CIDNOSIN, 1002

Dear Sophy,

Previously, I took comfort in this correspondence. I reassured myself that when I returned home, my notes would amuse and enthral you and spark all kinds of fascinating conversations about this place.

After my experience yesterday, though, I must force myself to acknowledge that these letters are nothing more than pretend. Perhaps one day I shall stop writing them altogether, but, at present, keeping up the façade comforts me still.

In some ways, this revelation is freeing. Now I may write whatever I like without fear of what you might say! For example – yesterday I had my hair cut short for the first time in decades. And it was I, not Arvist, who dropped the final piece of that octopus jigsaw behind the bookcase in the library, where it languishes to this day! There are all sorts of funny things I could divulge to a sister who can neither judge nor even respond. For the moment, however, I must focus on working through my thoughts about our present situation.

I travelled through the Structure to seek answers about my unusual "vision" and what Mother thought she knew. What I found instead was an odd assortment of related discoveries that simply produce more questions. While this may be the "city of Scholars" about which the Fleet dreamed, the island I visited and the poetic ramblings of Darbeni's associates apparently mean nothing here. And, most frustratingly, we failed in our attempt to investigate a means of escape. Like giddy children we've been in the library these past few days, playing with our illicit research and pretending we could solve our problems easily. How were we to know that these Structures are unidirectional? We might have realised this sooner if we were not both so weary and anxious, but now it is too late, and all ways home are barred to us.

Except, perhaps, for one, though that option relies upon the assistance of a most unbelievable ally. I expect I shall have to start over to explain that properly.

The day could not have begun more strangely. I would blush to mention it in any other context, but I can tell you in our pretend correspondence with no issue! You see, when I woke up, startled by some sounds at the door, I was surprised to find myself in Henerey Clel's bed.

Now, to be fair, is it really *his* bed? Like everything here, it is the property of our hosts. He does not own it and has not slept there regularly for more than a few nights, nor was he in it himself at the time in question. In fact, the bed is completely identical to mine in the adjacent room, and there is nothing about it that—

See how I digress already in my embarrassment? I must remind myself that you may never read this!

At any rate, I remembered in an instant that I fell asleep there after horrible thoughts tormented me for hours, and he was so kind and slept on the floor for the sake of my comfort. But Henerey was not down among his pillows when I woke up. No, he was at the door, whispering with someone.

As I tried to sit up, I realised my hair had burst from its braid and tangled into a nightmare of knots on my right side. I did not have much time to wrestle with it, for Henerey soon turned from the door, his eyes widening in the dim light as he noticed me (and, I assume, the horrible state of my hair).

"Good morning!" he said, which seemed funny and formal under the circumstances. "I'm dreadfully sorry if the noise startled you, but I'm glad you're up. Did you sleep well?"

"Very well. I am sure you didn't, though. I apologise again for the intrusion."

"I had a perfectly wonderful time," Henerey said. "I wish you could continue resting, but it seems our understanding of the appropriate hours in which to conduct business is not shared by our friends here. The Thirtieth Second Scholar already came to call, and I barely managed to beg a few moments for you."

"Then I must go. What will you do while I am away?"

"I hadn't considered it. Really, I should return to the library and see if there is anything else that can aid us."

"I think you shouldn't," I said as I rose. "You have worked tirelessly. Why don't you take a walk in the garden or something of the sort?"

"I shall find its wonders dulled without your company."

"O, you needn't say that out of politeness. I know there is nothing Scholar Henerey Clel enjoys more than spending time in nature and uncovering its secrets. Do you not remember that I have read all your books?"

"There may indeed be many things of interest to me there," he said with a smile. "I was, however, not being polite."

By this point, I had made my way to the door, and we both stalled there, a slight distance from each other. I felt I ought to say something — to thank him for helping me sleep peacefully, perhaps more peacefully than I ever would have thought possible, and to convey how grateful I was to have him here with me and how, despite the protests of my Brain, the truest part of me rather wished I could stay with him every night, and—

"I've not made your bed," I said. "I'll go back and do it now."

"The very least I can do is make the bed. I only wish you did not have to leave so soon." Henerey took my hand and held it firmly, his thumb running anxiously around the side of my palm. (Because you will not read this, sister, I may confess that the detachment with which I wrote the previous sentence is quite opposite to how I felt at the time.) "Please be careful, won't you, E.? You are all I have here."

"I will, I swear." I wondered if his mind, like mine, also hummed with thoughts he could not bring himself to express. Was there not something grand and heart-warming I could have said? We confessed in our correspondence that we were in love with each other, but there is something altogether different about signing off a letter and making such a proclamation in person. At this juncture, a kind of leave-taking, perhaps I ought to have reminded him of my feelings – but I could not, Sophy, because I felt so unbearably shy. Besides, the pressure of the Thirtieth Second Scholar's impending return cut short whatever might have happened had we more time.

While I intended to keep mostly to myself during my journey with said Scholar, I did not want to be entirely rude – so I obliged their attempts at conversation as best I could. (Our most significant discussion resulted in that aforementioned change to my hair!)

Then something happened that even the Thirtieth Second Scholar did not expect.

Because I had no way of measuring the passage of time, I tracked our journey by the changes in the quality of the water instead. At first, it was as dark as when Henerey and I arrived. Yet as we moved forward and the glowing bubble of the city diminished in our wake, I discerned a small pinprick of pure, purple light growing ahead of us, and it became steadier with each forward thrust of the Thirtieth Second Scholar's beastly depth-craft.

"This is not allowed," the Thirtieth Second Scholar said suddenly, going to the helm – really, a translucent triangle in the middle of the automaton's throat.

"I don't suppose you are allowed to tell me what is not allowed?"

"You understand our rules so thoroughly, Scholar Cidnosin!"

"Are we in danger?"

"In danger of me losing face with the council? Absolutely." Then, perhaps noticing my growing concern, the Thirtieth Second Scholar gave me a warm smile that was likely intended as a comfort.

Alas, no smile could prepare me for the sensation of finding myself floating in the purple water moments later.

First I gasped, and then I panicked because I had gasped underwater, which surely would cause me to begin drowning. I felt just as I did when I was washed away into that tunnel of water during the incident at the Deep House. The Thirtieth Second Scholar and I were suspended in the sea outside our vessel – I could see the Mechanical Beast behind me, resting as though anchored – but I could not perceive the sea against my skin.

This is yet another moment, Sophy, when I am relieved that you may never read this, because I fear you won't believe a word of it! Yet when I experienced the inexplicable in the past, I kept it from you, and I do regret that now. There is nothing I can do but describe what I saw.

Hovering in the water before us was an enormously tall woman whose torso ended in an impressive, dolphin-like tail, something I had only ever seen in old engravings for Fantasies featuring mythical sea-people. (Didn't we find such stories quite dull in our youth, as our family already managed to live underwater without scales or tails?)

Incidentally, I am not exaggerating my description of her height. She was at least four times my size, and I will confess that I felt as terrified as if I were faced with a whale or shark or squid or any other giant of the sea.

The water continued to sparkle dramatically as the woman watched me. Her eyes were fathomless like the ocean that surrounded her, and the lights that flashed before us reflected off her pupils. Before she could speak, my companion jumped in.

"This is why we call you the Illogical Ones," grumbled the Thirtieth Second Scholar. "Why must you remove us from our vessel in this most illogical fashion? Without even doing us the courtesy of explaining exactly *how* you are accomplishing such a marvel?"

"Is it unpleasant for you?" she asked – and o, I wish I could describe her voice! What sonority it had. "If only I could receive you at my home! I will fashion a home for you instead."

Sophy, do you remember learning about the cold waters of the Second Ocean as children? I recall Father reading to us, describing this impossibly different climate in which the water froze into sheets of ice the size of islands. (How we all marvelled at our icebox for the rest of the day, trying to imagine a frigid horizon!)

I mention this because the water suddenly began to freeze, forming a perfectly cube-like room around us. A box of ice, rather than an icebox! As I watched, baffled, lines etched themselves upon the icy walls. Any remaining unfrozen water seeped out through holes in the ceiling, leaving us vexingly dry. The Thirtieth Second Scholar and I slid about the floor of this remarkable construction as the sea-woman continued to float before us.

"Do you prefer this? Or does my art still cause you pain?"

"Well, it would be inaccurate to say any of it pains us," said the Thirtieth Second Scholar. "It is quite lovely to see the water from this perspective, I confess. Still, that does not make it appropriate! How are we able to do this?"

"Because I asked permission from the tiny pieces that make up the water and all the parts of your bodies, besides," sang the woman. "But it is your friend, not you, whom I have come to see. Her face feels familiar."

"I don't imagine it does," I said. "I am certain you and I have never met."

She turned her head to one side and examined me most exhaustively, her eyes diving back and forth with studious precision. The colours of her irises shifted constantly to match the seawater.

"Perhaps not," the sea-woman concluded. "Perhaps another shares your shapes."

"Perhaps she's confusing you with your sister," laughed the Thirtieth Second Scholar.

Before I had time to imagine the hilariously improbable scenario of this peculiar being encountering you, dear Sophy, the colour of the water transformed from purple to pink. I do not know what this change signified. For all I know, it was entirely for dramatic effect, as the sea-woman chose this moment to produce a goblet in the shape of a cone shell – a gossamer vessel wrapped in a spiral of light that looked more shimmering than substantial.

"Have you come to join me?" she asked.

Defying the slipperiness of our icy encasement, the Thirtieth Second Scholar sprang up in indignation once more.

"No! Decidedly not, Scholar Cidnosin! How dare you, Illogical One?"

"There's no need to worry," I said, shaking my head politely at the offering. "I avoid drinking or eating unfamiliar things when I can help it. Besides, there did not appear to be anything in that goblet at all."

The Thirtieth Second Scholar looked at me as though I had just failed the most elementary of examinations.

"It's consumable sound, not liquid. If you were close enough to listen, Scholar Cidnosin, she could have forced you—"

"I force no one," sang the woman in a mournful descant. "Where is your companion? Is he well?"

"How did you know about him?" I asked, though I neither expected nor received a straightforward answer.

"My siblings and I lead lonely lives. In our corners of your world we wait for you to come to safety. Your crossing heartened me, but there are many still who need our help."

A thought occurred to me, and I tried to conjure the courage to act upon it.

"Though I am already here, I continue to require help – if that is something you can offer," I said, hoping my voice sounded Sophy-like. "My companion and I simply must go home. My sister is there, and his brother, and everyone we care about."

"That is certainly not allowed!" exclaimed the Thirtieth Second Scholar.

Though my hearing was dulled by the sound of the water around us, I could discern a distant, disorienting melody harmonising with the sea-woman's voice when she spoke again.

"Why would you return when you know what danger lies there?" she asked.

"No one will tell me anything about this supposed danger," I said with a pointed glance at the Thirtieth Second Scholar.

"I could send you on a journey again," the sea-woman said. "But I fear it would not take you where you wish to go."

I repeated her words in my head.

"Again?" I repeated. "Did you send me to the island, through the Structure? I thought the Scholars—"

"I dare not tell you about that place. Nor can I return you home. All I may do is send my dreams through those – what name did you give them? Structures?"

"Sculpted Saviours," said the Thirtieth Second Scholar with a sniff. "And they are not yours to meddle with! Did we not already issue several written complaints about this matter centuries ago?"

"If someone else happened to find a Structure, could you send them a vision of me?" I pressed. "It is much to assume, but we still have that one in the undergarden, and if my sister goes near it ..."

"I will try," the sea-woman sang. "I shall strive to remember the colour of this conversation."

"Do not grow too hopeful, Scholar Cidnosin," said the Thirtieth Second Scholar. "If she sees a particularly compelling sea-vent over the next few days, she will forget your request completely."

"Then I will halt my studies of the vents, charming as they are," replied the sea-woman, her voice rising in one final crescendo. She swam towards me, arms outstretched. For a moment, I rather feared that this fascinatingly powerful being would enfold me in an unexpected embrace. (As you know, I fear such overtures from any stranger, mythical or not.) Imagine my relief when she simply twisted her hands in wave-like motions, causing purple light to emerge once more from the tips of her fingers.

"I miss my siblings as you miss yours," she murmured to me as the frozen walls collapsed. They did not melt, like ice would. Rather, as each wall diminished, the physical barrier seemed to be replaced by a ringing sound that was almost too high to be bearable – but just oddly melodic enough to be enjoyable.

No longer held back by the ice, the sea swirled around us in a wash of purple and gold. This time, I swear I could feel her enchantment at work. It was like – oh, Sophy, I know you'd be able to explain this better than I ever could, but I *must* try – I suppose it was like the ocean around me simply chose to stop for a few moments. No water could enter my lungs or sweep me away, because it was waiting – waiting on the sea-woman's word. I listened to the peculiar ringing melody and felt myself move. Towards the depth-craft, which stayed suspended in the still water, up to its sculpted sides, through the engraved metal and pipework and pistons . . .

Then we were inside the depth-craft as though nothing happened. Well, I suppose there was one change worth mentioning – the Thirtieth Second Scholar ended up in the passenger's chair, and I in that of the navigator! Afloat in the strangeness of the entire affair as I was, I became overcome by the urge to laugh. (That was no doubt a better option than the more intense reactions I was equally tempted to display.)

The Thirtieth Second Scholar, on the other hand, seemed extremely put out. The mood aboard our vessel only worsened when my companion reactivated the controls of the Beast and noticed the time.

"The Fifteenth First Scholar expected our return ages ago! She must have sent out search parties. What a disaster!"

"I don't understand," I said. "Were we not in the ocean for but a few moments?"

"Such is the way of the Illogical Ones! When you are with one, nothing works properly. Time does not pass, or it passes too quickly, or both, somehow."

"But how do they possess such powers?"

"We do not know, because they refuse to – well, really, I am not allowed to say," the Thirtieth Second Scholar said.

"Won't you answer but a single question for me?" I asked. "If you do, I shall answer a question for you about my life – and none of your fellow Scholars need to know."

"I suppose it is true that I will not be obliged to record this conversation, because it occurred directly after an encounter with an Illogical One."

"Were you recording every part of our conversation before now?"

"What is your question? Please don't ask anything dangerous, I beg you."

"Then – what are the Illogical Ones? Biologically speaking, I suppose," I clarified. "I have never seen someone like her outside of a Fantasy. The creative minds of our world have long imagined all sorts of hypothetical beings, but I did not think them possible in reality."

"I cannot answer that question – well, not all of it – it depends on what the Fifteenth First Scholar would consider essential information – but would she think—"

The Thirtieth Second Scholar began to pace around the cabin before speaking again.

"You and I are of the same species. The Illogical Ones are inexplicably unique. Greater than human. In an illogical way, I should say! They possess the power to do all sorts of unfortunately impossible things."

"She said she spoke to the water – what did she mean by that?"

"Our agreement was for one question alone, and I have far more significant things to ask." Then the Thirtieth Second Scholar grinned devilishly. "Now then! Is it true that the air and light of your world makes people more susceptible to their base emotions and passionate desires?"

At that, I could only smile. I did want to return to the topic of the Illogical Ones, but I was content to retreat for now – confident in the knowledge that the Thirtieth Second Scholar, despite their devotion to the rules, may be capable of revealing more than the Body of Scholars might like.

"Many of us are ruled by our emotions, though I cannot say if that is the result of our environmental circumstances. It varies, too, based on the Campus culture and the individual themselves. Some people process their feelings internally and do not express them, while many could not hide their emotions even if they tried. As for passionate desires, I'm afraid I'm the last person you ought to—"

I shook my head and started anew. "Well, that, too, varies from person to person. Our civilisation does generally valorise partnership and marriage, but many people are perfectly happy without either. Certain Campus departments also preach that strong emotions and personal attachments are not conducive to work and study."

The Thirtieth Second Scholar nodded. "That is right and true. It is my responsibility to focus all my attention upon adhering to our oaths. None of us dares to succumb to our own amorous whims when the consequences might be so very severe."

Their expression was so grave and earnest, Sophy, that I could not help but feel – well, rather sisterly. How peculiar to feel that way with anyone other than you! (Or Arvist, I suppose.)

"I once believed that myself," I said in a friendly whisper. "Our worlds may be wildly different, Thirtieth Second Scholar. Still, I know what it's like to live your life according to a set of elaborate rules that must be followed at any cost."

"Have you oaths of your own, Scholar Cidnosin?" they breathed.

"Oaths I have sworn to my own Brain, in a way. They have ruled me for years, and, in my dedication to them, I never thought I would be able to—" I stopped, realising that I had perhaps become slightly *too* open in this conversation with a near-stranger! "All I mean is that I am trying, in every small way I can, to consider what it is that *I* need, rather than what my Brain demands."

I wondered, then, what the other Scholars might think of the mischievous expression that soon overtook the Thirtieth Second Scholar's face.

"Is Scholar Clel, perhaps, an example of what *you* need?"

How fortunate that I, too, only promised to answer a single question!

When the Thirtieth Second Scholar and I finally reached the perimeter of the city, we were not alone. Other Mechanical Beasts swarmed near the entrance – all different from ours, with such a diversity of claws and tails and fins that I could hardly make sense of any one form – and the Thirtieth Second Scholar hailed them with a frantic call through the speaking-tube. Some conversation followed, though I had to cover my ears yet again at the unendurable volume. Then the Beasts assembled behind us in a rather terrifying line, and we all paraded back to the dome together.

"Will your colleagues be angry with me?" I asked the Thirtieth Second Scholar.

"With you? Not in the least. I may not be so fortunate. And the council will likely demand to meet with us immediately. It will be overwhelming, but it's also a little exciting, isn't it?"

I did not agree, but I did not say so.

When the Thirtieth Second Scholar navigated to the very edge of the barrier, I marvelled once more as a thin line of light began to crack the dome's surface, creating an arched opening large enough for a Mechanical Beast. Once every vessel passed through, the dome began to stitch itself back together as if nothing happened. The Scholars may call that sea-woman's magic "illogical", but I find their techno-logical feats just as perplexing as her ability to create delicately crafted cubes of ice!

Speaking of technological feats, I should explain what happens after you enter the dome, because I know it would interest you. (Or it would, I suppose, if you were truly reading this!) It's rather like our own dear Deep House's airlock system. When the dome creates an entrance or exit, some amount of water passes from the surrounding seas into an enormous basin that sits beneath the city. Once the door shuts, a vessel floats up in the collected water until it reaches the area that the Scholars describe as "the docks". Because the water level varies, said docks consist of many floating platforms to which Mechanical Beasts may be tethered.

If you debark from a vessel and walk along one of these floating pathways, you will eventually reach a much larger platform used for storing equipment, hosting seafaring trainings, and completing repairs. From this platform, one can also reach the pressurised doors that lead to the rest of the city. There are several such doors – all ovaloid, brightly painted, and connected by ladders to accommodate the shifting seas.

It was to this platform that the Thirtieth Second Scholar and I hastened when we disembarked. We joined a crowd of Scholars bustling about the storage cabinets and Mechanical Beast components. Several among their company spoke loudly and crossly to the Thirtieth Second Scholar. I felt exhausted, rather unsettled, and so significantly impaired by both feelings that I wanted nothing more than to see Henerey and be done with it all. When the collective din made me feel like great walls were pressing against my body, I retreated to the side of the central platform to avoid the mass of people.

As soon as I took refuge near a tall cabinet that held nothing but enormous glass Beast eyes, I spotted the unmistakable silhouette of Henerey Clel emerging from the jaws of a sizeable purple vessel. I did not dare return to the throng to find him, so I jumped up on a sturdy-looking box, hoping to catch his eye. What a comfort it was when he noticed me! The relief and warmth that animated his tired face in that moment of recognition made me feel distinctly bashful.

Sophy, I am convinced he intended to embrace me, which would have been especially romantic and a little overwhelming, but such a reunion was not to be. Following behind him with equal haste was the woman I recognised as the Fifteenth First Scholar, who increased her pace to reach me when Henerey did.

"We are most pleased that you are unharmed, Scholar Cidnosin," she said, while Henerey gave me a chagrined grin. "No doubt you are exhausted. Shall we speak briefly as I accompany you to your rooms?"

As the Fifteenth First Scholar led us away, Henerey fell into step beside me. I took his hand – I did not care what the Scholars might think.

"You cannot imagine how relieved I am to see you," he said in a very low voice.

"Did you really join their search for my sake? That was most courageous."

"I did not give it a second thought. I have been beside myself with worry, thinking you were lost, and——"

Yet before he could finish, the Fifteenth First Scholar cut short our emotional murmurings.

"The Thirtieth Second Scholar gave me a brief summary of your exploits," she said. "The Sixth First Scholar wanted to question you immediately, but I convinced him you must rest first. We shall meet in the morning, and I expect to hear every detail."

"I will share them as best I can," I said. "Though I still do not quite understand what happened."

"The powers of the Illogical Ones leave even the wisest disoriented."

As we neared our rooms, the Fifteenth First Scholar began speaking with more urgency.

"I fear we have not been the finest hosts, Scholars," she said. "I would like to change that, if I may, but in the meantime, I hope you will grant us some patience. We have never found ourselves in a situation such as this."

"Nor have we, for that matter," I replied.

"Well, we shall all do our best under the circumstances." The Fifteenth First Scholar bent her knees ever so slightly – which I recognised as the local equivalent of a parting bow.

"Get some rest, and I shall send the Thirtieth Second Scholar to knock for you in eight hours. No earlier." With that, she departed, leaving Henerey and me in the corridor.

"She is right that you should rest," he said, giving my hand one last companionable press. "But how are you, E., really? If you don't feel like speaking a single word, I understand completely. I don't know precisely what you endured, but the Scholars were very concerned about something illogical? O! Whatever happened to your hair? It looks lovely. The angles in the front really suit you. I guess that is all beside the point. Please, please tell me you are all right."

"I am fine! Worry not." In truth, I still felt dizzy from my brief encounter with so many people (and a little dizzier still upon remembering my new hair, and hearing that it was apparently "lovely"). "I'm sorry for troubling you. I hardly know where to begin – somehow time stopped, and there was this wonderfully unbelievable woman with the tail of a dolphin – you would have found it all most fascinating."

"With a tail? Like something out of *The Amphibious Fable*? Yes, I would love nothing more than to hear all about it." He cleared his throat. "Later, that is. It seems we have a busy morning ahead."

Then we stood there for an indeterminate amount of time in silence.

Why? Well, I cannot speak for Henerey, but I could not stop thinking about our previous sleeping arrangement and how much I wanted to repeat it. At one point in the night, I woke up in a panic, as I often do, and as I tried to ground myself in what I could see around me, I noticed him sprawled across the floor in a surprisingly elegant fashion. His presence gave me a feeling of calmness that I experience so rarely.

I am not suggesting that one man, remarkable as he may be, can magically cure my ills. But I am more than my condition, and the knowledge that Henerey was with me through the night gave strength and support to all parts of my being.

Did he feel the same, and was simply too shy to say so? Or had the whole thing been a little too much for him? I did not know, and I was not going to risk it by saying something forward!

"May we speak in the morning?" he asked. "After this council nonsense concludes."

"I would love nothing more."

"Excellent," Henerey replied in a nervous, distant way. "Well, I hope you sleep well."

"Good night," I said, though I knew I should say more than that!

Now I have completely disregarded all advice about sleeping by spending hours writing a massive letter you shall never read. And several times during the writing of it, I arose and stood by my door, wondering if I dared creep to Henerey's room to see if he was also awake. But I find myself ill equipped to contend with my Brain and my romantic inclinations and an extraordinary encounter with a sea-woman all at once!

I will try to rest, then, and imagine what advice the real Sophy might give me.

With my bewildered best wishes,

E.

P.S. After resting, I drew the "Illogical One" to show Henerey and decided to preserve the final sketch here for safe-keeping. I've made you a few drawings now, haven't I?

How I wish I could know what you think of them.

ANNOTATED SKETCH BY E. CIDNOSIN, 1002

I tried to capture her mesmerising expression, but you know I have always struggled with Portraiture! Because I do not wish to do a dis-service to her otherworldly visage, I discarded my previous sketches and decided to focus on her tail – the one aspect of her anatomy that does not require me to replicate the "human" figure.

OFFICIAL RECORD OF A COUNCIL MEETING BY THE FIFTEENTH FIRST SCHOLAR, 1002

By my Oaths, I, the Fifteenth First Scholar, attest to the accuracy of the following council record, which documents what transpired during an emergency meeting called by the Body of Scholars to discuss a reported encounter with an Illogical One.

All First and Second Scholars alike were in attendance. The Thirtieth Second Scholar, recused from recording duties, stood in the very centre of the chamber with Scholar Cidnosin and Scholar Clel.

The Sixth First Scholar began by asking the Thirtieth Second Scholar to describe what occurred after they stopped writing the record yesterday.

"Why, we encountered an Illogical One," the Thirtieth Second Scholar said. "She removed us from our ship by her anomalous arts."

All assembled reacted appropriately.

"How despicably nonsensical," said the Sixth First Scholar. "And then?"

"The Illogical One suggested that she interfered with the Sculpted Saviours again, and used them to send impossible visions, or something of the sort. In fact, the Illogical One implied that she had previously sent such a vision to our own Scholar Cidnosin."

"Could you elaborate, Scholar Cidnosin?" I asked.

Scholar Cidnosin spoke without raising her eyes from the floor.

"Before we came here, I went on an inexplicable journey – it seemed like a dream, and yet I felt its physical effects upon my body."

"We always assumed E.'s experience was facilitated by the Structure itself," said Scholar Clel. His companion looked grateful that he had taken over the conversation. "Are you implying that your devices are not equipped to work such miracles?"

"That is not an established function," concurred the Second First Scholar. "What grave tidings."

"Perhaps it is not so grave," I said. "We may disagree with the

Illogical Ones' reliance upon perplexing enchantments, but they share our mission of protecting those left behind. I argued this years ago, and I remain firm in my convictions. Is it wrong that the Illogical Ones use their methods, however questionable, to draw the attention of people who might otherwise ignore our creations?"

"What was the nature of this journey?" asked the Sixth First Scholar.

"She travelled to an island of darkness and luminescence – a place like nothing in our world," said Scholar Clel after consulting silently with Scholar Cidnosin. "That is where we expected to find ourselves when we came here, as I might have mentioned in my list of questions that have still gone unanswered. I ask again: is such an island known to you?"

My fellow First Scholars gazed at the Visitors in silence, revealing nothing of our secrets.

"Who can say what worlds an Illogical One might dream up," said the Sixth First Scholar. "What happened next?"

"Scholar Cidnosin asked the Illogical One if she could help our Visitors return home," said the Thirtieth Second Scholar.

The Sixth First Scholar let out a furious sigh.

"Why would you do such a thing?" he said to Scholar Cidnosin, who flinched at the attention. "Have you no sense?"

"I was not aware that I should have done otherwise," she said softly.

"Thankfully, that mercurial being likely has better things to do than cater to Scholar Cidnosin's whims," said the Fifth First Scholar.

"That does not ease my anxieties!" exclaimed the Sixth First Scholar.

Scholar Cidnosin grew more visibly anxious as the voices raged around her. She began to raise her hands. I hypothesised that she wanted to place them over her ears but was not sure whether that would be appropriate.

Soon enough, though, I realised I had neglected my recording duties by observing the wrong person. For I did not make note of Scholar Clel's behaviour before he suddenly stepped in front of Scholar Cidnosin, surveying my colleagues fiercely.

"This conversation has become rather unpleasant," he said in a tone as calm as it was cautioning. "Will you please speak more respectfully to Scholar Cidnosin? I do think you owe her an apology."

"I beg your pardon?" the Sixth First Scholar said.

"Not my pardon, as I said – hers."

The Sixth First Scholar continued to gape, so I cut in.

"We apologise. The topic of the Illogical Ones can make us behave rather oddly ourselves."

"I am sure you have your reasons, but that is no excuse for incivility. And let us suppose," Scholar Clel continued, "that these beings do have some way of helping us. Why may we not seek them out?"

"That is absolutely out of the question!" shouted the Sixth First Scholar. As he looked around at everyone's startled expressions, the Sixth First Scholar tempered himself.

"It is not that I do not wish to aid you," he said. "But going back to the Imperilled World is not safe, as the very name suggests. Neither is engaging with the Illogical Ones. We avoid them precisely because any knowledge of their incredible powers might be dangerous. If you were to learn, even by accident, how it is that they work their magic – your very lives would be at stake."

"I appreciate your desire to protect us," said Scholar Clel. "I feel you think of us as your wayward children. With respect, Scholar, we are all of us adults here, and if E. and I decide to take risks that affect only ourselves, you have no grounds to stop us. If these Illogical Ones can help us build or, I know not, dredge up some Entry from the bottom of the ocean—"

"But that is just it," interrupted the Fifth First Scholar. "Your actions could indeed endanger far more than yourselves."

"Is this not a sanctuary?" Scholar Clel exclaimed. "If you would like us to respect your rules, Scholars, perhaps you ought to help us understand them in the first place!" His face tightened, and I saw him fear, perhaps, that he had gone too far by gently and politely shouting. Yet I observed where his eyes travelled, and noticed whose gaze he caught, and how she looked back with the utmost admiration, and that seemed to calm him immensely.

(I should clarify, for the record's sake, that "she" in the preceding sentence refers to Scholar Cidnosin. I apologise for describing the moment in such a fanciful way. That is no example to set for my apprentice.)

"We cannot send you home at present. Nor can we allow you to lose yourselves in search of Illogical Ones who may never swim this way again," I said. "Still, we realise you will continue to seek answers unless we provide them. I propose, colleagues, that we induct the Visitors into our ranks, and allow them to learn parts of our history that are safe to teach."

"New Scholars? Preposterous," said the Sixth First Scholar. "Everyone here has been a trusted member of the Body of Scholars for hundreds of years."

"Did you say *hundreds?*" said Scholar Clel.

"There is no precedent for such a thing," the Sixth First Scholar continued.

"There is no precedent," I repeated, "because these are the only two people we have ever managed to save. If we hope to bring their entire world here one day, we may as well start establishing some best practices."

"Be that as it may, it takes time to develop such practices."

"I invite the Visitors to join me once this meeting is complete," I said. "Then we will begin to teach you our ways."

"What are you saying, Fifteenth?" sighed the Sixth First Scholar. "Surely you would not suggest that we accept this plan without further consideration!"

"This is but an introductory conversation. Their frustration is justified. Are we to force these brave souls to sit here like specimens on a sheet until we decide how to manage them? If they cannot return, they will have to make a home with us, and we cannot expect them to do so without a proper orientation. Any further arguments?"

Not a single objection-lantern swung from those assembled, and only the Sixth First Scholar grumbled to himself.

"Then it is settled," said the Second First Scholar. "What say you, Visitors?"

Scholar Clel walked back to Scholar Cidnosin. He whispered something and she made some reply.

"We accept your offer," he said. "But if we decide that what you say is not credible, perhaps we will pilot our depth-craft out of the city and find those whom you fear."

"We give you the gift of knowledge, never before bestowed upon any outsiders, and you dare to threaten us?" exclaimed the Sixth First Scholar. Even I had to nod along.

"It is rather bold of you," I said.

"If we determine that the threat you describe is real, then there will be no need to worry about us pursuing it," insisted Scholar Clel. "Shall we adjourn, then?"

"Let us proceed to the library," I replied. "Our library, that is, not the Visitors'. What manner of Scholars are you back home?"

"I am a Scholar of Observation, specialising in marine life," said Scholar Clel with a hint of pride, "and Scholar Cidnosin is an extremely talented illustrator."

"We have little marine life inside the city, and we are not especially fond of illustration, but I suppose it is something," said the Second First Scholar.

At this point, the meeting concluded. I will close my records here with a brief note to reassure my colleagues.

I pledge to provide for the Visitors:

- A curated retelling of our history with the Illogical Ones
- A summary of our city's general layout, beyond the Visitors' Quarters
- An introduction to our rules and society, and the nature of our Scholarly ranks

I also pledge the following:

- I shall determine what the Visitors currently believe about where they are (and whether they are dangerously close to the truth)
- I shall share with them only that knowledge which is inoffensive and unappetising to the one we fear

Signed in haste,
The Fifteenth First Scholar

Chapter 7

EXCERPT FROM THE JOURNAL OF HENEREY CLEL, 1002

To my dear future readers,

How dramatically have my fortunes improved since my last entry! You'll recall that I stopped writing yesterday because I was so concerned about E. A rather nightmarish few hours followed. I shall not document the wretched thoughts that troubled me when she failed to return as scheduled, nor my experience of taking to the seas again in one of those horrifying contraptions. When she resurfaced at last, all I desired was to embrace her for as long as would be practical. But we did not have much time to ourselves, and then I wanted to let her rest, and I was too much of a coward to do or say anything else, so I slunk back to my room and rather crossly slept – oddly missing the experience of being on the floor! And—

Once again, I find myself blathering on about romantical thoughts rather than discussing life-altering revelations about these Scholars and their city. Really, I must proceed with my historically important notes before indulging myself with other subjects.

I suppose I ought to address the most important discovery first, though I'm sure anyone reading this in years to come will disbelieve me entirely. Somehow, it appears that our new acquaintances unlocked the secrets of immortality, since every one of them was (allegedly!)

alive during the time of the Dive. I would say more if that were not the extent of my knowledge on the subject!

You see, during the latest overwhelming meeting with the Scholars' council, a brave soul who goes by the title of "Fifteenth First Scholar" promised to teach me and E. about the nature of this society – which was an enormous victory for us. Best of all, said victory was the direct result of my unexpected ability to stand up for myself and, more importantly, E., in front of a group of Scholars. (I am equally embarrassed and proud of my various outbursts.)

We retreated with the Fifteenth First Scholar to the Scholars' Library, a place forbidden to us until now. I thought it would be grander than the Visitors' Library. To my surprise, it was but a compact, crowded space, shadowed and cosy like an underwater grotto. The rooms seemed diminished because they were packed, floor to ceiling, with racks of scrolls and books. I spied a plethora of the fascinating sculptural books called "pyramidals", as well as cabinets replete with shells and gemstones and fossils that I simply ache to observe more closely. Amidst everything were crystalline bubbles of carrels, in which other Scholars resumed their own work. (Whatever that work may be!)

We settled down at a vast table – which the Fifteenth First Scholar freed from a thick covering of open scrolls – and she began her lecture, in a manner of speaking.

"Before I address anything else," she said in a rather bored tone, "I ought to mention that every Scholar here is well over one thousand years old, in your world's chronology. We are the contemporaries of your distant ancestors. That is all. I may tell you nothing about how we accomplished this feat, and we shall never discuss the matter again."

I looked at E., who was herself looking at the Fifteenth First Scholar with what I may only describe as an extremely attractive expression of scepticism.

"At any rate," continued the Fifteenth First Scholar, "you wanted know more about the Illogical Ones, did you not?"

"I am terribly sorry to interrupt," I said, "but do you truly mean to make an announcement like that without allowing us to ask a single question?"

The Fifteenth First Scholar sighed, as if she expected better of me. "I did not mean to announce anything. Thanks to my colleagues' insistence upon making suggestive remarks about the subject, however, I had little choice. As I said, you must simply accept this information and ponder it no further."

"But if you truly lived during the Antepelagic era, imagine what we could learn from you! What do you recall of the species that inhabited the Upward Archipelago? When did you become deathless: before or after the Dive? At the very least, will you please clarify whether you are immortal in the sense that you will not die from old age, or in the sense that no disease or injury can harm you?" I asked, desperately, as a thousand more queries spun about my mind.

"Is that last question really of any consequence?" Then the Fifteenth First Scholar shook her head. "I am sorry, Scholar Clel, but I dare not answer anything. You and Scholar Cidnosin will be in danger if you learn the wrong information. There are many other subjects I intend to explore, if you'll let me."

I nodded as politely as I could while sulking dramatically. I have read many Fantasies that feature various types of immortality, and the concept fascinates me. It's always been my impression that I would be well suited to living forever, which would give me ample opportunity to learn as much as I can about the universe.

Of course, an endless life of exploration would be meaningless if led alone. (When I tried to engage Vyerin in a hypothetical discussion of the matter in our childhood, he made it clear that a natural lifespan is more than enough for him!) I asked that last question not for my own sake, but because I wondered if E.'s death-related obsessions might abate permanently if the Scholars had some way of immunising her against any physical harm . . . and what she would think of that idea herself!

The Fifteenth First Scholar proceeded to spend the rest of the day lecturing us about a variety of tedious topics. Though I am now an expert on the etymological debates surrounding the phrase "Sunken Saviours" and the Scholars' opinions about the proper use of punctuation, I still do not know where exactly we are, the means by which this place was constructed, or how any of it relates to "A Luminous Circumference". As usual, I had little awareness of how much time passed, but I did find myself growing hungry twice. Not long after I did, the Thirtieth Second Scholar came by with more colourful and relatively tasteless dishes for us. Well, technically, there was a completed meal for me, plus a heap of fruit, some knives and spices, and a miniature cooking pot with a self-contained flame for E. This baffled me, but E. seemed touched by the gesture.

I'd already gathered that the Thirtieth Second Scholar and the Fifteenth First Scholar have some manner of working relationship, but I had not seen them interact before today. To my surprise, the Fifteenth First Scholar treats the Thirtieth Second Scholar with much more respect than is traditional in a typical Boundless Campus mentor/ apprentice partnership. Despite her better qualities, I'm afraid I must also note that the Fifteenth First Scholar is not a particularly skilled lecturer. She speaks in a kind of meandering, bombastic way, rather like how the Scholars in ancient texts use rambling metaphors and fictional dialogues to bring students around to their points.

I fear that recording the precise details of everything she said to us would put me to sleep. Instead, I will try to summarise the most notable tale she shared. (As someone with a fondness for Antepelagic Fantasies, I can say truthfully that this is unlike anything I ever read before!)

A (SLIGHTLY INCOMPLETE) HISTORY OF THE BODY OF SCHOLARS AND THE ILLOGICAL ONES

(WITH COMMENTARY BY ME, HENEREY CLEL)

After the destruction of the Dive, the Body of Scholars escaped to this place, which they had been building (somehow?) in secret (for reasons the Fifteenth First Scholar will not explain).

(I employed a few parentheticals in that first sentence, and yet they still cannot contain all my thoughts. I will group some more here! The Fifteenth First Scholar would only share one fact about the Dive. Just as the Fleet proposed, the Fifteenth First Scholar claims the calamitous event that brought an end to the Upward Archipelago was not an unforeseen tragedy, but a strategic response to danger.

Despite knowing full well that this "folkloric record" would never be suitable for publication at any Campus, I cannot resist the urge to contextualise the above statement in an appropriately academic manner – even if that involves summarising my current knowledge for future readers who are no doubt entirely imaginary. Before we journeyed here, E. received a most curious set of documents from Scholar Jeime Alestarre, who tasked herself with delivering the last words of the Fleet – a society to which E.'s own mother belonged. The core belief of this society was that the destruction of our old world was intentional. Considering that every child today is raised to mourn our lost cities in the clouds, this information is mind-boggling – even more so, now that the Fifteenth First Scholar confirmed its veracity.

Alas, we have learned nothing further. All the Fifteenth First Scholar will say is that the Upward Archipelago was sacrificed in service of a Greater Purpose that I am – can you guess? – also forbidden from knowing. Those who caused the destruction departed for this city and became the Body of Scholars, while those against it fled to the surface of our world and became our venerable progenitors. E. and I discussed this revelation at length over our luncheon, and I imagine we will continue to pick at it for days to come. So much of our culture – a millennium of thought and art – is tied up in our ancestors' loss of their former civilisation. Yet here we are, allegedly among the very people who orchestrated this loss – and they won't tell us a word about it! When the Fifteenth First Scholar glossed over this issue, I confess that I was perturbed enough by her stubborn silence to rather lose my temper.)

(By which I mean I murmured "I'm awfully sorry, but is it truly impossible for you to tell us more of the Dive?" and nodded genteelly when she demurred. What a pity that the bolder Henerey Clel who emerged in E.'s defence during the council meeting has abandoned me once more.)

(Now, I believe I was recording a story?)

As they settled into their new home, the Scholars began to shape it according to their own brilliant design. The city they built together (again, how?) – the product of their shared knowledge and innovation – was idyllic, a glint of enlightenment amidst an incomprehensible ocean. (That is roughly how the Fifteenth First Scholar described it and decidedly not a Darbeni reference of my own making, I promise!) In those days, the dome that roofs the city was thoroughly transparent, allowing the Scholars to gaze at the abyss surrounding them (a horrifying thought).

Yet they were not the only ones bringing light to these waters.

Soon afterwards, the Scholars noticed an uncanny entity through the barrier. The unexpected visitor was a true leviathan, a glimmeringly ferocious figure that rivalled the most formidable deep-sea scavengers. (That is my own imagining, anyway – the Fifteenth First Scholar simply said that the creature was "startling and shining".) Though the Scholars initially believed that the seas around their new home were uninhabited, they had grown accustomed to the occasional shape or shadow floating by. As a result, they assumed this peculiar visitor would simply grow bored and swim on – as any other sea creature might. Instead, it persisted. For nights and days on end it observed the Scholars, studying them with uncanny tenacity. Unnerved and dismayed, the Scholars decided that something ought to be done. (Their decision was also based upon the creature's unfortunate habit of baring its massive teeth and beating against the barrier with alarming gusto.) To escape its eerie scrutiny, they elected to cover the dome's interior with oversized curtains, leaving but a tiny window to the water at the very apex of the city.

One day, as a Scholar ascended to the apex of the dome to mend a

111

curtain-rod, they happened to glance at the small circle of uncovered glass (or crystal? I still do not know what materials they use here) as they completed their work. Through that window they spied something altogether unexpected. Regarding them with fondness and fierceness was a most beautiful being out of the pre-Dive culture's own fanciful tales, a creature with a human face atop a shifting body – at times with the tail of a whale or dolphin, then with the lit and limber tentacles of a luminescent jellyfish.

After many days and nights of debate in response to this development (I certainly believe that), the Scholars reached an agreement. Despite their misgivings, they would build a vessel and leave the city to investigate the stranger.

It was at this point in the story that the Fifteenth First Scholar displayed her first and only moment of theatricality. "How could we have known," she uttered in a monotone whisper, "that it was all a trap?"

(Though I do admire her for trying to infuse the lecture with a bit of character, I must admit that I do not fully understand what made this a "trap". I shall let you, dear readers, draw your own conclusions!)

As their new depth-craft set off from the safety of the city, the Scholars aboard plunged into an ocean of unexpected melodies. Even those who specialised in music could not identify the sequences of chords, nor the instruments that produced them. Then the Illogical One – soon to earn her name – swam to them, singing unrecognisable clusters of notes, and presented an unparalleled showcase of impossibilities. She could transform matter, including her own; produce sounds heard within and without the mind; and send sequences of light pulsing through the ocean.

The Scholars found these marvels deeply concerning. (When I asked the Fifteenth First Scholar to explain why – after all, such magical actions seemed unbelievable but also relatively inoffensive – she simply said that there is nothing more frightening than that which the Scholars cannot easily explain.)

"This is neither relevant nor expected!" some First Scholar no doubt exclaimed as the display grew complex and sublime. "Pay no heed, colleagues!"

The vessel turned and retreated to the city. How could the Scholars reckon with these wonders? That kind of knowledge must be unsafe. (There it is again – this recurring cultural motif about the danger of knowing things. I am dying to understand its origins!)

Yet the damage (or "damage", as I might be tempted to style it) was already done. Before the ship turned away, before the First Scholar intoned their words of warning, each Scholar beheld the creature's art and *admired* the impossible feats, if only for a moment. Could any person witness such beauty and mystery and not feel the same? It did not matter that each straight-thinking Scholar quickly suppressed these thoughts and cast them from their mind. As each burst of belief unfolded and faded in a Scholar's brain, the Illogical One began to truly embody her title by creating additional copies of herself. As they escaped, the Scholars could see the Illogical One multiplying in the distance, gaining a new sibling for each person aboard the vessel.

The newborn Illogical Ones crowded around the window at the top of the dome, congenial as ever. In response, the Scholars replaced the curtains with a filter of some material that leaves no vantage point uncovered. Yet the new barrier does allow those outside to see in – both to display the city's Organisation and Reason to deter the Illogical Ones, and to aid other Scholars when necessary. After encountering the Illogical Ones, the Scholars had very little desire to leave their home again, but they knew they must monitor the seas to rescue Imperilled people. Thus, they hoped any Scholar sailing through those waters on patrol would gaze through the transparent dome, note the industry and technology and order within, and remain immune to the Illogical Ones' charms.

These were not the only protective measures the Scholars implemented. They built themselves a fleet of depth-crafts – shaped like impossible, mixed-up beasts to distract the Illogical Ones from the Scholars the vessels contained – and they allowed only one Scholar to patrol at a time, to minimise the risk of further multiplication. In addition, for the first hundred years, the Scholars played the most dreadfully dull sounds – such as a single thrumming drum rhythm, just slightly offbeat – from speaking-tubes outside the dome to repel their unwanted guests still further.

Questionable as these methods seemed (such is my interpretation, at least), the Scholars were successful. Never again did a Scholar encounter an Illogical One (until yesterday, that is) and no more would their numbers grow. Reason reigned supreme in the city forevermore, and so forth.

Now, I personally find this conclusion rather unbelievable, especially since the latest chapter of the tale unfolded very recently. I discussed the matter with E. in quiet whispers when the Fifteenth First Scholar took her leave of us around dinnertime, and we agreed that there must be more to the story. If the Illogical Ones reproduce through human belief, why did two more not appear in the ocean beside E. and the Thirtieth Second Scholar during their encounter? What of the goblet of sound (what a marvellous notion) that the Thirtieth Second Scholar dissuaded E. from accepting?

(Indeed – the goblet, in particular, feels terribly significant. Earlier, I mentioned to E. that her experience reminded me of an odd meta-physical text I once read (recreationally, of course). Part Fantasy and part philosophy, *The Praxis of Our Great Reshaping* was published some three hundred years ago by Scholar Endeln Caris – a rather eccentric fellow who claimed he wrote every one of his publications while fully asleep. In the volume in question, Scholar Caris's dreams lead him to imagine what it might be like to transcend one's body – to trans-form into an entirely new being. Figuratively, I suppose. He describes Human Potential as a "hale and hallowed chalice" from which one need only sip to adapt and evolve.

"I suppose none of that really makes any sense," I said, after summa-rising the above to E. "Clearly, Scholar Caris simply enjoyed deploying the metaphor of a chalice. But the ideas feel familiar. Drinking vessels, transformation, dreams . . . even if that book isn't a particularly reliable reference, I thought it relevant to mention. Under the circumstances."

"I couldn't agree more," she said. "Especially since I've read it myself, twice."

"You've read Caris? Then why didn't you say so?"

"Because I should never like to deny you the pleasure of describing something about which you feel passionate. Nor deny myself the pleasure of listening to you."

I'm afraid I then found myself rather incapable of continuing our discussion. And now, upon recalling her statement, I may need to pause for a moment once more. Whatever was I even saying?)

(Our lingering questions of great import. Yes! Naturally.)

Another unresolved issue is why this sea-woman sent E. on a journey through the Structure to the island, of course. I'll sound like my brother here, but – *sink it all* – why have we still learned nothing about that accursed island, the spot we sought to explore in the first place?

Yet those inquiries are secondary to my larger questions about the Illogical Ones themselves. Since the story suggests the first Illogical One altered her original form to become more humanlike, does that mean she had never encountered our species before? If so, from whence did these beings originate? Are these Scholars truly insular enough to ignore the existence of another fully sentient life form – simply because said life forms do not adhere to established Scholarly protocol?

Of course, the Fifteenth First Scholar had no answers for me. Responding to questions is not part of didactic practice here. The Fifteenth First Scholar simply recorded everything I asked and stated that she would address my inquiries in due time. Imagine that—

SLIGHTLY LATER (THE NEXT DAY, REALLY)
My apologies for pausing mid-paragraph in a rather dramatic fashion. You see, as soon as I finished my folkloric explorations, I returned to the aforementioned romantical thoughts troubling me at the time.

Yes, observe me, yesterday – so pitiful! – recounting that unlikely tale of the Scholars and the Illogical Ones to block more pressing issues from my mind. I cannot believe I am about to write this down, but I simply must. Since I may not speak with my brother (I would forego my promise of never asking him about affairs of the heart if it meant I could see him again), it is upon my trusty journal that I must rely!

There is, however, something I ought to note first. Up to this point, I have addressed these notes to you, dear Scholars of the future. I understand that there is nothing I can do to prevent you from reading them long after I am gone – short of throwing this journal into the sea when I complete it. (I would never behave so insensibly as that, of course. Imagine what terrible digestive consequences might ensue if this book were consumed by some unsuspecting creature, like an Insatiable Gulper Eel!)

While I cannot prevent you anonymous Scholars from perusing the next few pages, I would like to take a moment to proclaim that what follows is decidedly not for you. I intend to write down this experience because I cherish it and do not wish to ever forget it. It is for me and me alone.

Now that I've ensured you feel appropriately ashamed *and* intrigued, I may recount what transpired between E. and myself.

What vexed me most last night was my unbearable desperation to see her. Have I not become frightfully predictable? Technically, we had already spent the day together, for she was by my side as the Fifteenth First Scholar lectured. Though it was rather unScholarly of me, I did derive secret joy from watching E. observing the Fifteenth First Scholar. Sometimes, it's difficult to tell where within her vast mind E. happens to be travelling, but when she truly listens to someone (best of all when that happens to be me), there is a fierceness in her eyes and a rhythm to her nods that I cannot help but admire.

Despite these frequent moments of admiration, we did not have a chance to speak, which rather destroyed me. After passing some time writing my tale and pacing about, I convinced myself to go to E., very briefly announce that I absolutely cannot be without her, and then depart immediately so she could process this information independently without feeling pressured by my presence. I would walk to my door with this conviction in mind, remember that it was all foolishness, return to my desk, and then repeat the process.

As I stood by the door, arguing with myself in this fashion, I barely heard her knock when it came. In retrospect, perhaps I should have waited a few moments before answering, but I could not prevent myself from flinging the door open immediately.

"Hello there!" I said cheerfully, in an unconvincing attempt at informality.

E. blinked at me. "Have you been waiting here by the door, Henerey?"

"Not for extraordinarily long. Is something the matter?"

"I just wondered—" and her voice dropped so that I could barely follow along "—if I might speak with you. The aftermath of the council rather foiled our plans to talk."

The revelation that she, too, apparently shared my desperation made me feel almost weepy – is that a typical symptom of lovesickness? I shall have to ask Vyerin.

Before I could offer her my chair, she sat on the corner of the bed as she had previously. I certainly did not mind seeing her there once more!

"Ever since we arrived," she began, "I have written letters to Sophy. But yesterday, I finally accepted that she may never read them. I am not abandoning all hope. I did ask that sea-woman for help. And I know you and I are quite resourceful and determined, despite the Scholars' attempts to keep us in the dark on trivial matters like how one goes about obtaining eternal life."

"I understand that feeling," I said. "Perhaps, if we dedicate ourselves to politely annoying the Scholars with our questions, they will become irritated enough to send us home. In the meantime, we may have to settle in. For now."

117

"But the longer we stay, the more likely it is that Sophy will think something horrible happened to me, and that thought makes me ill."

I have considered this as well. Lerin and my other colleagues on the *Sagacity* will have noticed my absence (and failure to return the borrowed depth-craft), and they might well have contacted Vyerin by now, and he must be worried sick, even if he allows no one (save Reiv) to see how much it affects him . . .

"Perhaps Sophy and my brother believe we are on a brilliant adventure," I said, as much for myself as for her.

"Now there is a most amusing thought," E. replied. "Sophy and Vyerin will have to meet, won't they? Think of the scandal. A famous Scholar and an eccentric recluse running away together. Made more shocking, I'm sure, by the fact that nobody would have expected anything of the sort from either of us!" Her playful smile would not convince anyone that she is incapable of such mischief.

"How fortunate that this adventure gave me such an opportunity," I said. "I doubt anyone as lovely as you would run away with me under any other circumstances."

E. reached across the bed to take my hand. While this has become a fairly routine activity for us, I am still not entirely accustomed to the feeling. It never fails to astonish me when her lovely left hand, the very one responsible for penning the letters that led me to love her, is intertwined with mine.

"I am beginning to form a hypothesis, Henerey, that both of us are completely convinced we are not worthy of the other," she said.

"To be fair, my self-critical nature is an adaptive response to living in a hostile Scholarly environment – exacerbated by the fact that you undoubtedly deserve a more suitable match than me."

"But I would say the same about you!" E. barely had time to blush by the time her exclamation was complete. "Perhaps we simply need to accept that we are both very fond of each other and, well, evolve accordingly."

Under her captivating gaze, I experienced a sudden and strange desire to express myself in a far less verbal fashion, but I should know better than anyone that evolution never happens so rapidly!

"Evolution – yes, that reminds me!" Then I stood up, without letting go of her hand, and reached with my other arm for the large box I'd stowed under the desk – all to distract her from the fact that romance is not one of the many topics I have studied extensively.

She regarded me wryly until she noticed the title I'd inscribed carefully on top of the box.

"Have you finished it? May I see?"

"It is all thanks to your contributions." I spread out the beautiful cards she'd made. "Would you care to play it sometime?"

"Why not now? If you don't mind. I know the hour is growing late." E. gestured for me to sit beside her, and I would not have declined that invitation, not even if it were past midnight.

Childish though this may sound, we passed a few hours playing our odd replica of this most excellent game. I took my time explaining the rules to E., because I knew I would have a distinct advantage otherwise. I considered playing a little less genuinely than usual – not letting her win, you know, but perhaps missing a few obvious moves here and there. I always employed such tactics with Vyerin, because he would become dreadfully cross when I beat him and would have foresworn such activities entirely if I did not secretly balance things. But that did not seem fair, and, besides, E. proved a fierce competitor. By the end of the sequence, the sublime symbiosis of her tidepool-dwellers put mine to shame. I fear she may be the one letting me win in the future!

When our game ended, it was undeniably late, and I tried to avoid yawning inelegantly as we restored the sea creatures to their box. With that distraction out of the way, the enchantingly unsettling tension we experienced earlier in the evening returned in full force. My desire to remain in her company for the rest of the night was so profuse that I dared not speak a word – for fear of humiliating myself by extemporising about how much I yearn for her. Might she feel the same? Even if she did, would she say so? I suspected E. could think it too impolite to simply help herself to my bed (though I would give it to her in an instant, as I would give her anything).

We sat in silence. I could barely imagine what she must be thinking of me.

"I fear it is now truly past any decent hour for sleeping," E. said at last, but she did not move from the bed – was it a sign, or simply a coincidence?

"I apologise for distracting you with the game, but I certainly enjoyed playing it with you. I suppose it is rather late."

"Undoubtedly time for bed," she concurred.

"That would be most reasonable." And – o, she was still not moving. I took a deep breath, glanced at the floor, and reminded myself that I have now endured two deep-sea depth-craft voyages and could certainly survive this, too!

"If it would help you avoid the dark thoughts of the night," I continued, not daring to look at her, "you are welcome to rest here again. The floor is unexpectedly agreeable and, if it's not too much to say so, I rather enjoy having you close by."

"I would very much like to stay. But you needn't abandon your bed – if you don't wish to," she said. Even if it were a fanciful impression rather than a genuine physiological symptom, I did feel as if my heart were beating faster than ever.

"What kind of host would I be if I made you sleep on the floor instead?" I said, because I did not know what else to do.

To my surprise, my statement caused her to rise and place her hands on her hips. "Really, Henerey Clel," she said, with a lightness to her fierce tone. "Your bravery in the council meeting inspired me to show some courage of my own. Yet you seem intent to thwart me at every turn!"

"I apologise!" I exclaimed. "I am no good at any of this."

She took my hand again. "You are too good at it. I am grateful for how considerate you are, even if that forces me to be unprecedentedly forward as a result."

"I would rather have you be forward, because I am terrified of putting you in an unwanted situation."

"I am not such a fragile, sick thing that I do not fall prey to the whims of the heart," she said with a sad smile. "Won't you please consider that all the hopes and desires you force yourself to dismiss might also exist within me, terrified though I am to reveal them?"

"That is beyond anything I ever allowed myself to consider," I said sincerely. "Somehow I managed to deceive you into thinking I deserve your attention, and I live in fear of you realising I am neither interesting nor skilled in the art of courtship."

She objected by praising some qualities of mine, and I fear it would be rather egotistical to include that verbatim.

"Besides," she concluded, "when I stayed with you that night, I was overcome by a sense of safety like none I have ever experienced. Since you happen to be merely a door away, I can't say I would like to deprive myself of that feeling when it is easy to achieve."

As if to prove her point, she shifted her way back up to the top of the bed in question and curled herself into the blanket.

I took a deep breath.

"Are you quite sure that waking up to find someone else – here – would not alarm you?" I inquired. "I simply do not want to make you uncomfortable."

"I also feel uncomfortable meeting correspondents at large parties, exploring mysterious islands in visions, sneaking into libraries, and leaving my dear, dear home to find out the truth about a most singular Structure," she said. "Yet I did all those things of my own free will, and I shall enjoy the rewards and suffer the consequences. My condition has many contradictions, and I am trying my best, Henerey, to ensure that it does not keep me from what I want."

"You are absolutely certain, then, that this is what you want?" Tentatively, I allowed myself to lie down on the very edge of the bed.

"More than anything," she murmured. Speechless as I was, I was grateful when she immediately continued. "And it is not my intent to make you uncomfortable, either! I am only asking you to lie here with me. Nothing more."

I did not wish to reveal how much relief this clarification gave me. At least I would be spared another uncomfortable confession this evening.

"I am relieved to hear you state it as plainly as that," I said before I could lose my courage. "I cannot describe how much I've yearned to – well, simply to be close to you. Yet I feared all this time that you are averse to extended physical proximity but too polite to admit it. When you first told me of your struggles, I took it upon myself to do some research so I would be better equipped to understand it all. Alas, the collection of medical texts aboard the *Sagacity* was disappointingly limited."

"Is that what all this is about?" E. asked. "Yes, if my Malady was but a footnote in a broader medical text, I am not surprised that you were confused. Have you not noticed me holding your hand frequently? You'll be delighted to know that there is practically an entire taxonomy for this mental condition of mine."

"I am nothing if not fond of a good taxonomy," I answered. "And I did indeed notice the hand-holding, I assure you. Sometimes I wondered if it was a kind concession you were making for my sake, and assumed you could only endure it through your great strength of will."

"I was not simply enduring it!"

To atone for this assumption, I took the opportunity to shift slightly closer to her. She noticed my feeble attempt, laughed, and then crept right next to me and very gently laid her head upon my shoulder. It was all rather intoxicating! At any rate!—

"As you'll note," E. continued, "I have no quarrel with touch. I mean, I cannot abide when physical contact is initiated by complete strangers. Some of Arvist's friends, for example, tend to embrace with little provocation."

"I would have qualms about that myself," I said with a shudder.

"What tends to trouble me most are thoughts – dark ones, like you wouldn't believe – about my actions causing harm. For example—" and here her voice dropped low and she spoke into my shoulder "—as much as I am delighted that we will share this bed, I am struggling to repel the pernicious worry that perhaps, while I sleep, I will roll my arm onto you in such a way that prevents you from breathing and I will be unaware until it is too late."

"That is highly improbable. And if I found myself unable to breathe, I would simply move your arm."

She looked at me with delight. "See, this is why Dr Lyelle always told me that it is useful to speak these things out loud, to see how ridiculous they sound outside of my brain. When that thought returns, as I'm sure it will, I shall try to remember what you said."

"If it would allay your fears further, you might sleep facing away from me. That would all but guarantee your arms stay at a safe distance, provided you do not make a habit of propelling them backwards in an acrobatic fashion."

"But if I turn away, well – is it not the case that the primary objective of this situation, so to speak, is maintaining proximity?"

"I may have a solution to that," I said, with no thought of propriety – so committed was I to helping her dispel this thought! Let us simply say it was a cosy solution that suited us both.

It is morning now, and we have briefly parted to dress ourselves and prepare for the day. And it seems I have chosen to "prepare for the day" by writing about the highlights of the previous evening.

(All right, I will indulge myself again and share one further highlight I wish to record. At some point in the night, I awoke to E. shuddering violently, as though she were battling a nightmare. I moved away, thinking she might prefer some space in such a frightened state. To my surprise, once her shaking subsided, E. murmured – and I am absolutely positive about this, because I keep reciting it in my mind – the phrase "wherever has he gone", rolled in my direction, and wrapped her arm around me once more. I'm sure she would have been relieved to know that her unconscious arm movements only impeded my respiratory functions in the sense that I felt too overwhelmed with affection to catch my breath.)

Forgive me, Vyerin – if I dare address you here – for on this wondrous morning, I find myself slightly less concerned about how soon we may return.

Chapter 8

NOTES PASTED IN THE JOURNAL OF HENEREY CLEL, 1002

Have you noticed that rather striking tapestry on the wall behind you, dear E.? I would say "the one with the triangles" if that didn't describe nearly all the iconography here. I refer to the tapestry on the right that appears to shake and shift occasionally, as though there were a door to a draughty passage behind it?

I had not noticed! I'll rely on your observations, because I fear our good tutor would notice if I turned my head away from my books so dramatically. How fortunate that you are facing that direction already. (And there I was, Henerey, thinking you were staring at *me* with such passionate focus . . .)

I find it most curious. Everything in the city is extremely obvious in its design – the lighted pathways, the exaggerated ornamentation, and so forth. The fact that this door (?) seems to be concealed is exceptionally intriguing.

Shall we investigate when the Fifteenth First Scholar leaves us, as she often does around mealtime?

*

Dare we? I suppose we must! (Also, in response to your prior parenthetical – I only had the opportunity to notice the anomalous tapestry
because I was indeed gazing at you in such a fashion. Forgive me?)

Then will you kindly conceal these notes in your journal so there is no
evidence of our conversation? (All will be forgiven if you also allow me
to gaze intently at you for some unreasonable amount of time.)

UNOFFICIAL RECORD BY THE FIFTEENTH FIRST SCHOLAR, 1002

By my Oaths as a Scholar, I attest that this account is intended for no
eyes other than my own. Though I will fulfil my Oaths by writing
exactly what transpired, it is my sincere belief that the information I am
about to record is not fit for our daily Compendium. Thus, if you are
reading this, I assume I have either granted my permission or perished
in some improbable way.

(In the unlikely event that I am deceased, let me urge any snooping
Second Scholars – namely, a specific Second Scholar who serves as my
apprentice – to resist that unbridled curiosity of yours and stop reading
immediately. There is information in this record that relates to the First
Scholars' Burden, and I hope you will allow me to uphold our Oaths
by protecting you from it.)

What has come to pass is no one's fault but my own. I, after all, had
the brilliant idea of allowing the Visitors to study with us. I did not
expect them to notice what lies behind the tapestry in the library, but
none of my colleagues can blame me for that. Would any of us dare
to open a door that we had not been explicitly granted permission to
enter? How illogical! But the draught from the tunnel, churned up by
the ferocity of the wave-pool that protects our sunken archives, decided
to intervene today, and the Visitors proved more fatally inquisitive than
I expected.

126

It is only by chance that I found them out. These Imperilled people demonstrate behaviours unseen among our company for a thousand years. They are mercurial and hasty and wildly nosy. Had I kept to my schedule as usual and enjoyed my mealtime appointment with the Tenth and Nineteenth First Scholars, I would not have noticed the disappearance – and I dread to think what might have happened then.

Fortunately, my colleagues did not have time for me today. After leaving the library, I encountered the Sixth First Scholar in the corridor, who told me that the Tenth and Nineteenth First Scholars had become caught in a complex epistemological debate from which they would not be roused. Though I took no offence, I ought to note for accuracy's sake that this is the third time in recent memory that such a thing has happened.

I journeyed back to the Library to check on the Visitors, asking myself whether I should invite them to dine with me instead. They fascinate me in a kind of childlike way – both in the sense that I find them childlike and that they give me a sense of wonder I'd long forgotten. What is it like to be so young and ephemeral?

By the time I returned, however, they had vanished. Perhaps only just, as the door to the passageway remained slightly ajar.

I opened it slowly, trying to mask my sounds and movements. I heard voices ahead of me, and soon discerned – with a sigh of relief – that the noise came from above. Scholar Cidnosin and Scholar Clel had gone up instead of down. Anything they spied through our great Periscope from the tower on the upper storey, far from the depths of the archives, would teach them nothing. They would see only an ocean and could never guess what secrets it holds.

I climbed the tower stairs swiftly and silently. The Visitors' voices resonated throughout the entire space, and it did not take long until I reached a step from which I could distinguish every word of their conversation.

"Henerey!" was what I heard first – an exclamation from Scholar

Cidnosin so spirited that I hardly recognised her voice. "This simply must be the ocean from my vision. It is unmistakable!"

"Is it truly?" answered Scholar Clel. "Remarkable. It is exactly how I imagined it when reading your letters. Why, indeed, are there no stars?"

"There may not be stars in the sky, but look—"

I knew precisely what had caught her eye.

"Luminescent plankton, perhaps? Could marine life exist in this seemingly empty ocean?" said Scholar Clel. "Something must prey upon that plankton. And you saw those shapes in the water when you visited the island . . ."

While I found their continued fixation on the island alarming, it relieved me to learn that they did not understand the significance of the scene before them. Really, I envied them. They merely perceived a sea dotted with small specks of light, likely a familiar sight back in their world, and they spoke of predators and prey as nothing more than abstract concepts.

"I would love to spy one of those shapes again," Scholar Cidnosin said. "I do feel much more comfortable seeing this landscape from a distance! But I worry we have tarried too long. We will have to return in the future."

"Of course we shall!" exclaimed Scholar Clel, who did not know that they could never do such a thing. "If we could find that island, E., I wonder—"

His voice and footsteps grew louder as they began their descent. I waited from my hiding place, listening to the whispering of the hidden waters I must keep concealed at any cost.

"If you think we have time to peek down the other corridor that leads under the city, I imagine I could steel myself against the thought of the depths – since you are with me," murmured Scholar Clel, his voice surprisingly loud at close range.

I sighed, knowing my moment had come.

"I am afraid that will not be possible."

I did feel rather guilty when they both flinched and grabbed each other's hands.

"Do not worry," I continued. "There will be no penalty for your actions – that is not how we do things here. The simple truth of the matter is that this place is not safe for you, and you may go no further."

"That is reasonable enough," said Scholar Clel. "I don't suppose I could trouble you for an equally straightforward explanation about why it is unsafe?"

"My colleagues do not know how to interact with you two, and I am hardly better," I replied. "You think us bafflingly bound up in our rules and customs. If I told you that what lies below us is incomprehensibly dangerous for you, would you heed my words? I imagine you do not find me especially trustworthy, considering that you snuck in here surreptitiously."

"You must understand our predicament," Scholar Clel said. "Everything that is important to us – besides each other, but that is too obvious to be stated—"

"I do understand," I said, and that was not inaccurate. "I too was once separated from someone I loved, as were most of my colleagues. Do not think for a moment that I cannot recognise your desperation."

"I am very sorry. But if you understand our plight, then surely you could assist us, even if your colleagues disapprove," pleaded Scholar Clel, his eyes still darting between me and the mysteries of the hall behind us.

"I can best assist by stopping you," I said. "For if you pass through this space and learn that which you cannot unlearn, you will never return home."

"Is that some kind of poetic expression about the dangers of esoteric knowledge? Because while I do appreciate it, I hardly—"

"There is nothing poetic about the truth." I thought of my Oaths and the Burdens we bear, and prepared myself to manage this conversation in a way that I would be proud to record. "I speak of a tangible, literal danger. If you discover that which we hide, you will not be able

129

to go back to your world without bringing doom upon everyone you hold dear."

"What is this doom, exactly?" said Scholar Clel. "If we are to prevent it, do we not need to know more about it?"

"The more I tell you, the more the danger increases." I paused, wondering if I dared ask a question that had weighed upon me since the Visitors first arrived. "Scholar Clel, did you not say that you specialised in marine life? In your years of study, have you noticed anything exceptionally unusual?"

"How funny you should ask! Well, I had been studying some bizarre migratory patterns in a particular species of ray, and E. spied these Elongated Fish—" he began, but I had already heard enough.

"Then it has begun, and the danger grows closer," I muttered. "And if you learn something forbidden and subsequently travel home, you will soon see anomalies like no other. You might awaken one morning to find that every creature in the skies has vanished, burying themselves deep within the sand and rocks for shelter. As if any shelter could possibly keep them safe! You could find yourself suddenly struck with a sense of sickening despair, a feeling that reduces you to a fleeing animal yourself."

"That sounds familiar," said Scholar Cidnosin in a quiet and strangely sardonic way. Still, I clung to her contribution.

"Have you felt it already? Is it indeed too late?"

"O! My apologies. I did not think you would hear me," she said. "I experience daily existential fear for – well, other reasons, not because of whatever it is you are describing."

"I don't suppose you're referring to the predator mentioned in the poem? 'A Predator – Awaits', you know? Was that a metaphor for, say, a monster of some kind? A species unknown to us, like the Illogical Ones?" asked Scholar Clel.

What is the nature of this cursed poetry they continue to invoke? I remembered this nonsense from the council meetings. Only the Illogical Ones could be to blame, but why would they send word of our

130

enemy into the Imperilled world? (It would be just like them to communicate such crucial information in the form of poetic expression.)

I decided that the best way to answer this question was to dodge it entirely.

"It would be most imprudent for me to say any more," I said. "Here is what I propose. If you consent to live here in compliance – to stop looking for answers and seeking out danger – then I shall indeed help you. As it happens, I have spent years working diligently and clandestinely on a project that you might find relevant."

Before you berate me for revealing any secrets, colleagues, please take comfort – there is no such project.

I felt a small jolt of fear writing that down, though I must remind myself that it is very unlikely any of my fellow Scholars will read this private record and know what I have done. Unless you *are* reading this, in which case I suppose I will state it plainly. I fed the Visitors a falsehood. It was a desperate act of protection that shames me. If it keeps them safe for just a little longer, however, it will be well worth it.

"In short, I believe I may be able to construct an Entry of my very own," I lied. "That said, my experimentation must remain entirely secret. I do not merely ask for your discretion. If you accept my terms, I will bid you never to mention this subject again until I approach you with further news."

"Why did you not say so in the first place?" said Scholar Clel. I was glad to see that my proposal had, like the luminescent lure of some clever carnivore, tempted him away from further inquiries about predators or poetry.

"If what you say is true, we would be forever grateful," said Scholar Cidnosin.

"Is there anything we can do to assist?" said Scholar Clel. "I can't say that either of us are mechanically minded, but E. spent ages observing the Structure in her garden."

"Does your vessel happen to have some kind of cistern that collects and distils water as you travel?" I asked.

131

"It does," said Scholar Cidnosin. "Though it is not quite *my* vessel. Henerey borrowed it for our purposes, and it's very old-fashioned. Still, its systems are similar to those at the Deep House – my home, that is, which is underwater. Whyever do you ask?"

"I require a small sample of water from your point of origin." If I had to lie about my supposed "project", I could at least tell the truth about how the Saviours work – not that the Visitors would know the difference. "Would you grant me leave to examine the vessel?"

"Certainly," she replied. "But I fear that whatever we absorbed before we left will be diluted by this point."

"I require only the slightest amount," I said, which was also technically true. "Does that mean we are in agreement?"

"I suppose so," said Scholar Clel. "Unless, E., you would prefer we take a moment to discuss—"

"No, I accept," she said, meeting my gaze for the first time. "You have my word. We will pry into your secrets no longer."

"Not only that," I intoned, "but I urge you to forget this place, as well as this conversation. Do not speak of it, even when you are alone together. Do not write about it in whatever private records you keep." At this, they exchanged a knowing glance – perhaps the customs of Imperilled people are not that different from ours. "And, as I said before, do not ask me about my work. In fact, it is probably best if you remain ignorant of our technology in general. I suspect I ought to conclude my lessons for you as well. If I must go to the trouble of building a Saviour, I do very much want you to be able to return home, after all."

"We are not to learn anything else?" asked Scholar Clel. "Not about the most insignificant of subjects? I can't imagine what I will do with myself otherwise. What are the specific limitations? What about – I don't know – you have little in the way of animal life, so what about botany?"

"Descriptive studies only," I clarified. "No experimenting with potential applications of plants and their by-products." If knowledge

132

of our mediocre plant life proved enough to lure the Predator out of hiding, he must be far less formidable than we believe.

"I do enjoy a good descriptive study," said Scholar Clel. "But what is Scholar Cidnosin to do?"

"Really, I am fine," she protested, but Scholar Clel proved persistent.

"Given your unique temporal circumstances, shall we say, you Scholars must possess a wealth of Antepelagic art and artifacts," he said. "May Scholar Cidnosin view and sketch from them, if she chooses?"

"I suppose that would be acceptable," I replied.

"I would enjoy that a great deal," said Scholar Cidnosin. The softness of her voice did not mask the strength of her enthusiasm.

"It is settled, then," I concluded. "Do not worry, and do try to enjoy yourselves. Anxiety is an inefficient use of energy, after all. No danger awaits you here. Is that not worth celebrating?"

They did not appear particularly celebratory, but I assume that is not relevant to this record.

Chapter 9

UNSENT LETTER FROM E. CIDNOSIN TO SOPHY CIDNOSIN, 1002

My dear sister,

I alluded to this in my last "letter", but now the time has come – what follows will be my final imaginary note to you. At present, it seems our lot to stay among these Scholars, learn from them, and hope a path home will emerge in time.

I have failed you. You were so concerned about leaving me behind after my accident, but I urged you to return to the Ridge, telling you that nothing would go wrong – I cannot begin to apologise.

Yet I am trying my best to keep these thoughts from consuming me, as I know you would not wish them to. All I can do is continue adapting to my circumstances, which I imagine will grow still more familiar in time.

Since we have no way of leaving, it seems Henerey and I are well on our way to becoming "Third Scholars". (They created a new category just for us.) How funny to think of me as a Scholar at last! We are now allowed to read various (pre-approved) volumes on our own in addition to "studying" with the Fifteenth First Scholar. When she occasionally treats us to a lecture, it always involves nothing more than the most basic, prosaic facts about this place. I wonder—

On second thought, please disregard the end of the paragraph above.

I have been discouraged from wasting my words by wondering about what we cannot know. (How cryptic. I fear I dare not elaborate further, not even in a letter no one will read.)

That said, I appreciate the opportunity to learn in a way that is not overtaxing for me. You know I never could have studied on any Campus – the crowded classrooms, the inevitable din, the seas of people crashing here and there – but now I am able to participate in an academic lifestyle on my own terms. Nobody ventures into our part of the library except for myself, Henerey, the Fifteenth First Scholar, and the Thirtieth Second Scholar. I use a private desk that stands parallel to the wall, which I can sit behind in comfort without constantly looking over my shoulder. I remain there for an hour or two, alternating between sketching from the extant Antepelagic art at my disposal and listening to the Fifteenth First Scholar lecture about something like mosaic placement rules. Then Henerey walks me back to the Visitors' Quarters so I can take some time to myself while he goes off to the garden to interrogate various Scholars about plants. My Brain always tries its best to interfere, of course, and some days are more challenging than others, but I would say I am rather enjoying myself. Though I know I am only able to participate because there are very few people, it does make me wonder if I was too hasty in avoiding all such experiences back home. Would any Campus have accommodated me and my needs, had I only asked?

(Boundless Campus certainly would not, according to Henerey. I know he did not have an easy time as a Scholar himself. It pleases me that this place also suits him.)

Still, despite the novelty, it is wearying. Even Henerey's irrepressible energy is beginning to flag. Yesterday, the Fifteenth First Scholar noticed our ennui and instructed us to take a day or two away from our studies. I suppose we did not exactly need her permission, since we set our own hours and are not conducting said studies for any formal purpose, but I appreciated her thoughtfulness nonetheless.

The change of routine was well-timed because I had a secret

plan – one entirely personal and free of the subterfuge we carried out previously. Because the Thirtieth Second Scholar no longer lingers around the Visitors' Quarters, I sought our new acquaintance in the library to inquire about something we discussed during our underwater adventure. As the Fifteenth First Scholar was engaged in an impromptu debate with a colleague, and Henerey had just stepped out to check the leaf structure of something, I did not need to fear anyone overhearing us.

"The Artificial Ocean! Yes, how could I have forgotten?" the Thirtieth Second Scholar exclaimed when I asked. "I will sketch you a map as we speak. It is truly a marvel of architecture – and artistry besides!"

"Thank you," I said, watching as their careful hand mapped out a perfect grid of the city. My draughtsmanship, as you know, is rather stylised and sketchy. I admire the Thirtieth Second Scholar's almost unbelievable skill at drawing straight lines with precision!

"Is there anything else with which I may assist you?" The Thirtieth Second Scholar passed me the map and smiled nervously. "I regret that my present duties prevent me from writing reports about – that is, spending time with you, but I am always happy to help you and Scholar Clel, should need arise."

"We did wonder what became of you. Is everything all right?"

"O, yes, of course! The First Scholars informed me that since you and Scholar Clel are now studying with the Fifteenth First Scholar, I may shift my focus to other responsibilities. There are hundreds of bibliographic records that need to be cross-referenced for safety's sake. Immediately, so I'm told!"

Remembering how diligently the Thirtieth Second Scholar tailed us during our first few days here, I could not help but suspect—

No – perhaps I daren't write about my suspicions either?

Instead, surely it is safe to note that I surprised myself with my response to this statement.

"If you wish to visit with us, you need only ask," I said.

136

Yes, Sophy, gasp all you like – me, E. Cidnosin, encouraging social interaction? The truth is that this bright young Scholar has rather grown on me.

"Do you truly mean that?" breathed the Thirtieth Second Scholar. Then they peered anxiously at the Fifteenth First Scholar, still extemporising on the other side of the room. "I shall have to ensure that such an activity would be in accordance with my Oaths."

"I would expect nothing else."

"And, as much as I would like to, I shall not accompany you to the Artificial Ocean," the Thirtieth Second Scholar exclaimed with a smirk the mysterious Oaths would surely forbid. "For you asked me in secret because you wish to go alone with Scholar Clel, do you not? How delightful! It is just like in *The Star Sailors*, when—"

Though I could already recall the exact scene from the Fantasy that was relevant to our current situation, I still felt disappointed when the Fifteenth First Scholar interrupted us. The apparently urgent bibliographic record project required the Thirtieth Second Scholar's attention once more!

The next day, after Henerey and I awakened together – yes, we did manage to overcome our mutual nocturnal shyness, but that's all I need say on the matter – I asked if he had any interest in taking a stroll with me to a specific location that I would not reveal.

"Scholar Cidnosin," he said teasingly, "are you inviting me on some manner of surprise outing?"

Much as I don't deserve it, I am now accustomed to everyone here referring to me as *Scholar Cidnosin*. However, Henerey has not called me that in private since his very first letters, and the old nickname thrilled me.

"You have all the evidence to consider, Scholar Clel," I said, "so I trust you will be able to draw your own conclusions accordingly." I had, the night before, packed some tea and our respective notebooks into a basket that I placed resolutely upon my shoulder. "As if the wonders of the garden were not enough, the Thirtieth Second Scholar

137

also informed me that there is some constructed inland ocean here. I thought it might remind us of home."

"Marvellous!" he said as we set off. "You know, E., nobody has ever asked me on a romantic excursion of this nature before."

"Never before?" I asked. "Was it not romantic when I offered to meet you at Arvist's party? Or when I asked you to brave unknown perils by travelling through the Structure with me?"

"Certainly it was, on both counts! With that in mind, I rather think it should be my turn next."

"I suppose it was actually you, not I, who originally proposed we meet at the Deep House so you could deliver that book to me."

"And it was you who suggested the party and were kind enough to face your fears by attending. I am grateful to that dear little book for giving me the excuse. I wonder what's become of it."

"Ideally, it is still on my bookshelf, untouched," I said, "though who knows how Arvist has meddled in my absence. I do not wish to dwell upon that. Henerey, if you had the ability to transport any book here, which would you choose?"

This topic occupied us for the rest of the journey. As we strolled along the blue path, another golden dome rose before us, its hemisphere decorated with abstract patterns I identified as cresting waves. The area seemed completely abandoned, which helped me breathe more easily. I had worried we might encounter other Scholars, though the Thirtieth Second Scholar reassured me that everyone was far too occupied with their various inexplicable duties to enjoy the recreational places constructed for people from our world.

A round, white door glistened like a pearl at the base of the dome, and we needed merely wave our hands for it to open. As in the gardens, the light shifted dramatically as we left the darkness of the city. Inside, everything was crisp and clear and blue and green and, o, Sophy, I almost wept to see it!

The interior of the dome was reasonably large – certainly greater than the main room of your Boundless Campus library I visited so boldly once – but what made it appear unbelievably expansive was the unknown artists' hands at work. Someone had carefully painted the walls with naturalistic murals suggesting a faraway horizon, using perspective to create the illusion of endless oceans receding into the distance. There was a faint breeze, no doubt produced by some hidden device, which felt bracing even if it lacked the taste of salt. A skilled sculptor, too, carved rock formations from resplendent black and purple materials that resembled the volcanic cliffs of the western Atoll – and throughout it all wild waters glistened!

While I have not spent much time on beaches, I found myself emotionally overwhelmed by this illusory equivalent. Henerey must have shared my feelings, for he grasped my hand tightly and seemed to brush away a tear himself.

We found ourselves a comfortable nook in the cliff-face – which, to Henerey's disappointment, was sadly bereft of hermit crabs.

"This is far more enjoyable than listening to the Fifteenth First Scholar pretend she has nothing interesting to tell us, don't you think?" I asked him, using my words as a diversion as I leaned onto his shoulder.

"Studying with the Fifteenth First Scholar has rather inflated my opinion of my own lecturing skills," Henerey agreed. "Yet there are some aspects of this Scholarly lifestyle that appeal to me."

"Considering what you and Sophy tell me of Boundless Campus," I said, "I do feel we have found ourselves a more hospitable environment."

"It is a most intriguing society. I know we hope above all to return home, but I wonder – E., if we could somehow move between worlds as we pleased, would you fancy living here?"

I took a moment to ponder the contradictions of the city. Immense beauty and unbelievable wonders amidst a bleak abyss. Incredible knowledge that we are not allowed to learn.

"I cannot say," I concluded. "In addition to my family, I would miss so much about the natural world. The ocean. Sunrises. Tide patterns.

Then again, the unique circumstances of this place grant me a rather fuller life than I ever thought possible."

"Yes, it is a wretched bargain to strike!" Henerey exclaimed. "Shall I choose to live in what is essentially a civilised aquarium, where all is artifice but the people are so eccentric that I feel almost normal among them? Or shall I choose the mystery and uncertainty of our home, where I remain perpetually at the mercy of my colleagues?"

"The trick, you see, is having no colleagues at all."

"Such is the benefit of your Deep House!"

In that moment, I found myself transported through my imagination to the dear Deep House parlour, where the temperature and light and silence felt exactly as I remembered. Yet as this beautiful vision overwhelmed me with all I've lost, I noticed one remarkable change – my mind allowed me to picture Henerey there with me. Not as a memory, but rather a wonderful suggestion of a potential future, in which the two of us sitting in the parlour and watching the water might become practically routine.

"Are you all right, E.?" he asked. "I know you yearn to be home again. I apologise if I saddened you."

"Quite the opposite, really," I said. "I was simply thinking that when we return, you are welcome to spend as much time as you like at the Deep House. In fact, if the thought is amenable to you, I wonder if you might——"

I trailed off, horrified by the ridiculousness of what I wanted to say. What would you think of it, Sophy? I can hardly endure my own brother's presence under the Deep House's roof. How could I invite someone else to live with me? And would I not be as bad as Arvist if I extended such an invitation without obtaining your permission first? Furthermore, was I not rather rebelling against Society's expectations for the proper duration of courtship by asking someone to share my home after we had only spent a few tides together?

"If your meaning is what I dare to hope it might be," Henerey

140

replied, his tone surprisingly confident, "I am sure nothing would suit me better."

"You needn't agree right away," I said. "Whatever possessed me to say such a thing? There is no guarantee that either of us will ever see the Deep House again."

"But it is not wrong to dream, is it? Though perhaps after you have shared quarters with me for more than a handful of nights, you will realise I am far too untidy to be a suitable household companion."

"You – untidy? There is a reason why I have not yet invited you to *my* quarters!"

We sat peacefully for a few moments, watching the waves go in and out. Directly below us, I noticed something new – a curious crystal walkway that emerged from the shore and projected forward on the surface of the water. The picturesque path stretched out about three fathoms, and, at its end, was topped with a bench that stood beneath a spherical, translucent wall upon which the waves continued to break.

"I believe that walkway leads to a sort of viewing platform under the waves." I pointed out my discovery to Henerey.

"I suppose that is perfectly safe on seas as placid as these!" he said. "Would you care to take a closer look?"

"Do you think we may?" I suddenly felt the cruel interruption of an intrusive thought, telling me against all possible reason that there must be some rule against going on that pathway. I thought it was but an innocent walkway, of course, but my Brain reminded me that I am immoral and corrupt and therefore no proper judge of—

As usual, I do not know what triggers such thoughts. There were no external signs of any danger.

When Henerey began making his way down the cliff, I followed more slowly, trying to remind myself that my Brain simply sought to ruin a most pleasant experience.

"Is something troubling you?" asked Henerey as he used his walking stick to launch himself over a rock with a little more gusto than I might have recommended. I offered my hand to steady him, which he accepted gratefully.

"You do not need to answer," he continued. "Only if it would help."

"O, I am just worried we are committing some unpardonable crime by going down here," I said lightly, relishing in how nonsensical my fear sounded when I explained it.

"By walking on this walkway designed specifically to be walked upon?"

"It could be some kind of private path that is not intended for regular use."

"There is a *bench*!" He laughed, but there was nothing mocking in his expression. "It will be worthwhile, I promise. This may be your best opportunity to feel underwater as you do at the Deep House."

He was correct, Sophy – for while I felt unsteady on the floating path, how my heart sang when we reached the viewing-wall at the end, which allowed us to practically sit beneath the waves! If I closed my eyes – which I dared do only briefly – I could pretend I was in my bedroom, curled up in the porthole in my typical fashion and listening to the water. Though it was painful to imagine the Deep House yet again, it was also pleasant to open my eyes and see Henerey there, regarding me with such fondness that I felt immensely shy.

"Dare I ask what you think as you scrutinise me so?" I hoped I did not look ghastly under the artificial sunlight.

"I am feeling slightly nostalgic, I suppose," he answered. "I was considering how remarkable it is that, at one point, I knew you only through your words. You had the advantage with my funny Scholar's portrait, but for a time, I hadn't the slightest idea of what you look like, or how you sound when you speak, or, er—" He smiled timidly and tapped his hand on my shoulder.

"My tactile experience, such as it is?"

"Precisely. There I was, receiving letters from a thoroughly mysterious correspondent. I had no sense of how old you were – though I suspected based on your writing style that we might be around the

142

same age – nor could I guess at your height, your gender, or the colour of your hair. Yet I was wholly transfixed by those words, E., and the bright mind that must be behind them."

"I, on the other hand, knew exactly to whom I was writing. Instead of the Scholarly detachment I expected, however, I found you exceptionally kind, unimaginably droll, and so alike me that I could not believe you were real," I said. "Now that all seems rather faraway, doesn't it?"

"It is remarkable how quickly we've adapted," he said, and then, with atypical self-assurance, reached out and ran his hand tenderly along the curve of my cheek! "While I shall always think fondly of the time we spent writing to each other, I will admit that our current situation has many advantages."

I felt dizzy and distant, as though both of my ears were pressed to seashells. Somewhere in the blurry background, the waves rushed and rushed onto the wall before us. His hand lingered still on the side of my face, but I could feel him trembling, and suspected we were dangerously close to losing our respective nerves.

"Did you intend for that statement to lead up to something, Henerey?" I asked faintly.

There it was again – that glance up to the right; that earnest, honest smile; that nervous angle in his dark eyebrows—

"Would it be all right," he said, his voice shaking, "if I did?"

Unable to speak, I nodded my assent, and, as the ocean continued to resound around us, he very gently brought my face to his and kissed me.

Now, Sophy, you'll understand why I am tremendously glad you are not reading this. You would exclaim, "Did you not confess earlier that you were already sharing a bed? How did *this* not occur until now?" Remember that not even the most romantic of circumstances can make me anything other than what I am.

Because this letter will never be sent, I may also note that what I characterised as a single "kiss" was, in truth, a rather extended and

143

passionate moment, which was fortunate (for obvious reasons) and unfortunate (because the pleasantly lengthy duration gave my Brain the opportunity to sneak in and sabotage my happiness). Though I fought valiantly, that cursed Brain insisted upon flooding me with images and recriminations. I tried to focus and ground myself in physical sensations – most appropriate in this of all contexts – but I felt so helpless!

To my horror, then, I eventually responded to this transcendent experience by bursting into tears and subsequently distressing my companion.

"O, E., I am dreadfully sorry!" he exclaimed, pulling away from me in a rush.

"It is not your fault." I attempted to seal shut my eyelids to stop the tears – with little success. "That was the loveliest thing ever to happen to me."

"You grew up in the Deep House, and yet this is the loveliest thing ever to happen to you?" I could perceive genuine concern mingling with the feigned lightness in his tone. "Then what troubles you?"

"I feel so guilty," I said, opening my eyes at last. "My sister and brother no doubt believe I am missing or worse, your family feels the same, the Scholars say everyone back home is in peril anyway, and here I am so selfishly enjoying myself with you like none of that matters. How vile I am!"

"I disagree, of course, but I do understand the feeling. That first night when—when you stayed with me," Henerey said, still with a shyness that I suppose shall take some time to dissipate, "I went to sleep convinced that I could not possibly be happier. But afterwards, I did think of Vyerin, and my parents and niece and nephew, and how troubled they must be."

He paused for a moment and looked out at the artificial waves, as though he hoped to catch a glimpse of his brother's vessel.

"What I concluded, after a time," Henerey continued, "is that those guilty thoughts do nobody any good. Let us assume the worst – that they have assumed the worst. If they believe we are gone, horrible as that is, we can do nothing at present to disavow them of that notion. And don't you think that perhaps, one day, they will be delighted to discover that we have been taking comfort in each other instead of having perished?"

"I suppose they would be," I said, ignoring the aggressive disapproval of my Brain. "In fact, if Sophy knew I have spent time living away from the Deep House in an unknown underwater world, started my first course of slightly formal study, shared a bedchamber with someone else, and vaguely managed to kiss that same person, she would be excited to an extent that would probably embarrass me."

"It seemed rather excellently managed, in my opinion."

"It was lovely, of course," I said, with unfathomable understatement, "but it was also rather quiet, and so my Brain decided to torment me. Regrettably, it's easier to keep that at bay when we are talking, you know."

He looked at me with such compassion and affection that I could hardly bear it.

"I cannot fully relate with your Brain preventing you from enjoying things, but I empathise in a slightly different way." Henerey bit his lip and peered about nervously. "I told myself that if I could work up the courage to kiss you, I could talk about this, too. Now, I feared the matter might have come up earlier, but given our mutual shyness, well—"

As he paused, I wondered what could make him more anxious than initiating what just occurred!

"The thing is . . ." he began at last. "O, it's not like I've never told anyone – my brother knows, remarkably – but I've never told *you* before. As I was saying, I'm afraid I find myself rather disinterested in most – not all, but most – of the, er, physical aspects of partnership that can be so very enjoyable for many people. Such things make me feel most unpleasant, like I am disconnected from myself, so I tend to avoid them, as a rule. I do apologise."

You can imagine that I felt relieved, though not surprised, by this confession.

"Do remember that you brought this up in the first place because it appears to be something we have in common. I did suspect, even from your letters. The only difference between us is that I have no experience with *such things* and can therefore speak only hypothetically about my disinterest in them. Why must you apologise when we are conveniently aligned?"

"It is due to my own anxieties, I suppose. And if that ever changes, or if you would ever like me to – well, as it happens, I am an excellent researcher, and—"

"I appreciate your thoughtfulness, but I think I might simply perish on the spot if you complete that sentence." I tried to punctuate this statement with a laugh, though it hardly felt like a jest based on how fast my heart was beating.

"I simply do not want to disappoint you, my dear, dear E." He pulled me into a sudden embrace and then released me just as swiftly.

"You never could," I said, returning his arms to my shoulders. "I am glad to have learned more about you, and I would not have you change any aspect of yourself. Am I safe in assuming that embracing like this may be on the list of physical activities you do enjoy? As is sleeping in each other's arms? Personally, I find both quite pleasant."

Ah, now it was his turn to respond by simply nodding!

"I shall note that down, then," I continued. "And if that kiss earlier was entirely for my benefit, I will not ask you to do it again."

"No, you ought to add that to your list as well!" Henerey exclaimed with a vehemence that made me smile, even as it somehow quickened my pulse further. "So long as it is in reasonable doses."

"Is there an established metric for what constitutes a reasonable dose? If not, you will have to let me know when things start getting unreasonable."

"With you and only you, I suspect my maximum threshold may turn out to be greater than ever before," he said in a low voice, and now here I am, barely able to write that statement out without blushing afresh! (Especially considering that his suspicion proved true later that evening. But I shall keep that strictly to myself!)

"You see, E.," Henerey continued, "you mustn't think I do not feel very passionately about you. I most assuredly do, despite it being against my nature to express it in particular ways. My primary concern is for you, and, if you are equally inclined to repeat what we just did, how we might overcome the obstacles set by your mind."

"I am most certainly inclined," I said automatically – and now I was the one to look away.

"Then perhaps there are some adjustments we can make," he said, readopting his characteristically quick and clever manner of speaking. "I imagine that the unfamiliar location, sublime though it is, is not making matters easier. Being in a private place where you do not fear some Scholar stumbling upon us would help, wouldn't it?"

"I suspect so," I said, feeling incredibly warm and peaceful. "You are keenly perceptive, Henerey, and I am so glad you understand me."

"Likewise."

"So perhaps – later?"

"Undoubtedly," he said, and kissed the top of my head to punctuate his point. "Though, at the moment, I feel disposed to stay here with you. What do you say to that? I keep glancing to the horizon for some kind of dolphin, or even just a fish jumping out of the water. While I suspect it's a foolish hope, I can't help but continue looking."

I share all this with you, Imaginary Sophy, not because I want to brag about my romantic accomplishments, or because I feel the urge to confirm their reality by recounting them to someone else (though I suppose both of those things are somewhat true). You cannot read these words, and yet, even so, I want to show you I am not suffering here. I have someone to care for, and he will care for me in return, and the two of us will keep surviving for as long as we are able. I could not ask for a better companion – imagine the bleak reality in which Arvist and I were exiled to another world together, for example!

O, Sophy, I fear you are frantic with worry, but I know your character better than anyone. You cannot rest until you have solved a problem, and you will never accept that I simply vanished. I have the utmost faith in your ability to weather this experience. While I will no longer write to this imaginary version of you, I shall continue to await the moment when we are reunited and I can tell you everything (well, perhaps not *everything*) in person.

In the meantime, dear sister, I promise I will be quite all right.

Chapter 10

AUTOMATED POST MISSIVE FROM "L." TO THE THIRTIETH SECOND SCHOLAR, 1005

To my dear 30,

May I call you that? Have we grown close enough for me to leave off the "ii"?

I hope everything in my package was to your satisfaction. I strove to prepare and pack the documents appropriately. I even placed protective sheets between the pages of Henerey Clel's journal so the ink would not smudge onto the versos! (Yes, I do feel a little guilty about tearing out those first few pages to send in my initial letter. I shall atone by treating the rest of Scholar Clel's manuscript with uncharacteristic archival care. I presume you were responsible for selecting that lovely blue cover while rebinding the manuscript? It is pleasingly lavish, and therefore suitable for a secret diary. Well done.)

Though I must confess that after expending so much effort to obtain these documents of yours – beginning with befriending the certain wife of a certain incorrigible cartographer who is the certain sister of a significant figure in this narrative, which led to said friend inviting me to visit your world by way of the Cidnorghes' Entry, which led to me encountering you by "chance" in your city's library, which led to us taking tea together – I needn't go on, since you know what followed, but I did want to catch you up on the prior events – at any rate, after going to all that trouble for documents that my employer yearns to add to his collection, what did I find when I read them?

Well, that they are all overlong, overdetailed, and contain far more sentimental blathering than I expected. Why were so many pages of documentation dedicated to the process of these two finally daring to sleep in the same bed? (Whenever I meet someone vaguely interesting, the very first thing I do is invite them to my bed – rare though that may be.) If they are indeed so remarkably shy, does it not boggle the mind that they were comfortable committing these intimate encounters to paper in the first place? And if we grant that perhaps they might write down such things in secret, why in the names of all the seas would they allow said papers to be archived and consequently read by strangers in the future?

Unless, in fact, they did not consent to such a thing. Is there something you are not telling me, dear 30?

(I will admit, however, that I did rather enjoy your reports. Like Scholar Cidnosin, I was disappointed when you seemed to vanish from the record towards the end. Thankfully, you seem to have changed significantly over the past few years. I would feel terrible about stealing anything from your younger self!

Terrible enough that I would have to charge my client additional fees for the trouble, I suppose.)

While I am pleased that I fulfilled my employer's request by obtaining your papers, I do feel I have the worse side of our bargain. For the documents you still possess – those that belong to me, as I hope you'll remember – are of far greater historical import, and if they do not return to my possession, I am afraid the consequences may be dire.

By the way, you may wonder how I managed to send you a package full of physical objects when our worlds are connected only by a few errant Automated Post machines. Well, I tell you this now because you will need to use a similar method when returning my documents to me (which I anticipate you will do shortly, won't you?). Relying, once again, upon my friendship with Niea Cidnorghe (which, incidentally, is one of the most rewarding fake friendships I ever developed – so committed am I to this ruse that we are meeting tomorrow to go shopping for aquarium supplies, simply because it seemed like a pleasant thing to do) and her access to one of those transporting Structures, I leaped between worlds to carry these documents to your door. While there, I intended to see if I could rob you of my missing files and save you the trouble of postage.

Unfortunately – and I say this as if you were not the one who put this clever scheme into action! – when I arrived at the docking-place where this inexplicable device deposits its travellers, there was a fierce-looking guard patrolling the area! Unperturbed, I dived off the dock and clung to its underside, with only my very nostrils above the water to allow me to breathe. I watched as the guard's boots tromped dangerously close to said nostrils, though I was protected by the docking-boards between us. When my enemy retreated at last, I placed your package by the edge of the water. It was labelled with your name, so the guard would know where to deliver the package after confiscating it!

At any rate, if you wish to deliver my documents in a similar fashion, you need only send word, and I will brave your docks once more to retrieve them. (Unless you would prefer to visit our world? Have you ever done that? You previously claimed to be acquainted with Sophy; I imagine it would not be too difficult for you to use the Cidnorghes' Entry yourself . . .)

I await (and expect) your immediate response.

Firmly,

L.

AUTOMATED POST MISSIVE FROM THE THIRTIETH SECOND SCHOLAR TO "L.", 1005

Dear L.,

What a funny one you are! You never cease to amuse me. That fearsome "guard" you encountered on the docks was simply one of my colleagues, the Twenty-Ninth Second Scholar, who made plans with the Fortieth Second Scholar to do some maintenance around the perimeter of the city. Now, the Fortieth Second Scholar is so well regarded that they are often delayed by more pressing requests from the First Scholars, so the Twenty-Ninth Second Scholar was forced to take up a lonely vigil at the docks for some time. He mentioned catching a glimpse of a stranger's nose, but brushed it off as mere illusion, as he has been busy with a project and has not slept well recently! You certainly made an impression.

Don't worry, I have no intention of betraying you. I am working now to complete my copies of the information from your documents, and I shall send along the originals shortly. I admit to some reluctance about doing so, however, because I find myself sorely offended by your dismissive interpretation of what you termed the Cidnosin Papers.

Yes, perhaps I am biased. Despite your compliments about my records, I regret that you now know all too well the role I played in Scholar Clel and Scholar Cidnosin's visit to our city. What you do not know yet is that I grew rather close to them in the end. But that was a different time. Though it's only been about a year by *our* calendars since they first came here, I would like to think I have matured. Back then, I had been given responsibilities that were previously incomprehensible to me, because I formerly occupied much of my days with Frivolous Tales and illicit Second Scholar gossip. These two surface-dwellers – who were so kind and peculiar and so kindly and peculiarly in love with each other – became dear to me. As a result, I am perfectly happy to spend pages reading about all the experiences they shared.

(How amusing that you find it odd for people to write down their personal experiences in such detail. By any decent record-keeping standards, the majority of those romantic descriptions were remarkably sparse and could have benefited from much more specificity!

I say that only in jest. Naturally.)

You made a most critical error, by the way. I do indeed have the appropriate permissions to preserve these documents. Really, what do you take me for?

It is true that I am also well acquainted with the Cidnorghes. Still, I don't know if it would do for me to pass into your world at present. While our rules are slightly more flexible these days – and the Cidnorghes and Ambassador Mawr often pop in and out – no one has dared to broach the subject of whether we are allowed to leave ourselves. Rules aside, I remain far too busy! I shall place the documents in a safe-box at the docks for you to fetch. If it would entertain you, I may even set a guard or two for you to avoid.

(What an illogical waste of time that would be! I fear you may have contaminated me with your influence.)

I imagine everything will be ready for you tomorrow – that is, tomorrow *here*. I do not know when that will be for you. Simply keep an eye out, won't you?

With fondest regards,

30.ii (or "30", since that's what you prefer! No one has ever called me by a shortened title before. How delightful!)

P.S. I am not familiar with the customs of your world, but should I feel hurt by the revelation that you do not find me "vaguely interesting" enough to merit an invitation to your bed?

AUTOMATED POST MISSIVE FROM "L." TO THE THIRTIETH SECOND SCHOLAR, 1005

Dear 30 (since you do approve),

I suspected there was something off about that guard. Any true sentinel worthy of their title would have noticed me in an instant. When they turned to chase me, I would have folded back my arms like the fins of Brisk Porpoise and swam away at top speed. I was, in fact, expecting this outcome, and regretted missing the opportunity to practise my strokes.

As I trust you will keep your promise, I will allow myself to relax a little as I await the delivery. My employer grows most impatient. He is busy constructing an archive of documents relating to every stage of this family affair – he recently got his hands on a collection of relevant papers that Sophy Cidnorghe and that captain friend of hers had stashed somewhere. (Fortunately, that acquisition did not require my involvement.) Today he (the employer, that is) asked if I could lend him the logbook from the *Perspicacity*, which remains your prisoner. Of all things, too! I said he could not have it – not because the shorthand copy is currently in the possession of a fanciful young Scholar who is far more cunning than they appear, but because I am in the midst of restoring the slightly waterlogged pages. (I chose this lie because I know my employer, disinterested as he is in the practicalities of everyday life, would never guess that captains have made use of waterproof paper for centuries.) I do require those documents soon, dear 30! Do not disappoint me!

Though I now comprehend your personal interest in the Cidnosin Papers (and I do admit, begrudgingly, that there was something vaguely pleasant about people finding comfort in each other in dire circumstances, &c), I think you will discover that my documents provide much more valuable context for the events that so recently reshaped both our societies!

L.

P.S. On the contrary – you are one of the most interesting people I've ever had the pleasure (or misfortune?) of meeting. Who knows what might happen if you deigned to visit our world one day? (I am, indeed, disappointed by your reluctance to travel here. I had hoped I might return the favour by inviting you to tea and seeing what you would steal from me next.)

Chapter 11

EXCERPT FROM THE LOGBOOK OF THE *PERSPICACITY* BY VYERIN CLEL, 1004

A mutiny today, courtesy of Sophy Cidnorghe. My husband will be relieved.

ANNOTATION TO THE LOGBOOK BY SOPHY CIDNORGHE, 1004

I feel it is my responsibility to expand upon the concise remarks of our dear Captain – not simply to defend my own good name, but to chronicle a grand step forward in the search for E. and Henerey that has gone on far longer than I care to admit. (Though if I might return to the former matter for a moment, I would like to emphasise that Vyerin is – by his own confession – a family man. Our decision to spare him from a potentially treacherous endeavour is certainly not malicious, mutinous though it may be!)

As I have never annotated this logbook before, and because I suspect the rest of Vyerin's entries are as terse as the one above, perhaps I ought to establish some facts about said mission and its present frustrations. Tides and tides ago, I stood upon the deck of the *Perspicacity* for the first time, thrilled by how everything fell into place. When nobody associated with any Campus deigned to answer our advertisements, Vyerin managed to engage a crew of unaffiliated Navigators recommended by his seemingly ceaseless network of captain's acquaintances. There were five of them in total, all pleasant people who were not bothered in the least by the prospect of seeking out Antepelagic technology that may or may not provide access to another world.

In addition, as I hoped, Niea and I also recruited some former colleagues from the Ridge expedition. Not all of them, alas. Ylaret Tamseln insisted that our shared experience at the bottom of the ocean had rather spoiled her appetite for adventure, but she did introduce Vyerin to some experimental celestial navigation techniques that could make our journey easier. Irye Rux and Vincenebras offered to join us aboard with taciturn curiosity and overwhelming enthusiasm, respectively. The final crew also included Cidnosin family associate Jeime Alestarre (apparent expert on the subject of the Entries) and my wife's inscrutable friend Tevn Winiver Mawr (apparent expert on the subject of the generally mysterious).

Such was our crew. I use the past tense intentionally, though not because some tragedy did away with them all! In fact, what occurred next was merely a series of disappointments and scheduling conflicts. You see, finding an Entry in operable condition proved more difficult than Vyerin and I hoped.

The original document from the Fleet that Jeime shared with E. included coordinates for only a handful of Entries. Further investigation of the Darbeni archives led us to an additional Appendix, which predicted the emergence of several more Entries in the year 1004. A promising start! Yet every time we reached a new location, we found nothing more than detritus, with the device already having been blown up by its own unstable components (as in the case of the Second Potential Entry), turned into breeding grounds for approximately a thousand squid that we could not stomach the thought of evicting (like the Fourth Potential Entry) or nibbled beyond repair by some shark with no gastronomical standards (which was the fate of the Seventh Potential Entry).

None of our companions signed on for such an extended venture. Our numbers dwindled. Vyerin's colleagues book jobs for set intervals, so it was no surprise that our Navigators had to depart when our journey continued beyond its promised duration. Irye might have stuck it out for tides more, happily making field recordings, but then they received the summons of their dreams: an invitation to serve as a consultant for an independent theatrical recording company near Intertidal Campus. After Irye's departure, Vincenebras moped about for days until Niea kindly suggested that perhaps he ought to go back and see how Irye was getting on – only as a favour to Niea, of course.

Consequently, the *Perspicacity* is presently crewed by myself, Vyerin, Niea, Jeime, and Tevn, as Captain Clel has no doubt recorded on our updated roster—

I have just glanced across Vyerin's desk at said roster and realised that it is horrifyingly basic, with nothing more than names. Considering that I once furnished my sister with detailed visual descriptions of my Ridge colleagues at the start of that fateful expedition – even when they were still strangers to me – the least I can do is provide, for posterity's sake, a little more information about these companions whom I know so well. (We departed in a rush, after all, and had no time to take any portraits to commemorate our journey.) I shall copy out Vyerin's lacking manifest here and annotate it accordingly.

PARTICIPANTS (STILL) ABOARD THE PERSPICACITY
Captain Vyerin Clel. I dare not write anything about you in your own logbook, dear Captain. I *wanted* to say that you are an exceptional Navigator, a devoted brother, and one of my dearest friends besides, but precedent suggests you would tear out this page if I marred it with any such drivel! It is, however, challenging to resist the urge to describe you, since you cut such a striking figure at the helm in those blue captain's

robes with your black hair, the same length as mine, curling about your face in the most dramatic fashion ...

Yes, I know. Drivel.

Sophy Cidnorghe. O, why must my name appear second on the list? There I was, teasing Vyerin for not wishing to be described in this record, and now I feel quite unwilling to write about myself! Well, I am a cartographer (how much nicer that sounds than "disgraced ex-Scholar of Wayfinding"), a wife, and a sister. I keep my hair short, my waistcoats tidy, and my disposition relatively cheerful. Unlike my red-headed siblings, who could never survive long in the sun, I inherited my late mother's look, and I appreciate how much the tanned, careworn face I see in the looking glass after days at sea resembles her.

Surely that suffices.

Scholar Jeime Alestarre. Jeime is an Architect (still actively affiliated with a Campus, unlike most of us aboard) and my mother's dearest friend and former partner. In addition to her actual field of study, Jeime's areas of expertise include aquadynamic construction, depth-craft design, and the defunct secret society known as the Fleet, whose notes guide our current movements. She somehow manages to appear both resolute and ethereal. Her waist-length hair, often pulled back with a ribbon, is gold streaked with grey, and the soft whitish-blue cast of her skin reminds me of my brother's. Jeime's lips are almost always pursed primly – I have never seen her smile properly – but her eyes are constantly alert. In that keenness I recognise the very quality that led my mother to love her.

Eliniea Hayve Cidnorghe. I am tempted to simply write "my indescribably superlative wife!" and leave it at that – but I would never do such a disservice to her many accomplishments. Niea (the name she prefers) is a brilliant former expedition leader, the enterprising founder of an independent Institute of Knowledge, and a skilled aquarist, among many other things. Her departure from Boundless Campus after our Ridge mission was likely the greatest tragedy ever to strike the Scholars of Life.

Still, I intended for these annotations to include descriptions of personalities and physical characteristics, not accomplishments, so I suppose I ought to rein in my wifely pride and focus on the essential facts.

Personality: empathetic, resilient, exuberant, and a confident yet compassionate leader.

Physical characteristics: bespectacled eyes, evening-dark hair that falls in soft waves (on the rare occasions when she wears it down), a deep brown complexion, remarkable height, graceful hands that almost dance when she speaks excitedly, and eyebrows eternally raised in a kind expression.

Other sundries: Niea is in possession of a quick wit, a wardrobe of pastel-coloured dresses, an adorable nose that crinkles in a most charming manner as she gazes out to the horizon, and—

I do absolutely cherish her. Shall we leave it at that?

Tevn Mawr. As I mentioned previously, Tevn is here by virtue of his long-standing friendship with Niea (and because of what he previously experienced with us at the Ridge). Though I still do not quite know what to make of him, I can describe Tevn well enough – quiet, refined, and curious in both senses of the word. He is of average height (which is to say that both Niea and I tower over him), pale-skinned and wide-eyed like certain abyssal fish species from my wife's research, and blessed with grey-brown hair that always ends up looking stylishly tousled whenever a tempest troubles us.

Now that I have satisfied my inescapable urge to document everything properly, I shall return to the main point: despite all these obstacles, we found a functioning Entry at last!

Spotting an Entry in the first place is challenging enough. The Fleet's calculations are rarely accurate, as changes in the currents shift the positions of the Entries over time. In fact, we might have spent hours circling the wrong waypoint today without the surprising assistance of Tevn Mawr.

I do not mean to imply it is surprising that Tevn would assist us. He may not be the most gregarious member of our crew, but I've learned to appreciate his dependability. What surprised me was that he provided said assistance by receiving an inexplicable vision from a mysterious being whom none of us could ever forget.

The vision in question occurred yesterday, right as we were bickering collegially over which wave would bear us most swiftly to our intended destination. Tevn rarely takes part in these conversations, except when he cuts in to take Niea's side when necessary. (I have come to appreciate, not envy, his unerring loyalty to my wife.) On this occasion, however, he interrupted the proceedings by falling to the floor as his eyes filled with tears.

Niea reached down and caught Tevn, while the ever-ready Captain Clel, stolid as ever, tossed her some pillows from a convenient hatch below the helm. We all crowded around and fussed over the fellow – perhaps in the hopes that his natural distaste for such things would restore him from this swoon.

"She remembers me." Tevn's face was alight with sorrow and shock.

"Your friend, you mean?" asked my wife, exchanging a meaningful glance with me, which I then tried to exchange with Vy, though he had turned back to the helm and did not notice. Tevn's intense distress and delight could only be caused by his enigmatic sea-woman "friend" – an inexplicable apparition of the deep who first appeared to him alone. Tevn, Niea, and I last encountered her during the final expedition of our Ridge mission.

"I don't suppose she had anything useful to say about the location of the Entry?" I said, because I am incorrigible and rarely think of anything other than our mission.

"Technically speaking, she had nothing to say at all," Tevn replied. "It was not like how we communicated back then. No, this time, she sent me a series of images. I saw her, in what I imagine must be her natural habitat. And, well, Sophy, I suppose I ought to mention that I saw someone else, too."

"Please elaborate." My calm tone did not, in any way, reveal the rush I experienced as he spoke.

"Is your sister very like you, but with auburn hair that just reaches her shoulders?"

"That could not possibly be her." I steadied myself on the ship's railing. "She would never wear her hair short."

"Sophy!" exclaimed Niea. She threw her arms around my waist: either to comfort me or prevent me from tumbling overboard in my confusion.

"Are you certain?" I asked. "If you are not, Tevn, I swear—"

"My focus was on my friend, so I apologise if I misinterpreted some minute aspect of E.'s appearance. I can say with absolute confidence that someone who looked like she could be your sister was there."

"Did you see a fashionable bearded fellow – a gentler version of me?" bellowed Vyerin from behind us. Somehow, in a manner of moments, he leaped from the helm, turned to Tevn as if to grab him by the lapels, thought better of it, and then retreated once more. I understood the feeling.

Seemingly unaffected by Vyerin's outburst, Tevn shook his head. "I saw only E. and my friend."

"We should not put too much faith in hallucinations," said Vyerin, but I could tell that he already had.

"Regardless of what Tevn saw, this may yet be useful," I said. "Have we not determined that people tend to have inexplicable visions – or more, in E.'s case – when in proximity to these Entries?"

"Could it really be that simple? That an Entry is right beneath us?" asked Niea. "But we are still some fathoms off from the coordinates."

"Well, considering that the Fleet's coordinates failed us eleven out of twelve times thus far, I am open to following Tevn and his premonitions. Captain – drop anchor!"

"As you wish, *Captain*," Vyerin grumbled, giving me a long-suffering smile.

Everything proceeded efficiently after that point. Niea, Vyerin,

Tevn and I assembled into a depth-craft. As is typical on our first surveying dive of a new area, we were also accompanied by Jeime, who was tasked with providing a mechanical evaluation of any device we might find. (Unfortunately, we did not need an expert to determine that all the prior Entries were completely useless, so she has felt rather bored of late.)

As we neared the ocean floor and I spotted a small, shadowy shape just ahead of us, I feared the Entry had met the same fate as the others. Was it so thoroughly destroyed that only a tiny part remained? I never saw the infamous Structure by the Deep House – outside of my sister's sketches, that is – but it was apparently large enough for a depth-craft to dock upon, and that seemed impossible with the one before us.

When we drew closer, I observed that this piece of seafloor detritus was, in fact, a delicately carved miniature arch with barely enough space beneath for a particularly agile person to crawl through. (For the record, I believe E.'s Structure did not quite look like *that*.) We were not at a depth that any of us Ridge alumni aboard would consider deep, but the waters were surprisingly dark due to the overcast skies. I mention this because the low light levels made it possible for me to discern a pale green luminescence emanating from the object.

"I don't suppose we have any chance of finding the other half of this one?" asked Vyerin.

"I think it may be intact." I pointed out the glow that ran along the arch like the curve of a rainbow. "None of the broken Entries lit up, did they?"

"If this is truly an Entry, then I question the reason of its creators," said Jeime crossly. "Why use such different shapes for objects that all fulfil the same function? Surely it would be more reasonable to find the most effective form and then repeat it. I imagine your brother would debate the matter with me, Sophy, were he present."

I did not have much to say in response to that, and will not make much note of it here, either – other than admitting that I did rather intentionally leave someone out when discussing the make-up of our

163

crew. I suppose I should mention that my brother Arvist spent but two days aboard the *Perspicacity* before fleeing at the next port. Against my better judgement, I let him beguile me with his apparent investment in finding our sister. In fairness, during those two days, Arvist was in fine form – pitching in most heartily whenever we needed (though his efforts inevitably caused more work for everyone), sharing suppositions aplenty about the "Phosphorescent Place" we sought (though he always used such conversations as an excuse to bring up the art he wished to make there), and even expressing a vague interest in joining me for dinner both evenings (though, on each occasion, Vyerin and I were too busy planning together to step foot in the galley).

Then, out of nowhere, my brother apparently succumbed to intense seasickness and had no choice but to depart for the nearest Infirmary. Though I do not intend to diminish the struggles of those who fall ill while on the water, I do wish Arvist had shown me the courtesy of inventing a more convincing lie. He has been out and about on boats and depth-crafts and vessels of all kinds since we were children, after all!

Really, I don't know what else I expected from him.

"Can you evaluate it from here, Jeime, or do you intend to dive?" I asked.

"I can certainly review it at this range, assuming our mechanical arm survived after being so ill used."

"Again, I do apologise!" Niea exclaimed as Jeime pulled the depth-craft closer to the Entry. "But I had never seen a Volatile Anemone preying upon a member of its own species before, and that rock was in the way—"

"I was jesting, Niea, but apparently I am better at wrecking jokes than you are at destroying depth-craft components," said Jeime. "How curious! Sophy is right – this appears to be an entire Entry. The intended application of the device is fairly simple. People swim through the arch, one by one, and are transported to the desired destination."

"That is what I feared," I said. "If we pursue this route, we will not have a depth-craft at our disposal on the other side like E. and Henerey did. That complicates matters."

"There is an additional complication." Jeime activated the depth-craft's periscope and directed it beneath the arch, where we could see a network of small cracks forming beautifully alarming textures on the unknown material.

"I do not think highly of its structural integrity," she said. "As we learned from the Deep House's Structure, massive amounts of energy release when these things activate."

"How many people do you reckon could make it through before the device explodes?" I asked.

"I have no way of knowing. I wouldn't take a chance with it myself, as my fiancée would never forgive me. The fewer go through, the better, in my opinion."

"So, for example, no more than two?" Against my better nature, I took this opportunity to smirk smugly at Tevn. (Since he joined our mission, Tevn and I have been engaged in a rigorous debate about the nature of the Entries that neither of us dares to drop.)

Tevn sighed. "For the last time, Sophy – though I suspect it will not be – my friend never meant to imply that there is a restriction on how many people can enter an Entry at once."

"I can quote the exact words as I transcribed them in my letter, Tevn. She said, 'So many Scholars, though I asked only for one more!' She wanted you and another person – a pair, just like Henerey and E."

"Her statement reflected the reality that I have few friends, and she could not possibly expect me to bring more than one. The fact that a pair of people crossed over shortly thereafter was due to coincidence, not a capacity limit!"

I could see Vyerin mouthing along to our oft-repeated arguments, and I wanted to scold him until I saw how much his antics made Niea smile.

"I do not wish to support either side of this conflict," said Jeime hurriedly, "and perhaps my assessment of the Structure's stability is too bleak. Besides, I realise I am aboard this vessel with people who have spent more time living underwater than anyone else. Couldn't your Ridge training prove useful?"

"O, why didn't I think of that?" said Niea. "We have three long-range depth-suits and two of those Bubble habitations. I do not know how Vincenebras obtained them, and I do try to avoid asking him too many questions! I nearly forgot that I packed them before we set off. As many as three of us could go without a vessel, if we wished."

"*Three* of us can certainly try to go," I said, giving Tevn one last frown.

"Then Niea and Sophy shall have to tutor me in deep-water diving," said Vyerin.

"With pleasure!" said Niea. "How many years of standard diving experience do you have, Vy?"

"None. I suspect I will be a quick study."

My wife possesses impressively formidable optimism, but even she looked concerned by this response.

"You can fight amongst yourselves to choose who else goes, but one thing is certain – I shall be one of the three," said Tevn, suddenly rising from his corner of the depth-craft.

Vyerin eyed him warily. "Have you also lost a sibling who travelled through an Entry recently?"

"You already know whom I seek. Since she is our best lead to the whereabouts of E., you will not get far without me."

"This is ridiculous," Vyerin grumbled. "Sophy, I'm sure you'll be able to tell him why. Much more energetically than I could, no doubt."

I looked around the depth-craft at the odd party I'd assembled – my beloved wife, my dear friend, my mother's lost love, and my former replacement-turned-colleague-turned-reluctant-ally. I placed my hand on Vyerin's shoulder, and he sighed.

"I'm sorry, Vy," I said. "But I agree with Tevn."

"And she really must agree, if she's willing to take my side," said Tevn.

166

"Besides," I continued, "travelling long distances underwater without a depth-craft is a dangerous enterprise that requires skills you lack. Do you think your husband and children would rest easy if you took such a risk?"

Vyerin twisted away from my consoling touch, and for a moment I thought I would see a demonstration of the latent fury he once told me he possessed. He did not turn back to face us for several moments, and some faint sounds soon suggested that Captain Vyerin Clel was weeping.

"If you return without him, or if you enter that confounded thing and never come back at all, Sophy, what am I to do then?" he murmured, still facing the wall of the depth-craft.

"We will all come back," I said firmly. "Based on what we've read, I don't think it would be possible to bring E. home without Henerey, anyway. I shall return with them both in tow, and they will have a laugh about the fact that we're such good friends, won't they?"

With another reluctant nod from Vyerin, our plan was confirmed. Now Tevn, Niea, and I are preparing to go into the unknown. It has been a long time since I put on a proper diving suit, and the feeling is both nostalgic and unsettling. With that glossy, thin material wrapping around my legs once more, I felt instantly transported to the waters outside of the Spheres station – to the time when my days were marked by the joys of falling for my wife and the frustrations of working for the pernicious Chancellor Rawsel. And the bittersweet delight, too, of receiving letters from my sister up above.

Nostalgia aside, I pledge here and now that I will do whatever it takes to find E. and Henerey. I've written this pledge down so Vyerin may read it in times of need. (I will, of course, continue to reiterate this pledge in all our future communications – since it is our understanding that we will be able to exchange Automated Post missives even after I depart. In the tides before our journey, we worked with some discreet Scholars of my wife's acquaintance to see how much one might maximise the distance between Automated Post devices while still managing to send messages effectively. Early testing proved most promising, so I remain comfortably optimistic.) Now it is time for me – and Niea, and Tevn, too – to follow in my sister's footsteps. I hope that E. awaits me, and that I do not go to my doom. My sister was brave enough to make this choice on her own, so I will follow her lead.

AUTOMATED POST MISSIVE FROM ELINIEA HAYVE CIDNORGHE TO SOPHY CIDNORGHE, 1004

Sophy, are you there? The Entry shattered before I could make it through, but do not fret! I am fine – back on deck now with Vyerin – wishing desperately to be with you. I hope beyond anything that this works!

AUTOMATED POST MISSIVE FROM ELINIEA HAYVE CIDNORGHE TO SOPHY CIDNORGHE, 1004

Perhaps my first message did not send? I shall try once more! The Entry fell apart but did not "burst", so you needn't worry about me. But I cannot stop worrying about you! Be safe, please?

EXCERPT FROM THE LOGBOOK OF THE *PERSPICACITY* BY VYERIN CLEL, 1004

Unforeseen complications. Dropping anchor to keep a lookout – and to look after N.

AUTOMATED POST MISSIVE FROM ELINIEA HAYVE CIDNORGHE TO SOPHY CIDNORGHE, 1004

It's unlike me, I know, but I grow terribly concerned. A whole day has passed now, and I continue to check the A.P. machine constantly. You are most likely alive and well, but I do not enjoy the uncertainty! If you can read this, please know that I love you immensely and I wish—no, it is no good to dwell on that now. Where have you gone, my dear Sophy?

AUTOMATED POST MISSIVE FROM VYERIN CLEL TO REIV CLEL, 1004

Dear Reiv,

I'm afraid I haven't the time to provide any context for this note. I simply wanted to say the following:

I miss you terribly, and I am not going anywhere.

I can picture the exact expression on your face as you say, wryly, "But *Vy*, whatever do you mean? You are on a moving ship, going places constantly!"

Yes, yes. You're very clever. I only meant that I will be remaining in our own familiar world with you for the foreseeable future. I shall explain all presently.

In the interim, don't you dare fret. We'll ring the house Echolator just as soon as the *Perspicacity* gets back into dialling range.

With twenty times more fondness than I am typically willing to put into words,

Vy

AUTOMATED POST MISSIVE FROM SOPHY CIDNORGHE TO ELINIEA HAYVE CIDNORGHE, 1004

My brave Niea,

What a terrible day (or more) you must have endured! I am so sorry and wish I could hold you for hours in recompense. I promise you that I am well, if extremely distressed by our accidental separation. Yet something is most certainly amiss ... temporally speaking! Your A.P. messages appeared – one after the other – on the machine a few moments ago, but less than an hour has passed since Tevn and I departed. (That is an estimate, of course. None of our timepieces are working, which is most distressing to Tevn – you know how fond he is of his smart watch-pin.)

How could this be possible? An hour ago, I glanced over my shoulder to draw strength from you before swimming through the Entry. I should have kissed you again before we latched our helmets – I would have done so a thousand times if I knew you could not follow me here. I am so relieved that this Entry did not perish with as much fanfare as the Structure at the Deep House. I feared the worst, but my suffering was nowhere near as intense as yours: as I mentioned, I have spent merely an hour or so worrying about your fate. (Tev, too, feared for you. He decided to express his concern by calculating the odds of you surviving an underwater explosion at close range. It turned out that a positive outcome was slightly likelier than I expected, and I did find his efforts vaguely reassuring.)

I never intended for this mission to separate us. It is indescribably upsetting. Perhaps I am also upset because my brain is engaging in what my sister learned to identify as "magical thinking" – a type of flawed processing in which someone assumes that their thoughts caused a particular consequence. Because you see, Niea, there was a moment (hours ago for me, days ago for you) when we were discussing the fragility of the Entry and I suddenly felt an urge to dissuade you from joining us. Not because I do not need you – if I must do the seemingly improbable and bring back my sister, I could ask for no better companion than my wife! – but because I began to realise, a little belatedly, that there are some profound risks to this enterprise.

It all felt rather exciting at first, didn't it? What a lark it was to conspire with Vyerin and our old friends from the Ridge and make our grand plans. Yes, how simple everything seemed – we would rely on ancient and unpredictable technology to reunite us with Henerey and E., who are obviously well and living happily at the bottom of some unknown ocean!

I know I am glibly overstating the matter. I know we worked diligently to make this as safe as possible. But when the time came to swim through a mysterious gateway without a depth-craft to keep us safe, I forced myself to consider that enlisting your aid might be selfish. If E. is out there somewhere, it is my responsibility to find her. Yet I never should have let you become so involved.

Could the Entry – or the broader metaphysical Universe – have known about these secret feelings and trapped you on the other side as a result? See, therein lies the flawed processing. I acknowledge that my thoughts alone could not tear us apart, but I do still feel somewhat responsible.

(Speaking of flawed thoughts, is it so wrong of me to cite our separation as further evidence that only two people may use a single Entry? Tevn objects and says it is a mere coincidence, and that I am far too fixated upon this notion of mine. I oscillate between believing and denying him. I admit I have become strangely stubborn about this issue, but how am I to tell whether I am following a good instinct or worrying myself for no reason? Again, I feel there is something E. could teach me about sorting through one's thoughts in situations like this!)

What a relief it is that you are safely aboard the *Perspicacity* with Vyerin. In a way, I am almost pleased you have accidentally joined the part of the crew that will oversee the second phase of our plan, because

I know your brilliant mind will be an unbelievable asset. Still, I yearn for you, and I am exceedingly glad that I must spend the night on the floor of a Bubble when next I rest. The thought of getting into a proper bed without you is devastating.

You have probably watched all these words materialise as the A.P. machine types them, and perhaps you are laughing because I spent so much time in self-recrimination and sentiment and mentioned nothing about where we are! So far, I have little to report. Tevn and I currently float in deep, lightless waters that are practically indistinguishable from those around the Ridge. (I wish we were there instead, with you following behind us on a cetacean automaton!)

Despite my relative familiarity with the depths, there is something about this ocean that feels eerily unfamiliar. I can't tell you why, exactly. Whether it is instinct or simply imagination, Niea, I cannot shake the sensation that we are well and truly *someplace else*. I can only hope it's the same someplace where E. and Henerey went.

Our present plan is frustratingly opaque by my standards, but I have no choice in the matter! Tevn is convinced that his friend will find us. Since she has yet to show, I will soon recommend that we start swimming upward, towards the general direction of what must be the surface. If E. and Henerey came here in their depth-craft, they would have done the same – though I do hope their depth-craft was the sort that can adjust its pressure automatically. I will try not to think of that overmuch . . .

In the meantime, I accept that we must wait here for a while. Tevn and I brought almost a full season's worth of rations, so that is of no concern. I know the Bubbles can sustain life for extremely long periods. Still, if you, Vyerin, and Jeime can proceed with the plan as efficiently as possible, I would be most grateful.

At any rate, please do not forget that Tevn and I are both well and shall continue to navigate about in the dark until we find something more conclusive. (Something like my sister piloting a depth-craft with Henerey by her side, ideally!)

172

Look – as if the ocean senses how my mood has changed after thinking of your lovely face and writing you a letter, I could swear there is almost the slightest tinge of pink to the water. (You know all too well, Niea, that I grew up despising that colour – so seemingly lack-lustre compared to more vibrant hues – but I now find it very precious because it reminds me of you and your various coral-coloured dresses.)

Sending you all my love (which, fortunately, requires no Entry to travel your way!),

Sophy

AUTOMATED POST MISSIVE FROM ELINIEA HAYVE CIDNORGHE TO SOPHY CIDNORGHE, 1004

Dearest, dearest Sophy,

Well, you needn't worry about Tevn's watch-pin – I will endeavour to track the time for you! I have waited loyally (and most anxiously) at this Automated Post machine for several days, and only just received your message. There is indeed a substantial delay, which is fascinating! I'll confess I am a little displeased that we will not be able to commu-nicate more normally.

That is not true – I should never again say that I am displeased or unhappy or anything of the sort, now that I know you are not lost, my cherished one! Yet – o! – how sincerely I miss you. Despite your stated desire to keep me safe, I would much prefer to be by your side. (To keep the peace between you and Tev, if I could help in no other way!)

I do hope his "friend" appears by the time this message makes its long journey to your A.P. machine. And yes, going to the surface as your next step is brilliant! Do remember to proceed slowly. The Bubbles can serve as decompressors, but they are not as effective as a depth-craft, and you may still feel ill when you ascend (assuming you do not end up someplace with a convenient depressurisation chamber available for your use). Surely there could not be an ocean without a surface?

In the meantime, now that I am functioning again, the three of us shall focus on the next step of the journey – though it is the part that gives me the most pause. Jeime gathered up all the pieces of the Entry you used (fortunately, the damage was not as substantial as we anticipated) and we are off to find and retrieve an additional Entry, if we can! Then the real work may begin.

I know we have keen Scholarly minds working on this project (not including mine, no matter what a lovely flatterer like you might say!), but now that you are gone, I find myself terrified by the non-negligible notion that you may struggle to return home. Finding another Entry, for me, is also a security measure. If all else fails and you are stuck on the other side, I will simply step through that Entry and seek you out, and we can make an agreeable home together in some other reality. Wouldn't that be romantic?

Yet I continue to hope that our plan will work, and that, by studying an Entry, we will be able to construct one ourselves.

I shall say little more than that, because you know our objective all too well, and I find myself uncharacteristically paranoid of late.

Do you remember seeing any unusual vessels during the past few tides of our journey? (I assume you would have mentioned it, if so!) Well, Vyerin and I are now both grimly convinced that we are being followed!

At first, I thought I had merely spied the dorsal fins of some unknown whale slapping the surface of the water several times. The Discerning Toothed Whales carry out their courtship rituals at this time of year, and I have spotted a few making all kinds of lusty jumps to impress each other. (Much like I did when we attended that ball last month – I suppose you can best judge the efficacy of such attempts at wooing!)

A certain specimen has been circling the *Perspicacity* for some time, and I found its movements rather atypical. The dives and breaches of this whale seemed oddly predictable, as if it only knew how to move in one predetermined manner. Now, I will confess that I have noticed many unusual animal behaviours over the course of our voyage – including my infamous encounter with the all-consuming Anemones – and the bizarre whale once again reminded me of Henerey's observations about the rays from two years ago. What would he make of this, I wonder?

When I sought out Vyerin's spyglass to examine the creature more closely, I noticed that the upper part of its body was constructed, with the rivets and manufacturing streaks prominently visible. There is a sinister shadow of a depth-craft chasing us, Sophy, and I am impressed and unsettled in equal measure by how much the vessel resembles a real whale!

To fulfil my duties as a reasonable first mate, or whatever my position may be aboard this ship (I do not aspire to co-captaincy as you did!), I hoped to share my concerns with Vyerin over dinner. We have taken to dining together to become better acquainted in your absence. Vy insists on doing the cooking himself. It is nothing more than a simple sailor's stew most of the time, but it is hearty and pleasant and makes me feel better, since I find myself relatively helpless in the kitchen without you to assist me. (Jeime does not join us, as she prefers to take her meals in the darkest hours of the night.)

We often sit in a companionable silence that I am only rarely apt to break. Today, however, our dear captain seemed distant and sad. I felt irrepressibly joyful because you are alive, so I succumbed to the urge to meddle sooner rather than later.

"May I ask what is on your mind, Vyerin?"

He fixed me with that powerful stare of his, and I could almost identify the moment when he decided that the risks of emotional vulnerability were worth the benefits of confessing his worries.

"I know I should not be troubled by the vision that Tevn allegedly experienced," he said at last. "But it terrifies me that only E. appeared in it."

"That does not mean something happened to Henerey," I said. "Perhaps Henerey was there, but simply out of the vision's range. Are visions like cameras?"

"It would be rather unlike my brother to hide from a camera, especially if he were pleased with his outfit."

"We must trust in Sophy. Isn't it a marvel enough that she and Tev made it through, Vyerin? If they can do that, surely anything is possible."

"It is unlike me to say it, but I do trust your wife, Niea. More than I have ever trusted somebody from outside of my family." He gave me a wistful smile. "I don't know how I would have muddled through all this without her."

"And she feels the same about you," I said. "I am ever so grateful you two found each other!"

Perhaps this was all getting a bit sentimental for poor Vy's taste, for he responded by taking a swig of stew and promptly changing the subject. "Have you noticed, Niea, that there is an artificial whale tailing us?"

"Absolutely!" I exclaimed. "It is an astonishing replica. Most automata are so stylised. What do you make of it?"

"I do not like it. And I have had enough of its captain's nonsense. What do you say to giving them a bit of a fright?"

He winked at me, and in the schoolboy delight that illuminated his face I could see the young Vyerin Clel you've described to me, Sophy, as he described himself in his letters. It would not surprise me to learn that he was a masterful prankster in his youth!

"What exactly did you have in mind?" I whispered with conspiratorial relish.

Vyerin stood up, lifted his bowl to his lips, and consumed his remaining stew in one long gulp. Then he threw on his coat and made for the door.

"Won't you accompany me to the helm? I'd wager these mysterious strangers think they've been exceptionally clever and stealthy. Nothing would surprise them more than if we swerved towards them, don't you think?"

"How intriguing!" I followed him onto the deck. "Is there anything I can do to help?"

"For my sake, I would kindly ask that you hold very firmly onto the railing."

"For my own sake, certainly, but why for yours?"

"Because I dread to imagine what fury Sophy Cidnorghe would raise if she returned from the depths only to find that her wife was flung overboard in my care." He stretched his shoulders and gave me one final nod. "Let's sink those scoundrels, shall we?"

Anything I might have said in response was drowned out by the rushing and creaking that began as the ship commenced a dramatic turnabout. I did hold onto the railing, but I must also confess that I leaned slightly forward to experience the wind rolling about me as we carried out this manoeuvre. How freeing it felt to face the horizon like a figurehead, moving in symbiosis with the sea! Who is to say which was in control: the ocean, or Vyerin? As someone who has spent most of her life in either classrooms or depth-crafts, I try to enjoy these pleasures when I can!

It did not take us long to reach the creature. The beast endeavoured to breach – perhaps in the hopes of convincing us that there was nothing afoot.

"A true whale would never breach facing downwards, nor with its tail jutted out at such an angle, don't you see?" I said as we pulled closer. "And they would slap their fins by making one quick, fluid movement, not by tapping them against the water several times."

"There is also the matter of the visible paint flaking off its eyes," said Vyerin.

As we drew within less than a fathom of the whale, it dived down and vanished from sight.

"Cowards!" exclaimed Vyerin bitterly. (I do wonder if he *tries* to behave like a stereotypical captain from a novel when he is at sea, or if that is simply his nature by default?)

To rebut Vyerin's insults, the whale surfaced again, bobbing close to the *Perspicacity*. From this vantage point, I could discern its artifice more clearly. I also appreciated the genuine barnacles growing on its fake skin!

The whale turned to face us, its vacant, mechanical eyes staring straight ahead. Then a human head began to rise from the creature's blowhole like a spout of water.

"Good day, stranger," said Vyerin, barely waiting long enough for the unknown person's torso to emerge from its peculiar vessel. "We're eager to hear why you are following us. Who are you?"

"I am Lady Coralean, captain of this vessel," the stranger announced in a clear, confident voice.

"Lady?" I asked, thinking of those Star Sailor stories you and your sister love! "I did not know that title remained in use outside of Antepelagic literature."

"It is not a title," she said. "It is my given name, by which I mean it was a gift from and to myself."

While Captain Lady Coralean's brown hair was clipped back by the most elegant pearl barrettes – a style I am tempted to try myself when we return to land – she was dressed informally, in a dingy blouse and trousers smeared with oil. I wondered if she was the sole person aboard the vessel and therefore required to act as ambassador and mechanic and everything in between.

But I was soon distracted by something still more troubling.

"Chancellor Rawsel sends his fondest regards for your mission, Eliniea," Lady Coralean said, giving me a rapid curtsey. "He looks forward to seeing where you will find the next Entry."

"Are there no regards for me?" scoffed Vyerin.

The woman scrutinised him from across the water, then pulled out an enormous folio from some impossible pocket in her trousers. "And who are you, sir? Tevn Mawr, I presume?"

"Decidedly not!"

"Then I am puzzled. I have no Scholarly portrait of you in my files, and I assure you that I study my materials fervently and make errors only rarely." She looked through her papers once again and shrugged. Then, at last, I landed upon an explanation for Lady's presence and behaviour – she must be one of those gossiped-about few who specialise in Document Acquisition. And "Lady Coralean" must be her alias. How exciting!

Or so it would be, if she were not working for the one person who I hoped would never again possess any documentation related to me.

"This mission is a private research inquiry, conducted outside of the purview of any Campus," I said, trying to channel your ferocity! "What business is it of Chancellor Rawsel's?"

"Anything to do with the Entries is his business. I am merely here to inform you that he is watching." Lady Coralean turned back to her notes before restoring them to her pocket. "Yes, I suppose that is all. I hope you have good sailing today – the water is sure in a chipper mood, isn't it?"

"Chipper winds never did chafe a ship," said Vyerin automatically, and then gaped, horrified, as though he had committed a crime.

The woman looked at him with surprise. "Familiar with the Captain's Axioms, are you? Then you cannot merely be an anonymous assistant. Are you in disguise for some ill purpose? I always adore meeting a fellow captain. I had a mail-boat for years, and now I sail a repurposed two-masted research sloop for my *business*, shall we say, but the whale seemed a better disguise, and I couldn't turn down this commission. Chancellor Rawsel offered me—o, what am I saying? Farewell!"

With that, Lady lowered herself as oddly as she had emerged, and the whale glided into the deep.

Naturally, this encounter sent Vyerin and me into rather bleak moods. As you know very well, there is no love lost between Vyerin and Rawsel, who misused his position as Chair of the Department of Classification to treat Henerey so ill. When I attempted to logic away my own intense fear of encountering the Chancellor again, I'm afraid I found every concern to be perfectly rational. The notion that Rawsel

179

is dangerously manipulative, for example, is quite tidily proven by the fact that he forced me to lie to the world about Tev's participation in the first Ridge mission – a lie that continued to torment me in my position as Expedition Specialist. The idea that he will stop at nothing to fulfil his unknown agenda is evidenced by his attempt to threaten us and our colleagues after we discovered that sunken door in the depths of the abyss. See? There is simply nothing unreasonable about my fears! O, Sophy, it frightens me to think that he is here, watching and waiting, trying his best to impede our mission – but to what end? Because of his inexplicable interest in what we found at the Ridge? Must we return to that, and to him, after all this time?

Vyerin and I did not speak much after the encounter, but after finishing the above paragraph, I decided to seek him out once more. Together, we reached a conclusion that is rather different than what I envisioned when I started writing this letter. We will not abandon our plans to find another Entry – we are well on our way to the next set of coordinates. But when we acquire that one (assuming it is functioning) and bear it homeward, we will then seek Orelith Rawsel to ascertain what he wants from us . . . and what it will take to make him go away.

What a thrilling tale I've spun for you tonight, my Sophy! I think of you every moment, radiant as you must be in that unfamiliar darkness. I hope Tev is not bothering you overmuch. You have a mutual interest in cartography, as you already know – perhaps you ought to strike up a chat about maps to break the ice?

It is very lonely here without you, and I suspect it will only feel worse when I return to shore, visit our home, and find you are not there. It reminds me of long ago, when you were up at the surface with E., and I down at the Spheres by myself – when our love was relatively new, and I was so burdened by my secrets. With all that in mind, it's almost a relief that our main obstacle at present is simply the fact that you are physically elsewhere.

I cannot wait to see you again, and I shall do my best to stay out of trouble (even if it insists upon following us!).

Your wife across worlds,

Niea

P.S. Though this ship's berth is much more comfortable than the floor of the Bubble, I do agree that your situation is slightly more favourable. Sleeping alone in an unfamiliar place would be easier than doing so in a place we already associate with togetherness. To this end, I asked Vyerin if I might pull out a cot on the deck because I could not bear to be alone in the cabin I shared with you only a few days ago. He nodded solemnly and then vanished – I was relieved, at least, that he did not laugh at me – and, moments later, ushered me off to the captain's quarters instead. Despite my protests, he and I have swapped rooms! May this plush captain's bed give me the rest and strength I need to ensure that you return as quickly and safely as possible.

Chapter 12

**AUTOMATED POST MISSIVE FROM
SOPHY CIDNORGHE TO ELINIEA HAYVE
CIDNORGHE, 1004**

Dear Niea,

What more did you encounter at sea after writing that message? Certainly you have already endured your fair share of unusual happenings! Did Chancellor Rawsel, somehow sensing that you and I have been cruelly separated, decide to reappear to add insult to injury?

It was my general impression that as soon as we abandoned our Scholarly posts (and confirmed that the door in the abyss was destroyed), Chancellor Rawsel never deigned to pay us another thought. You are remarkably courageous for planning to confront him, but I hope you will take care of yourself. If our dear friend Captain Clel is empathetic enough to trade cabins with you, I have no doubt he could storm a recalcitrant Chancellor's quarters single-handedly if he thought that would spare you pain!

(I am also pleased to hear how much Vyerin behaves like the literary archetype of a captain when facing conflict at sea. I expected nothing less.)

I feel reluctant to spend too much time discussing your letter, because I fear whatever I say will be obsolete by the time this reaches you! Let me simply note, then, that I hope your journey to find the third Entry will be swift, with no further pursuit by false whales.

In the meantime, I have promising news to share. We shall not need to make for the surface after all, though I did appreciate your thoughtful reminders about the importance of depressurisation. Tevn's friend arrived at last!

It may startle you to learn that, by my reckoning, no more than a single night has passed since I left you. When Tevn and I parted yesterday and retreated into our respective Bubbles, he had not experienced any further visions. Now, if I were a mythical being with a notable flair for the dramatic, I would leap at the opportunity to visit my friend as he slept. Consequently, when I awakened the next morning, I activated the Bubble's communicators immediately to check for any updates. (At the risk of becoming repetitive – how I wish we were back at the Ridge and you were the one listening at the other end!)

"Are you awake, Tevn?" I asked, hoping I had not startled him from a dream in which the sea-woman was providing clear instructions for finding E. and Henerey.

"I did not sleep, so I am most certainly awake," he said morosely.

We joined our two Bubbles, and I soon found myself faced with a shockingly sad Tevn.

"I presume you did not receive any communications?" I asked.

He blinked at me. "How did you know?"

"You look about as miserable as I have felt since we left Niea behind."

"We still have not yet enjoyed a proper conversation," Tevn groused. "Before, we would talk for hours. Days, even, because I would forget myself entirely, and she paid little heed to time!"

"Perhaps now we understand why, considering the temporal oddness of this place."

"She could have said anything to me!" he continued, ignoring my aside. "And yet she showed me your sister instead."

To my surprise, Tevn suddenly gave me an uncommonly anxious look.

"I do not mean that. I am glad we saw your sister. I suppose my mission is selfish when compared with yours."

"I wouldn't say that. I am not some hero, Tevn, rescuing my sister because that is my duty. I simply wish to see her again, and there is a selfishness to that wish that I will not deny. Isn't it funny that we have embarked on this perilous, improbable journey so I may spend time with E. and you can court a monumental sea-woman?"

"Court?" he spat. "Do you think I would waste my time going to balls and – I don't know – engaging in other such frivolities with someone like her?"

"I was merely joking. I know courting is not of interest to you. And besides, she appears to be roughly five times your height and would likely be very difficult to kiss. Another joke! I will stop now," I reassured him.

"Well, I do not wish to kiss her, incidentally."

I nodded and turned ahead to watch for any signs of the un-kissable woman in question.

"However," he murmured, "if a decree were issued, mandating that every person must kiss another person at least once, I suppose I would choose her. Is that satisfactory?"

I turned back to him, speechless, and Tevn Mawr surprised me by laughing riotously.

"O, you were utterly convinced! As you said, it is difficult to explain," Tevn said. "When I am with her, I do not have to be anything other than what I am. I needn't worry about performing according to the standards of human society – since she does not understand society herself!"

"I see," I said. "You do seek companionship with her, then, but simply not in an amorous way. Like what you have with Niea, for example?" I felt proud of how far I've come, because just a year ago, I would have said that in a darkly jealous tone!

"Niea! No. She is like a sister to me, but she and I could not spend our lives together in a platonic manner. She requires passion and romantic commitment and consuming sophisticated beverages while gazing at the stars and suchlike."

"Don't worry," I said. "It is my pleasure to ensure she has more than enough of all that." (I hope I am successful!)

"What hurts the most is that I have no inkling about what my friend thinks of me," Tevn said. "Does she consider me a precocious child, playing at acquiring knowledge he can never comprehend? My desire, Sophy, is for her to see me as an equal – someone worthy of her companionship."

"Ultimately, that is also how Niea and I feel about each other. You merely desire all that without the bonus of romantic attachment and physical affection."

"Bonus is an interesting term. Once, when I asked her, Niea confirmed that when people kiss, their mouths are in close contact, and, if one is not careful, each person's teeth may collide with the other's. Can you imagine anything more revolting?" Tevn shuddered. "I detest teeth. I try very hard not to think about them. And don't get me started on tongues."

It was just as well, for it did not seem appropriate to tell Tevn my opinions on that subject!

"I hope this will not offend you," I said instead, "but there are many things about you, Tevn, that remind me of my sister." I thought, naturally, of his discomfort in social situations, and that intense awareness of himself and his surroundings, and . . .

"Does she share my distaste for teeth?" he said. Before I could clarify my intended meaning, he waved me away with a laugh.

"I do not know the details of your sister's situation, but here is how I see it. My particularities and peculiarities are merely part of how I operate. Because I could never fully cure them, it is unproductive to think of myself as having an illness. For that reason, I am not overfond of the phrase 'Malady of the Mind'. If I were to remove what makes me peculiar, I would not be myself."

"I simply meant that I feel you two experience the world in similar

185

ways. I think she would be glad to meet you and learn about how you see yourself."

"Ideally, she will meet me soon. That is why you've agreed to put up with me, is it not?"

I did not know how to respond. It is true that Tevn and I are not exactly the best of friends, and he would never believe I was rather enjoying my time with him. I decided, instead, to follow your excellent advice.

"I know many Scholars of Wayfinding prefer contemporary cartography, but I wondered if you happen to have any interest in historical maps?"

His eyes widened with excitement, but then he shook his head.

"Did Niea instruct you to ask me about this subject?"

"Do recall that I specialise in the same field as you. Have you seen the Pelagic Circle Map in person, I wonder?"

"I cannot believe the curators make you walk through a long hallway lined with several reproductions of the map before you see the true artifact on view!" Tevn shouted at a volume that startled even him.

We passed some time in this manner. Your advice is sage as usual, my dear Niea! We made it through about three hundred years of historical map production before Tevn interrupted our discussion.

"Have the sounds of the water changed?" he asked.

"Can you describe what you mean? I can't quite hear the difference. If only Irye were here."

"I suppose it is rather like everything is slowing down."

After a few moments, I sensed it too. The hums and bubblings now occurred rarely, with each noise lasting far longer than usual. Outside, the dark seas transformed into a light purple colour.

"Either we are in terrible trouble, or your friend is coming, or both," I said.

Before he could reply, we heard an uncanny crackling, as though the water had frozen around us. (Is it silly that I could not help but think of studying the bitterly cold Second Ocean with my siblings

186

and father years ago?) Then a much-diminished version of the sea-woman squeezed inside our shelter. Her head scraped against the top of our joined Bubbles and she had to bend her graceful shoulders most dramatically.

It was mightily odd to see her again, Niea! There was much about her aspect that appeared different from what I remembered. When we met her in the depths, wouldn't you say she seemed almost transparent? That was why, in my unsent letter to E. about the subject, I tended to refer to her as a kind of spectre, or an odd automaton. Well, perhaps that quality was the consequence of her travelling to our world. Here, she appears as solid – I dare not say "flesh and blood", for I suspect her anatomy is unlike ours, given the preponderance of scales on her face and torso – but she was decidedly more physically present.

"My clever friend!" she sang, and I found myself spellbound once more by the musical sound of her voice. "I have missed you!"

"And I you," murmured Tevn. "It has been too long."

"Alas, I cannot comprehend your time. But I am heartened to be here with you, and the little ones too, I see?"

"The little ones?" I asked. "Whatever do you mean?"

"Those lovely little signals!"

At once she burst into a thousand tiny flashes of light, which hovered in a cloud over – of all things – this very Automated Post machine!

"I saw them, brave little things, trying to push across. Courageous and feeble! I made a path for them, and now they can travel just as they are meant to." The lights rushed together in an awesome cloud, and the sea-woman appeared before us once more.

How silly I was, Niea, thinking we somehow modified Automated Post technology effectively enough to create a device that allows communication between worlds! I am grateful we had a little help in the end. (Admittedly, it is disappointing to learn that it would not have worked otherwise. Do you think she interfered with "the signals" at the Ridge on that fateful night of our expedition when we saw the lights of the Spheres flicker out?)

187

Now it was my turn to be studied by the sea-woman.

"The sister of the sister," she continued in a more melancholic melody. "She bid me to find you. I placed that task in my mind like a shell and clung to it until you drew close. And then I saw my friend, and I could not help but send the dream to him instead."

"So my sister is truly alive?" I said, barely daring to speak the words. "Where is she now? Is her companion with her?"

"They are in the city." This time her tone was harsh and dull. The music sounded like – well, Niea, this is strange to write, but imagine that the ocean had turned to solid rock, and all you could see for fathoms and fathoms was a flat expanse of stone.

"The city of Scholars where I was to go?" asked Tevn. "Can you take us there?"

"I will," she sang, "for they require assistance, which is why I wanted to bear you to them. They do not believe in anything that unsettles them, but he is interested in everything strange, aren't you, my friend?"

"Then you are not one of them?" I said. "We assumed you were working with those Scholars in some way." I did not say, *I based that assumption on information from my mother's secret society, and I continue to wonder how they even verified their information in the first place!*

"I help when I can, for those funny little machines are not quite enough."

"Speaking of the Entries," Tevn said, "can you clarify for us how many people are able to pass through one? Would you say the number is greater than two?"

Unfortunately, by this point, the sea-woman faded into light yet again – well, not light, I suppose, but rather a kind of motion? She became an energy that infused the walls of our Bubbles, and we started moving at a speed so incredible that Tevn and I had to activate the safety harnesses!

It is all rather terrifying, and I am trying to type this letter to calm myself. O, Niea, can you imagine – am I about to find E.? Could it really be that simple? I promise I shall write to you and Vyerin as soon as we reach the city.

    With excitement (tempered only by my yearning for you),
    Sophy

AUTOMATED POST MISSIVE FROM VYERIN CLEL TO SOPHY CIDNORGHE, 1004

Dear Sophy,

    I hope you are well. I returned home today to reunite with my beloved husband and children. Unfortunately, said beloved husband let in an unwanted trespasser.

    Even more unfortunately, your wife encouraged said trespasser to stay – because he is your brother.

    I miss the stability you bring.

    Be safe and take care,
    V.

AUTOMATED POST MISSIVE FROM ELINIEA HAYVE CIDNORGHE TO SOPHY CIDNORGHE, 1004

Beloved Sophy,

    After I read appropriate selections from your letter aloud, Vyerin refused to discuss the matter of Henerey and E. any further. He is stunned yet shyly hopeful. We cannot stop checking the A.P. machine!

    Yes, it is so peculiar to write while knowing you are behind me in time. Almost two tides have passed for us already. At this rate, Sophy, I might be an old woman when you return! (I jest, but also, I hope you will be able to retrieve E. before we gain too much of an age difference.)

    Since your last letter, Vyerin and I returned home. We were so put off by our encounter with the curious captain that we did not tarry in our quest for the third Entry. It required heaps of effort and good humour, but all you need to know is that we did retrieve what we sought!

Well, I suppose there was one other occurrence that may interest you. On the way to the relevant coordinates (off the Atoll's Ragged Coast this time), the *Perspicacity* crossed paths with a small research vessel piloted by a sole occupant. As Vyerin politely hailed the sailor, I was reassured to see that the vessel seemed entirely ordinary and not the least bit whale-like – nothing more than a humble Illustrator's boat, laden with paints and easels.

I felt more relieved still when the occupant introduced themselves as Scholar Lerin Zuan Vellen, a name Vyerin and I recognised immediately!

"Were you not acquainted with my brother, Henerey Clel?" called Vyerin, just as I said, "Did you not produce that gorgeous illustration based on my description of the Abyssal Nautilus?"

"My goodness!" exclaimed Scholar Vellen, tossing over the anchor immediately. "Is that you, Scholar Forghe? And Captain Clel, we never had the pleasure of meeting in person. I don't know if you ever received my letter. I was truly sorry to hear about your brother."

"I was not capable of reading your letter until recently," said Vyerin. "I endeavoured to send you a reply last year, but we heard from your Department that you were voyaging and relatively unreachable. You asked about publishing Henerey's notes, didn't you? I'm sorry to say that he kept his scientific journal in his possession when he – departed."

"What a shame." Scholar Vellen sighed. "I thought our meeting was to be a fortuitous one. During my most recent voyage, I saw some anomalies that led me to recall Henerey and his atypical rays."

"Anomalies?" I inquired.

"Well, perhaps it is even more fortuitous that I have a Scholar of Life to pester with my odd observations, Scholar Forghe!" said Scholar Vellen. "At present, I am sailing homeward after spending tides painting Immoderate Ospreys on a glorified rock off the southern Atoll. I've visited the spot several times, and I always enjoy seeing the various species of hermit crabs gambol about as I prepare my canvases."

"A delight, I'm sure!" I exclaimed.

"But no such delights awaited me this time. I could not spy a single crab. At length, I found the entire cluster hiding in deeper waters."

"As they are prone to do."

"Tell me, Scholar Forghe—" at this point I suppose I ought to have updated them about my married name, and the fact that I am no longer a Scholar, but it did seem rude to interrupt "—are hermit crabs prone to abandon their individual shells, work together to seize a single plate-sized rock, and hold it over themselves as a collective?"

"That is most unusual indeed!" I said. "I imagine you reported this to the Department of Classification?"

"I did, of course, but perhaps my report was not classified correctly," muttered Scholar Vellen. "In any case, I must press on if I seek to stay ahead of the wind. I only hope you will keep your eyes open, Scholar Forghe. There are some impressively peculiar things happening in the natural world of late, and I wish Scholar Clel were here to ponder them with us."

I dared not mention to Scholar Vellen that we were already well acquainted with peculiar things, and that we hoped to find the newest one before the day's end. And so we did!

This third Entry is the most unique of them all – carved in the shape of a humanlike figure. Jeime proposed that one activates it by taking the figure's hand. Naturally, we wrapped all appendages securely to prevent any inadvertent transportation. Now the device sits in the harbour along with the pieces of the Entry you used. As soon as Vyerin can tempt some colleagues to help bring our treasures ashore, we shall take everything apart and ascertain how it works.

(You might wonder why we established our centre of operations at Vyerin's home, and not ours. Well, the reason is mostly personal.

I still fear that if I were to go home, I might simply become too sad to speak. That is quite uncharacteristic of me, but so is being without you.)

After docking in the Atoll's South Harbour and hitching a ride on a canal boat, we returned to that cosy little house you and I first visited some time ago, laden with letters! (I have grown rather fond of the South Harbour neighbourhood, with its wide sea-canals and brightly painted coral mosaics. How lucky the Clels are to live there!)

Vyerin was disappointed to find no one home. When boisterous calling yielded no answer, I hoisted my bags and asked Vyerin if we should proceed to his study.

"Do you mind, Niea," Vy said in the shyest voice I ever heard from him, "if I wait a moment? I would rather like to sit by myself for a spell and – take it all in."

"Why, certainly!" I exclaimed. I left him in peace and headed on to unpack our materials. I'm not sure if you noticed during our previous visits, but the hall to the study features gilt-framed silhouettes of Avanne, Orey, and Reiv, each proudly holding a different musical instrument in every frame, followed by one of Vyerin, stubbornly holding nothing. (Perhaps we ought to have silhouettes done of us and my fish once you return home?)

At any rate, I reached my destination and set down a box of papers on Vyerin's desk. As I began organising all we brought – the logbook, coordinates from the Fleet, notes by Jeime about the various Structures we encountered, and so forth – I thought I could hear a tapping from the left side of the room. I hypothesised that it must be some imperilled creature, like a wayward Perplexing Sea-Bat, and I felt a sudden desire to provide any necessary assistance! After a moment of walking about and listening carefully, I traced the noise to a large chest – a beautiful thing, carved with waves and flowers – a Clel family heirloom? On second thought, I do not know why I am discussing the ornamentation, because the chest's external appearance ultimately proved much less important than what it contained.

Can you imagine my surprise when I opened the lid to reveal your very own brother?

"Dear Niea!" Arvist exclaimed, as I gave a warranted shriek. "How was your adventure?"

"It was successful, though you ought to know that you disappointed Sophy most awfully when you abandoned us." For your sake, I had to get that out before I started addressing the more pressing matter at hand! "But Arvist, however did you wind up in the Clels' study? How long have you been in there?"

"O, some number of hours – perhaps half a day? Time ceased as I lay encased! It was a most riveting experience." Arvist rose from the chest and brushed off his jacket. "I am here, of course, because Mr Reiv Clel kindly let me in to await your return."

"He asked you to wait inside this chest?"

Arvist raised his eyebrows in what I think was intended to be the equivalent of a conspiratorial wink.

"I assured good Mr Clel that hiding here was in keeping with my newest series of Unperformed Occurrences – spontaneous bits of theatre to interrupt our dull lives. I promised to cite his home as a location in my upcoming Compendium of Performances, and he was delighted! But then your arrival took much longer than anticipated, and I feared perhaps this performance might be my last." He gave me a friendly pat on the shoulder.

"Now, Niea, I wonder if you would let me surprise Captain Clel as well. Think of the artistic beauty that will generate! Come, I shall return to my wooden incubator."

"Niea?" called that stern voice from the hallway. "Who in the world are you speaking with?"

Moments later, Vyerin entered the room, took in the scene, and immediately looked much glummer.

"Surprise!" I said. "It's my brother-by-marriage!"

Arvist gave me a worn look, no doubt appalled that I deprived him of his grand reveal.

"Are you not shocked to see me?" he greeted Vyerin. "Do you not wish to know how I came to be in your study?"

"Not especially," said Vyerin darkly. "I assume Reiv let you in. Then he started his afternoon composing session, ran out of his preferred staff paper, dashed into town to fetch more, and promptly forgot you were here."

"How did you manage to guess all that?" asked Arvist.

"The music room is in total disarray, and you are eminently forgettable."

"Vyerin!" I cried.

"He deserves it. He upset Sophy grievously by not participating in our expedition as promised."

Are you not pleased, Sophy, to have such loyal supporters defending you against your brother's mercurial nature?

"Yes, I know," drawled Arvist, "but I simply couldn't bear it. Can I be blamed if I have the heart of an adventurer but not the stomach? The Physicians at the Boundless Infirmary had never seen such a pronounced case of late-onset chronic seasickness! Besides, Seliara then informed me that our little Eri cannot sleep a wink without the soothing influence of my Soporific Stagings. What choice did I have? You know how much I wanted to seek my mother's fabled Phosphorescent Place and find E. and that other fellow—"

Vyerin started grumbling under his breath as soon as those last three words were uttered.

"O, all right, it was more than that," Arvist continued. "I confess that my nausea was only caused by a decidedly undercooked tart I was forced to prepare and consume alone when Sophy refused to join me for dinner in the galley. And Eri's taste in lullabies, to my distress, has always been painfully pedestrian."

"You admit, then, to being a liar as well as a coward?" seethed Vyerin.

"What led you to lie?" I asked, more gently. "Knowing the truth would mean a great deal to me, Arvist."

Arvist swung out his arms, as though he were about to stage yet another performance – and then, to our surprise, he crumpled to the carpet in a startlingly ungraceful and improvised fashion.

"The truth is that I knew I would slow you all down," he murmured. "I dreaded the thought of standing in Sophy's way. It all seemed so simple until the moment I stepped aboard that ship. Then I witnessed her being brilliant and practical and so very *Sophy*, while I – what was I? No more than bothersome ballast! Saving E. could not be more important to me, and that is why I removed myself from the mission. What help could a liar and a coward like me bring to a team of the brightest Scholars ever expelled from any Campus?"

"That is laughable. You, sir, are unbelievable. I can't imagine that—" Suddenly Vyerin turned to me, and I'm afraid my face was more tearful than it ought to have been. "Sink it all, Niea! Don't tell me that you are the first person besides my husband to be convinced by a performance from this man?"

"I know he can be dramatic when trying to get out of trouble," I said, "but I perceive a ribbon of honesty, Vy."

Vyerin gave me one of those careful looks that make me feel like a chart of currents he is studying to determine if the waters are safe.

"I admire your tendency towards compassion, Niea, since I do not seem to possess it myself. I shall try to follow her lead, Arvist Cidnosin."

"Cidnan, actually, is my married name," he clarified.

"Mr Cidnan, then. If you would like to atone, you may help us now."

"But of course! I am happy to assist in any way. Why, I possess rudimentary knowledge of just about every field in the School of Inspiration!" Arvist reached out to shake Vyerin's hand and was instantly rebuffed. "Where is Sophy, by the way? O, perhaps it is providential that she is not here yet! I don't suppose you'll let me carry out one more performance when she arrives?"

Before he could climb back into the chest, we told Arvist about your present circumstances and The Plan, and he seemed far more enthusiastic than you might expect. He mentioned that he had, for artistic purposes and in tribute to your mother's legacy, spent tides observing

195

and sketching the original Structure. The fellow even drew it from memory right before our eyes!

Suddenly, a knock on the study door interrupted Arvist's sketching session.

"May I come in? I do hope I've not missed the Unperformed Occurrence, Arvist?"

Vyerin bolted to his feet and flung open the door. There stood Reiv, struggling to balance several cylinders of staff paper upon his shoulders!

The cylinders soon rolled across the floor, however, when Vyerin swept Reiv into an embrace and kissed him.

"I am happy to go back into the chest and repeat my performance, Reiv," Arvist proclaimed. "Simply say the word!"

No word, of course, was said.

Then a clamour in the outer rooms announced the return of Avanne and Orey from their studies, and I kept Arvist occupied while our friend reunited with his children. I confess that seeing Vyerin and Reiv together again (when you and I are not) made me a bit melancholic.

Eventually, though, I could not stay away without seeming rude – nor could I possibly stymie Arvist's desire to speak with Reiv, who may be his only true admirer – and so we joined the Clel family for a pleasant dinner. O, you might recall that you cleverly arranged to have our mail forwarded to the Clels' address during our time away. Well, Reiv presented me with a horribly large pile of things – mostly correspondence about the Sunken School, or letters from former colleagues of mine. (There also appeared to be a wedding announcement from Vincenebras, but I assume that is yet another one of his inexplicable jokes.)

Most surprising of all, however, was an envelope from Chancellor Rawsel containing an invitation to a "casual yet compulsory dinner party" that we were obligated to attend. Tomorrow, of course.

I suppose Vyerin and I shall have to look sharp and prepare to defend ourselves!

O, dear Sophy – by the time you read this, that confrontation will have already occurred. This delay is exceedingly vexing! I have never felt so far away from you. I wish you and I could sit as Vyerin and Reiv are tonight, settled onto their couch with such familiarity and comfort. Avanne is playing her harp, Orey is clapping along, and Vy occasionally leans over to whisper to Reiv – or stop their son from clapping his hands *upon* his sister's harp strings. I am honoured to share such a cosy evening with the Clels. Yet I ache for our little drawing room and the joys of watching my aquariums with you – and to regain that, I am even willing to put my faith in your brother.

With the maximum amount of affection that A.P. is capable of transmitting,

Niea

Chapter 13

AUTOMATED POST MISSIVE FROM TEVN WINIVER MAWR TO ELINIEA HAYVE CIDNORGHE, 1004

Dear Niea,

Do not fear – Sophy remains perfectly well. As she is rather pre-occupied, I promised to send an update in her place and let her enjoy some time with her sister.

Are you surprised?

Surely the revelation that I would willingly render assistance to Sophy Cidnorghe is more shocking than the news that we found E. (And Henerey, too – I suppose you ought to mention that to Captain Clel. If he's not already reading this over your shoulder in secret while feigning disinterest, that is.) Well, I am unexpectedly happy to assist, under the circumstances.

I don't know how much Sophy told you of our encounter with my friend, but I think it's a safe guess that your wife's letters are as verbose and energetic as she is. I assume you already heard that my friend found us in the water, but then she left me soon after, and you cannot comprehend how miserable this made me.

I may not be like you, Niea, with your charming love story and your incredibly devoted wife who simply will not stop talking about you. (I do appreciate your good qualities, but there is only so much I can stand hearing about your "peerless kindness" and "inexhaustible effervescence".) I simply wish to spend all my time conversing with my friend and learning from her. It is not unfair to say that I seek to study her, because she freely admits she is studying me, and who knows what we might uncover together?

While I do not fully understand the details of the dispute between my friend and these Scholars – and I have spent but a few moments among the latter – I can tell you what transpired when we arrived.

After several hours in transit, we caught our first glimpse of the city – a substantial blue hemisphere, which rather resembled an enormous version of the Spheres. At first, we saw the city from an angle that revealed only the top of the dome, and I did not know how far down it extended. When our vantage point changed, I realised the entire structure is suspended in the ocean by some mechanism unknown to me. It is not installed on the seafloor, as the water continues below it to depths I cannot estimate.

As we approached, an impressive flurry of lights appeared on the dome, followed by gentle, glowing lines that began to intersect over its surface like a route charting itself on a map. We followed the brightest of those lines for a moment before my friend reformed inside our joined Bubbles.

"They will not grant you entry." She laughed in her musical way. "I shall ask them to do it as a favour! Won't that make them cross?"

"Tevn, this place is unbelievable!" Sophy exclaimed once our escort vanished. "I cannot believe it – my mother and E. were correct!"

"Well, as you'll recall, I also predicted this," I droned. In truth, I felt just as excited. Since leaving the Ridge, Niea, I have lived liminally, yearning for more of the unknown but never being able to find it. Now I have been delivered to its very doorstep.

"How do you think they make the—" started Sophy, but she was interrupted by the reappearance of my friend.

"They are furious!" she sang with delight. "They dare not open their silly gates. I must send you in myself, and then bid you farewell!"

"You are leaving?" I said.

"They are not fond of me, my friend, and there is much else I must do."

"Will you visit me? In ... in my mind, like you did before?"

"May I? If I may, I shall, and I will return sooner than you can imagine!"

With this insubstantial promise in place, she disappeared, and we found ourselves instantly transported to the end of a pier crafted from unfamiliar purple stones.

It took a moment to adjust to the light, since we'd spent such an extended period in the near-complete darkness. Through the film of the Bubbles I observed the stony boat-ramp, etched with the same glowing lines I saw on the exterior of the dome. I could identify the sounds of machinery, and, more distant still, people speaking. I felt overwhelmed already.

"I suppose we ought to get out, oughtn't we?" I said, turning to deactivate the Bubbles. Sophy remained still.

"Are you afraid?" I asked. "She would not have sent us someplace dangerous."

"I am not afraid of the place," she said. "Tevn, I suddenly feel almost ill. Is E. truly here? What if she is not? That is what I fear most. I fear this is all an illusion and my sister is dead, lost at the bottom of the sea. If I step outside, I have no choice but to welcome whatever tragedy awaits me."

"And if you stay here, you will be forever trapped with the uncertainty," I said. "Besides, if you do not come, I shall have to go alone. I am not particularly fond of people, as it happens. If your sister is alive, I trust she will find me poor company. Shall we?"

Sophy took a deep breath and nodded, and we emerged into the light together.

The space itself was some kind of vast harbour, filled with automata that were anchored as though sleeping. These creatures, Niea, would delight you! Each one was a composite animal, made from three distinct anatomical components – one possessed the head of a dolphin, the mid-section of a crab, and the tentacles of an octopus. Others featured appendages all scaled and finned that I cannot connect to any known species.

As we ascended the ramp, two people ran to us. They were dressed in highly ornate garments and appeared astonishingly anxious.

"Greetings," said the first person in a high-pitched, shaky voice. "Do you attest that you are real, and not illusions fabricated by the Illogical Ones?"

Sophy seemed almost thrilled by this perplexing question.

"I do not know how you expect us to prove that we are real, but we most certainly are," she said, warmly.

Both strangers shook their heads.

"But do you attest to that fact?" asked the first one again, and the second one nodded approvingly.

"I suppose—" Sophy began.

"Attest, not suppose!"

"I promise we are both corporeal individuals rather than illusory ones," said Sophy. "Does that satisfy you? My name is Sophy Cidnorghe, and this is Tevn Winiver Mawr. We travelled here from—"

"Yes, yes, we know! You could only possibly hail from one particular place," the stranger continued. "We must fetch the Thirtieth Second Scholar."

"I shall seek them out," said the second stranger, turning to leave already.

"What is the name of this place?" I asked.

"This is your sanctuary, your refuge, your safe harbour," said the stranger in an odd, rote way. "You need fear no longer. We will protect you, as we protect all visitors."

"Then you have had other visitors?" asked Sophy. "Well, we seek—"

She was interrupted by the extremely expedient return of the other Scholar, accompanied by a young person who seemed uncommonly excited and could not stop tugging at their curls.

"More visitors?" said the apparent "Thirtieth Second Scholar", who then let out a quiet gasp after seeing Sophy's face. "You look most familiar. I apologise if this is mere coincidence, but I don't suppose—"

The other Scholars were clearly having none of this dramatic reveal. They ushered the younger Scholar away, promising to return.

That was inaccurate. The Scholars did not, in fact, return. Instead, after Sophy and I passed the time by discussing the curious depth-crafts, in walked two different people.

I know you and Scholar Clel were formerly acquainted, so you know what he looks like – but you've never met your sister-by-marriage, have you? Even if Sophy's shown you a portrait, I suspect you've not seen E. Cidnosin like this. She does indeed wear her hair closely cropped around her shoulders, with a small pencil perpetually present behind her ear and a string of pearls with a pendant around her neck. On this occasion, she was dressed, like her companion, in clothes identical in style to those of the Scholars, but she had none of their simpering mannerisms.

No, indeed – E. Cidnosin appeared to be a confident, energetic woman, who greeted her long-lost sister by whispering, "Dear Sophy. I knew you'd find me eventually."

For the first time since I've known her, your wife had absolutely nothing to say.

There were tears and embracing and those sorts of things, during which I politely averted my eyes and nodded to Scholar Clel, who also stood to the side. Not too long afterward, though, E. ran back to Scholar Clel.

"Henerey, this is Sophy! Though you've met before, haven't you?" she said. Then she perceived me at last, or so it seemed. She surely noticed me when she entered the room, as she seems the sort of person who notices everything. Perhaps she needed a few moments to mentally prepare herself for the experience of greeting a stranger, which I found relatable.

"O, and who is this?" E. Cidnosin said. "I don't suppose this is your brother, Henerey?"

202

I should be flattered, as I imagine this is the first and last time anyone shall ever confuse me for the likes of Vyerin Clel.

"Goodness, no!" said Sophy to prove my point. "This is Tevn Mawr."

Scholar Clel gave me a neat bow. "Scholar Mawr — I thought you looked familiar. Did you not join the Ridge expedition towards the end?"

"Have you and Tevn become friends, Sophy?" E. asked. "I didn't think you two were close."

"Nor did I," I said (o, Niea, don't click your tongue at me!).

"And what of my brother?" asked Scholar Clel. "Is he all right? Have you spoken with him? Is he horribly angry?"

"He is only angry that he was not able to join us," said Sophy. "Your brother is safe at home with his family and my wife. Vy and Niea desperately wanted to come, but Tevn and I were the ones who made it through in the end."

"I am sorry to disappoint," I said.

"At home with his family," Scholar Clel repeated in a slightly delayed fashion. "Goodness, the children must have grown, I'm sure! I missed Avanne's birthday, I'm afraid — a transgression she will never let me forget — but by my calculations, Orey's is but a few tides away, so perhaps I shall not be the most neglectful of uncles."

I suspect Sophy wanted to share a significant glance with me here, but I could only stare back blankly. I certainly knew nothing of Vyerin's children's birthdays and how they related to the matter at hand!

"I must tell Vyerin we found you. Better yet — you may tell him!" Sophy said, recovering from whatever surprised her. "I have an Automated Post machine, and if I am able to set it up somewhere, you can write to him."

"An Automated what?" asked Scholar Clel. "No matter! Whatever it is, it cannot surprise me more than the technology here. Before we do anything else, I shall ask our colleagues to give us some privacy. They will be extraordinarily curious about the two of you."

As he turned to go, he gave E. a broad smile that I am sure he thought I would not see. After her companion departed, E. ran over to Sophy and embraced her once more.

"I still feel as if I am in a dream," she said. "I included plenty of details about my plans in my letter, which gave me some reason to hope, but I did not know if you could follow us."

From over E.'s shoulder I saw Sophy eyeing me again.

"A letter?" she said at last. "E., whatever do you mean? I had no idea where you'd gone – at least, not at first."

"Yes, I left a letter for you on the table in the parlour. Did you not find it?"

"I ... suppose I did not. But I am so very happy you are alive and well."

"Whatever could have happened to it?" E. asked. "Don't tell me that Arvist—"

"O, never mind Arvist. I'm simply delighted to see you. And Henerey, too! You two seem as close as ever. If not more so."

E. blushed slightly. I was feeling increasingly uncomfortable about witnessing this conversation, so it was a relief when Scholar Clel returned at last.

"We are in the clear," he said triumphantly. "They are eager to meet you and carry out their Visitor protocol, but will give us some time to catch up first. I tried to emphasise the familial significance of the situation."

"Do you expect me to believe there are Scholars capable of valuing familial significance over established protocol?" said Sophy, and she and Henerey exchanged bleak smiles. "Thank you, Henerey."

"No trouble at all. Where shall we go, then? To that Refectory-like room in the Visitors' Quarters, I suppose?" He paused and turned to E. "If that setting suits you, my dear?"

"I would brave any setting to speak with my sister," she replied.

"As would I," said Sophy. "I'll set up the machine for you, Henerey, when we are settled."

"I shall set it up," said I – how noble, etc. "I will write a note to

Niea first, to ensure the A.P. still functions, and then you may have at it, Scholar Clel."

As we all walked down a most peculiar corridor (everything is so bright and fascinating here, Niea, and I feel I have never experienced colours so intensely), I was surprised, again, to hear the elusive E. Cidnosin chattering at a remarkable speed.

"I do hope you've been seeing to the algae?" I caught her saying to Sophy. "It must be the blooming season now, which is always most trying."

"The algae?"

"Why, at home, of course! Don't worry if you have not. It is slightly gratifying to know the Deep House misses me."

Sophy kept silent for so long afterwards that even I could grasp how socially odd her behaviour was. Perhaps she could not find the words to tell her sister what had become of the family home. For the second time that day, I felt the irregular and unexpected urge to assist Sophy Cidnorghe.

"The Deep House—" I began.

"Surely we can discuss such matters later," Sophy interrupted, giving me a pleading frown behind E.'s back. "Right now, I feel rather astonished by this place. What can you tell us about it, E.?"

They talked for the rest of the walk, with Scholar Clel occasionally jumping in with some note or observation. Then we found ourselves in a rather ill-lit but cosy room, and the chairs there were excellent, Niea – made from the most comfortable fabric I ever touched! In any case, I kept my word and let them speak while I wrote to you, and now I ought to let Scholar Clel connect with his brother.

I wish I could write to *her*, but she does not visit me yet. Perhaps she will in time.

In the meantime, I remain your friend,

Tev

AUTOMATED POST MISSIVE FROM HENEREY CLEL TO VYERIN CLEL, 1004

To my dear brother,

This is one of those rare occasions when I find that I hardly know how to begin a letter.

(Isn't this machine marvellous? I cannot believe you experienced such a significant change in technology during the short time in which we were away!)

There, I have already made a mistake that I wish I could strike out.

A few moments ago, Sophy revealed that E. and I have, in fact, been away for nearly two years. I cannot begin to comprehend this.

I suppose it should not come as a surprise that the passage of time in this world is not entirely aligned with that of our own. Yet I feel sick when I think of all I missed – birthdays and celebrations, visits to you and our parents, and discoveries in the world of Natural History! There might be full extinctions of which I know nothing!

Still, not everything is so discouraging. Sophy says that you and Scholar Niea Forghe (Cidnorghe, I mean!) have hatched a plan to travel here – she will say no more, though, because E. rightfully urged Sophy not to tell us the details of your plotting. (There are some odd restrictions on knowledge in this society that now weigh heavily upon us. Particularly E., I'm afraid.) It is much to take in. Yet I hope this letter is but a prelude and that we will be together soon. I have ever so much to tell and ask you!

For the moment, though, please know that I am as fine as I can be. In fact, in a surprising turn of events, I've had a rather pleasant time down here. E. and I built a wonderful little life together – over the course of what we thought was just a season or so – and her curiosity and kindness make every day remarkable. I cannot wait for you to meet her. I think you shall like her very much. O, again, there are so many things I wish to discuss, Vyerin, but I could not even begin to address them all in one note. Besides, Sophy says it will take several days for this to reach you, and for your reply to reach us.

I will close simply by saying that I hope you will forgive me for giving you such a fright. I swear I shall never do so again.

Sending my apologies,

Henerey

AUTOMATED POST MISSIVE FROM SOPHY CIDNORGHE TO VYERIN CLEL, 1004

Dear Vy,

I could have written to announce that I found your brother, but assumed I ought to let him speak for himself. So he has, and I hope you will enjoy his letter and not feel obliged to read this one until you're ready!

Because it bears repeating and celebrating – yes, Henerey is here, as is E., and I have joined them in this improbable city. At present, we sit within an enormous Refectory, except it is made of what looks like gemstones instead of shell-brick and glass, and the tables are curved and irregular, unlike our rectangular ones, and instead of lamps, the faint light comes from the very walls themselves—

Well, I suppose it is really nothing like a typical Refectory, save the fact that we are eating here. Or I was eating a rather flimsy salad, at any rate, while E. and Henerey told me about any number of things they've experienced.

Though I have not seen my sister since her disappearance, I've not glimpsed this version of her – whose energy could power several small depth-crafts – since long before that. At present, she is like the E. of several years ago, when, on her better days, she would spend hours delightedly lecturing me about some obscure historical fact or principle of Natural History she read about. (Also, and most importantly, she has indeed cut her hair! To preserve my pride, I tell myself it must be

207

a practical decision and that she will grow it out presently. You know that *I* am the Cidnosin sister who wears a signature short hairstyle!)

(Isn't it grand that E. and Henerey are alive and I can say such silly things about my sister again?)

Though I have always conceptualised this as a rescue mission, I suppose I never considered – *we* never considered? – that being stranded in an underwater city might be good for our respective siblings.

I must stop now, because there is so much to ask E., but I did want to share this moment with you as best I could.

(O, and do tell Niea, to whom I assume you've read this letter, that I will write to her later when I have more privacy. These Scholars are strikingly prying. After only a day, I have already learned too well the cultural significance of record-keeping. I half suspect there is someone sitting in the corner looking over my shoulder as I write! If I return to my quarters to find a Scholar peering out from under my pillow, pen in hand, I shall do whatever it takes to stop them from copying every single note between wives!)

With unbelievable relief,

Sophy

P.S. As I don't intend to spoil the aforementioned letter to Niea with anything other than unabashed amorousness, I'll address one final matter here instead. If you and Niea have not done so already, would you please tell Arvist that we found E.?

If it is not too much trouble, would you also thank him for me?

I was initially displeased to hear that he had inserted himself in your work, but if what he told you and Niea is true – if he does, truly and wholeheartedly, want to help – then I am glad of it.

Despite our differences, I do wish all three of us could be here, enjoying our reunion as a family. Perhaps I am too hard on him.

(Or perhaps the strain of my journey has inclined me to far more fraternal sentimentality than is reasonable!)

AUTOMATED POST MISSIVE FROM VYERIN CLEL TO HENEREY CLEL, 1004

Henerey,

If you, of all people, struggled to write a letter to me, imagine how I feel.

I thought I ought to send you a short and clever reply to disguise my true feelings. I cannot. I am weeping.

I am extremely relieved to hear you are well. I have not been, but my situation improved dramatically after I met Sophy. I would have gone through the rest of my life mourning you if it were not for my friendship with her.

I look forward to meeting E., as well. I do not know how long it will take for this reunion to occur. Niea and I are hard at work, but it is thankless and difficult.

Reiv and the children send their love and amazement.

I don't have much more to say, but I find myself reluctant to stop writing.

I know there is a delay, but please write to me again soon, won't you? But only if that is acceptable to you.

Love,

Vyerin

Chapter 14

AUTOMATED POST MISSIVE FROM ELINIEA HAYVE CIDNORGHE TO SOPHY CIDNORGHE, 1004

My treasured Sophy,

How do I begin? We have been simply beside ourselves with joy since we read your news. Isn't it all so wonderfully surreal? When that first message from Tevn began appearing on our machine, I called Vyerin over because I knew something significant must have occurred. I read aloud as the A.P. typed each word, and enjoyed the distinct pleasure of watching him react. As soon as I uttered Henerey's name, Vy spontaneously gave me a brotherly embrace – and did not even pretend afterwards as if nothing had happened!

(While I appreciated Tevn writing on your behalf, I am also grateful for the glowingly AFFECTIONATE letter you sent just for me afterwards. I most certainly did not read that one aloud! I took the liberty of removing the stored file from the A.P.'s records and retained the physical copy for myself. I continue to sneak it out whenever I am most in need of you. That is all I shall say, since I know you could be reading this, Tev!)

This is rather less important than reuniting with E., but o, Sophy, you must tell me more about the underwater city! We've spent so much time researching the Fleet's lore and seeking out the Entries that the idea of this sunken society in another world seems rather commonplace, doesn't it? But the fact remains that it is astonishing! Have those Scholars truly lived there since the time of the Dive? Did anything remind you of that peculiar room we found in the depths of the Ridge? (O, but perhaps not, since you discovered that Tevn's friend operates separately from the Scholars ... whatever does it all mean?)

Despite my questions and curiosities about your current location, I am quite sure I know one truth about it already – there is no readily available method for you to return home. Well, you needn't fear. Our work on that front does continue, though a troubling little wrinkle has emerged that I hardly know how to smooth.

Between this and your last letter, we did indeed attend the dinner party proposed by Chancellor Rawsel. Vyerin dressed up in some fine Atoll-style robes, and I wore my iridescent "emergency gown" – the very one that you teased me for carrying around in my valise! (To my great embarrassment, Reiv found my get-up so glamorous that he insisted upon taking a photograph "for Sophy to admire when she returns", as he said. I wish I could send it to you!)

Rawsel now resides where Intertidal meets the Atoll, in a little houseboat docked several neighbourhoods away from Intertidal's arts and theatre district. Off-campus accommodation is rather unusual for a Chancellor, I imagine! Haven't we done so well by detaching ourselves from the very thought of Chancellor Rawsel these past few years? Before today, I hadn't the slightest idea where his life had taken him since our expedition ended – though one does hear gossip from questionable sources named Vincenebras on occasion – and if he experienced a kind of fall from grace, I cannot object.

I felt deeply anxious as we waited for the card-claw to announce our arrival. (We gave the device one of Vyerin's calling cards to carry inside, because I feared the Chancellor might disdain my new, non-Scholar ones.) When we entered, I worried that Rawsel – so long the villain of our story, Sophy dear – would emerge like a spectre from the darkness, wearing a velvet cloak that made him appear half-shadow, as a sinister tune played upon a gentle harp in the distance!

Instead, we found him seated in a comfortable armchair and clad in an antique-style dressing gown with scalloped sleeves and the texture of a tapestry. By appearance alone, this immensely powerful and subtly vicious Chancellor seemed transformed into a rather grandfatherly sort of fellow. (That is rather confusing, in retrospect, since I consulted the Scholars' Compendium when we returned home and learned he is but fifty-six.)

"Eliniea," he said without rising from his chair. "I never thought you'd be clever enough to return to me. Yet here you are. And you've brought a charming companion, I see."

Vyerin, to his credit, treated me to an unabashed eye-roll and refused to return Chancellor Rawsel's seated bow.

"I am Captain Vyerin Clel," he said, emphasising the *Clel* with such ferocity that it sounded like the clanging warning of a ship's storm-bell. "Consequently, Chancellor, we must be enemies."

Chancellor Rawsel let out a hauntingly familiar chuckle – that, at least, had not changed. "Enemies? O, do let me guess at why. Did poorly in one of my classes, did you, sir? If that is so, my apologies. I cannot help that my standards are exacting."

"My brother, Scholar Henerey Clel," said Vyerin, "once told me that if I were ever to meet you, I would – and I quote – either 'shame you into silence or silence you into shame'. You treated him cruelly, so any civility between us is impossible. Surely you understand."

How I admire Vyerin's unwillingness to waste time bantering with the unworthy!

Chancellor Rawsel's eyes scanned back and forth, as if he were searching through an extensive catalogue of everyone he had wronged.

"O, Clel," he mused, "that soft-hearted Scholar who simply

wanted to poke about in tidepools instead of doing any real research. I see you are aggrieved, Captain Clel, but take it from me: if that boy didn't learn the tough truths of the world from someone, there was no chance of him ever amounting to anything. He could not receive constructive criticism without trembling, nor sit with his back to a doorway without flinching at every sound! Scholarship is a most formidable profession, not made for the weak of heart or mind."

This sounds fanciful, Sophy, but I swear I could see a current of rage jolt through Vyerin's entire countenance!

"As you mentioned in your generous invitation," I said, hoping to calm the conversation, "we are here to discuss the Entries."

"If the Boundless Board of Chancellors sent you on this quest of yours, Eliniea," Rawsel replied in a quick, desperate voice, "then I will tell you exactly what I told them all those times before. The Entries are unquestionably real, and indescribably dangerous. There is no task more critical than finding every single Entry and any rogue Envoy that may yet exist, and if they won't accept that and reinstate me, then—"

"Reinstate you?" I asked. "Are you no longer Chancellor?"

"Yes, go ahead and pretend you don't know. Deception suits you. Your superiors from the Board surely thought that you and Sophy Cidnosin—"

"Cidnorghe," Vyerin and I corrected, in unison.

The Chancellor sighed. "Really, Eliniea? Had you no better option? At any rate, you surely thought you could draw me out by hunting for Entries. And that, in my desperation, I'd let slip some foolishness for you to report to the Board in your misguided quest for revenge."

"We are not employed by anyone but ourselves," said Vyerin. "Hasn't your spy told you as much? Sophy and I have a more personal investment in finding these Entries."

"So you truly are working independently? Fascinating. And,

all on your own, you've managed to find Entries?" Rawsel said. "My associate provided me with your most recent coordinates, but I am less interested in where you were than what you found there. What stages have the Entries reached? How long do we have before they burst?"

"We are not here to share information!" Vyerin exclaimed. "We are here to tell you to stop sniffing around like an enfeebled seal and leave us be."

"I fear I cannot," said the Chancellor. "Because I have a – how did you phrase it? – a more personal investment in these Entries as well, Vyerin Clel. Let us jump to conclusions and assume that perhaps you are developing a scheme to go through one. In that case, I would like to observe."

I was relieved, at least, to learn that the Chancellor does not know you and Tevn already went "through one". Either Lady Coralean is a subpar spy, or the Chancellor is simply too self-centred to absorb much information that does not directly involve him.

"That is absolutely out of the question!" Vyerin spat back.

"I presume he intends to force our cooperation somehow," I said, attempting to give the Chancellor a look that would adequately convey my immense disappointment. (I suspect, however, that my expression ended up amounting to nothing more than a nervous grimace.)

"I'm glad you have not lost all your wits, Eliniea. If you do not invite me to join your little investigation, I shall have to drop a few anonymous hints about how you and your colleagues are secretly investigating dangerous Antepelagic technology that ought to be studied through the proper channels."

I suppose I should have responded in kind by reminding him that I, too, could share some "hints" about the truth behind the Ridge expedition that any Journalist would be delighted to hear. Still, I didn't want to risk Rawsel making good on his threat. If any Department did learn of the Entries, Scholars would swoop in with their regulations and permits and documentation requests and make our clandestine activities practically impossible. (Didn't E. once note a similar fear about the Structure in her past letters?)

"There is nothing quite so pathetic as intimidating someone with anonymous gossip-mongering," said Vyerin. "Though perhaps that is all you have left. I am no Scholar, Rawsel, but I think it mightily strange to see a person of your position exiled to a houseboat a good day's sail from the heart of Boundless Campus. Did you not previously admit that you were stripped of your role?"

"Right, that," the Chancellor (or is he?) said. "You must have misheard earlier. Really, it's all a wretched misunderstanding. I became so caught up with these Entries that I no longer had sufficient time and energy to focus on a Chancellor's duties. The Board knows how important my work is, so they offered me a private leave of absence – I would remain a Chancellor in name, but would be granted a reprieve from all responsibility."

"That sounds rather unlikely," I said.

"Of course," he continued, "I needed to recover, in truth, from their machinations and manipulations. In my time away, I've taken the opportunity to start seeing a Physician of the Brain. While there's nothing wrong with my mind, the Physician taught me how to establish boundaries and demand the respect I deserve from those powerful parasites."

"Is this Physician accepting new patients? I should like to acquire such skills before our next conversation," said Vyerin. "In the meantime, if you have nothing more of substance to say, then Niea and I shall take our leave."

"Calm your seas, Captain." Rawsel smiled. "I have spoken with substance enough. Regardless of my current situation, many Scholars will listen if I choose to spill your secrets. Do we have an accord?"

"What exactly is it that you want?" I asked.

"Nothing more than to be included!" he said with a simpering smirk. "Is that so much to ask? If you manage to travel through an

Entry, I want to be there when you do. It is just a little thing – a trifle. When do you return to sea?"

I acquiesced. What else could I do? I do not want a thousand Scholars swarming about us. I cannot allow anyone to keep me from bringing you and Henerey and E. home (and Tev too – my goodness, there really are many of you over there now, aren't there?).

"We shall take to sea no more," I relented.

Chancellor Rawsel examined me in that keen, dissecting way I remember so well.

"Don't tell me you have one," he said with delight and disgust. "And you are trying to understand how it works? That is ambitious and likely to fail."

"We have many experts involved." I did not mention that one of them was Arvist Cidnan!

"I am sure you do," he answered. "But none will hold a candle to me, I presume. At what time shall I join you, and where?"

"Must we really do this, Niea?" pleaded Vyerin. "What would Sophy say?"

I knew, if you were here, that you would never put up with such nonsense. Sadly, my dearest, you are elsewhere, and I must make whatever sacrifices prove necessary.

"We have taken up residence in an empty shipwright's storehouse on the Windward Docks," I informed the Chancellor as Vyerin groaned. "We gather there during daylight hours."

"Excellent," Chancellor Rawsel crowed. "I know the area well. There is a rather pleasant inn just down the road, is there not? I shall book a room so I may be close by. I look forward to seeing you soon."

O, Sophy, I hope I have not shamed you with my behaviour. When I imagined meeting Chancellor Rawsel again, I envisioned myself as the very picture of quick wit, talking circles around the shell of a man who used to torment me. Yet even if Rawsel's power is all but gone, I remain simply swept up in the currents of old emotions.

I am grateful for Vyerin, of course, who is as reliable as ever. Now

216

we have returned to his home to rest and recuperate (and enjoy a proper dinner, which the former Chancellor never offered us!). How lovely it is to be in a normal house again, with sinks and bath-basins and warm water, after so many months at sea! I do not mean to brag – I do not know what manner of facilities will be available to you in your underwater city.

At any rate, once I was fed and comparatively calmed, I borrowed the Clels' Vocal Echolator to ring a certain infamous friend of ours! (Since I could not speak with you about Chancellor Rawsel, it seemed fitting to contact the Ridge expedition member who was most likely to have all the gossip.)

It took fifteen rings before Vincenebras deigned to answer, but that is only slightly above his average of ten!

"Dear Niea, I feared you'd perished!" he greeted me. "If you are a spectre, I offer my condolences. If you are not, I hope you are calling to apologise."

"Apologise? If I've offended you, Vincenebras, I don't know—"

"You missed my wedding, of course! Don't tell me you've been at sea all this time?"

I recalled the puzzling invitation, which I fear was scribbled upon by Orey after I discarded it.

"In fairness, Vincenebras," I said, "do you not make a habit of regularly submitting false wedding invitations to Campus circulars – indicating that the date is set and all you require is a willing partner to join you in matrimony?"

"I do indeed, so you ought to have taken this one more seriously!"

"But who is your new spouse?"

"I am, I'm afraid," cut in Irye's familiar voice in a more distant crackle. "Hello, Niea. Have you heard about the Composer who recently wrote an opera based on the sounds made by a Nautiloid's cirri as they flee from danger?"

"You two are wed? O, many congratulations!" I cried (though I did wish to hear more about this opera).

217

"In fact, we are just about to leave on our nuptial voyage," said Vincenebras. "At least we were able to share the pleasant news with you before leaving. How fortunate you are!"

"But I called for a reason!" I insisted. "Chancellor Rawsel is threatening to involve himself in our ... venture. You know all the rumours and whispers, Vincenebras: how do you imagine he found out, and why?"

Vincenebras, for once, had nothing to say. I suddenly grew exceptionally concerned.

"Are you still there?" I asked, "or has Irye hushed you in order to analyse the silence of these intervening moments?"

"Apologies, dear Niea," said Vincenebras with a cough. "We did not wish to tell you."

"You are only making matters worse, my fine fellow," chided Irye. (Though it was not the first time I had ever heard Irye refer to Vincenebras in such a way, the "fine fellow" contained far more fondness this time around.) "Niea, before we joined your voyage, both Vincenebras and I received personal notes from the Chancellor of a rather demanding nature."

"So that is why you left before our mission concluded?" I said. "O, my friends, I am exceptionally sorry. What did he say to you?"

"No, Irye and I ignored him entirely!" Vincenebras insisted. "The Chancellor asked us to report on your discoveries in exchange for various vague rewards – or else receive various vague punishments. How demeaning! There is nothing more offensive than someone conflating the fine profession of Journalism with something unsavoury like Document Acquisition."

"We did not wish to alarm you and Sophy by revealing that Rawsel had taken an interest, and we thought the matter settled when we refused to respond," said Irye. "Can you not do the same? He is on administrative leave, you know. Any threats he's made are likely meaningless. His influence is not what it once was."

"But he seemed so very confident."

"Because empty confidence is all he has left!" Irye sighed. "If you must deal with him, why not take control by giving Rawsel a fright with your photographs of what we found in the abyss?"

Irye's tone was terribly casual. So very light and relaxed, as though they were simply recommending that I listen to a particular symphony. As though they did not remember what it felt like at the end of the Ridge mission, when we all huddled together in the communication room trying to explain to Rawsel about the door and the chamber and the sea-woman – when he snapped and sneered at us, at *me*—

I suppose that's not entirely fair. Irye no doubt remembers exactly what *they* felt at that time. Their experience is simply distinct from mine.

"Wouldn't that only make matters worse? If I recall correctly," I said, "Ylaret's threat to publish the photographs only irritated the Chancellor. Made him threaten to put us all on forced sabbatical, as a matter of fact. Isn't that why we all resigned?"

"But that's precisely what proves Irye's point!" exclaimed Vincenebras. "Rawsel never could have gotten away with putting the entire Ridge expedition team on disciplinary leave. That idle threat was the act of a desperate man. Ergo, the thought of those photographs reaching the world was powerful enough to send him into desperation. The conclusions draw themselves! Again, there is naught I dare say but ergo! I assume Rawsel assumed we had reached an unspoken understanding – he would let us go, and we would keep those images to ourselves."

"And I assume," muttered Irye, "that you recently dreamed up the phrase *there is naught I dare say but ergo* and have been waiting for the perfect opportunity to say it, despite it making very little sense in any context."

"How well you know me, dear Irye!"

"We are powerless Scholars no longer, Niea." Now Irye's voice was no longer a mutter – nor casual. In fact, I had never heard them speak so clearly and passionately. "I understand it doesn't feel that way. Not all the time. Not after what Rawsel put you through. But I do think you ought to see how he reacts to those photographs. You do still have them, don't you?"

When I assented, Irye clicked their tongue in approval.

"Then take whatever action you must, Niea, to keep him in check. I know you and Sophy are simply unstoppable together."

"Speaking of which," interrupted Vincenebras, "did you and Sophy ever take a nuptial voyage? Perhaps you ought to wash your hands of Rawsel and spend some time together on some abandoned shore instead!"

How fanciful – and how I wish I could follow his advice!

At the very least, I will take Irye's suggestion to heart and seek those photographs. I don't know if they will do any good, and I am reluctant to visit our home to prise them from our safe-box, but if that is what it takes . . .

May this message reach you soon! I don't suppose you could ask Tev's friend to send the signals along a little more quickly, could you? I kept my eye on the Automated Post machine all evening, hoping to spy the keys starting to move as your words type themselves upon the sheet of coral-pink paper I keep there. But I am just being greedy. You have already sent me welcome news enough. It is now my turn to send you all my affection and the fondest good night kiss for good measure!

Yours,
Niea

AUTOMATED POST MISSIVE FROM VYERIN CLEL TO SOPHY CIDNORGHE, 1004

Dear Sophy,

I have been a bit of a sneak. Earlier this evening, I composed my letter to Henerey before letting your wife take her turn at the A.P.

machine. But now I am back because I wanted to write to you in private. I trust Niea told you about our encounter with Rawsel. Yet I'd wager she has not told you everything about the past few hours.

As you might imagine, all seems a bit fragile at present. Seeing that message from Henerey made me feel as overwhelmed as I did when you first shared his letters. I find it so terrifying to accept that my brother is alive. I presume I shall grow accustomed to it in time, and what a privilege that will be. For the moment, however, as I am unable to see Henerey in person, I remain vulnerable and cautious and adrift.

And I am not the only one.

What was the tone of your wife's letter to you? In truth, I do not need to ask. Surely it was written in accordance with the character she presents to the world – unfailingly optimistic and immensely supportive. Niea is a sensitive, thoughtful person, and I suspect she is unwilling to admit to her own suffering because she does not want to upset you. Likely you know this already. Likely she does this routinely.

When I bid her good night, I noticed Niea turning in the direction of my study rather than her room. I worried she was spending too much time fixating on the Entries and our project, and I told her so, but she insisted upon keeping at it for your sake.

I pretended to retire for the evening, but really, I left Reiv to his reading in our bedchamber and crept to the kitchen to brew Niea some tea. When I approached the study again, I could hear her weeping.

I did not let the matter rest. I sat with her for a time and we spoke of our various feelings. (That is, we did so once she managed to stop crying while muttering seemingly disconnected phrases about safe-boxes and Vincenebras and nuptial voyages.) Though she dreads to think of distracting you from the joy of finding E., your wife misses you very much and is most concerned about getting this device to work as we intend. I have no doubt she will manage

221

to do so. I just thought you ought to know about the other bit. I worry for her.

(She is, obviously, not the only one who misses you. And I am incredibly envious that you may now spend time with my brother at your leisure. Please give him my best regards.)

V.

Chapter 15

**AUTOMATED POST MISSIVE FROM
SOPHY CIDNORGHE TO ELINIEA HAYVE
CIDNORGHE, 1004**

Dearest Niea,

I hope the sight of these words appearing on that coral-pink paper you mentioned will give you some joy after yet another long wait! I too wish we could speed our letters along.

I have much to say, my love, but I wanted to start by emphasising that I long to be with you. I find it near-impossible to endure the various emotions of this experience without you by my side. As miraculous as it is to be with E., I sometimes become so overcome with sadness and yearning for you that I fear I might lose myself entirely. (Yes, even I, the rational Sophy Cidnorghe, succumb to such thoughts!) Have you found yourself feeling the same? It won't make me worry to hear it, I promise – I would rather know we are equally troubled by our mutual separation than leave you to bear that sorrow alone. No circumstance other than this could ever draw me away from you. In fact, when I am home, I would very much like for us never to part again, even if that means I must accompany you to those annual aquarium-keeping conferences you enjoy so much.

I mention this because I understand how difficult it was for you to meet Chancellor Rawsel and shield yourself against his barbs. If

I heard him speaking to you in such a way ... well, let us say that Vyerin Clel would not be the only quick-tempered and dramatic one among us!

I do not blame you for allowing Rawsel to work with you under extreme duress. I am also fascinated by his apparent investment in the Entries, which is corroborated by his interest in our discovery at the Ridge. Wasn't there something in one of Jeime's letters to E. about a former member of the Fleet who fell from their ranks? If he truly is fifty-six, Rawsel is not much older than my mother would have been.

Well, Niea, may I now trouble you by asking for some advice and comfort? I did not want to open my letter with this, but I may have made a mess of things with E. already. Let me explain; I shall address everything in time.

Before I do — you asked about my present location, and I will do my best to describe it. Truthfully, I am so busy marvelling at my sister's survival that I have hardly acknowledged the marvels of my surroundings! The city makes me wonder what would have happened if we built a true long-term habitation at the Ridge instead of simply dwelling there for an extended period. This is the ultimate form of underwater architecture. Obviously, their technology is sensationally advanced — I cannot begin to think of how they manage to maintain oxygen, light, temperature, and all the other qualities that make this place so comfortable! Based on what E. and Henerey told me when we first arrived, this is indeed a society from before the Dive, so they have preserved some degree of lost Antepelagic artistry. Everything is glowing and domed and abstract, and the geometric iconography is perfectly in line with Upward Archipelago style. (Still, to answer your other question, nothing resembles the singular chamber where we saw the sea-woman in the abyss. I wonder if she redecorated that Antepelagic ruin to suit her own tastes.)

The Scholars themselves leave us to our own devices. They are curious and quiet people who, Henerey told me, managed to learn our modern Academic Vernacular simply from speaking with their first two visitors! We attended an odd and surprisingly short meeting with their "council" soon after arriving. For reasons unknown, their grand reception hall is only equipped with two additional chairs. When you picture this scene, imagine Tevn and I in those seats amid a crew of strangers, with purple light casting the room aglow in haunting cold tones. E. and Henerey sat on the floor, off to the side, and I saw them passing notes to each other like Apprentice Scholars!

The meeting itself was relatively dull, and primarily involved strangers inquiring after our Entry and whether its various functions remained intact (especially the luminescence). To Tevn's satisfaction, we also learned there is no limit on the number of people who can travel through a single Entry. Yes, my extended fixation appears to have been for naught. I am not too disappointed, of course, because that certainly makes things easier for you. Imagine if you had to construct an extra Entry for each pair of us who needed to return home!

Curious as they are, the Scholars are nothing but hospitable. Though I'm sure the quarters they offered us cannot compete with the charming guest bedroom at the Clel residence, we are comfortable enough. Last night, E. stayed with me until my much-belated bedtime. We talked for hours, and she told me so much about her recent activities – but I did not quite return the favour.

You see, Niea, since I arrived, I have struggled with a burden I did not anticipate. Somehow, my sister did not know what became of the Deep House. She and Henerey had already departed by the time the explosion occurred. I realised this horrifying truth soon after our reunion, and then Tevn almost revealed everything to her by accident – though I did appreciate his counsel on the matter later.

At one point, during that first night, Tevn approached me in a conspiratorial manner.

"You are lying to your sister," he observed. "Do you wish me to follow suit? I would prefer not to."

"I simply need to find the opportune moment to tell her." I glanced

225

at E. on the other side of the room, laughing at something Henerey had said, and felt nauseous. "In the meantime, I don't expect you to pretend that the Deep House is in good condition, but I would be most grateful if you could simply remain silent on the matter."

"I shall endeavour to do so. But I do not like it, and if I were E., I would rather know sooner than later. Wouldn't you?"

I agreed, of course. Still, as I spoke with my sister throughout the evening, I could not find the right moment to raise the issue.

At any rate, yesterday began rather excellently. Because E. and I spent so much time together in my temporary quarters, I had not yet seen whatever had become her home. I rose early and wandered the corridors until I encountered the young Scholar from the day before. To my surprise, they directed me away from the metropolis of a building, which I assumed made up most of the city, and across a narrow, glowing street to a small assortment of homes like you might find inland on the Atoll. I did ache to think how trapped my sister must feel in a city of this nature, which lacks the solitude and beauty of the Deep House! (O, how fitting and unfortunate that I should mention it again.)

The Scholar I'd asked for assistance told me to keep an eye out for E. and Henerey's "mark", and I discovered what that meant when I spied a detailed tympanum painting of a Nautilus in my sister's own dear style. Just as I started to knock, I noticed a long spiral of some crystalline tubing extending from the side of the door. Moments later, E.'s voice sounded from it.

"Is that you, Sophy?"

"Do you receive no other visitors?" I asked, first to myself and then, realising my folly, into the speaking device.

"Not commonly, and that is just how we like it!"

The door opened, revealing a room that was much more spacious and homier than the sterile Visitors' Quarters. I entered their parlour, where the walls were painted a merry shallow-sea blue and graced with several framed sketches – which must have been due to Henerey's influence, for my sister tends to be most unwilling to display her artwork. There were books and scrolls stacked (or rolling upon) practically every surface. A proper school of scrolls surrounded a wondrously tidy desk in the corner, which sat adjacent to a comfortable-looking chair with an unusual collection of rods and sticks that I later understood as this place's equivalent of an easel.

Then I came upon the most striking sight of all – E. and Henerey together on a long, nest-like sofa covered with a tapestry of tessellations. They held scrolls in their hands and sat on opposite sides of the couch, with their legs companionably crossed over each other's in the centre. I'm sure they might be embarrassed to know that they put down their respective reading materials and smiled at me almost in unison.

"I'm glad to see you two have not suffered overmuch down here," I said.

"Do you like it, Sophy?" said E., beaming yet again – is it an illusion caused by time, or have I never seen my sister so consistently happy? "I think we've done quite well at making it homelike. Though it's no dear Deep House."

My stomach sank, but I tried to force a smile. "This place is charming. I'm glad to see your artwork receiving the attention it deserves."

"As am I," said Henerey. "I only convinced her by pointing out that we hardly receive any visitors save the Thirtieth Second Scholar, so there's no risk of any Scholars of Inspiration judging her artistry. Even if they did, I'm sure they would be most complimentary."

"You clearly have not spent much time around Scholarly artists, my dear," said E. with a fond smile.

"Is this Thirtieth Second Scholar a friend of yours?"

As I spoke, E. began gesturing at a scalloped, shell-shaped chair until I took the hint and sat down.

"You've met them already – the younger Scholar who first recognised you. The Thirtieth Second Scholar is clever, gregarious, and a bit of a romantic, which is uncommon here. I have tried my best to be a sort of mentor."

I felt a pang of jealousy – you, Niea, know more than anyone how I am prone to it – and I tried to reframe that feeling as a positive sign of how much I care for my sister.

"I seem to have forgotten all surface-world manners," said Henerey, saving me from further introspection. "May I get you something to drink, Sophy? There are many odd teas available here, made from the plants in that vast garden. I've yet to fully study any of them, but I have become more familiar with their established properties. Because there are so few creatures around these parts, I have been toying with the idea of picking up botany."

"By which he means that he has already written a monograph of about ten thousand words on the subject," said E. They shared a laugh so endearing that I felt only a weak pull of envy.

"You needn't trouble yourself, Henerey. Thank you."

"As you like," he replied. "O, and perhaps I ought to give you two some privacy? I don't mean to intrude."

I said, "That would be lovely," just as E. said, "You needn't go!"

He laughed at our cross-purposes, stood up, kissed E.'s forehead with a confidence I would not have expected from him, and made for the door.

"If you need me, E., I shall be in the conservatory, messing about with assorted leaves."

"I need you always," she called in response, "but I shall try to leave you to it!"

"I never thought I would see you like this," I said after Henerey departed.

"In a parlour in an underwater city, lost to the world?"

"I meant living with a partner, in fact," I replied. "And happily, too. Do you no longer feel the need for solitude?"

"I wouldn't say I ever truly needed utter solitude," she said. "That was a protective measure, for the most part, though I remain loath to attend any of the Scholars' social gatherings or go out unnecessarily. Besides, living with Henerey does not feel like being with another person at all – in the sense that it is no burden. I am perpetually surprised by how well we suit each other."

"Well, I am pleased to hear that." I had long suspected that E. would never share her life with someone else. I sometimes wondered, Niea, if I would always feel bound to serve as her closest companion, since she would have no other.

"How I dreamed of sitting here with you, just as we are now! Henerey and I tried to make this our home when we accepted that we might never return, but I suppose that is no longer the case?"

At this point, I told her more about what presently occupies you and Vyerin – though I left out that Rawsel was involved, since I did not want to upset Henerey when E. inevitably passed the news along.

"And I am even more hopeful now that I better understand how the Entries work," I concluded. "You see, E., ever since I began the journey to find you, I've experienced a peculiar obsession with the idea that only two people can use an Entry before it breaks. Tevn tried to dissuade me, and there was plenty of evidence to the contrary. Still, it has bothered me against all reason for some time – it is difficult to explain."

To my surprise, my sister laughed.

"You certainly needn't worry about explaining that sort of thing to me," she said.

"O, I am sorry – it was not my intent to equate our experiences. I apologise for any offence."

"It does not offend me in the least. I find it oddly validating when people's unexpected fixations give them even the slightest insight into my brain. Every time Henerey prepares plant specimens, for instance, he goes back to his conservatory once, just once, to check that he sealed their drying chamber properly, even if he is certain he did. Dr Lyelle – I hope she is well, by the way – told me that everyone must wrestle with challenging thoughts or behaviours from time to time. It only becomes a condition like mine when that sort of thing intensely affects your daily life, you know."

"Well, I wouldn't say this thought affected me to that extent," I

229

replied. "And I feel silly now that it's been disproven. I just thought I ought to mention it, to show you how confident I feel in our ability to take you and Henerey home."

"I can hardly believe that is possible."

I cannot describe how relieved I was to see genuine delight on her face.

"We shall see how it develops. I suspect building an Entry may be a difficult enterprise, to say the least. Then again, I thought it impossible that I might find you – and here we are."

E. glanced nervously about and leaned closer. I find myself perpetually surprised by the experience of being in her presence again. I never forgot my sister, but I forbade myself from imagining her with such clarity – the impossibly fast movements and gestures, the constant quiver in her hands and shoulders, the sound of her biting her lip when she is unsure of what to say – when I thought she was gone.

"I believe one can successfully build an Entry, or Sculpted Saviour, as they call it here. Soon after we arrived, Henerey and I had a peculiar conversation with one of the First Scholars. She said that if we promised to stop prying into the Scholars' secrets, she would make an Entry for us."

"Prying into the Scholars' secrets?" I exclaimed. "You and Henerey?"

"It was nothing impressive, I assure you," she protested. "If either of us were the slightest bit assertive, we would have responded more firmly when the Fifteenth First Scholar's promise proved an empty one. As months passed and we attempted to bring up the matter again, she said only that we must be more patient. I think they are desperate to keep us here, Sophy, and – as I said before – you should not mention any of this when we are among them."

"That suits me well enough. But there's no need to worry, E. If you wish to return home, I swear no rogue Scholars shall stop you. If I have faith in anything, it is my wife and her tenacity." (Yes, I did say that, I promise!)

"How thrilling it is to hear you refer to your wife!" E. said, and

I welcomed the change of subject. "Though I am heartbroken that I missed your wedding. I ought to have asked about that last night instead of blathering on about me and Henerey! When did it take place? What did you both wear? What did *Arvist* wear? Tell me everything!"

"It was nearly a year ago now. We held the ceremony privately – it was just Niea and me, on an Intertidal platform near where she'd grown up, with her sister and Arvist in attendance. We didn't feel in the mood to do anything splashy, you see, since—"

"Since I had just died," she said in a bleakly humorous tone. "O, Sophy. How miserable I made you. What must I do to earn your forgiveness?"

"There is nothing to forgive." I took her hand and squeezed it. "Only please continue being alive, won't you, and come back with me?"

"Of course I shall!" she said. "Henerey and I are in accord. He is desperate to see his brother and the rest of his family. And don't tell Arvist, but I am eager to reconnect with him and Seliara."

"I'm sure he will craft a suitable performance to commemorate our reunion. Incidentally, I did tell Father about you – or tried to, anyway – but I haven't heard anything from him in a long while."

"That is unsurprising."

"But o, E., I understand him a little better now. The grief I felt for you was so sickening. Worse than it was with Mother, for you and I were always together, weren't we, and to think that you were gone—"

I felt myself choking back the tears that I knew would inevitably emerge during this visit. E., to my surprise, came over to my chair and embraced me like we were children once more.

"I am so profoundly sorry," she said. "But, Sophy, I am gone no longer. We're together once more, as we ought to be. When I am home, we'll do the most mundane things as though nothing ever happened. We can gather for family dinner parties, and Niea and Henerey can chatter about species of Shrimp or suchlike as you bicker with Arvist and Seliara helps me make dessert. Won't it be lovely?"

231

"I resent that your imagination consigned me to bickering with Arvist." But I smiled, too, because it was indeed the loveliest thing I could picture. Our family has been so fractured, starting with Mother's death and Father's Seclusion, and worsened still by E.'s disappearance. The prospect of being together again felt like such a gift that I almost forgot – or didn't care – that the Deep House was gone.

"How is Arvist, by the way?" E. asked. "Please don't tell me he sculpted some kind of ridiculous memorial to me and consecrated it with a dance."

"He's matured somewhat, though he is still very much Arvist," I said, not wishing to mention either the disappointing chronic sea-sickness or his more promising involvement in your mission, Niea. "I would say that fatherhood suits him."

"O, how did I forget? Seliara said she hoped they would have a child soon!" she exclaimed. "Why, that baby must be nearly speaking now. What is their name?"

"You won't like it," I said with a knowing glance.

"Please don't tell me that my dear brother and dear friend felt called to preserve my memory by passing down *Erudition*."

"She has been going by Eri for short, which I find sweet," I said. "But yes, all three are well, and they live near Intertidal now, closer to Seliara's parents."

"They've finished their incursion into the Deep House, then?" she said, with a shy hope that broke my heart anew.

"I suppose they have," I mumbled.

"In that case," my sister continued, "Sophy, there is something I must ask of you."

"You may ask me anything." If only she could have asked me anything but this!

"Would you mind awfully if Henerey joined me in the Deep House?" E. said. "I suggested the idea to him before, but we discussed it properly yesterday evening. Henerey always loved the Deep House, nearly as much as I do, and he's thrilled about the prospect of us caring for it for the rest of our days."

I could imagine it perfectly, too, as clearly as if I were seeing a vision like the one that E. experienced of the island. I pictured myself stepping out of the airlock and hearing the eternally recognisable click of the door as I entered the parlour, greeting my sister when she looked up from repairing one of Father's stained-glass portholes. I would settle down with her in the Crystal Room – which would be newly strewn with frames and books just like their quarters here – where we would chat and watch through the window as Henerey pursued octopi across the undergarden with a camera in hand. I envisioned the pleasure of staying the night there and leading you up to my old, familiar room, where I'd find everything tidily dusted and straightened up, with all the maps I'd used to decorate in my youth welcoming me home. What a joy it would be to wake in the morning and hear the comforting symphony of the Deep House's machinery and the sounds of voices and dishware below! (I am somehow convinced that Henerey Clel, like me, is an exceptionally early riser.)

I imagined it all and that imagining shattered me, Niea, because I know any possibility of this pleasant life is gone forever, consumed by the sea. Even if I've managed to salvage my sister from the wreck, there is no chance I will find a fully intact Deep House tucked away in this city.

"Was that too much to ask?" E. said.

"It is not that, dear E.," I murmured, as slowly as I dared. "I would give you and Henerey the Deep House in a moment, if I could. But I'm afraid it is lost to us."

"Lost?" asked E. in such a loud, desperate voice that I wondered if Henerey would hear from the next room and come running. "Have some Scholars taken it over to study the Structure? I feared such a thing might happen. We can contest it, Sophy, especially now that Henerey and I are returning."

"I have no doubt that you would." I gripped her hand. "Yet it's impossible. The Deep House is truly gone, E., gone for as long as you have been."

"But how?"

"Do you recall what happened when Arvist manipulated your Structure and it reacted rather dramatically?"

"And damaged the parlour, yes, but I thought that was repaired? Was the damage more substantial than Jeime thought?"

"No, that is not the issue. You see, E., it appears that when the Structure – the Entry—" I stalled, fearful of every word that brought me closer to what I must reveal. "When that device completes its objective, it releases a burst of energy more powerful than the first."

E. breathed in a shaky gasp.

"The house is beyond repair?" she said in the faintest voice.

"There is nothing to repair. It is a hole in the ocean floor."

Perhaps I expected her to start sobbing; indeed, there were already tears running down my face again. Instead she staggered a bit and slid back on the couch, her rough breathing continuing.

"E., I am so sorry," I said. "I hardly knew how to tell you."

"It is my fault." Her expression could not have been blanker. "I destroyed the Deep House."

"What? Of course you didn't!" I exclaimed. "According to Jeime, the Entry would have exploded anyway in due time."

"I thought it was the best way to fulfil Mother's legacy, and instead I destroyed her creation. Sophy, I stole your home from you!"

There was a darkness in her tone that frightened me.

"It is a loss that we will continue to mourn together, but aren't you treating yourself unfairly?"

"How could I not?" she said. "I caused such a loss because I followed my own selfish desires. You should not forgive me. How can you bear to speak with me? Why hasn't this destroyed you, Sophy?"

"It devastated me! But the loss of my sister far overshadowed the destruction of a house, as unique and beloved as it may have been."

"I do not agree that I am worth more than the Deep House," she replied. "You would still have your home – you would have never suffered in the first place! – if it weren't for me."

I took a breath and let go of her hands, which I had been holding quite firmly. I tried to remember all I had learned from reading her letters.

"E., I know you are prone to thinking you have committed some wrong when you have not. Do you think that perhaps your brain has latched onto your grief and is forcing you to feel shame when it is unmerited?"

"It is my brain's prerogative to make me fixate upon things that have not actually happened," E. said, tearing at her fingernails. "Yet this is undeniably real! I will not blame my condition for something that is my responsibility."

"The destruction of the Deep House is real, yes, but blaming yourself for it is not right – that is what I am trying to say!"

This was not the first time I engaged in such an argument with my sister, but never before had it involved so much genuine sorrow for both of us. What was I to do, Niea? I felt utterly helpless. I am no Physician of the Brain, and the only reason why I ever succeeded in calming E. in past circumstances was because I knew her better than anyone.

Is that still true, considering that I have not seen her in so long?

I was only making the matter worse. She did not need a debate; she needed care. And not, I feared, from me.

"I am sorry, E.," I said. "Please try to consider the possibility that this is not your fault. I cannot bear it when you are cruel to yourself."

I touched her shoulder again, but she continued staring away, and I could imagine, in her mind, the whirring gears of self-recrimination, powered by the genuine grief she felt and accelerated by that part of her mind which persecutes her beyond reason.

"I will return soon, I promise." Then I departed. I left her alone, Niea.

Logistically and physically, it was easy enough to accomplish. My body merely had to walk out of the parlour while my mind begged it not to. It pained me to proceed to a small glass conservatory at the back of their residence. There, among a rainbow of extraordinary plants that might well have caught my eye under other circumstances, I found Henerey examining the veins on the underside of a vividly orange leaf through a magnifying glass.

"Ah, Sophy, hello again!" he said. "Have you changed your mind about the tea? This plant produces a remarkably purple brew." He placed down his magnifying glass and looked up at me with a gentle smile. "Is something the matter?"

"E. needs you," I said. "The Deep House was destroyed, Henerey, and I told her, and most probably she would like to be alone, but I do not think she should be. I leave the rest to you."

"The Deep House? Whatever happened?" He stood up instantly and made for the door.

"I cannot stay – I am sorry. I know you will take care of her," I replied in haste. I could feel my own tears returning yet again, and I did not want Scholar Henerey Clel to see me weep right then.

My decision haunts me still. When she feels better, I will tell E. everything that I could not when I panicked in her parlour. Perhaps after she has time to adjust to the initial shock, she will understand that I do not hold her responsible in the least.

O, I do wish you were here, because you would know just the things to say – first to comfort me and lift my spirits, and then to gently chide me into doing whatever is right.

My dear Niea – I know you are hard at work doing the impossible, but I don't suppose there's any room in that brilliant mind of yours for a plan to reconstruct the Deep House, is there? Surely my mother's technology is much easier to reproduce than whatever arcane nonsense powers the Entries?

Yours as always,
Sophy

236

P.S. – Henerey has been waiting politely for me to finish writing this letter, and he sends his best regards. (Do not worry; he says E. is well. I hope he cannot tell that I almost resent him for knowing my own sister better than I do, at present.)

Chapter 16

AUTOMATED POST MISSIVE FROM HENEREY CLEL TO VYERIN CLEL, 1004

Dear Vyerin,

As a result of the rather funny delay between our messages, your letter arrived at a most opportune time.

E. and I recently learned what you already know – namely, that the Deep House was destroyed when we passed through the Entry, and there is no way of repairing it. I cannot fathom what E. has lost. That house was not simply her entire world, the one place where she felt confident and in control, but also a family treasure passed down from her mother. When E. and I first met, I witnessed first-hand how at ease she was there, and how she knew all the small secrets of the Deep House that no one else did.

I, too, find myself devastated by the news. You know how much the Deep House fascinated me as a boy, Vy, even if you never under-stood my fixation. It began as this kind of fantasy-place for me, a famous architectural marvel I took pleasure in imagining. Then I happened to fall in love with the very person who lived there, so it became still more precious! Future visions of the Deep House, I'll confess, helped keep myself and E. afloat throughout the uncertainty of our experience. The thought of spending the rest of my life there with the woman I adore seemed the most unbelievably ideal fate.

Of course, I would be content with the smallest dormitory if only E. were with me. Now that our vision of the future has burst apart and dispersed into detritus across a sundered coral reef, it becomes our task to simply build a new dream for ourselves. For the moment, however, E. has just begun to grieve. She is understandably quiet, but not withdrawn. I had thought someone like E. might require isolation and silence to work through her feelings. As it turns out, she decidedly rejected the former by seeking the latter from within my embrace. Yesterday evening, I lay with her soundlessly until sleep consumed us both. Sophy gave me the impression that E. could be struck by the urge to behave compulsively in response to the unwarranted guilt she feels, so experiencing the normal symptoms of grief seems an improvement upon those ceaseless cycles of checking and rumination that oft overcome her.

Ah, while we are on the subject – let us discuss, dear brother, your friend Sophy Cidnorghe. Did you two enjoy reading my private notes and correspondence for the better part of a year?

You see, I sought out Sophy today because I suspected she would be eager for news of her sister. Our friend, the Thirtieth Second Scholar (I suppose I should mention that they do not use personal names here), happened to visit E. and me this morning. To my immense surprise, E. said she would be happy to entertain the Scholar if I desired a moment to myself. I did not, but I also did not wish to pass up the opportunity to speak with Sophy.

When she was not in her room in the Visitors' Quarters, I remembered that Scholar Mawr set up your rather ingenious "Automated Post" device in the place we compare to a Refectory (I am there now, in fact). Under the circumstances, I assumed Sophy might be writing to her wife about the situation. I would have done the same! (Vyerin, is it wrong that sometimes, in my most automatic thoughts, I think of E. as my spouse, though we have not undergone any official commitment ceremony? Such rites are not part of the culture here, and I daresay we've managed to intertwine our lives quite thoroughly without the formalities.)

239

At any rate, Sophy was indeed where I suspected, tapping out a letter to Scholar Cidnorghe. Not wanting to be impolite, I paused in the entryway as she finished. I didn't mind waiting. A pot above an adjacent awning happened to hold a particularly charming example of a certain thorned micro-bush with a questionable form of photosynthesis that I have been trying to wrap my head around for some time!

"Henerey?" said Sophy, startling me from my botanical reveries. "Has something happened to her?"

"No, she is well enough. Good morning! I didn't want to interrupt you," I replied. "Though, if you have not yet finished, would you please send my best regards to Scholar Cidnorghe?"

Sophy smiled and returned to the Automated Post system. "P.S. – Henerey has been waiting politely for me to finish writing this letter, and he sends his best regards," she said as she typed. "Are you satisfied with that?"

"Perfectly! That device is remarkable. Would you mind if I used it to write to my brother again?"

"I wouldn't mind in the least! If I did, Vyerin would never let me hear the end of it," she said. "I am glad there is no emergency. But how is E., really?"

"She continues to grieve, of course."

"And you thought she ought to be left on her own?"

"She is not alone, and I left at her own request." There was an uncharacteristic sternness to my words – my goodness, Vyerin, has love finally made me assertive? "The Thirtieth Second Scholar is with her, and I am glad of it."

"Yes, right, E.'s substitute sibling," Sophy muttered. "That was a jest, Scholar Clel – no need to look so aggrieved."

"I am most certainly not aggrieved," I said, which you know is something I often say when I most certainly am.

"I am sorry for behaving oddly," she said with a sigh. "I never expected that our reunion would turn out like this."

"Despite it all, I know E. could not be more pleased that you are here."

Then Sophy gave me a genuinely kind smile, allowing me to perceive the family resemblance for the first time. As I'm sure you've learned over the course of your friendship, Vy, Sophy lets herself come across as competent and collected because that is what she needs to be – but there is a gentleness in her, as in E., that helps me understand why the sisters are so close.

"That does reassure me. Still, I cannot help but worry that E. and I will never be as we were." She placed her head in her hands. "Since Vyerin and I began our project, I have felt increasingly close to my sister, and I thought reading her letters had changed me – by helping me see her in an utterly new way."

I fear Sophy was not quite finished with that speech, but I could not help cutting in. Something surprising (can you guess what?) caught my attention.

"Pardon the interruption, Sophy, but I might have misheard. Did you say you read E.'s letters?"

Sophy's mouth dropped open.

"Yes," she declared. "I did, I'm afraid, and yours as well. That was how Vyerin and I met in the first place. We read through everything, because we thought you were dead, and when we realised you might not be – well, I don't regret it, as we could not have found you without the documents. I do apologise for invading your privacy."

"O, I suppose it's really no matter in the end, is it?" I said, surprising her – and perhaps you too, Vy? Yes, it's perfectly all right with me. Of course I had to give you a bit of a talking-to in that earlier paragraph, didn't I? You've spent so much time studying my letters, so I have earned the right to tease you in this one.

"It's no matter?"

"Not at all. I always assumed – perhaps Vyerin told you this – that Scholars of the future would read anything I put to paper. That simply happened rather sooner than I anticipated."

241

"But I do feel a little odd speaking with you after examining your private correspondence and learning your secrets," she said.

"What secrets?" I replied. "The only secrets I kept in those letters fell into two categories – the secrets of the Structure and so forth, which brought you here, and, secondly, my love for E., which could not be less of a secret. In fact, I would happily proclaim that to all the people in the world if she asked it of me."

"I have no doubt that you would, and no doubt that she wouldn't."

"Am I right to assume you have not yet told her about this?"

Sophy heaved another sigh. "How could I? She is so burdened already. I don't suppose I could convince you to keep that information between us?"

"I would never lie to her," I replied. "But for the moment, I will leave it to you to inform E. as soon as you can. And who is to say? I suspect, in the end, it will not bother her overmuch."

"I hope you are correct." Then, more tentatively, Sophy said, "May I ask – before she learned this terrible news, E. was doing rather well, wasn't she? She was happy?"

"Well," I said, feeling suddenly shy, "I would like to say she was. She is still troubled by obsessions – particularly as they relate to a certain Scholar's instructions that we were not, under any circumstances, to—I won't go into that. Most of the time, we rather enjoy ourselves. We take walks around the city, the garden, and the Artificial Ocean, and play games together, and study with the Scholars, and we always have the most fascinating conversations."

"I can't fathom how someone so ideally suited for my sister exists, Henerey Clel, but I am grateful that you do."

"In many ways, this place is ideally suited for the pair of us," I replied before I grew too embarrassed. "There are hardly any people, and the Scholars mostly keep to themselves, so E. feels comfortable most of the time. Besides, I'm not overfond of society myself, as I'm sure you've read."

She flashed me a guilty grin.

"I confess I am rather concerned about returning to the world, especially the academic one," I continued, "and that is why losing the Deep House is so heartbreaking. We both hoped our happily isolated existence could continue there. Yet we will find ourselves a new home in time."

"Undoubtedly," she said. "Well, I will delay you no longer, as you must long to write to Vy."

"Where will you go now? I'm sure E. would love for you to call upon her."

"Dare I show my face again after I simply left her yesterday?"

"If you do not wish to show your face," I answered, "you could always try writing her a letter."

I did not mean this entirely in jest. When you are here, Vyerin, and we reunite – will it be bizarre to speak to you after so long? Will you think it odd to interact with me when you have spent so much time inspecting my letters and private journal entries?

I suppose we shall find out, and I have not forgotten how fortunate it is that we may do so.

Hoping to see you sooner rather than later,

Henerey

AUTOMATED POST MISSIVE FROM ELINIEA HAYVE CIDNORGHE TO SOPHY CIDNORGHE, 1004

My lovely Sophy,

How I wish I could embrace you instead of writing this miserably ineffective note! Won't you indulge me by pretending we are back home in the window seat, watching the sunset with your head in my lap, as I attempt to comfort you?

I am terribly sorry you had to break the news about the Deep House to your sister. I, too, never realised she did not know! It is perfectly natural that you would imagine an alternative future and feel so attached to thoughts of what might have been. I confess there were times earlier in our courtship when I would envision being at the Deep House with you. I'd dream of that clever look on your face as you showcased your home's ingenious features or swam with me around the edges of the reef. I regret never having the opportunity to step inside its airlock even once.

I cannot rebuild what is lost, my darling, but when this is all over, I promise we shall find ourselves the loveliest little house you could ever picture. I know we chose our flat because it was convenient for my work. (I did briefly visit the school other day, incidentally – I do ache to return, though they are proceeding admirably without me!) Have we not reached the stage in our lives when ease and convenience are less important than comfort and permanence? I want a proper home with you, Sophy, with historic map reproductions practically everywhere and, if you consent, rows and rows of aquariums set in the walls to give the impression of being underwater. (I shall have to consult with Jeime about the most efficient way of engineering such a marvel.) In the absence of the Deep House we shall have our own House, and we can prefix it with any adjective that seems fittingly poetic! And I cannot wait to meet E., and to see what adventures we shall all get up to there.

I hope that glowing vision makes you feel a little better. It helped me to write it out. You perceived correctly, Sophy, that I have not been very well without you. As always, I marvel at your ability to discern the emotions I try to conceal. (If I did not know better, I would suspect that Vyerin confided in you about a moment of weakness I experienced some time ago, but I cannot be sure!) Although I know you are perfectly safe in your impossible underwater city, I fear that at any instant, you will vanish like E. – that I shall never see you nor read your words nor hear your voice again. (I ponder your voice often, dear Sophy. I am so accustomed to hearing it at all hours of the day. Sometimes, I vex myself by thinking that perhaps I have not properly remembered the exact inflection you would use to say a particular word, and then I rehearse every option in my head until something sounds right.)

Yet I am using my sorrow productively by flinging myself into our work on the Entries. Thanks to the mechanical knowledge I acquired as the Ridge Expedition Specialist, I am not as out of my depth as I feared. It is doubly fortunate that these Entries are, surprisingly, extremely simple in their construction. If you open this one (as we have), you will see not a complex labyrinth of wires and circuits, but an unadorned chamber containing a crystalline core that defies all understanding.

This is the puzzle we presented to our visitors this morning – for Chancellor Rawsel did make "good" on his promise of joining our enterprise. Thankfully, I took Vincenebras' advice to heart (what an unprecedented statement!) and came equipped with the photographs in question. By the time we arrived (at seven bells as usual, which barely gave Vyerin enough time to say farewell to his sleepy children and fully alert husband – Reiv having been up with the sunrise to practise his scales, as usual), Chancellor Rawsel was already there, in the company of another familiar face.

"I brought my associate," Rawsel announced. "I thought it would be useful for her to see how effective coerced collaboration can be."

"I assure you that voluntary cooperation is far more effective," I said. I wanted to show Chancellor Rawsel the photographs at this precise moment, but my heart thrummed so fiercely that I feared it would burst if I dared remove the folder from my valise. I turned to Rawsel's companion instead. "Good day, Lady Coralean. I hardly recognised you without the whale!"

"Right, that is precisely the amount of time I allocated for pleasantries," interrupted Rawsel, slamming shut a pocket-watch and tossing the chain over his shoulder. "Eliniea, take us in."

With great reluctance, I ushered them forward – once again without revealing the photographs, which led Vyerin to eye me with surprise. The storehouse is a funny place, Sophy, built in a vintage 900s style with extremely low ceilings and a rather unexpected architectural focus on the figure of the cylinder. The halls are cylindrical tubes that lead into a spacious room made of sea-stone – which is why we chose this building, because we were slightly concerned about the destructive capabilities of an exploding Entry on land. In the middle of it all is our place of operations, with the walls lined with sketches by Jeime and Arvist.

As we entered, Arvist gave a magnificent bow. "Why, Chancellor! How kind of you to visit."

"I suspect it is quite the opposite of that," muttered Jeime.

"She is correct!" said Chancellor Rawsel. "I am here for our mutual edification, Scholar, er—"

"Arvist Cidnan," he said, "Scholar of Art. Shall I introduce you to our project? I will tell you all you wish to know—"

"If I wished to ever hear anything from a Scholar of Art," said Chancellor Rawsel, "I would not wear earplugs when I visit museums."

I think even Vyerin might have felt a little sorry for Arvist at that point!

"Arvist," I whispered, "last night, when I failed to sleep, I found myself reconsidering a certain aspect of the original Structure. I would love to see that very fine retrospective blueprint you produced. Would you kindly fetch it for me?"

"Of course, Niea, of course!" he said in a tone more desultory than exclamatory.

As Arvist departed, I sighed and nodded to Jeime. "Might I ask you to provide our guests with an introduction to the general problem?"

Jeime observed Chancellor Rawsel dispassionately.

"If we are to be bullied into allowing the Chancellor to observe, then I feel the very least he owes us is an explanation," she said.

"My reasons are my own business," said Rawsel. "I already made that perfectly clear to Eliniea and Captain Clel."

246

"Perhaps circumstances have changed since you did," Vyerin commented, tilting his head at me in a most encouraging manner.

I, of course, said nothing. I love and admire you so, Sophy, but I must confess that I have never wished to *be* you – until this moment, anyway. You would have thrust those photographs into the Chancellor's lap, handling the situation with as much courage as when you rescued me and Tevn from the sunken room or sped after our colossal Nautilus! I am not like you, and, normally, that suits me well enough. I fear if we were too similar, we would not enjoy each other's company as much as we do. Still, I cannot contest that it would have been far better if you were the one in the storehouse with the Chancellor and I were taking tea with E. and Henerey underwater.

"Niea," Vyerin pressed, "is there nothing you wish to say to this man before we begin?"

"Wouldn't you do a better job of it?" I asked miserably.

Vyerin placed a hand on my shoulder.

"I know none could handle it more capably than you."

"O, enough of this nonsense!" exclaimed Rawsel. "What do you have for me?"

"Nothing you haven't seen before." I extracted the photographs from my valise and spread them out before me.

I know we examined the photographs recently, after all the revelations about E.'s disappearance came to light, but I suppose I shall never grow accustomed to the sight of them. I brought only the best three – the initial image of the door, unopened, surrounded by dark water; the staircase, thick with algae; and, most importantly, the blurry, haunting photograph of that room, which shows a fleeting glimpse of the sea-woman's eyes amidst haloes of distracting light.

I felt pleased with myself, all things considered, and Vyerin gazed at me with the self-satisfaction of a proud mentor.

Then the Chancellor laughed.

"I can hardly believe that these trivialities are what you used to threaten me years ago," Rawsel scoffed. "You've captured nothing more than some crumbling Antepelagic building. Only this—" he jabbed his finger at the sea-woman. "—is significant, and yet the composition is appalling. Based on your menacing claims, I assumed you had a proper portrait of the Envoy. I expected more from you, Eliniea."

"I charge you to take a better photograph of a magical being in an underwater room full of mysterious light," snapped Vyerin.

I expected Vyerin would soon challenge the Chancellor to a proper verbal brawl, so I thought of you, Sophy, and forced myself to intervene.

"If you are unconcerned, then surely you won't mind if I distribute these after all," I said, my voice shaking only slightly. "I have a certain Journalist on call who would delight in publishing them." (I did not mention, of course, that said Journalist was currently on his nuptial voyage and thus as out of reach as Vincenebras could ever be!)

"I could not be more disappointed in how far you've fallen, Eliniea," Rawsel seethed. Yet he did not discount the photographs again, and while he would never admit it, I could tell that my attempt at intimidating him had proved moderately successful.

I also had the distinct impression that Chancellor Rawsel becomes angriest when he is afraid.

"We are united in the desire to keep our respective missions out of the public eye, are we not?" I continued. "So long as this ill-fated partnership continues, Chancellor, I expect you will be a little kinder and more cooperative. Won't you start by telling us why you are so concerned with these Entries and Envoys in the first place?"

The Chancellor, to my great surprise, gave me a subtle smile.

"You suspect me and my motivations. Perhaps I can clear the air by assuring you that I do all in service of the greater good. The crux of the matter, my friends, is that the Entries – and what lies beyond them – pose a threat to our entire civilisation that I have spent the better part of decades striving to quell. Single-handedly, at that!"

Chancellor Rawsel surveyed us one by one, nodding emphatically.

"To be clear," the Chancellor continued, "I do not expect you to believe me. If you know of the Entries, that can mean only one thing – your mind was poisoned by an unscrupulous society, now blessedly defunct, that relished in spreading misinformation. Am I correct?"

"I am best equipped to answer that question," said Jeime. "You are the member who defected from the Fleet years ago. Aren't you, Chancellor?"

"Is your friend also involved in Document Acquisition?" murmured Lady Coralean, appearing behind my shoulder. "I am impressed with her spy-craft."

"You know of my past life? That is impossible. Unless you are one of them yourself," Rawsel said to Jeime. "How unsettling. Don't tell me the Fleet has been resurrected after all these years. So you are the genius behind this operation?"

"I am here out of affection for the Cidnosin family, and to satisfy my own inescapable curiosity. I am no member of the Fleet, and do not entirely disagree with your negative opinion of them," Jeime replied. "Still, I loved someone who supported them ardently, and I do not feel comfortable sharing secrets with the enemy of my former partner's secret society."

"And I am not comfortable being in a storehouse full of fools with a floor that feels like it is about to cave in at any moment – what an awful design! – but we must all make sacrifices, mustn't we?"

"Remember, Chancellor, that our new bargain includes no allowances for rudeness," said Vyerin in an ominous voice I would never want directed my way. "I will not stand by and see you treat my companions unkindly."

"Is that a threat, Captain?"

"Certainly not. Threats are the toys of those who dare not take action. And I think you'll find, sir, that I am not among their number."

"My word!" exclaimed Lady Coralean, stepping between the two men. "I never expected this to be such an interesting assignment. I'll simply thrill to see what happens if you provoke Captain Clel further, Chancellor. Though I'm afraid I'll have to increase my fees accordingly."

"Everything could remain quite civil – and affordable," said Vyerin, "if Rawsel would stop splashing about and explain his motivations more clearly."

"Fine. I shall explain it as though you were but Apprentice Scholars. I joined the Fleet as a boy, in the foolishness of youth. I soon learned that Darbeni and his circle aimed to create nothing but fear. Their myths and mysteries made people worry unnecessarily about extremely unlikely occurrences. And worry is the quickest path to weakness." He grinned. "We need look no further than your own brother as an example, Captain Clel."

"Chancellor—" Vyerin warned.

"Do you really think," the Chancellor persisted, "that the root of Scholar Clel's problems was not an inherent weakness of character caused by his inescapable anxiety? Surely you saw how his frailty made him a liability. How could *you* not notice? A strong man like yourself, who was so eager to threaten me just moments ago?"

In response to all this, Sophy: can you believe what Vy did? He simply chuckled. In the face of Chancellor Rawsel himself, Vyerin Clel laughed in his dry and resonant way. (O, if only we'd had him as a colleague at the Ridge!)

"If you believe me the epitome of strength, you are more ignorant than I feared," said Vyerin. "There is no man weaker than I. Why, simply compare me to the company I keep. Niea has been separated from the woman she loves, and yet she always summons the strength to greet me with a smile and a kind word. And Sophy herself dived into the unknown to search for E. and Henerey."

"You would have done the same, Vyerin, had you been able," I whispered. "Sophy knows that, and so do I."

Vyerin shook his head. "That's because I've deceived you all. Didn't I do well? Didn't I put on a proper show of being torn up about it?"

Jeime and I, as the only two crew members of the *Perspicacity* currently present (Arvist still being out on my manufactured errand!), exchanged a confused glance.

"You were weeping aboard the depth-craft, were you not?" said Jeime. "I did not think you the sort of man who could weep simply because he wished to."

"You even complained about being left behind in your own ship's log!" I objected. "You called it a mutiny!"

"If there's one thing I've learned in my time as an accidental archivist, it's that people do not always write exactly what they mean." Vyerin sighed. "My tears were real, Jeime. Unfortunately. I did fully intend to accompany Sophy. But, in the end, when it turned out I couldn't – I was relieved. You can imagine why."

"You couldn't leave Reiv behind," I said. "Nor your children. Vy, you simply ought to have said so. We would have understood."

I kept my words gentle, but, o, Sophy, I wanted to shout them. How very well I understood Vyerin's predicament now that you and I are apart!

"Considering that you've now progressed to another subject entirely, I suppose that means you are finished interrogating me?" interrupted Rawsel. "Could we possibly return to the present issue of the Entries and their construction?"

I squeezed Vyerin's hand in what I hoped was an understanding manner. "Jeime, would you please explain what you are doing?"

"Happily," said Jeime, sadly. "Here is the issue. These Entries function by the grace of an incredibly strong crystal object at their cores. It is this object that somehow creates the door in the world, so to speak, through which you are transported to another place. The Entry itself simply focuses that energy. The problem is that these engines, if you will, are powered by something too strong to be contained by the now-ancient Antepelagic casing, and that is what causes the devices to become unstable."

"Is there a way of putting a damper on it?" asked Lady Coralean.

251

"I have tried many things," said Jeime. "I do not even specialise in this kind of work. I am an Architect by trade, and there is little about this that relates to my background, other than the fact that it involves taking things apart and putting them back together again."

"Well, isn't it fortunate that I offered my services?" said Rawsel.

"Don't tell me that your ill-begotten Fleet knowledge included guidance on how to control an Entry," said Jeime.

"Then I shall simply have to show you," he said with a most unfortunate wink. Before any of us realised what was happening, he grabbed a large basin (normally used to mix ship sealant, I imagine), seized the core from Jeime's hand, and threw it into the basin with a horrifying crack.

Vyerin reacted first. He took my arm – not ungently – and Jeime's too, somehow, and shuffled us towards the door.

"What possessed you, man?" he screamed at Rawsel. "You'll blow us all up!"

"I will do nothing of the sort, Captain Clel. I think you'll find that everything is perfectly fine."

"Vyerin Clel," I said sternly, "were you about to use your own body to shield me from an explosion? What a terrible idea!"

"I told you," he said, not meeting my gaze, "if anything happened to you, Sophy would become a most perilous explosion herself."

"I did not realise Sophy Cidnorghe was so concerned about my wellbeing, as well," said Jeime with a rather dark merriness to her tone.

Vyerin looked bashful. "I just did not want either of you to be injured."

"Reiv wouldn't be pleased," I chided. "Did you not make a grand profession, moments ago, about how you dared not leave him without you?"

"I meant every word I said! But Reiv married me knowing full well that I have an unfortunate tendency towards impulsive heroics. You shall have to ask him about our very pleasant fifth anniversary

252

dinner, which resulted in me saving three people from tabletop candle-fires – unrelated incidents, you know."

We returned to Chancellor Rawsel and looked down into the basin at the ruins of the crystal. The hard exterior had broken neatly apart, revealing two halves like the sides of a hinged jewellery box.

And swimming around the basin in a viscous purple liquid were what appeared to be luminescent microplankton.

"What in all the seas are these little fellows?" I asked, kneeling closer and reviewing my knowledge of microplankton taxonomy. Of course, most creatures of this type are not completely visible to the human eye. I retrieved my microscopic spectacles from my pocket and leaned in to get a better look.

The dark background of the liquid proved an excellent visual contrast to the creatures, making my investigation all the easier. I observed a series of bright lavender lines, each topped with antennae and tapering into a long tail (or perhaps it was in reverse, and they are double-tailed with a single antenna – further investigation is required!). They pulsed slowly around their odd aquarium, and I swear I could spy flashes of light in various colours as they moved.

"I am astonished that none of you completed the bare minimum of research into Antepelagic technology," said Chancellor Rawsel. "These are Scintillating Isopods – bred long ago from some ancient stock up above. Extant accounts from the time claim such creatures naturally release potent energy, and, when properly contained, can continue generating that energy for centuries."

"Are you saying these creatures are a thousand years old?" I asked, gazing at them with appropriate reverence. Then my reason returned and I swept together the halves of the crystal, scooping all the plankton and liquid inside.

"What if they have existed in perfect equilibrium inside this crystal since before the Dive?" I exclaimed, glaring at Rawsel. "We might have killed the poor things by altering their environment!"

"They look fine to me," Chancellor Rawsel said. "Haven't I

told you, Eliniea, that there is nothing to be gained from anthropomorphising simple animals? A good scientist never indulges such fancies."

"It is my scientist's reason that tells me we should not have disturbed them. If they are exposed to stimuli that affect them negatively, they may be unable to continue generating energy."

But I should have more faith in the resiliency of microplankton! Moments later, the engine started to glow and quiver once more, and Jeime returned it safely to its chamber.

"Despite the questionable circumstances under which it was made, this discovery gives me several thoughts," Jeime remarked. "I am loath to ask, but would you agree, Chancellor Rawsel, that the Entries are volatile precisely because these creatures were left alone for a thousand years? In that time, I imagine they reproduced prolifically enough to rather overpower an Entry today."

"Exactly so, dear girl, exactly so," he said.

"Please never refer to me in such a way again. Would you also agree that if we were to, say, divide the creatures – for the time being, at least – that we would find ourselves possessed of two power sources?"

"Which could allow us to construct another working device that might be far more stable," I said. "But how would we contain both groups of isopods? We only have the one crystal casing, after all."

"We try to melt it down," said Jeime. "And produce two smaller versions from it, filling each with half of the creatures."

"That seems rather excessive. What if we destroy everything?" asked Vyerin.

"If we do," I said, "then we will simply find another Entry and start over. At this point, I suppose we may as well try."

"I happen to have a talent for smithing and glassmaking," came an uncharacteristically quiet voice from the door. "Especially with unusual materials. One can never succeed as a sculptor without experimentation, you know."

"Arvist, have you been standing there all this time?" I asked. He nodded with a broad grin.

"Then we have a plan," said Chancellor Rawsel. "I shall make assignments. Eliniea, you—"

"That was not part of our agreement," said Vyerin testily. "Scholar Alestarre is the most mechanically minded among us, so she shall give our assignments."

I fear this has grown long and dull, but the gist is that we have a concrete plan at last. How gratifying it is to tell you about our specific progress rather than simply and vaguely saying that "our work continues", as I have in past letters! (Perhaps I shall continue with the specificity by typing up some of Jeime's research notes for you over the next few days. Feel free to share them with E. and Henerey, as well – and Tev, if he likes, though I know from first-hand experience that he is not overfond of reading other people's notes. That makes him quite unique among us!)

As you know, the most pressing challenge was determining how to bring everyone back safely. If we construct an additional Structure that we can carry with us, we could set it up on the other side and depart in that way. After all, the original Structure was able to transport something as large as E. and Henerey's depth-craft. I do not know whether the crystal-smelting will be successful, nor how long it will take until we are satisfied that our new Entry is safe for use, but Vyerin and I shall not stop until we exhaust all possibilities.

And sooner than you can imagine, my dear Sophy, I shall hold on to you and strive very diligently never to let go again.

Until then (soon, I suspect!),

Niea

P.S. I hate that I feel compelled to add this paranoid postscript, but after typing my hopeful conclusion, my head continues to swim with concerns. I think we all assumed that Chancellor Rawsel's hatred of the Entries and Envoys was merely based on a personal vendetta against the Fleet. That is not incorrect, as it turns out. Still, as I believe I wrote earlier, I cannot shake the belief that he is truly afraid of those mysteries we seek. Especially the Envoy.

I am reluctant to trust Chancellor Rawsel, and I know Tevn's mysterious friend has been nothing but helpful (she did try to warn us, after all, when the underwater room collapsed into sound at the end of our mission). Yet what if there is danger? What if your mission has taken you dangerously close to it?

And, most troublingly, what if this nebulous, undefined danger finds you before I can?

EXCERPT FROM THE RESEARCH NOTES OF JEIME ALESTARRE, 1004

Construction, Day the First:

As the above header proclaims so ambitiously, our project has entered its final stage at last. Following is a summary of today's preparatory activities:

- All necessary materials have been acquired. We determined previously (see Analysis, Day the Third) that the Entry's exterior was crafted from the variety of Antepelagic stone informally known as "primordial serpentine". V. leveraged his captain's connections to locate a purveyor of antique rubble, who proved more than happy to assist – for a price. (Their currency of choice turned out to be rare books from N.'s collection.) Our struggle to identify the decidedly non-oceanic metal that lines the Entry's interior (see Analysis, Day the Fifth) reached a satisfying conclusion today as well. That same rubble-dealer (really, a Scholar of Life with a peculiarly entrepreneurial spirit) glanced at a sample of the interior and declared it to be sky-silver, an alloy formed from meteoric substances that were far more prevalent in the days before the Dive. We now possess several sizeable shards of the coveted metal, acquired at the low cost of additional tomes from the Cidnorghe library.

- A. asked if he could craft the new Structure in a design of his own making. We concluded that he ought to copy the original to keep the variables as consistent as possible. He grumbled but accepted his fate, as he is wont to do. Thereafter, A. produced several mock-ups – sketches, clay statuettes, even a driftwood carving – of his replica for our approval. I believe even V. was impressed by the quality of A.'s creations.

Construction, Day the Second:

- Smelting proved successful. This morning, A. brought in his "portable" furnace – "the sort one employs for impromptu glassblowing, you know" – and the two of us settled before the flames in our protective aprons and spectacles. To our great surprise, the crystal core liquified almost instantly at a moderate temperature. A. lovingly funnelled the molten material into the moulds he'd designed, and nearly leaped into the air with delight when he opened them to reveal a pair of perfectly formed casings.
- This feels rather inappropriate to include in my research notes, but I must admit (for Ami's sake, if no one else's) that this enterprise has given me a new-found respect for her son. A. jumped into this project with unbelievable enthusiasm. He was an eager colleague during our Analysis phase – always happy to offer a new sketch or design, even as I lambasted every one of his previous attempts – but the Construction phase seems especially suited to his particular talents. I do think his sisters and parents would feel proud of him: as I, rather improbably, do.
- Update to the above: I'm afraid he accidentally set his sleeves aflame in the furnace while I wrote the previous note.

Construction, Day the Third:

- Thanks to yesterday's efforts, we are now in possession of two identical crystal casings. With the aid of a delicate specimen transportation tube, N. divided the Isopods into two groups that now occupy separate spheres ("Sphere A" and "Sphere B"). N. observed that Sphere A glows more brightly, despite containing slightly fewer plankton, and wondered if their ability to produce more light in smaller numbers is some sort of protective adaption. V. wondered if Sphere A's plankton were simply more antisocial.

- A. began carving the rubble for the replica today, starting with the head. He spent hours gazing in silence at the sculpted face of the Entry before he dared pick up his tools. I do not know why his artistic process required him to press his forehead against the forehead of the sculpture, as though they were moments away from sharing a kiss – but I am begrudgingly glad it did. For, in doing so, A. made a remarkable discovery. In the head of the statue is a small glass phial of water – seawater, to be precise. We do not know what this means but will continue to investigate. I have a hypothesis and may need to sleep on it first. (I have not slept in some days. Nor has N., despite V.'s firm insistence that she rest. A., somehow, always manages to collapse comfortably on the very floor of the storehouse and does not stir until morning.)

- In case I forget in my weariness: let this note be a reminder to tell Min how baffled A. was when he learned the two of us have remained betrothed for nearly two years now. "Do you truly never intend to wed?" he gasped. I told him we did not – that M. simply enjoys the word "fiancée" – and enjoys wearing a fine betrothal brooch, besides. (How I miss that *fiancée* of mine. I do not, however, require a note to remind me of that.)

Construction, Day the Fourth:

Several of the following observations could be categorised under the third or fourth days of construction, since much occurred during those odd hours that mark the transition from one day to the next:

- N. and I did not, in fact, rest. V. went home to his family, and we passed the night on the storehouse floor (our environment enlivened by A.'s snores) to discuss all we had learned. Thanks to a late-night revelation, we arose in the morning feeling ready to test our replacement Entry for the first time. In forming a hypothesis yesterday evening, N. and I thought back to another significant question with which we have grappled. Even if we make our own Structure to carry people home, how will it know where to carry them? When we found the phial, ideas blossomed. Somehow – and I will be the first to admit that I cannot begin to wrap my head around it – the creatures seem able to distinguish between water from different places (???), and that is how the energy is directed. (N. argued that this is not entirely unprecedented in the natural world. There are some forms of migratory plankton, she said, that travel in great purple waves in search of seawater with familiar levels of salinity and acidity – which draws them to the same geographic locations year after year, across the generations. I appreciate her perspective, but the apparent serendipity of it all still frustrates me.)
- Consequently, we conducted experiments. As none of us wished to test the process personally, we enlisted the assistance of a diving automaton from N.'s collection. V. and N. sailed a few fathoms offshore into a protected cove, where they collected a small sample of water. Upon their return, we placed the water into the chamber, and prepared the automaton for the journey. When its hand was placed upon the hand of the Entry, the automaton vanished, and we took up a raucous and excited cry.

259

Then all of us (save the Chancellor, fortunately, who felt tired, and his retainer, who seemed disappointed to be excluded) returned to the cove, where we found that blessed automaton washed ashore. The process was repeated until we felt satisfied with the safety of both Entries: the reassembled original and A.'s replica.

- But I am continuing to write – despite the late hour, when even N. has returned to V.'s house for much-needed rest – because I, myself, am not satisfied. Everything feels too . . . tidy, I suppose. We have spent tides toying and trifling with Antepelagic technology we cannot fully understand. The Entries should have been wildly complex and impossible to replicate. The greatest wonders of our society – depth-crafts, Automatic Post machines, Echolators, underwater habitations – all of them are intricately crafted from thousands of tiny components that an amateur mechanic could render useless with one wrong move. Meanwhile, these devices that can *send people through worlds* are nothing more than hollow sculptures filled with water phials and apparently invincible plankton. How could that be?

- Our twin Entries stare at me from across the storehouse as I write. Their sculpted expressions reveal nothing. How Ami would laugh to see me now! Here I am, faced with incontrovertible evidence of the hidden world she believed in, and I remain nothing but sceptical. I suppose that is simply my nature. I will not apologise for it, but I do not wish to let it diminish our accomplishments, either.

- We have, after all, accomplished exactly what we set out to do. As soon as we send a few more automata through to make sure our earlier successes were not simply good luck, N. and V. may be ready to start the final part of this journey. Though it is foolish and sentimental, I imagine Ami's kind regard upon me as I help reunite her children.

- (And, while I am being foolish and sentimental, let me also note

260

that I hope she would not judge me for declining to join them on their journey. It is too painful to consider seeing the world that I refused to believe existed. Yet I expect she would be pleased beyond measure by my role in facilitating the Cidnosin siblings' own independent voyages of discovery.)

AUTOMATED POST MISSIVE FROM VYERIN CLEL TO HENEREY CLEL AND SOPHY CIDNORGHE, 1004

Dear H. and S., two of our dearest people,

Niea and I are on our way. Unfortunately, so is Chancellor Rawsel. I am sorry, Henerey.

Our party will consist of us three alone. We have conducted every possible test, but we still fear something may go wrong. Thus, Jeime will stay behind to seek a solution if the Third Entry fails.

Arvist will stay, too. To my surprise, he confessed he could not stomach being away from his wife and child for much longer and, consequently, must retreat homeward for a time. He did promise to return immediately to lend Jeime his fabrication skills if they are forced to create another Entry. Arvist declared that he looks forward to seeing E. when we all return. I hope Sophy will feel heartened rather than disappointed when she learns that he is immensely regretful about this. (He even managed to convince *me* of his sincerity.)

I said short farewells to my family and urged Reiv to use the A.P. as often as he needs, *if* we become stuck. If all goes according to plan, we will only be with you for a short while before bearing everyone back to where we belong.

We shall see you soon. Niea sends her love as well (the vast majority of it for Sophy, I am sure).

P.S. Henerey, I'm not ignoring your letter. It only appeared this morning – the time delay is the most baffling thing. Why don't we plan to talk through everything in person?

AUTOMATED POST MISSIVE FROM THE THIRTIETH SECOND SCHOLAR TO LADY CORALEAN, 1005

Dear L.,

Or shall I now call you by your full name, dear Lady?

It appears I am not the only one of us who appears in these documents. Do you still make a habit of captaining artificial whales? And is your employer truly that awful man? (I met him only once, but I suppose you'll read about that soon enough.)

Enclosed you have no doubt already found what I promised you – absolutely everything from your files. Now it is time for you to send what remains of mine. Then this entire communication shall end at last.

The files you currently possess happen to be the most valuable of everything. I expect them immediately.

30.ii

P.S. Please?

P.P.S. I was very proud of my firm tone, but then I had to go and ruin it! Won't you kindly disregard that postscript?

AUTOMATED POST MISSIVE FROM LADY CORALEAN TO THE THIRTIETH SECOND SCHOLAR, 1005

Dear 30,

I am strangely flattered (but not surprised) that you noticed my appearances in Niea's letters. Piloting an artificial whale is an intense technical challenge!

I'm afraid my list of active clients is completely confidential. Let me simply say that my current employer is not an "awful" man. A middling one, at worst. To his credit, he is driven by that noblest of all motivations – familial loyalty. (I say "noblest of all motivations" simply because that is the general understanding given unto me by society, not because of any particular experience with such things on my own part.) That is a far cry from my previous clients. Besides, even if his motivations were less decent, I am here to procure documents, not pass judgment.

In this case, I am also here to bestow documents upon you, apparently. Never fear. If I were to play you false, you might stop writing to me. If our communication ceases, how will I know what schemes you might plan next? (At present, I can study your letters to see what secrets your handwriting reveals about your current state of mind. It has been a rough day, hasn't it? Why don't you take it easy tonight?)

That is all to say that I shall continue as planned with no betrayal. (I hope that does not disappoint you overmuch.)

Earnestly (by my standards, anyway),

L.

AUTOMATED POST MISSIVE FROM THE THIRTIETH SECOND SCHOLAR TO LADY CORALEAN, 1005

L.

All I shall say is that despite the changes brought about by the appointment of Ambassador Mawr, I do find our society dispiritingly rigid at times. I'm sure you will discern the specifics of my frustrations through further analysis of my penmanship, so I need not provide additional details.

I will be grateful for your continued cooperation – or as grateful as anyone can be to the person who caused them so much trouble in the first place.

(We do not tend to "take it easy" here, though I shall try, just for you!)

"30"

Chapter 17

LETTER FROM SOPHY CIDNORGHE TO E. CIDNOSIN, 1004

Dear E.,

I must admit that this feels very artificial. Please humour me by reading my letter in its entirety before you dismiss it! Your own true love himself suggested I might find success in writing to you, and I thought it was worth a try.

Before I say anything more, I need to make a confession. Vyerin and I read your letters, yours and Henerey's and anyone else's we could find, to obtain a sense of closure in our grief. In the end, though, what we discovered gave us a glimmer of hope – that you might still be alive! – and so the nature of our mission changed. I did not like the idea of reading your letters. But I would not change my decision for the world, because, firstly, it enabled us to reunite, and secondly, it allowed me to understand you anew.

In your letters, you were as clever, eccentric and delightful as I knew you to be, but you were also confident, inquisitive and self-assured. Now that I am here, I find myself almost intimidated by you! You adapted skilfully to your new life, and I do not know that there is a place for me within it.

I told you I felt little grief for the Deep House because I was too busy grieving you. That is not entirely true. In a way, I have you and our home impossibly intertwined in my mind. I dreamed about the both of you frequently. I still do.

I am not prone to cataloguing, checking, or monitoring things as you are, but there are so many details of the Deep House I remember clearly. I know exactly how many panes of glass Father set into the lower lunette over the front window; I can recall all the times as a child when I occupied myself with counting them, because I was rather overtired of whatever you and Arvist were chattering about! I am exceptionally well acquainted with the texture of the tiny bit of carpet behind the bookshelf on the left side of the library, because once I kissed Seliara there and then fixed my eyes on the floor as she said she thought of me only as her friend. I can summon a full and complete sensory impression of sitting with you in the parlour as your voice echoed through our dear halls, which modulated your tone more dramatically than anyone else's. Before I told you the terrible news, I stitched together all these inconsequential memories to imagine what our lives would be like if the Deep House had not been reduced to driftwood.

When I arrived and you started talking about the algae as if everything were normal, I wished so desperately to delay the inevitable. I wanted to dive into a way of being with you in which we understood each other perfectly. I thought that would be easy, because, well, I had read your most private thoughts and correspondence! How could I not know exactly what to say?

I feel I understand the E. of the past, but know very little of you now. If the Deep House is gone, do you wish to go "home" at all? You do not need to answer immediately, as I imagine it will be some time before Niea and Vyerin manage to create an Entry. In the meantime, I don't suppose we could take this opportunity to become better acquainted again?

I miss you terribly, though you are right here.

Sophy

LETTER FROM E. CIDNOSIN TO SOPHY CIDNORGHE, 1004

Dear Sophy,

Because I just placed this letter under your door, I presume you may feel tempted to simply seek me out instead of reading further. Resist that urge, for my sake! If you find yourself so accustomed to understanding me through my letters, surely you would not say no to the opportunity to read one more?

I do not fully remember what occurred at the end of our last conversation, when my physical sensations overwhelmed me so thoroughly. I am faring a little better now. The loss of the Deep House still feels like something from which I will never recover. I can acknowledge that feeling and how real it seems while also accepting that life must continue. Sometimes I wonder if I am in denial – after all, I have not seen evidence of the Deep House's destruction with my own eyes. Yet I do prefer simple mourning to battling against my Brain.

I cannot fault you for reading my letters. Granted, before I "died", I would have been horrified by the idea of someone accessing my personal correspondence. I might have even been a little cross if you simply told me this outright when we reunited. I can say now that your letter changed my opinion. If studying my silly words brought you comfort, I could never truly disapprove. (How shocked you must have been by the unsubtle flirtations between myself and a certain correspondent!)

The one thing I shall chide you for, Sophy, is assuming that my letters jointly create an authentic portrait of my true self. Please remember that those letters are but written manifestations of my feelings as I expressed them in certain contexts! I am quite familiar with that distinction by this point. Henerey and I have spent a great deal of time getting to know the similarities and differences between our "true" selves and the versions we communicated to each other in the earlier stages of our courtship. I loved the Henerey Clel who wrote to me, but I find my relationship with his real-world counterpart far more fulfilling and marvellous.

You needn't chastise yourself for not knowing what to say or do. While I am the same person who wrote those letters, I understand why you struggle to recognise me now. Sometimes, I can hardly recognise myself – and I mean that in the best of ways. Can you comprehend how free I've felt, existing in a world where I may go places and try new things without interacting with others? I am no less susceptible to the whims of my Brain, but I would like to think I am better at finding creative solutions to help me live on my own terms.

The truth is, dear Sophy, that while I have not been cured of my mental travails by some deep-water magic, you need no longer worry so much about taking care of me. Bittersweet though that is, I suspect you secretly feel such relief now that I've said it. You are my younger sister, and it is not your responsibility to be my sole protector and confidante. While I could hardly have survived the dark years of my young adulthood without your support – and I will always be grateful for your compassion and understanding – we cannot always be two odd young women looking out for each other in the Deep House's isolation. You are married now, and I – I have found someone who not only cares for me with fierce kindness but also turns to me in his own times of need. I never thought that someone like me, who can hardly help herself at the best of times, could provide comfort to another.

That is not to say that I do not need you, because I do, and only you can understand the grief we will carry with us for the rest of our lives. (Well, only you and Arvist, technically. I imagine he was equally distraught to see the Deep House disappear!)

With that in mind – shall we talk about it?

E.

OFFICIAL RECORD BY THE THIRTIETH SECOND SCHOLAR, 1004

By my Oaths as a Scholar, I promise to report all details from my various conversations today that the Fifteenth First Scholar deems I am authorised to document.

It has been some time since I enjoyed the opportunity to record a moment of historic importance. When Scholar Cidnorghe and Scholar Mawr arrived, I played such a brief role in the proceedings that my reports were dismissed as "negligible". (That is saying something, considering the many matters we do not find negligible!) Yet, in confidence, the Fifteenth First Scholar advised me to monitor our new Visitors in a more surreptitious manner – in case they needed anything and were too shy to ask for help, I suppose! I aspire to emulate the Fifteenth First Scholar's hospitality and empathy! Consequently, I semi-regularly bring myself to the part of the Visitors' Quarters where they set up their extraordinary letter-writing machine.

When I arrived there today, the sound of spirited voices indicated that our Visitors were already present. Because I felt it only fair to interrupt during a natural break in conversation, I pressed my face to the door and awaited my moment.

"Vyerin – here?" It was easy to identify this exuberantly awed tone as belonging to Scholar Clel. "Sophy, I cannot thank you enough."

"I am afraid it is not entirely good news," said Scholar Cidnorghe. I might have struggled to distinguish her voice from Scholar Cidnosin's, but Scholar Cidnorghe speaks more loudly and slowly. "Here, Henerey, read it yourself – it's addressed to both of us, after all."

As a suspicious silence ensued shortly afterwards, I could not help but peer through a slightly less opaque panel in the door. The blurry figure of Scholar Clel stood surprisingly still, with a letter clutched tightly in his hand.

"I certainly did not expect *him* to accompany them," Scholar Clel said. "What an unexpected surprise."

Scholar Cidnosin, peering over her companion's shoulder, took his hand with such self-assuredness that I assumed her action must be exceptionally significant (and therefore worth recording).

"You needn't see the Chancellor if you don't wish to," she murmured at a volume that made me squeeze my ear still more uncomfortably against the glass!

"I am quite sure that nobody here ever wishes to see Chancellor Rawsel again," said Scholar Cidnorghe. "But he may well be the least of our worries. I am more concerned about Niea and Vyerin's safety."

"Because of the temporal difference?" said Scholar Mawr. Despite the heightened energy of the general conversation, Scholar Mawr maintained a steady voice that is very much in keeping with the tones required by our Oaths!

"O, I see," replied Scholar Clel, more urgently. "We received this letter today, but for all we know, Vyerin and Niea sent it tides ago. They could have been floating around for ages!"

"They are aware of the delay, so they may have planned accordingly," Scholar Cidnorghe reassured him. "Perhaps they brought a depth-craft, as you and E. did. Still, the ocean out there is difficult to navigate. We must seek them immediately."

"Hello!" I said, feeling proud of myself for choosing the most socially appropriate moment to enter. "I was just about to take a turn about the city in *Ieneros*. Would anyone care to join me?"

"Thirtieth Second Scholar!" exclaimed Scholar Clel. "How fortuitous! You see, two more of our companions – plus a third – made the crossing. Could you possibly assist?"

"I assume so, since you have been standing outside the door for several minutes listening to our conversation," said Scholar Mawr.

Scholar Cidnorghe gave him an incredulous glance.

"I am very attentive to changes in our environment, and I saw the shadow cast against the door!" he protested. "It is no great feat. Any one of you could have noticed."

"I did," said Scholar Cidnosin. "I am relieved you were the one eavesdropping, Thirtieth Second Scholar, and not some malicious stranger, as I feared."

"Despite the circumstances of my arrival, I am here to help," I continued. "We shall find your companions as speedily as possible."

"I presume Tevn and my sister will join you," said Scholar Cidnosin. "If it is quite all right, I would prefer to stay behind. I fear that being confined in *Ieneros* with so many people would be too much for me."

After saying her part, Scholar Cidnosin turned to Scholar Clel and placed her hand on his shoulder.

"But what about you, Henerey? If having me there would help you in even the smallest of ways, I shall brave the journey. I recall you once writing to me that you would rather swim with all the predators of the ocean than—"

"—brave one hour in a depth-craft with the Chancellor. Yes, that was no exaggeration. Unfortunately, I doubt all the predators of the ocean would assist me in finding Vyerin," he said. "I fear there is no choice – if my brother is out there, I must venture onto a depth-craft once more, regardless of its occupants. Perhaps I will find depth-crafts perfectly homelike after living underwater for all this time! But you needn't accompany me, dear E. I would prefer knowing you are safe here."

Some expressions and gestures were exchanged between them that I struggled to interpret – though I did notice Scholar Cidnorghe watching the pair intently as well.

"Shall we go?" I asked, and an immediate chorus of assent was all the confirmation I needed. I bid farewell to Scholar Cidnosin, who asked Scholar Clel to hang back for a few moments more. Once he caught up to us in the Visitors' Quarters hallway, I overheard Scholar Cidnorghe questioning him.

"Were you wearing that necklace earlier, or did you acquire it recently?" she asked.

"You are correct in assuming the latter – o, perhaps it's because you recognised it? It is your sister's."

271

"A token of affection," said Scholar Cidnorghe. "How fanciful."

"It is more than that," he replied. "When we first arrived, E. gave me this necklace to distract me from an unpleasant attack of the nerves. I hope it shall lend me strength in her absence."

"You had an attack of the nerves, and my sister was the one who comforted you?"

"Is that so surprising?"

"Not truly, I suppose," answered Scholar Cidnosin. "But it is lovely."

It is fortunate that we were interrupted soon after, because who knows what other "personal opinions" I might have been forced to record in response to that?

We had just made our way to the docks when we encountered the Fifteenth First Scholar. I greeted her as is customary and appropriate, and she asked what occupied us.

"There are two more Imperilled who may require our assistance!" I told her. "Scholar Clel's brother is one of them! Isn't it wonderful?"

"Do you not think that the Twenty-Ninth Second Scholar seems a little restless today?" inquired the Fifteenth First Scholar in reply. "Perhaps you might leave this mission in his capable hands. I require your assistance, Thirtieth Second Scholar."

"So much the better for you!" I said to the Visitors, hiding my own disappointment. "The Twenty-Ninth Second Scholar can execute a full turn in *Ieneros* much more gracefully than I."

After I waved them off, the Fifteenth First Scholar gestured towards a small bench some distance from the path. We sat in silence until I could endure it no longer.

"Is something the matter?" I asked. "I am happy to provide any aid I can."

"That is reassuring," responded the Fifteenth First Scholar. "The matter is this. New Visitors are arriving with increasing frequency. While I am relieved to see them brought to safety, I worry that perhaps these particular people may endanger themselves without realising it."

"What do you mean?" I asked. "What danger could they encounter here?"

To my surprise, the Fifteenth First Scholar fell silent again. This time, however, I resisted the urge to interrupt until she had a chance to gather her thoughts.

"I know it has been an age since you completed your initial training," she said, "but you do remember the Burden of the First Scholars?"

"How could I have forgotten?"

She nodded at me, so I dutifully brought the old creed back into my working memory. "The First Scholars enjoy the honour of authority and bear the burden of secrecy. The Second Scholars provide the gift of support and receive the boon of protection."

"Just so. You will understand, then, that I cannot tell you what I fear. You will have to consent to assisting me without knowing my aims. Is that acceptable?"

"Undoubtedly," I said. "What would you have me do?"

"It is simple, really," she replied. Then she glanced at me with sudden horror. "Have you been taking notes?"

"Why, of course. How could I engage in any conversation without recording it appropriately?"

"Your commitment to your Oaths is admirable," the Fifteenth First Scholar said, more gently. "Yet there are some matters – those related to our Burden – that are too dangerous to write down. It is imperative that you drop your stylus and give me the record for safe-keeping."

So I shall stop here, I suppose. (And when you read this, Fifteenth First Scholar, please note that I did not intend to offend. I am eager to help you protect our Imperilled Visitors – I shall spare no effort!)

Though you may never read this annotation, I thought I ought to record that I value your enthusiasm more than you know. – 15.i

AUTOMATED POST MISSIVE FROM VYERIN CLEL TO REIV CLEL, 1004

Hello there, dear old Reiv,

Don't keep my supper warm. I've been delayed. Nothing is wrong, but after splashing about in that depth-craft longer than any of us would have liked (in the company of a certain unnamed ex-Chancellor, to make matters worse), Niea and I require a bit of rest before we make the return journey. Her idea of sending the A.P. message to Henerey and Sophy several days before we left was clever, but that intentional pause was not quite enough to make up for the unsettling difference in time between this world and our own. We spent nearly a full day awaiting rescue. I presume you did not worry. You know nothing short of a calamity can take me down.

Well, Henerey is alive! Perhaps I should have said that first. He is in fine form. In fact, I have never seen him happier or healthier, and he only appeared more at ease when we debarked their monstrous excuse for a vessel and returned to dry land.

You'll be proud that it was I, not my brother, who suggested retreating to somewhere private for a chat. (I am sure you do not need prompting to imagine the appropriately stoic tears rolling down my face as Henerey and I had our first proper conversation.)

I forgot so many small things about him. How he takes a deep, anxious gasp between phrases when he speaks about something at length, because he's so eager to get the words out that he forgets to breathe. That little look of earnest and vulnerable inquiry he makes to determine if his listener is still paying attention, which he has done since he was a boy. I enjoyed reading my brother's letters last year, but I would have flung them all into the sea in exchange for this single conversation with him.

At any rate, he showed me the little place where he and E. reside and told me a bit about their life there. (That was after he apologised approximately forty times for leaving without telling me anything.)

Here's the funny thing, Reiv – though he hasn't said as much, I don't think the poor fellow wants to come back with us. Especially now that the Deep House is gone. I suspect the appearance of Henerey's old tormentor, Chancellor Rawsel, also highlighted all the reasons why he does not wish to return permanently.

I should not say that. Henerey does wish to return, but I am the only reason why. (Besides all the creatures of the air and sea, which he desperately misses observing. O, and our parents. Third on the list, I presume.) I suggested to him – rather against my better judgement – that perhaps, if our cobbled-together Entry proves resilient, there might be a way for him to move between the two worlds regularly, so he could visit our family and live the life he desires. My greatest wish has always been for Henerey to find the place that is right for him, which was something he rather struggled to accomplish in the past. Even if these Entries do not support long-term travel and I end up losing my brother to this place, it will be different this time. I shall know, from the beginning, that he is not dead but rather as close to contentment as one can be.

That is, needless to say, assuming that E. also consents to staying here. He will not do anything without her. O, yes, I suppose that is worth mentioning – I have met my brother's fabled partner at last. E. spoke little but observed me with fervent curiosity. There is a kind of severe beauty to her. She reminds me of a haunted portrait, which I mean in a complimentary way. Yet there's nothing severe or ghostly about her aspect when she looks at Henerey, so she secured my approval.

Sending hugs to A. and O. and a separate batch for you,

V.

Chapter 18

OFFICIAL RECORD BY THE FIFTEENTH FIRST SCHOLAR, 1004

By my Oaths as a Scholar, I pledge to record all recent developments of note – even those which reveal my own errors.

Let us start with an uncomfortable truth, then. Our Visitors made a fatal mistake, but the greater part of the responsibility is mine. I ought to have noticed sooner.

After a thousand years of isolation, should it not have alarmed us when a total of seven Imperilled people made the crossing to our city in but a few months? When I heard that a third group arrived yesterday, I grew concerned at last. I had to act. I risked exposing my apprentice to the First Scholars' Burden in my desperation to keep the Visitors in check. I tasked the Thirtieth Second Scholar with monitoring the new arrivals' activities, but my apprentice did not initially understand the grave importance of this responsibility. At the very least, today the Thirtieth Second Scholar fulfilled their duties to the letter by informing me about a confrontation unfolding in the Visitors' Quarters. I am proud of their initiative, but I fear it is still too late.

We concluded long ago that the Predator could return at any moment, which is why we must remain vigilant. This morning, I awakened to a primal panic that I had not experienced in a millennium.

The body does not forget that fear he brings. Like a startled animal, I felt a drive to run and hide.

When I last experienced such an urge, I was in my summertime quarters in a garden on the Fifth Islet that I loved well. I remember, even now, every sound and sensation of opening the door to the pavilion and creeping down its spiralling stair – though there is no logical reason for me to retain these details. Waking there, I would linger between sleep and alertness, hearing the birds call to their lovers as I lay with my own.

O, colleagues. I do apologise.

I fear my time with the Thirtieth Second Scholar has corrupted my prose. I did not intend to reminisce about days gone by, when we were all of us innocent enough to waste mental energy upon frivolities. I only mentioned the memory to demonstrate how familiar I am with this feeling and what it portends. I suppose it is fitting, however, that I felt compelled to recall the man I have not seen in a thousand years: for what happened on that particular morning ultimately augured the end of our partnership. While we both felt the inescapable fear, he rejected it and I did not.

Our research into the matter suggests we may be last to know when the Predator is on his way. Our fellow creatures sense it much sooner. Most of them cannot understand the source of their fear, yet it causes them to behave erratically. It is only when the danger grows closest that we start to dread it, too. We may be safe from the Predator in our great sanctuary, but I have long hypothesised that some of us – like myself – might be subconsciously primed to recognise when he takes up his prowl once more.

Especially if his intended prey is the planet we once called home.

Upon identifying my fear this morning, I proceeded immediately to the library in search of my apprentice. As I walked, I started to wonder if I had frightened myself over nothing. Yet after I nearly crashed into the Thirtieth Second Scholar, who was moving at quite an irrational pace in the opposite direction, I soon confirmed that my instincts were correct.

"Good morning, Fifteenth First Scholar!" they said after we detangled our respective robes. "I believe I just witnessed—"

"In here," I said, drawing them into a nearby vestibule. That proved a prudent decision, because the Thirtieth Second Scholar began speaking loudly and animatedly as soon as we were concealed.

"I do not know if this qualifies as the information about the Visitors that you seek, and I question whether I perceived the situation correctly at all."

"What did you see, Scholar?"

"You will think me without reason," the Thirtieth Second Scholar murmured.

"One can experience something unreasonable and still describe it reasonably."

"Then I shall try!" They did sound slightly more resolute. "In short, I believe this third group of visitors transported a Sculpted Saviour here."

"I assume you chose those words intentionally, and that you do not simply mean they were transported here through a Sculpted Saviour."

"I warned you that it would seem unbelievable! They call it an 'Entry', as Scholar Clel and Scholar Cidnosin mistakenly do, but it is undoubtedly a Saviour. At least, according to the texts I've read, it certainly resembles one. I was too young to have seen any myself."

"I believe you," I said, somewhat relieved. The Visitors must have brought a Saviour because they believed it would allow them to return home. Still, they could not possibly understand how the device works. The Predator would not care about the Imperilled learning how to carry something from one place to another.

What, then, of my fear?

"You did well. I am grateful you shared this with me."

As I spoke, I detected a glimmer of pride across the Thirtieth Second Scholar's features. I resisted the urge to mention that such emotions are not entirely in accordance with our Oaths.

"We must go now," I continued. "I am eager to understand these aberrant happenings."

I did not engage the Thirtieth Second Scholar in conversation as we wound our way through the corridors. My thoughts kept returning to the Predator, and the speed of my step increased apace.

And my feet were wise to carry me more swiftly. For when we arrived and I glimpsed the scene before me, I realised in a sick instant that all I feared would come to pass, and I would be helpless to stop it.

There was indeed a Sculpted Saviour in the centre of the room. It appeared to be No. 3, "The Belligerent Dreamer". When I looked closer, however, I discerned several oddities. This was not a statue carved a thousand years ago. It was, somehow, a copy, fabricated by a masterful artist to match our own work. Truly, the Imperilled accomplished a wondrous feat, and I confess I am impressed by their ingenuity.

If only it would not spell the end for their people.

"I shall fight with you no longer!" exclaimed one of the new Visitors. "Seeing this treacherous city only confirmed my concerns. All evidence of the Entries must be destroyed as swiftly as possible."

"No one is fighting with you," replied another man, whom I took by appearance to be Scholar Clel's brother. "You demanded to come along. How were we to know that you wouldn't last a day here?"

Before he could respond, Scholar Cidnosin seemed to notice me – or worked up the courage to announce to the rest of the room that she had noticed me. She tapped Scholar Clel's shoulder, and he turned to greet me with a smile.

"Good morning, Fifteenth First Scholar!" he said. "You haven't yet met my brother Vyerin, have you?"

"What was that? Are you saying one of them is finally here?" interrupted the furious Visitor, turning to me.

"You have no idea what chaos you cause with your poems and portals," he raged. He paused to catch his breath, then continued his tirade before I could provide clarifying information about said danger (and deny any involvement in this wretched poetry business).

"Do you know what would happen if word spread that our world was threatened by some unidentifiable danger? And that everyone must abandon their lives and travel through unstable machinery to escape it? Academia as we understand it would crash to a halt. Progress would become a thing of the past. Society would crumble. Can you imagine how people would lose themselves to needless panic – and because of what? The superstitions of some underwater recluses?"

In keeping with my Vows, I ought to mention how I froze at his words.

I did not know this man. I had never seen him before, and, quite frankly, had no particular desire to encounter him again. The substance of his words, however, haunted me. I am obliged to say that this was not the first time such an argument had been directed at me.

"Since I left the Fleet, it has been my objective to find this place and persuade you to see reason," concluded the Visitor – conveniently unaware of my plight. "I hope you believe me when I say I will do whatever it takes to ensure that no one besides this lot hears about your city. If, by some slim chance, your fictional danger is real, then our society shall face our fate bravely when it comes – as we should."

"You say *bravely*, Chancellor, when I believe *obliviously* would be more appropriate."

I did not recognise this second speaker, either. She sported both an impractically gauzy pink garment and a fiercely stern expression – and held tightly to the hand of Scholar Sophy Cidnorghe.

"Use whatever word you like, Eliniea. I certainly haven't the time to care. Now that you and Captain Clel have confirmed, once and for all, that these Entries *can* function, I shall be able to continue seeking their destruction with abandon. Farewell for now."

"You break our hearts, truly," said Scholar Vyerin Clel as the man grasped the arm of the Belligerent Dreamer and vanished before our eyes.

The room seemed to breathe a collective sigh of relief that I could not share.

"Apologies about that, Scholars," said Scholar Clel to me and my apprentice in a wan voice. "That man is no friend of ours, and I am already worn from spending a short spell in his company."

"What have you done?" I said, ignoring Scholar Clel entirely and addressing Scholar Cidnosin's sister and Scholar Clel's brother.

Scholar Cidnosin and Scholar Clel exchanged a nervous glance, but it was Scholar Sophy Cidnorghe who spoke.

"You are the Fifteenth First Scholar, are you not?" she asked. "I believe we met at your council meeting. My wife, Niea—" She gestured to the woman beside her, who gave me a sweet smile. "She managed to reproduce one of your Entries. Isn't that marvellous?"

"It was a group effort," said Scholar Niea Cidnorghe. "We divided up the, er, planktonic core, if you will, in the original Entry, and developed a more stable version that can accommodate the creatures' growing population."

Against all reason, I found myself fascinated. It never occurred to me that the creatures might multiply over the years, making their energy much more concentrated. At present, however, that mattered little.

"Those isopods were native to the ponds and rivers of our home in the sky," I said. "It took us centuries to discover that their luminescence generates energy. Why do you think that was?"

"Because the isopods had so many natural predators that the population only rarely reached numbers sufficient to produce these effects?" said Scholar Clel with unabashed excitement.

"I did not expect you to give me a genuine answer," I said. "You are, in fact, correct. The light helps the isopods identify their fellows, so it is a helpful adaptation, but it also exposes them to danger. For that illumination draws the eyes of all that would prey upon them. That is what I must tell you – we are ourselves no larger than microplankton in this vast universe, and your discoveries are the luminescence that will bring forth the one who hunts us."

A nervous silence descended upon the group, which satisfied me. I was pleased to have impressed the significance of the Predator upon them.

"Pardon me?" asked Scholar Sophy Cidnorghe. "What precisely do you mean by 'the one who hunts us'? Are you being metaphorical?"

"It's like the Predator from the poem," said Scholar Vyerin Clel.

"Don't tell me that my untimely death forced you to appreciate Darbeni at last!" whispered Scholar Henerey Clel.

"Henerey and I reached that very same conclusion when you spoke with us privately, Fifteenth First Scholar," said Scholar Cidnosin. The intensity of her frown shamed me appropriately. "If there is some imposing monster out there, why didn't you simply say so when we asked?"

"It is rare for a Scholar to admit such a thing, but I made some errors, Scholar Cidnosin," I said. "When I found you and Scholar Clel in that place that I bid you forget, I panicked. I knew if I told you anything about what you saw there – or the Predator himself – you could be at risk. To keep you safe, I swore you to secrecy and spun a lovely tale of building an Entry. At the time, I felt confident that such a thing was impossible. Now the Predator approaches, and my efforts were for naught."

Scholar Cidnosin did not seem entirely settled by this explanation and pulled Scholar Clel away to partake in furious whispers.

"I think I'm still a little behind," said Scholar Vyerin Clel. "Do you mean to say that there is an actual Predator coming to attack our world – because we built a machine? Unbelievable!"

"If you will not believe me, I suppose I have but one choice," I said.

Assuming – correctly – that they would follow me, I turned and led the group into our greatest secret.

I know that you, Sixth First Scholar, may read this record later and wonder why I did not take more conservative action. Why not convene the Body of Scholars to discuss the matter when I found Scholar Clel and Scholar Cidnosin so near to our archives in the first place? Why would I bear the group there now without obtaining the necessary consensus from the First Scholars? Well, colleagues, there was simply no time.

Out of politeness, I did not listen as my guests cautiously admired the architectural aspects of the passageway that are all too familiar to me. Their general mood remained elevated (though Scholar Cidnosin and Scholar Clel lagged behind), and I did not say anything to dispirit them. Why should they not experience some wonder while they still could? Granted, these particular people would be safe from the Predator either way, but it would no doubt be most upsetting to have their world consumed. If they wanted to coo over the columns that lined the entrance, I would not stop them.

After descending through the lower hallway, we reached the deepest alcove. I helped myself to the diving equipment kept in place for the rare Scholar who visits. Both of the Scholars Cidnorghe were intrigued by the make and style of my suit, but I did not grant the wives any time to examine it. I simply dived.

As our records confirm that some thirty-eight years have passed since we last dared to visit our archives, I understand I am obligated to provide an update on their condition. Life flourishes apace in these waters. The floating rings that the Seventh First Scholar so ingeniously installed to lead us safely through the depths now house peculiar barnacles that shuddered on their trembling stalks as I swam by. A gleaming green fish widened its solitary eye at me, then vanished into the darkness. As I neared the very heart of the archives, where our oldest truths are catalogued, I noticed the surrounding vents were far more active than usual. The cloudy plumes of minerals that projected from these fissures made it twice as difficult for me to find our cache of waterproof chests, but I am pleased to report that all thirteen remain intact. The particular chest I sought was thick with purple algae, which I removed with my archivist's knife. I bore the chest to the surface and presented it to the Visitors.

"I shall give you an hour to read," I said firmly, ignoring how they all gaped at me. Perhaps it surprised them that archival materials could be stored in this manner, but that is no concern of mine. "When that time passes, we will determine a course of action."

It was Scholar Cidnosin who took the chest from me. Under her shaking fingers, I caught a glimpse of the chest's contents through the stained-glass observation window set into the lid. There it was, after all those years. That silvery stationery, no doubt still slightly scented with the noxious ink of an old-fashioned writing machine. That angular typeface he always used without fail – even in his very last letter to me.

Exaggeration is neither productive nor polite, so know that I am not exaggerating when I claim to remember every single word of the letters and documents our Visitors are about to read. At times, I wish I did not.

I will end my recording here – not because they said nothing afterwards, but because I have far more important tasks to complete. I shall see if by my reason I can predict with more accuracy when the Predator may come. We may have no choice but to collaborate with the Illogical Ones if we aim to save the Imperilled world. Such cooperation will not please most of you, dear colleagues, but I have not gotten this far by virtue of my ability to please.

Signed,

The Fifteenth First Scholar

Chapter 19

LETTER FROM INITIATE ELUVIAL TO INITIATE GREYLY, PENNED THE SIXTIETH DAY OF YEAR 3'1 (Sk.E) ON THE FIFTH ISLET OF THE UPWARD ARCHIPELAGO

Dear Initiate Greyly,

I suppose you never expected to receive a personal note from me, of all people. Certainly not after I trounced you so thoroughly for the *fifth* time in yesterday's theoretical debate. Would you feel more inclined to continue reading if I flattered you by saying that your closing arguments, at least, were inspired?

That's not entirely flattery. They were, after all, far superior to the arguments you made during our four previous debates.

If I can't appeal to your ego, allow me to appeal to your rebellious spirit. I'm writing to you – rather than any other learned person of my acquaintance – because it is my impression that you are less offended by rule-breaking (or, in this case, questions that delicately skirt around the notion of rule-breaking) than anyone else in our Coalition.

I know we are forbidden to speak of what we learned in our Initiation today. Please do not assume that I am violating this rule because I am ignorant. On the contrary, I have personally read all five hundred and eighty-three pages of *On the Sanctity of*

Cosmic Knowledge and could recite from memory any edict contained therein.

I understand that the very act of writing this letter is an affront to everything we've been taught. But I'm still writing it, Greyly, because I'm absolutely dying to talk to someone. What did you make of it – the great revelation newly imparted to us by our cherished Instructors? My mind spins.

Initiate Eluvial

LETTER FROM INITIATE GREYLY TO INITIATE ELUVIAL, PENNED THE SIXTIETH DAY OF YEAR 3'1 (Sk.E)

Well met, El. Where'd you find my address, anyway? I go out of my way to ensure that nobody knows Father and I live on the Third Islet. I fly over to the Fifth every morning for our lectures. It's awfully inconvenient, but I wouldn't trade the privacy and peacefulness of the Third for anything so cheap as convenience. There's nothing I value more than a little quiet. It takes something truly exceptional to draw me out of my solitude.

That's why I decided to reply to you. In case you wondered. What could be more intriguing than the model of a model student feeling so eager to chat about forbidden knowledge that she would deign to write to *me*?

You must be truly desperate. Consider me captivated.

For my part, I read only the first chapter of *On the Sanctity etc.* before giving up. Why couldn't they simply print "Learning can be *dangerous*!" on those five-hundred-plus pages and save us all the time?

So, yes, you thought correctly. I am not offended in the least by your all-consuming interest in what we just learned. It was a great deal to take in. I was quite excited for our Initiation, as a matter of fact. One hears such fascinating whispers about them. As a child, I fell prey to the seductive rumour that all new Initiates learn how to work proper enchantments – you know, like in *The Star Sailors* or . . . well, take your pick of all the modern epics based on legends from our Prior World ancestors. I fancied myself riding the very clouds themselves and taming the winds after I came of age. Or catching a falling star, befriending it, and soaring upon its back across the seas of that mysterious planet beneath us . . .

My father thought me a fool for believing all that. He doesn't think highly of the Body Esoteric. "You've dedicated your youth to them, and for what? They'll only share some useless, abstruse knowledge at that Initiation of yours." That's what he said to me over dinner last night. Perhaps I should have listened to him, but I sometimes find it impossible to determine whether he is telling the truth or simply expressing his own rage against the "Fickle Faithful". His term, not mine.

Curious as you are, you're probably wondering why a man such as my father would allow his only child to study with the Body Esoteric in the first place. Father may be a Planetary Empiricist – and a most outspoken one, at that – but my grandmother was an Esoteric Instructor of great renown. I joined the Body in her memory.

At any rate, I welcome your question, because I seek to ask it myself. Do our venerated Instructors truly expect us to accept that the universe is a literal ocean, rather than a collection of stars and planets and empty space? Where is its shore? What was the source of the water in the first place? Why have we not met others who sailed across it to find new worlds like ours?

Why bother teaching us false Astronomy in the first place?

I fear you expected me to provide a more intelligent answer. I am sorry to disappoint. I might, however, find myself more able to address the matter were we to discuss it in person. Despite your ungenerous views about the quality of my oration, I think of myself as a far better speaker than a writer.

There's a lovely fountain three paces from the southern landing

287

station on the Third Islet. A proper crowd of Scintillating Isopods inhabits the water and a gentle breeze usually shows up around sunset. I go there in the evenings to think. Perhaps you'll soar over and join me one night?

Grey

LETTER FROM INITIATE ELUVIAL TO INITIATE GREYLY, PENNED THE SEVENTY-FIRST DAY OF YEAR 3'1 (Sk.E)

Greyly,

"Lovely fountain" is a misleadingly romantic description of a crumbling stack of stones from which water occasionally spills. I flew past that ruin three times before realising it was the very landmark you'd mentioned. How fortunate that you happened to arrive moments later. I might have been circling the area all night until my very arms collapsed under the weight of my cloud-craft.

Despite your inability to provide accurate directions, I did very much enjoy our conversation. I cannot stop thinking about it, as a matter of fact. If you participated in academic debates as enthusiastically as you do in impromptu ones, I suspect I never would have beaten you once.

Philosophically speaking, I am entirely unlike you. I have not spent the better part of my life questioning the Esoteric values and methods of our great Instructors. For years, I've accepted everything they taught me without hesitation.

Yet there is something about this cosmic discovery that frustrates and fascinates me. Just as I said when we met, I am still consumed with the impractical desire to soar up through the atmosphere as far as I possibly can. How it would gladden my heart (and renew my faith) to touch a single drop of the water they say surrounds us! (More likely I would asphyxiate or fall to my death, alas.)

288

I won't go so far as your father and say that it's utter nonsense. (I felt too embarrassed to admit this to your face earlier, but – yes, I do know your father. Who doesn't know the Primary Planetarian? His insistence upon parading a crowd of Planetary Empiricists around the entrance to the Esoteric Halls, preaching Rationality in the face of Misguided Academia, is infamous.) But I want to learn more. I want proof. I want clarity. I could not be more elated that you feel the same.

Here's what I'd like to propose. You know the only way to truly learn more than your average Initiate is to become a fully vested Instructor. Obviously, only two people are selected from each Coalition to join the Instructor ranks – but we could be that very pair.

I've made it clear how highly I think of your curious mind. I can't imagine you feel the same about mine, especially considering all the ridiculous questions I asked you today, but I would like to imagine that the two of us could prepare decently enough as a team. What do you say?

Eluvial

LETTER FROM INITIATE GREYLY TO INITIATE ELUVIAL, PENNED THE SEVENTY-SECOND DAY OF YEAR 3'1 (Sk.E)

Dear El,

Thought you'd never ask. I do, by the way, think highly of your mind. Don't they always say that the surest sign of a quick mind is the ability to ask questions without shame? I also cannot help but admire your endless desire to explore this "ocean" of the cosmos. It is the same curiosity I feel whenever I gaze through the clouds at that strange world below us. The Instructors say it is barren, uninhabited, inhospitable. Still, I see those deep green seas reflecting the light and I cannot imagine that life does not thrive there. Even if it is not life as we understand it. I may not be a Planetary Empiricist myself, but sometimes I do understand why my father and his fellows wish so desperately to abandon our lofty academic retreat in the skies and focus upon the real world, so to speak.

Might we choose a different place to meet, though? I grow weary of my father's meddling. He asks me time and time again to reveal what we discussed in our Initiation. I am concerned he might take even more of an interest in my activities if he knew I was meeting with a fellow Initiate.

This time, you can pick the location. Just tell me where.

Grey

LETTER FROM INITIATE ELUVIAL TO INITIATE GREYLY, PENNED THE SEVENTY-SECOND DAY OF YEAR 3'1 (Sk.E)

Grey,

I attached a coordinate scan to this letter. In case the coordinates fail you – it's the pavilion in the back garden of my family's home on the Fifth.

It is also decidedly not a ruin.

Eluvial

LETTER FROM INITIATE GREYLY TO INSTRUCTOR ELUVIAL, PENNED THE FIFTH DAY OF YEAR 3'2 (Sk.E)

Hello, you.

Here's an unexpected letter for your enjoyment. I figured you'd find it nostalgic, under the circumstances.

I'm mostly just writing to congratulate you. Yes, we did promise to meet on the First Islet to view the announcement mosaic together, but I flew in early instead. I knew what I expected to see, and I wanted to surprise you with glad tidings.

Sure enough, there was your name – first on the list, spelled out in a beautiful array of silver tiles. And, right there next to you, was ...

Funny thing is that I can't even remember who it was.

Definitely wasn't me, though.

Really, I'm flattered. I suppose I could jokingly say that your success, at least, reflects the excellence of my tutoring skills.

Apologies. This is all nonsense. I truly did wish to congratulate you. I hope you and – whoever it was – will become fast friends as you ascend through the Instructors' ranks together. Rumour has it that your research focus for the next season will be isopods, of all things? If you ever need to examine some in the wild, you know I know a place ...

I can't say I have any more faith in the Instructors than I ever did, but I do hope you will keep asking them questions.

Yours,

Grey

LETTER FROM INSTRUCTOR ELUVIAL TO INITIATE GREYLY, PENNED THE SIXTH DAY OF YEAR 3'2 (Sk.E)

Grey,

I'm flabbergasted and nothing but sorry. It ought to have been you. I am quite convinced that it would have been you *and* me, were the Instructors not so ruled by their desire to keep everything just the way it is.

I will not stop asking questions, and I hope you will not either.

In fact, I have a new proposal for you. It is true that I have Ascended and will no longer see you in the Initiates' courses.

However, there is nothing to prevent me from speaking with you independently. If you ask me one question each day – only that which strikes your curiosity the most – I will see what I can learn on your behalf. (Even if it's just about isopods. Apparently an Instructor recently made a discovery about their bioluminescence functioning as an energy source – thrilling stuff.)

El

LETTER FROM INITIATE GREYLY TO INSTRUCTOR ELUVIAL, PENNED THE SIXTH DAY OF YEAR 3'2 (Sk.E)

El,

May I ask my questions from the comfort of your pavilion?
Starting tonight, perhaps?
(Two questions. Apologies. I'll make it up to you later, I promise.)

PUBLIC ANNOUNCEMENT BY THE PRIMARY PLANETARIAN, RECORDED BY AN OBSERVER ON THE FIFTIETH DAY OF YEAR 3'2 (Sk.E)

To my own never-fickle faithful, united by your scepticism –

I have learned what those Esoteric Instructors tell our own children who study with them. (Including my son, whom they dare to call "Initiate" Greyly.) The Scholars preach that we are but shrimp – shrimp! – in a vast ocean of a universe, rather like the sparkling sea rolling over that elusive planet below. This is the lie they peddle in secret to the ardent youth! Never has this information been revealed to anyone outside of the Body. I came across it only by fortunate chance. Now I share such knowledge freely, as it ought to be shared.

But perhaps you feel this curious cosmology alone is not enough evidence that the Instructors have gone rogue. After all, there is nothing particularly offensive about believing that the universe is an ocean. Many of us hold our own privately unbelievable beliefs, stories passed down to us through our families from the Prior World that shape our lives in ways we may never be able to dissect.

The Body Esoteric, however, aim to use this fictional threat as a means of controlling us – us as a society! They believe this sea is haunted by a so-called Predator, some kind of celestial monster from before time, who preys upon knowledge – as though knowledge ever filled anyone's belly – and approaches our world even now, salivating for what we have learned in our thriving city in the clouds. And what solution do they recommend? The Esoterics propose that we may only stop the Predator by abandoning everything we've ever known. They intend, in fact, to oversee a full evacuation of the Upward Archipelago!

Dear friends, I am not an unreasonable man. Long have we Planetary Empiricists believed that our civilisation ought not to waste time studying hypotheticals in the skies when such a fascinating world exists on the ground. If the Body Esoteric had ordered us to leave the Islets and fly down to the planet itself to build a more sustainable home, I would have been the very first to agree with them!

But that is not their intent. They believe we need to flee to an entirely different sanctuary. Some questionable refuge in the cosmic sea, built according to their own design. In the meantime, they command us to cease learning, cease thinking, cease creating, cease living in the world into which we put all our efforts – to abandon all for a life in exile that they believe will be our salvation. They believe it is no longer safe to *do* anything other than idle study that will never amount to any tangible progress.

How convenient for the Body – considering that idle study is their specialty.

If the time comes for lines to be drawn, we must be ready to save ourselves from those who would destroy our existence. I do hope, friends, that you are with me.

LETTER FROM INSTRUCTOR ELUVIAL TO INITIATE GREYLY, PENNED THE FIFTIETH DAY OF YEAR 3'2 (Sk.E)

Grey,

I heard about the speech. I can hardly believe it. How did he find out? Do you agree with him? I would like to see you, but I imagine the Body will forbid our association if I wish to retain my position as an Instructor. We shall have to be secretive. (I suppose we've never struggled with that.)

The Fifth Islet is in chaos at present. All the Instructors are flummoxed. They fear your father's rhetoric will strike fear into the hearts of the entire Upward Archipelago, and that anyone who refuses to accompany us will surely be consumed by the Predator ...

I share their concerns, obviously. But I suppose I am a poorer Instructor than I expected, for what troubles my heart with equal strength is whether this changes anything for us?

El

LETTER FROM INITIATE GREYLY TO INSTRUCTOR ELUVIAL, PENNED THE FIFTIETH DAY OF YEAR 3'2 (Sk.E)

It's my fault, El. All of it. I should have been more careful. I've been so caught up in – well, *you* – that I didn't notice.

Father has been reading our letters. Every note we've exchanged since you became an Instructor. His curiosity consumed him until he could resist no longer, I suppose. He tore through my desk. He took

294

what information he needed and burned the rest. (Fortunately, I still have your earliest letters tucked away in a folder elsewhere – the first ones we exchanged, up through your Ascension. I will give them to you for safe-keeping.) He detests the Scholars, and I—in a way, I understand his quarrel with them, though I do not agree with his actions.

If you can forgive my indiscretion – this changes nothing.

(But I suspect you should write to me no longer. I shall meet you at your pavilion, as always.)

THE COMPLETE AND FACTUAL NATURE OF THE PREDATOR AND A PLAN FOR OUR FUTURE, DISTRIBUTED TO THE PUBLIC ON THE FIFTY-THIRD DAY OF YEAR 3'2 (Sk.E)

Respectfully we Scholars write to you, citizens of the Upward Archipelago who seek safety –

We regret that a sizeable minority of your fellow citizens have turned against us. Yes, we admit to one deception. For centuries, our Instructors have known that the area in which our planet hangs in the heavens is not a vacuum, but a kind of odd celestial water in which we float. We did not think this worth sharing. Realising the true nature of the universe is an astonishing, sublime experience, but it does not necessarily change one's day-to-day life. Consequently, we kept this secret to ourselves and passed it down, as tradition dictated, from generation to generation of Initiates.

Only recently did we learn of the Predator and what he seeks. We waited to announce it because we hoped to conclude our preparations first, but now all must be revealed.

It began with a single stroke of bright light.

Our learned Astronomers spent many years using the instruments bequeathed to us by our spacefaring ancestors to monitor the cosmos for any wayward comets or suchlike. The screens they use for this purpose are rudimentary. Our colleagues simply see a rendering of the sky in miniature and, on occasion, shapes that flash against it. A massive meteor, twice the size of the Fifth Islet, might appear on this screen as a circle no larger than your fingernail.

When the Astronomers noticed a line stretching across one side of the screen, they assumed something had gone wrong with their machinery. Technicians were summoned to restart the device. Then the line expanded into a ridged, fin-like frill that soon consumed half the screen. Next, the monitor's entire display was occupied by a vast and empty oval – rather like an eye.

The teeth appeared last.

Something enormous approached, but we knew not what. Then the youngest Astronomer spoke with their great-grandparent, whose own grandfather survived the journey across the stars – or sea, as the case may be – to the place we call home today. We do not wish to bore our readers, but in the interest of mutual understanding, perhaps it is worth recapitulating the essential history of our society. Our people did not always live upon these islands in the sky, circling an empty world. As most accounts would have it, our ancestral home was destroyed by an accident of fate, and only those who happened to be stationed off-world at the time were able to escape. This Astronomer's great-great-great grandfather had an alternative hypothesis, which he kept to himself lest others think him mad. The world was consumed instantly after a series of magnificent techno-logical discoveries unfolded over the course of a single year. Could there be a connection?

We reached the following conclusion as we studied lost texts from our old world. When civilisations grow too strong, the Predator, sali-vating for new knowledge, strikes them down. This force will come for us in turn, unless we take action.

It is now time to reveal another secret – an experimental inquiry into dimensional technology that a select group of Scholars began testing after the discovery of the universal ocean. Our newest findings suggest there is a way to push through the boundaries of our atmosphere and into this vast ocean to build a place no Predator can find. Dear friends, rejoice – for the very discovery of this technology is a testament to the miraculous nature of human ingenuity! Earlier this year, one of our Instructors, weary from extended research, experienced a most peculiar dream. In this vision, an eerie melody filled them with inspiration as a parade of machines – each in its own unique shape – floated past their curious eyes. Then they awoke, scribbling down blueprints with fantastic speed. Is it not fascinating how our imaginations work?

After the Instructor presented their ideas to the rest of the Body, we began to develop these devices in earnest – devices that allow for expedient travel between our home and the cosmic sea. What beautiful serendipity has coloured every phase of our research! All we've learned over the past decade – our research into isopodic energy, the water-collecting satellite we sent out into the cosmos – it has, by providential coincidence, proved essential for developing the passageways that will be our Saviours.

While the testing process has been less rigorous than we would have liked, we are confident about our chances of success. Some brave souls already trialled these passageways and presently occupy themselves with constructing a sanctuary on the other side.

In due course, we will join them. Our plans will be implemented on the eightieth day of this year. We realise that is not a great deal of time to pack up one's entire life, but it is the best our estimates will allow. Then, once we have passed through the gateway to our salvation, the last to leave shall strike our islands from the sky – sending them crashing to that empty world of water below so that the Predator will have no trace of our knowledge left to tempt him.

We urge those of you with questions to speak with the Instructors who have been trained to handle your queries. We look forward to the day when we can live in peace and no longer fear that light that approaches.

297

LETTER FROM INITIATE GREYLY TO INSTRUCTOR ELUVIAL, PENNED ON THE EIGHTIETH DAY OF YEAR 3'2 (Sk.E)

Dear El,

You expected to see me, not a letter. I cannot apologise enough, and I wish there were some other way. The truth is that I would be miserable if I were to go with you. And I swear it is not simply due to my father's influence.

I fully intended to join you. I was prepared to take your hand and pass into that unknown world, safe from the reach of the Predator (if such a Predator exists). I was ready to see the very moment when you glimpsed the cosmic ocean for the first time. I could not think of anything more beautiful.

But your colleagues – the Instructors – I fear they are letting their fear of the Predator overcome them. Won't we be safe from the Predator's reach in our new home? Wasn't that the entire point of all this? In that case, why have the Instructors still forbidden us from studying anything of great significance there? Aren't we being overcautious? That is why I cannot come with you. I loathe the notion of never asking questions, never innovating, never developing anything new. I do not want your fate to be forever intertwined with that of someone who wishes so desperately that he could be elsewhere.

I know not what awaits me on the planet below. My father and his allies say there is at least one island. We will pilot our cloud-crafts there, drop our anchors, and see what kind of life we can build for ourselves. And always we will progress, not wasting any time mourning the society we lost – or, technically, that we will lose very shortly, once your compatriots are satisfied that all of us have evacuated so they may send our cities crashing down.

Though we will not look backwards, I shall allow myself the occasional pleasure of thinking of you. I hope you will do me the same courtesy.

With my fondness for all time,
Grey

REFERENCE NOTE BY THE FIFTEENTH FIRST SCHOLAR, YEAR (?)*

*Alas, our debates over the format of our new calendrical system have not yet been resolved: even though we have now lived in our new home for well over a year.

I have created this reference note for the benefit of any future Scholars who may find themselves curious about the inclusion of these documents in our archives. We were discouraged from carrying an excess of ephemera with us. (This edict was, for the most part, implemented to keep Instructors from weighing themselves down with far too many books and papers.) It was not my intention to bring these letters here. I did not think I'd have any need of them.

When I discovered – at last and too late – that they would become my only remembrance of someone very dear to me, I stuffed them in my robes before leaving my quarters on the Fifth Islet for the last time.

What a silly, impulsive thing to do. My embarrassment waned, however, when I realised that the letters I brought as sentimental mementoes have become our sole surviving primary sources documenting what brought us to this place.

They are, therefore, both essential historical records and potentially dangerous. There could be no better home for them than the new archives we are constructing far below our city. When the Third First Scholar first proposed that we hide our most precious documents within a deep-sea vent, we all thought the suggestion a bit fanciful. Was it not impractical to create a library in the depths of

299

the ocean, requiring any seeker of information to dive through the waters of the cosmos to find it?

Yes, it is terribly impractical. That is precisely why it suits us.

Though it now feels an age since we inhabited the Upward Archipelago, little time has passed at all. We know not what has become of the people whose paths diverged from ours.

Before departing, we sent down a variety of additional gateways. Sworn to secrecy, cloud-craft pilots soared through our skies and dropped the devices into the water, with no sense of where they might land and in what condition they might be found. The Eighth First Scholar (who always did have a flair for the dramatic) dubbed these devices "Sculpted Saviours", in the hopes that they might one day bring our missing fellow citizens – or, more likely, their descendants – home.

One day, all being well, some Imperilled people may manage to travel here. If the Imperilled learn dangerous information and return to their own world with that knowledge, they might thereby draw the maw of the Predator. All among us agree that secrecy is of the utmost importance.

I suppose I ought to note here, for the record's sake, that "we" are not as numerous as before. The past year has been one of endless debates and dissensions. Not every soul who travelled to our new home believed in the vitality of our mission. Factions emerged and collegial relationships fractured until one day – we lost nearly half of the Body.

No. What I should say is that they *left* us.

Their departure has already been well documented in our records, so I will not resurrect it here. Dwindled as we are, we have adopted an entirely new Society to suit our needs. We left behind our old names and developed a system of classification for ourselves – a new, complete system, in which no one appears to be missing. This system also protects our young Second Scholars, who are but children, from understanding the truth about our history until they are ready.

(*When* they may be ready remains a most unanswerable question, considering that they continue to age at an alarmingly slow rate. But our concerns about that matter, too, are documented elsewhere.)

Most importantly, we have all reaffirmed our unwavering commitment to restricting the knowledge we possess. For safety's sake.

It matters not that *we* are now eternally out of his reach. It matters not that the very reason we gave up our home was to retreat to this sanctuary in the cosmic sea, where the Predator is practically microscopic. We have grown accustomed to our rules and rituals. Protocol protects us. There is a great power in it.

I shall wield that power, then, by locking away these letters of mine.

Here ends this record. What follows is an inconsequential footnote for the benefit of an individual who will decidedly never read it:

When I saw the celestial ocean around us – frightening and fathomless though it is – I thought it a wonder.

EXCERPT FROM THE JOURNAL OF HENEREY CLEL, 1004

I have not written in this journal in too great a time to quantify. I make no apologies for that. Yet considering that I found it necessary to record every moment of my early bashfulness with E., I really ought to document the historically significant time in which we are currently living.

Also, I am terrified, and I do not know what to do otherwise.

Well, I suppose I must begin somewhere. For the benefit of anyone reading this in the future, I shall provide some explanatory context. It appears that the combination of rapid technological advancement from the past few years or so – including innovations like the Spheres station, Vocal Echolators, and that new Automated Post system, to name a few – somehow attracted the attention of a creature intent upon consuming knowledge. All the recent peculiarities in the

301

natural world (including my own rays!) portended his approach – and Vyerin and Niea's attempt to bring us home hastened his arrival.

This is an incomprehensibly frightening prospect with horrible implications for the world at large. If I think about it in depth, I can hardly—

At any rate, we presently seek to determine whether there is any hope of preventing this Predator's arrival. The information we gleaned from the documents in the Scholars' archive feels over-whelming and rather challenging to comprehend.

The Fifteenth First Scholar (who we now know was once a young Antepelagic Scholar called Initiate Eluvial, though she advised us that her personal involvement in the documents was of no importance – I disagree!) offered to clarify some aspects of the story, and I brought out my journal to record her account as effectively as possible.

AN APPARENTLY VERACIOUS ORIGIN MYTH FOR OUR UNIVERSE

Imagine, if you will, an endless ocean topped by an equally endless sky. It seems impossible, of course. Everything must have its end eventually, mustn't it? Yet if there is a place where this ocean ends – where the waves crash onto a continent of nothingness – we cannot find it ourselves. Surely, then, we are justified in describing this ocean as functionally infinite.

Now, despite its perplexing vastness and astonishing scale, the ocean is not altogether unlike the one I call home. Like any ocean, the cosmic sea features currents and tides, layers ranging from mild shallows to depths and darkness, and, most significantly of all – life in many forms. At the base of the celestial food chain, as in the ter-restrial one, are the smallest creatures. These are microplanktonic forms that appear, to the naked eye, like nothing more than distant twinkling stars drifting through the waves.

That is an appropriate simile, because what do we understand about stars? Only that the visual dots we perceive in the night sky are but small signifiers of exceptionally enormous astronomical bodies. Neither are these supposedly microscopic entities "organisms" as we understand them. Each infinitesimal form afloat in the ocean of the heavens is what we would consider a planet. And many – not all, but many – may well be populated by creatures similar to or unbelievably different from us.

In a way, there is little difference between this account of the universe and the one taught by our own Scholars of the Skies. Long has it been assumed that life may exist on planets outside of ours. In fact, the persistence of ancient texts such as *The Star Sailors* only further supports this idea. That beloved epic suggests that our ancestors came from elsewhere, and that there was once a time when people travelled between worlds as easily and as often as we take to the seas.

According to the Scholars' lore, that impression is not far from the truth. (Is it time for me to tell my origin myth at last? What an impressive preamble!)

Many thousands of years ago – a time only quantified before the Antepelagic genealogical records went down with everything else in the Dive – calamity struck a bustling planet. In what felt like a single moment, the entire world and all the life that inhabited it simply vanished, consumed by some incomprehensible force that left nothing in its wake.

For all we know, such calamities may have occurred many times throughout the history of the universal sea. If an entire world vanishes overnight, what records will remain to substantiate its existence? In this case, however, the destruction was not quite so complete. This world, you see, was home to people whose knowledge of spacefaring knew no equal. After centuries of progress and effort, they established a cluster of habitations on a neighbouring moon. The outpost was by no means extensive, but it sheltered a few hundred residents – who soon became the last of their kind.

303

(I cannot imagine how they must have felt, and I shan't even try. I may have first-hand experience with this feeling soon enough.)

Knowing their world was gone, these brave souls made a decision that put their very survival at risk. They were not equipped to reside permanently on the moon without support from their planet; they had a reserve of supplies, but even those would run out eventually. So, by unanimous decree (according to legend, at any rate), they set out to find another place more hospitable to their needs.

What these people did not know as they sailed through the stars was that they were, in fact, making their way through this universal ocean. The watery planet they discovered – one with no major landmasses save an ancient, dwindling atoll – was yet another microplanktonic speck, itself just as vulnerable to the same fate that befell their original home.

I have already discussed the lowest part of the food web, but what of its upper echelons? When microscopic life flourishes, it is not unreasonable to expect that creatures might feed upon it. Everything sounds so simple when I put it biologically, doesn't it?

Even the Fifteenth First Scholar, with her vast knowledge, can provide only scraps of hints and myths about the other creatures that inhabit our shared celestial ocean. It has been hypothesised that incomprehensibly enormous filter-feeders, each more than twenty billion times larger than a single planet, rule the cosmos. Like our whales, they sweep through the stars with mouths wide, unaware of the lives swallowed into their vast maws. The First Scholars have no quarrel with the filter-feeders, terrifying as they seem. They are forces of nature. You cannot fault a tidal wave for destroying a research station; the wave did not act out of malice.

Amidst these waters of life and death and feasting and destruction, there remains one creature unlike the others. He is possessed not merely of sentience, but vast intelligence. He is the last of his species, which consisted of (comparatively) tiny creatures driven almost to extinction by the appetites of the filter-feeders. To survive, he adapted, developing a cunning desire for that which will make him all the swifter and cleverer.

He is the Predator, and his prey is the collective knowledge of any world he encounters.

Unlike the unknowing filter-feeders, the Predator intentionally seeks out societies that have advanced furthest, those rich with new discoveries and ideas he never tasted before. The Scholars, in their folly, built a robust, thriving world – the sky-society we describe as Antepelagic – that proved sophisticated enough to attract his attention. A faction of the Scholars destroyed that society to put him off the scent, but now we (by which I do mean specifically all of us assembled here right now) have lured him back again.

(Now, I would like to note – since the Fifteenth First Scholar is still talking and will not think it odd that I continue to write – that I question much about her story and its veracity. How much of this is myth and how much is fact? Is there a chance that the Predator is nothing more than a metaphor for something less fanciful, like a gravitational void or other cosmic catastrophe? After all, these Scholars have not been especially forthcoming or truthful with us on other matters. That mystical tale of the Illogical Ones, for example, that the Fifteenth First Scholar shared during our first day of study with her – in which she described the sea-woman magically duplicating herself while the Scholars looked on in disdain. I found it difficult to believe then, and now, after reading the Fifteenth First Scholar talking about the loss of some Scholars, I wonder—

But that matters little. What is most important is how furious E. feels about the Fifteenth First Scholar's misdirection, even though the Scholar's intent was not malicious. E. puts so much effort into determining whether her anxieties are intrusive thoughts or legitimate concerns. I fear the revelation about this impossible Predator makes E. question her very reality. I wish I could take her away from

305

all this and help calm her. Dare I, under the circumstances? Though Natural History inevitably involves the study of life and death, I fear I am utterly unequipped to handle situations of this nature, and my own anxiety overwhelms me . . .)

Chapter 20

OFFICIAL RECORD BY THE THIRTIETH SECOND SCHOLAR, 1004

I write today to record a meeting between the Visitors and the Body of Scholars, held in response to the approach of the Predator.

(I wrote that statement with full knowledge of this terrifying secret, supplied by the First Scholars. It seems their burden will be a shared one from this point forth.)

O – under the circumstances, I neglected my attestation. Let us simply assume that I will record the meeting accurately. Is that acceptable, Fifteenth First Scholar? It is most evident that I could not have invented any of this!

As a result of the revelation in the parenthetical above, I have been quite preoccupied and therefore missed several opportunities to observe our Visitors' activities. They kept busy in my absence, so I will summarise their movements for the record. Understandably, my Imperilled friends and acquaintances find themselves faced with a most unexpected dilemma. They know their world is in peril – or fear it might be, anyway, even if many of them remain somewhat stubbornly sceptical – and yet they have neither the time nor the ability to warn their fellow people. Before the council meeting began, I came across the Visitors waiting in the outer chamber, where a spirited discussion about the aforementioned dilemma was underway.

"Regardless of the waterlogged documents we read, are we truly going to accept that our entire world is about to meet its end – simply because these Scholars say so?" Scholar Mawr said as I entered.

"Of everyone here, Tev, I thought you'd be most likely to believe the unbelievable," replied Scholar Niea Cidnorghe.

"I am, as a rule. But in this case, I would prefer to ask my friend for her counsel before we make any rash decisions." He sighed. "She has not, of course, appeared in my mind yet."

"What if she never does – and what if the Scholars are indeed telling the truth?" Scholar Cidnorghe persisted. "Is there anything we may do? Must we simply accept that we are incapable of convincing every person in the world to follow us here before this danger comes?"

"And how would we convince them?" asked Scholar Mawr. "Through some kind of public announcement? A newspaper article? Who would believe us? And how much harm would we cause if we issued a false alarm when the Predator is nothing more than myth? This would not be the first time, Niea, that some Scholarly authority forced our cooperation by invoking the greater good."

"Though I hate to reference that particular Scholarly authority, our conversation rather reminds me of what Chancellor Rawsel argued himself," said Scholar Sophy Cidnorghe. "He claimed he opposed the Fleet because their premonitions of danger would produce mass chaos. Even with the time delay, I imagine we would not have the opportunity to speak to everyone in the world before the Predator came. If it does come."

"Then the question comes down to whether it is worth issuing smaller-scale warnings, in the event that the Scholars are correct," said Scholar Niea Cidnorghe. "Jeime said she wanted to spend some time with her fiancée while awaiting word from us, so I do not know where exactly she is. Arvist will have gone back home by now, as well. He and Seliara and Eri live on the farthest ring of Intertidal, Sophy, don't they? That's a day's sail at least."

"Arvist," Scholar Cidnosin echoed in the faintest of voices. Scholar

Clel, seemingly the only person besides me to hear this utterance, enfolded her in his arms.

"What about your own sister, Niea?" Scholar Sophy Cidnorghe asked gently. "Where is Alie right now?"

"On her research vessel," Scholar Niea Cidnorghe whispered. "I imagine we could not . . ."

"Well, one matter is settled. I'm going through for Reiv and the children, as soon as I can escape you lot," said Scholar Vyerin Clel grimly. "I can't say I'm particularly convinced by this Predator nonsense, but I've experienced enough impossible things to know it's not worth taking any risks. I'll leave now, in fact, if you'll allow me."

"Without question," said Scholar Henerey Clel. "But our parents, Vy. They are so far away, too!"

"You know they wouldn't trouble themselves with trekking all the way to another world just because a cosmic Predator *might* be coming," replied his brother with a grim smile. "Thankfully that stubbornness doesn't run in the family."

"Clearly not," agreed Scholar Sophy Cidnorghe.

Scholar Vyerin Clel departed immediately – which is what excused him from this meeting. The rest of the Visitors then dutifully paced into the council chamber, where each person politely insisted that someone else should take one of the two chairs. Ultimately, all Scholars ended up on the floor, with the chairs empty behind them.

An uncharacteristically sombre mood has overtaken my colleagues today. The Second Scholars, like myself, are sobered by this overwhelming revelation. After all, we were but infants and children when the First Scholars instigated the Dive, and we were never told of the specific danger that caused them to abandon their world. And, besides—

Well, I suppose my personal opinions about this development are not the point of my record, are they?

The First Scholars range from resigned (the Seventh First Scholar, for example) to furious (the Sixth First Scholar, obviously). In contrast to her colleagues' unScholarly reactions, the Fifteenth First Scholar remained the calmest – and was, therefore, the natural choice to lead the proceedings.

"I shall not waste time with formalities," she said. "The Predator approaches. The fate of the world we left is at risk, just as it was a thousand years ago."

"What can we possibly do?" asked the Sixth First Scholar. "His destruction is inevitable – in fact, every one of us Scholars cast aside our homes and disbelieving families because we would stake our lives on the fact that the Predator cannot be stopped." He turned to the array of Visitors on the floor.

"I apologise for sounding so cold," he continued. "It is out of respect that I tell you the truth, harsh as it is, instead of deluding you into thinking that there is a chance."

"But is there no chance at all?" asked Scholar Henerey Clel. "You Scholars may have sworn to stop learning anything new, but this city alone proves that you possess many technologies unknown to us. Can nothing be done to stop the Predator – if he is indeed pursuing our planet?"

"There is no logical course of action," replied the Sixth First Scholar.

Of course, it was at that very moment when illogical things started to happen.

Before writing anything down, I dashed to the crowd of First Scholars and found the Fifteenth First Scholar, who looked at me askance.

"May I have permission to record inexplicable happenings, under the present circumstances?" I asked, ignoring the shouts of outrage and surprise from my fellow Scholars.

"Under the circumstances – why not?" she replied, and that was all I needed to hear.

Now I may, with permission, say that soon after the Sixth First Scholar's statement, an Illogical One appeared in the centre of the room, suspended halfway between the ceiling and the floor. Perhaps out of kindness to us, she did not make any further changes to the environment, though beams of light still shone through her skin as if she were a prism.

To my surprise, the Visitors reacted more strongly than any of my colleagues.

"There you are!" exclaimed Scholar Mawr, running towards the Illogical One until he stood directly below her. "I awaited you for days. You promised to return."

"And I remembered, I did, but I was prevented – how cruel!" she said in that oddly melodic voice. I cannot be sure, but I had the distinct impression that she was the very being whom Scholar Cidnosin and I encountered outside of the city.

"You are not welcome here, Illogical One," said the Sixth First Scholar. "These matters are far too serious for your interference."

"Let her speak," allowed the resigned Fifteenth First Scholar. "You are not simply *any* Illogical One, are you? Have we met before – long ago?"

"You recognise me?" sang the Illogical One in a high and ebullient melody. "Many years have passed since your friends became my family."

"What has become of them now?" asked the Eighth First Scholar in a quiet voice.

"You do not need to ask!" exclaimed the Sixth First Scholar. "They chose their fate."

"They were brave, waiting in the other world to see if someone would pass through your little doors!" the Illogical One sang. "Yet he has returned, so I called them back before their vigils ended."

"I knew it!" exclaimed Scholar Henerey Clel – perhaps louder than he intended, because he glanced at the floor as everyone turned to look at him.

"I was puzzled by the Fifteenth First Scholar's claim that the Illogical Ones multiplied when people believed in them," he said, more subdued. "Because you did not tell us the truth about that either, did you? I have formed a hypothesis already."

"Yes," said the Fifteenth First Scholar. "I am sure you are correct, so you needn't take the time to say anything further."

She said this at the exact moment when Scholar Clel said, "Some of your own logical Scholars became Illogical Ones, didn't they – o, my apologies."

"Of course," Scholar Cidnosin whispered. "The chalice was not metaphorical after all."

"But how exactly did it work?" Scholar Clel persisted. When my colleagues declined to answer, he turned to the Illogical One.

"You are evidently quite remarkable, Illogical One," he said. "O – pardon me. I know the Scholars use that name for you, but is there a name *you* prefer?"

The Illogical One rolled her head upon her graceful neck.

"There were none to name me when my life began," she mused. "I collect them from others now. It amuses me to see what they create. My friend once named me Iridescence, and I found that the loveliest of all."

At that, Scholar Tevn Mawr turned away most dramatically – in embarrassment, perhaps? I, too, would be embarrassed to have diluted the definition of a perfectly good word by using it as a mere nickname! (Why are my colleagues and I alone in the universe when it comes to the effective use of titling conventions?)

"How aptly poetic!" Scholar Clel smiled – rather illogically, under the circumstances. "At any rate, Iridescence, I have heard from E. – and see right now, with my own eyes – how you can transform the world around you. Could you truly change another being's form moments after meeting them?"

"Moments after meeting them?" sang the Illogical One in a strange, stilted rhythm. "That is not correct. They became my friends first. We spoke for hours and days and ages, even after the curtains were hung. Nor do I change my friends myself. They seek to transform. I merely teach their bodies what songs to sing."

312

"Fools, all of them," groused the Sixth First Scholar. "I suppose they've long since learned the folly of wasting their lives chasing Fantasies in the form of frightening fish-people."

"Would you like me to call them here so you may ask?" The Illogical One's voice shook the very walls of the Chamber! "You call us Illogical – yet we would never say anything other than the truth of how things are."

"Why have you returned to our city, after all this time?" interrupted the Fifteenth First Scholar.

"I had nearly forgotten!" the Illogical One exclaimed. "The Predator returns, and I wish to stop him."

"This might seem like an impertinent question," said Scholar Sophy Cidnorghe, "but I fear I have not even been fed explanatory falsehoods like E. and Henerey."

She gestured to the Illogical One. "We saw you, didn't we, at the Ridge? When you took up residence in that Antepelagic ruin? Still, I do not know the first thing about what or who you are. What connection do you have with the Predator?"

"You saw her before?" asked Scholar Cidnosin, but I do not think her sister heard.

"The Predator and I should be friends," replied the Illogical One. "For we share the same grief. Like me, the Predator is alone in the vast sea."

"You are also from this cosmic ocean?" asked Scholar Niea Cidnorghe. "What other beings call it home?"

"It is immense and lonely," sang the Illogical One. "I was born in a burst of song to an empty sea. For ages upon ages I trailed the waves, seeking others like myself. I saw nothing, but I heard everything. The richest sounds imaginable, flowing from speakers and singers I could not trace. The mystery drove me to despair. Why did it seem as though life was all around me, when I floated alone in the ocean?

"In my thoughts, I was never alone. When I rested, dreams overtook me, filled with conversations I could not remember with beings I never saw before. It tormented me until I realised these thoughts were not lost memories of my past, but images of my future. How I laughed, then, to learn I was not entirely lonesome! All I needed to do was find my friends – and they were, as it turned out, right before my eyes."

The Illogical One extended her finger and waved it idly, illuminating the chamber with coloured light.

"What a miracle it was," she intoned. "Everywhere I swam, I marvelled at the specks of light around me. I thought them tiny, inconsequential things. Then I recognised that the very sounds I heard originated from those luminous little forms. Each was a world like yours. So beautifully sonorous.

"I tried to visit them. I reshaped my very essence. Diminished myself until I could see each world, so vast and bright before me. But I could not enter them, not at first. I was far too young. Instead, I sent my dreams. Rare it was that someone heard me. When they did, I made it worth their while. I sang of myself, to start, and then, when I grew bolder, I sang of more."

"Do you truly expect us to believe all that?" demanded the Third First Scholar.

"Is it even safe for us to know this in the first place?" whispered the Fifth First Scholar.

"I can hardly imagine the life you must have led, in that great ocean—"

That third voice sounded very much like the Fifteenth First Scholar's. Why, I even saw her mouth move as the words came out! But this must have been an illusion crafted by the Illogical One. I cannot imagine my mentor, of all people, *marvelling* over the mysterious . . .

In any case, the Fifteenth First Scholar then proceeded to clear her throat. "While we appreciate your storytelling, Illogical One," she said, "should we not return to the topic of the Predator?"

"Then I shall. Once it was that I conversed with the Predator about the nature of loneliness. Long ago, before I changed my form to match yours. We met by the shores of the island – I lounged on the beach where the waves broke, while the Predator floated alongside me, small enough to fit in my fins. I told him of my desire for companions. He said he had no time to waste on friendship, so committed was he to his own survival. But the Predator, despite his greed, is not without curiosity. It was then that he and I created the pact."

"You spoke with the Predator?" asked the Sixth First Scholar. "That is an abomination."

"An abomination!" laughed the Illogical One. "You should be grateful, silly Scholars, for it is thanks to this pact that you may yet halt his feasting."

"Tell us more, please," said the Fifteenth First Scholar.

In response, the Illogical One produced a goblet of sound, just as she did when Scholar Cidnosin and I met her in the water. This goblet, however, was of a different sheen – the material was still thin and iridescent, but darker in hue, and it was cast in the shape of a spiny shell that does not match any in our Historical Taxonomies. Instead of the careful border of pearls and sea glass I remembered from the other goblet, this object was decorated with painted starlike tiles, feathery fronds of kelp, and tiny crystalline fish that seemed to move. The overall effect was rather stunning—

Stunningly illogical, I mean!

"The Predator promised to entertain my pleas under certain circumstances. If I wished to stop him from devouring a world, he would consider a . . ." She paused for a moment and met the eyes of Scholar Mawr. "Which word would these Scholars find most persuasive, my friend? I placed an image in your mind."

Scholar Mawr pondered this for a moment and then nodded. "Perhaps you'd like to describe it as a petition. Or an argument?"

"You are incandescent, Scholar Mawr," she said, smiling broadly.

"Sometimes I think better in pictures too," he said with a shrug.

"Do you mean to say that the Predator might show mercy?" asked the Fifteenth First Scholar. "That does not seem consistent with his disposition."

315

"It certainly does not!" exclaimed the Sixth First Scholar. "Why would he consent to such a nonsensical pact in the first place?"

"Because I entreated him," said the Illogical One. "Because I sang and argued and begged. Because the fault was mine – not yours – that he scented out your world in the first place."

Please note, colleagues, that I employed the word *said* on purpose. For the very first time, the Illogical One spoke just as we do. Firmly, flatly, and without a hint of melody.

I suppose, however, that the content of the Illogical One's statement is of far more import. My apologies for the distracting description of her delivery!

"It was not my intention," continued the Illogical One. "How foolish I was! I only wished to show my friends how to visit me. Instead, I inspired you to build that which you could have never invented yourselves."

A harsh sound followed. All evidence suggests that it was a wordless exclamation from the Fifteenth First Scholar – yet surely she would not have made such an unScholarly outburst?

"We attributed the success of our journey here to the power of Science," the Fifteenth First Scholar whispered. "Our gateway. Our Sculpted Saviours. All of them exemplifying our brilliance as Instructors. Could it truly be that our greatest achievements were nothing more than—"

"Nonsense! They might have been inspired by a dream, but *we* sculpted the Saviours!" persisted the Eighth First Scholar. "The Body Esoteric laboured over them for ages. I, personally, designed the isopod core!"

"And I varnished the Belligerent Dreamer," added the Fourth First Scholar.

"I do not mean to diminish your accomplishments." The Illogical One gave a great and sweeping bow. "Your hands and minds worked wonders. But were it not for the songs I sang across the worlds, those wonders could not have come together so easily."

316

"She helped," murmured Scholar Sophy Cidnorghe. "Just like she did with our A.P. signals."

"And it's just like Jeime thought, too!" exclaimed Scholar Niea Cidnorghe. "Those Entries were so simplistic in their construction that they seemed near-miraculous."

"Are you daring to suggest, Illogical One, that the very foundation of our society was built upon unreliable enchantments that cannot be explained logically?" said the Sixth First Scholar.

"Perhaps that is true. But I'm afraid it matters very little now." The Fifteenth First Scholar hung her head in a most exhausted manner. "Will you tell us more of the pact, Illogical One? I beg of you."

"He will await someone on the island, where they may make the case for survival. This will bear you there." The Illogical One dropped the goblet in one fluid motion. When it landed, it produced a melody that I could not transcribe with the musical notation systems known to us.

"I suppose none of you Scholars would like to be considered as potential petitioners, would you?" asked Scholar Sophy Cidnorghe. My Oaths mandate that I describe how my kindred shrunk away from her gaze.

"I would volunteer," I said – and, because I must write all that is true, I confess that I enjoyed the shock this created among the Body of Scholars! Unfortunately, nearly every one of my colleagues and the Visitors shook their head at me.

"Are you not rather young for such a risky enterprise?" said Scholar Sophy Cidnorghe.

"Technically, I have an age that is equivalent to four and twenty years of development, though I have existed much longer than that," I explained cheerily. "Besides, based on your physical attributes and the biographical information conveyed to me by Scholar Cidnosin, I was under the impression that you yourself were not much older than—"

"We need you here, Thirtieth Second Scholar, to record everything

317

that comes to pass," Scholar Cidnosin interrupted in a gentle voice. "There is no Scholar we trust as much as you."

"That is most unfortunate," intoned the Sixth First Scholar drily, but I cared not, so bursting was I (I must tell the truth, mustn't I?) with pride.

"Then it is down to us," said Scholar Mawr.

"You've accepted the truth of the Predator now, have you?" asked Scholar Sophy Cidnorghe.

"If my friend — if Iridescence believes the Predator is coming, I cannot deny it. To that end, I propose that Sophy or Vyerin bargain with the Predator. I'm sure we can all agree that they are the most physically strong and emotionally resilient among us."

Scholar Sophy Cidnorghe practically grinned at him. "Do you really think so, Tev?"

"Sophy," began Scholar Cidnosin. I fear none heard but me.

"And," Scholar Mawr continued, "it is my impression that while Captain Clel is the more imposing, Sophy is more persuasive."

"I may be up to the challenge. I shall confer with Vyerin when he rejoins us," said Scholar Sophy Cidnorghe. "What exactly is expected of me?" She paused and looked to her wife. "And how will I return?"

"My siblings shall bear you back when the task is complete. First, you will travel to the island, where you may await the Predator for some time. There is a dwelling there, built in some time unknown to us, in which you may shelter. You will make your plea, and if he is convinced, he will alter his course."

"And if he is not?" asked Scholar Niea Cidnorghe in a hushed voice, wrapping her arm tightly around her wife's waist.

"No harm will come to you. The Predator is uninterested in individuals. Your world, however, will not be so fortunate."

"Sophy, I wonder if you would—" said Scholar Cidnosin.

"That seems simple enough, doesn't it?" asked Scholar Sophy Cidnorghe. "I know our time is limited, so I will keep my preparations brief, but what shall I do shortly when it is time to depart?"

The Illogical One proffered the glowing goblet once more. "You will drink of this, and the music will carry you to the island. We have a way of watching what happens there, to make sure you arrive safely."

Scholar Sophy Cidnorghe glanced again at Scholar Niea Cidnorghe, who nodded with a tight smile. "Then I accept. I shall gather my things and make my farewells."

"Sophy," said Scholar Cidnosin once more. "Would you please hear me out, just for a moment?"

"There is no need to worry about me, E. I am best suited to this task. Since time is of the essence, we needn't even wait for Vyerin. Now, Tev, I wonder if you would be willing to lend me that handy pocket-tool you used to tune up the Bubbles when we were floating about together?"

Then a series of unexpected occurrences began, which I shall try to record in the proper sequence. Scholar Cidnosin dashed to the centre of the room and seized the goblet. The melody it played began to change, with chords that seemed comprised of a thousand notes resonating around us. (Though I know my colleagues will scoff, I must report that as the music transformed, I could swear the sounds took shape in the air, creating a shimmering picture of that inscrutable island and a rather illogical onshore kelp forest. Did anyone but me spy it, I wonder?) At a rather unbelievable speed, Scholar Cidnosin sipped from the goblet and then stood blinking with surprise.

"O," she said. "I did not expect it to have a taste as well as a sound."

"E.," said Scholar Clel in what is objectively the most sorrowful voice I ever heard. "What are you doing?"

"What have you done?" uttered Scholar Sophy Cidnorghe almost simultaneously.

"I am terribly sorry," Scholar Cidnosin said. I could not confirm who was the intended recipient of this statement. "I do not wish to make this journey. But I must spare you, Sophy. It is more my responsibility than yours."

Scholar Sophy Cidnorghe took the goblet from her sister's hand,

319

trying desperately to catch even a single note of its tempting melodies – but it had run empty.

"How could you?" she shouted. "We just agreed that I would go!"

"I agreed to nothing, because you wouldn't let me speak! I am your elder sister, Sophy, and I tell you I must do this. I am the only one who has visited the island, and I am familiar with its terrors and wonders. It is my fault that the Deep House is gone, and my fault that you suffered for so long, thinking I was dead. This is my way of atoning."

"But you mustn't atone at all!" Scholar Sophy argued. "I can't bear to have you gone again, E., not after all I did to find you. You needn't bear every burden simply because you are a few years my senior!"

As Scholar Sophy spoke, I noticed Scholar Cidnosin starting to fade. As illogical as it sounds, she was becoming transparent, with the outlines and colours of her body still present but losing their strength by the moment. With each part of her that vanished, new notes joined the ever-present chords.

"I know you, Sophy. You could not bear waiting in isolation for the Predator to arrive. Tell me this – have you ever been alone, truly alone, for more than a few hours? What if the Predator does not come for some days? It would consume you, but not me. Never me," she said, "O, but, Henerey—"

He ran to her side in an instant, even though I never would have thought him a skilled runner, and embraced her, even though she was semi-transparent and every Scholar I knew was watching them closely.

"You are something of a marvel, aren't you, my E.? And I love you most thoroughly," he said. "I shall not rest until you return."

"He means that quite literally. Please make sure he does rest," Scholar Cidnosin said to her sister. "And don't worry, my dear. You know I speak very quickly, so I will return—"

Then she was gone. Scholar Sophy Cidnorghe released a terrible cry, and Scholar Clel appeared frozen in shock. I can truthfully and accurately state that none of *us* had the slightest idea of how to respond.

"Sophy! What in the world is the matter?" interrupted a stern voice from the door. I turned to see that Scholar Vyerin Clel had returned, accompanied by a thin, pensive man, a young girl with a defiant expression, and a small child who simply seemed delighted to see everyone.

I think it may be fair to say, at this point, that the formal meeting concluded. I will conclude my account as well.

UNSENT LETTER FROM SOPHY CIDNORGHE TO E. CIDNOSIN, 1004

Dear E.,

How can you be gone again?

I did not mean to speak over you. I did not intend for this to happen. I do not know why I am writing this letter that you will never read, but I am lying in Niea's lap trying to do something that makes me feel like I can reach you.

I am a cartographer, E., and yet here I am, thwarted by that which I cannot map. Long ago I read your letters to Henerey describing that island you visited, but I do not have the slightest idea where you are and I cannot navigate there. I do not fully understand where I am in space right now – in this galactic ocean that apparently exists.

I know the stakes are much higher. I know the entire world is at risk. Our wayward father. My family-by-marriage. Jeime, who has honoured Mother by doing so much for us. Seliara and our niece. I cannot begin to think of them without weeping. And our brother. O, Arvist. If he were to fall into the Predator's maw now, vanishing dramatically before I have a chance to tell him how much I do care for him, despite everything – why, that would be so very like him, wouldn't it?

Yet it is not just those whom we hold dearest. I keep mentally cataloguing everyone I have ever met. My colleagues from the Ridge expedition, my classmates from when I was but an Apprentice Scholar, even pitiful Orelith Rawsel. In days or hours or moments, all could be gone. They will not suffer (or so I hope), but they will likely cease to be.

Unless, that is, you succeed.

You are right that I am not accustomed to being alone. I can hardly bear being in a Bubble for a night by myself. I spent my idle young adulthood falling in love aimlessly again and again because I could not fathom the thought of going through life without a companion. Perhaps I would have struggled on the island, but will I not struggle more knowing that you risked your own wellbeing for my sake?

I feel guiltier still when I think of how much your Henerey grieves you. There must be a part of him that blames me. After you disappeared, everyone dispersed so the desperate waiting could begin. The Illogical One left to "glimpse" the island, whatever that means, and Tevn accompanied her. The Scholars had little time for us, though I witnessed the Thirtieth Second Scholar shedding some unScholarly tears. I think they have not seen something this dramatic in a thousand years!

Then Henerey, Niea, and I were alone. Vyerin departed with his family in tow, promising to return once he settled them in – and once he figured out an age-appropriate way of explaining the situation to his children. Niea was trembling, clutching my hand, and I had never seen her look so exhausted.

"Are you all right?" I whispered to her.

She nodded solemnly and pressed her forehead against mine. "I forced myself to accept that you might leave. I am truly glad you did not, Sophy – I know that is selfish of me. I cannot be without you again."

"O – Niea. I am terribly sorry," was all I could manage to say. "I promised I would not leave your side, and yet—"

"I understand why you needed to go," she replied. "And you can understand why I am so terribly happy that you did not. But there is someone else in this room who might not share my excitement. Won't you look after him for now? I shall await you in our chambers."

Niea gave me a quick embrace, and I kissed her thrice before she departed.

Then I turned to face Henerey Clel, who still stared straight ahead, gazing at nothing. I recognised the expression, as a matter of fact. I've seen it on you, E., when your thoughts trouble you most seriously.

"Henerey," I said, as gently as I could. "It should have been me."

"Would it be impolite to agree with you?"

I wasn't sure if he was trying to lighten the mood or simply stating facts as they were.

"She acted impulsively," I replied. "But the circumstances are dire, and I am only impressed that one of us managed to make a decision before it was too late."

"She was—I was about to say that she was not quite herself at the moment, but that would not be fair of me," he said breathlessly. "I only mean that this guilt – this all-consuming, misplaced guilt she believes she must bear alone – it has shaken her immensely. And she told me only hours ago how angry she felt about the Fifteenth First Scholar's deception. I'm afraid all this in conjunction pushed her to make a choice she might not have made otherwise. For if she was not so burdened, Sophy, do you think she would have gone without me?"

I felt a painful kinship for this man that I never thought we would share. I recognised the feeling – not from this moment, but from everything before – when I first learned you had vanished, and then again, when I learned it was not an accident, and that you *chose* to go on your journey and leave me.

(I can admit such things only because you will never read this letter.)

"I agree that her sense of guilt is misplaced," I said. "But Henerey, there is something else. Is it not possible that, in our shared grief and anxiety, we are overlooking something important?"

He nodded at me, and I let myself continue.

"My sister says that one of the most destabilising aspects of her brain is how difficult it is to tell who she is, and which decisions are truly hers, as opposed to being the products of her obsessions. On top of it all, E. has the kind of mind that wants her to obsess about how much those obsessions impact her choices, which leads to the kind of recursive struggle I am sure you know all too well by this point."

"But, to me, it is always evident who E. is and what her decisions are," he said. "Even when she thinks she is being ruled by her condition, every choice and statement that she makes herself is so vibrant, so clear, so loud—"

"Surprisingly loud," I cut in.

"Yes, I should say! And the truth is, Sophy, that despite her feelings about the Deep House and the Fifteenth First Scholar and everything, she's done an exceptionally brave thing, hasn't she?"

"Exactly," I said. "Something she chose to do."

"And I cannot help but admire that, but, sink it all . . ." I had never heard him say something with such ferocity ". . . I wish more than anything that her nobleness of spirit manifested itself in less dangerous ways."

"It does hearten me to see your devotion to her. I know you would give anything to ensure she does not come to harm."

"That may be," Henerey agreed, "but my motivations are far more self-serving than you understand."

"What could be self-serving about wishing to protect the one you love?"

"Because it is not just about that!" he exclaimed. "I am sorry, but the truth is that I wish E. hadn't gone because, quite plainly, I cannot be without her. Did you happen to glean from my letters, or from my brother, or from Chancellor Rawsel, that I myself am rather afraid of everything? I do not have the same condition as your sister, but I too can be rendered shaking and speechless by worries about what will happen when I go out in public. And I am also, apparently, deeply incompatible with enclosed underwater spaces. There is no one, not even Vyerin, who has ever made me feel more like myself – made me feel practically brave – than your sister does. If she can never return, Sophy, what will become of me?"

324

O, I wish you could see how much you mean to him. At present, though, you are not here, and there was only so much comfort I could offer Henerey in your absence.

And now I am writing to you and wondering what you are experiencing. In our past letters, we typically asked each other questions about our current activities and opinions, did we not? But I cannot even dare to keep up that pretence. I will simply wait, once again, to be reunited with you.

With all my love,
Sophy

EXCERPT FROM THE JOURNAL OF HENEREY CLEL, 1004

I find myself alone in this beautiful garden once more. I cannot say why I am bothering to write, as simply opening this journal set my emotions raging. I looked back on my whimsical notes from earlier today about myths and the Predator and the cosmic ocean and I despise myself for writing them in such insipidly cheerful handwriting. I feel sickened by every exclamation mark and witty aside, every upbeat loop on an *l* and optimistically curved *o*. Even then, when I bore the full knowledge of the calamity that might unfold, I behaved like the fanciful fool I have always been – by taking secret pleasure in the fact that I discovered something new, and that thoughtless desire to experience the sublime wonder of the unknown made me incapable of acknowledging the danger.

The worst thing is that I have only now acknowledged that danger because it affected me so personally. There is a dark, terrible part of me that I must describe here because I will not confess it to anyone because it is not a part of myself that I want anyone to know because it is horrible and selfish, but I do not care. This part of me says to forget the world and let it face its fate, so long as I do not have to be apart from her.

325

I shall not allow myself to think of such things and I will not say such things to anyone. I needed to get all this out of my head before writing a letter to her. She may not read it, but it is important that I write the best letter imaginable, and I hope that by some miracle of romantic connection she will feel my words from wherever she is. How cruel it is that I cannot even tell E. herself that there is nothing I wouldn't do to stay with her!

UNSENT DRAFT OF A LETTER FROM HENEREY CLEL TO E. CIDNOSIN, 1004

To my dearest E.,

It occurs to me that I have never written you a letter without the comforting knowledge that you would read it. I know that is not the case for you! When you sent me that first letter — an act of remarkable courage for which I am eternally grateful — you said yourself that you not only assumed I might not have time to read it, but also that you rather wished I wouldn't. Of course, you had not yet met me, so you could not know that I never received a letter I didn't read! But you must have felt anxious about taking the time to compose something without any assurance that my eyes would ever look upon it.

Now I understand that feeling all too well.

UNSENT DRAFT OF A LETTER FROM HENEREY CLEL TO E. CIDNOSIN, 1004

To my dearest E.,

I just spoke with my brother, who tried to comfort me so I will stop feeling sick with worry. Is it wrong that I felt a little angry as he advised me to hope for the best? It is easy for him to say such things

326

when his entire lovely family is here, safe and sound, and I utterly adrift without you!

UNSENT DRAFT OF A LETTER FROM HENEREY CLEL TO E. CIDNOSIN, 1004

To my dearest E.,

I am trying my best to picture you in my mind's eye, just as I did after we first met and I wanted to cling to your fleeting image. It is easy to imagine you, but I struggle to envision the landscape. You described that island so lucidly to me, yet I cannot work out how you look in the darkness, lit only by the plants and seas. Was that shape you spied in the water one of the filter-feeders, ready to sift thousands of worlds through its baleen? I hope you will stick to the shoreline. The Illogical One mentioned a house – you didn't see that when you visited before, did you?

I only wish I could be there. What cosmic cruelty is responsible for this rather impractical goblet-based transportation system that only allows one person to travel at a time? If circumstances allowed, and you consented, I would have accompanied you in a heartbeat. In that scenario, I would not worry for an instant about whether we could return. What would it matter if I were with you? I would happily confine myself to any island for the rest of eternity if we remained together. But I did not even have that choice, did I?

Is there any hope that I still might?

Chapter 21

LETTER FROM E. CIDNOSIN, 1004

I dare not begin my letter with a salutation, because I know not who will find it. Fortunately, I have grown accustomed to the notion that my correspondence may be read, so it does not trouble me (overmuch) that this particular note might prove historically significant. Please think of what follows as a letter to my world, then – and perhaps, I fear, the last I shall ever write.

If you are reading this, I assume you already know something of my present circumstances. But I suppose there is always the chance that this letter will be scooped up, like a message in a bottle, by a stranger aboard some hypothetical cosmic trawler. For their benefit, I shall summarise. I came in search of the Predator. I passed into a place outside of time – an island in the vast ocean that makes up the known universe.

Because I visited this island before, elements of it are familiar. The infinitely dark skies, the seaward spectrum of luminescence, the spongy shore that shudders under my step. When I travelled here in the past, I felt overwhelmed by the strangeness of it all. Now, I am not afraid, because I understand why everything looks the way it does. For example, the reason why there are no stars in the sky is because they are all in the sea. The waves that oozed at my feet as I waded ashore are home to countless places and planets. From the beach, I spied the faintest glimpse of the coruscating waters, illuminated by small orbs the size of phytoplankton – each one a world. I can't pretend to understand the scale. Here, I have ascended, becoming a giant of legend, and I fear to displace a single grain of sand lest it too contain a Galaxy.

While I am terrified of causing undue harm to whole worlds without any awareness of my actions – the thought makes my breath quicken – I myself face no threats here. Such is the nature of this bewildering shift in perspective. Released as I am from the limitations of scale and size, I imagine that even the filter-feeders who swim through the stars, consuming millions in great, gasping gulps, are nothing more than docile whales to me.

Only one being shall seek me out. Though he holds the power to destroy my home – every drop of water in that microscopic puddle we considered the ocean – he will not prey upon me. By the scale of this island, the Predator is but a small, frightened fish, struggling for survival like all of us.

To return to my previous subject, the primary difference between my first trip to the island and my present circumstances is that I understand I am truly here, in the flesh. When I drank from the shell, something indescribable happened – some arcane art rearranged and transported me in a flash. Well, that is not entirely correct, you see, because a "flash" is visual. I felt as if I ceased being physical matter and transformed into sound, soaring through unknown space via waves of a very different sort. It is a most disorienting mode of travel. There I was, standing in the council chamber, clutching on to you – by which I mean Scholar Henerey Clel, because this letter is not written for anyone in particular, as mentioned previously – so perhaps my other readers will simply disregard this sentence?

All that matters, I suppose, is that one moment I was there, and the next, I was here, stumbling out of the sea. I do not know how long I waited by the water, but I am sure my sense of time is as skewed as my understanding of scale. Certainly it was not an atypical number of hours for me to be alone with my thoughts. Besides, the Predator

329

made an appearance soon enough. Like any good host, it seems he expected my visit.

I should note some things I've learned about my new acquaintance. I refer to the Predator as "him" at his own request. He speaks my language – my own, familiar dialect, not the Archaic Scholar I've struggled with since Henerey and I came to the city. I do not understand how that is possible, because he is an exceedingly small fish who, I imagine, is not in possession of a voice box or a tongue. Yet the sounds resonate from him, circling around me and echoing through the air.

His words of greeting were, *Follow me.*

I assumed the Predator could not survive on land. In a way, his slender teeth and tapered body make him resemble a Glowering Telescope-Fish – about which I remembered reading in a certain Scholar's fourth Natural History publication – and, like the Telescope-Fish, he is noticeably gilled. To my surprise, he rolled out of the water in an unexpectedly substantial bubble, which surrounded him like an aquarium of star-coloured glass.

At first, I marvelled at his ingenuity. Where had this creature gained the power to comport himself in what was effectively the opposite equivalent of a depth-craft? Instead of ensconcing him in a comfortable pocket of air, as our devices do, this system preserved the Predator in a sloshing swirl of water. Then I realised he likely gained this knowledge by consuming a world, or several. To think that such an unfathomable number of lives might be lost to enable this sinister fish to walk!

During my first visit, I never had the opportunity to grasp the true size of this place – if it can be said to have a set size, as the island appears to expand and contract. I wonder how you would even begin to map it. (And by "you", I mean my sister, Scholar Sophy Cidnorghe. Please disregard that misstep as well.) Previously, I stopped at an enormous stalk of kelp and rested there until I was carried back. This time, we pushed past the kelp forest (or, rather, I pushed, and the Predator rolled at his soft speed) until we reached a truly astonishing sight.

A house, tidy and cosy, built from a rainbow of driftwood. Though its architecture was unlike anything I had ever seen before, I say "house" with such confidence because clearly that was its purpose. The shelter is shaped like a low dome, with algae-covered, cylindrical forms jutting out at every which angle. While several beams are unpainted and exposed, other parts appear almost scaled, graced with layers and layers of triangular crystals overlapping each other in a reptilian mosaic. Two blue lights protrude from the sides like the eyes of a Perpendicular Shark.

"What is this place?" I said, more to myself than to the Predator – for how could I ask him such insignificant questions when the fate of the world rested upon my shoulders?

Its origins are unknown to me. The Predator spoke without pausing the quick rolling of his bubble. *It has always been here. Until I learned to travel in this way, I did not know it existed.*

"But someone constructed it! It is not a cliff-face, nor a kelp forest. Someone took these materials and fastened them into place. Who designed it?"

It is unknown to me, spat the Predator again. What could be more reprehensible to such an entity than knowledge he cannot acquire?

Then, remarkably, the Predator appeared to notice my cowed response to his harsh tone and tried to make it better. From which consumed planet did he learn compassion?

It is certainly strange, he remarked in a kindlier tone. *I've heard the Filter-Feeders sing of this house. But they do not know its story either. Some whisper that it simply grew, plant-like, from the very island itself. Waiting for someone to call it home.*

He nodded at the door. (Even with his many abilities, the Predator still lacks fingers.) I touched what looked like a piece of driftwood made of shimmering oil, and beneath my hand it took on a series of pulsing patterns. The marbled liquid breathed into circles, then squares, then hexagons, then proceeded through all known geometric forms until it reached shapes that I could not begin to identify. Finally, all melted away, and the door rasped open for us.

To my surprise, this ineffable, prehistoric house was rather welcoming. More glimmering mosaics made from gems I could not name – all streaked with a spectrum of quartz-like veins – covered the walls, with each diamond-shaped tile nestled companionably into the next. A bed-style nest hung from above, its expansive round net stacked with long pillows. And in the centre of the room were two small hollows in the floor, both lined with similar cushions. To these "chairs" the Predator and I proceeded.

I intended to focus on the Predator and our conversation, but all who know me will understand that I cannot stop wondering about this extraordinary place. Though the forms and structures of the furnishings were alien to me, I could tell that they complemented each other, creating a cohesive and impressive interior. Some person (being?) wanted to feel at home here. They loved it, I reckon, as much as I loved the Deep House. But who were they? A visitor like me who came to this place for some worthy cause? Or were there others, long before us, entities for whom our vast universe was truly just the ocean that swirled at their doorstep?

I will never know the answers to these questions, of course. Perhaps it matters not. Perhaps all that's really worth mentioning is how strangely comfortable I felt there.

I should not have been surprised that the Predator continued observing me as I considered my surroundings.

What I admire most about beings of your type, he said, *is your fatal curiosity. No matter the situation – no matter if your very lives are in danger – you remain in thrall to your desire to know more. I feel much the same.*

"Is my very life in danger?" I asked him. "You are, at the moment, but a tiny fish in a bubble."

The Predator leaned closer to me. *I did not perceive you as the threatening type, little one. I don't suppose you are proposing that you save your world by trapping me in an aquarium?*

"The idea hadn't occurred to me," I said, "but now that you mention it—"

Before I finished speaking, I suddenly felt myself falling through water, just like when I had my accident at the Deep House, while a nightmarish leviathan – the Predator magnified thousands of times, with menacing eyes larger than moons – swam closer and closer—

Then we returned to the house, and the Predator appeared harmless once more. Aquarium-sized, if you will.

I diminished myself to suit the scale of this island, he snapped, *but if I wished, we could return to the ocean as it really is, where I am vast and you could not be more insignificant. Do you understand?*

I nodded, feeling that familiar panic rising in me yet again. I feared I had made a grave mistake. Surely someone else – a trained scientist, a courageous mediator, anyone – would be better suited to this task. They would not sit here sobbing after a cosmic predator temporarily dropped them into the sea to make a point.

But I took a moment to evaluate my thoughts. No amount of Scholarly training could prepare someone for this experience. I reminded myself that my reaction was not solely caused by my Malady of the Mind (which I mention for the benefit of any unknown readers who are not familiar with my personal history). One could have a perfectly "typical" brain and still react negatively to these most unusual circumstances.

I dried my tears and took a moment to count the tessellations on the wall before turning back to the Predator.

"I acknowledge your power, Predator. If you can eat worlds at any moment, why bother respecting this pact at all?"

Didn't I make it clear earlier? he said – smiling, perhaps. It was difficult to tell with those teeth. *I am curious, and I must follow that impulse wherever it takes me. I am especially curious to hear what you have to say, little one.*

333

"My name is E.," I said firmly. "I don't suppose you have one yourself?"

Some see fit to give me names. I don't care for them. They make me sound rather fearsome – a destroyer of worlds – and pay little attention to my intellect.

"Perhaps it is understandable, considering that you do, in fact, destroy worlds."

But who does not? he cried. *On your own planet, do you not destroy a world every time you step into a tide pool or turn up a rock? Are there not thousands of small ways in which you can harm those around you without knowing it?*

I stiffened, blinking like a Glowering Telescope-Fish myself. Did the Predator know he'd hit upon the very theme that has troubled my Brain for years now, or was it simply a coincidence? Should I say I agreed with him? Recount the story of the time I discarded six perfectly good pies, because I could not shake the feeling that I had accidentally poisoned them and would subsequently sicken my entire family? Or when I banned my siblings from the undergarden for a tide because I feared I had not sufficiently checked the area for toxic Cone-Shells? Or when I—

"The difference," I said, before this line of thinking led me into distressed dissociation, "is that you do know. You intentionally seek out worlds that appeal to you, and you understand the cost of consuming them."

That I do, conceded the Predator. *Now, why do you think your world does not deserve the same fate?*

The moment had come, then. The negotiation. I felt utterly unprepared. Had I not been so impulsive, perhaps the First Scholars would have equipped me with scrolls upon scrolls of rhetoric and logic before I came here, giving me the tools to sculpt a passionate plea that would touch the heart of any person.

But I was not here to convince a person, exactly.

As though I had spoken my thoughts, the Predator continued

conversationally. *I could tell you all about the worlds I've seen – the knowledge I've obtained. The sparkling cities glimmering deep within their planet's core, fuelled by the very motion of the magma itself. Do you know all the habitations and gardens I could design, if I so chose? There are places where beings have crafted songs that can heal or harm, and where everyone grows protective shells upon their backs through clever manipulation of their own biology. I carry all their discoveries and innovations. I stand as witness to how they lived and learned, and it makes me stronger. What makes your planet superior to those that are gone?*

"I do not claim that our planet is superior," I said. "We cannot boast of such wonders as you describe. We always seek to expand our knowledge, but often we set ourselves back without understanding why. I do not imagine that you will spare us because we are singular."

Of course that was not the reason; it never could have been. A mediator or scientist might have taken that approach – cataloguing the wonderfully unique and impressive aspects of our civilisation – but those words would ring false if I spoke them. After all, I am a recluse, not a Scholar. The little I know about our world and its happenings comes from what I read in books and letters. I have not attended the Symposia to hear radical ideas debated in public. I chose not to receive formal academic training. I enjoy music and the arts from a distance, but I have not been to a museum or a theatre since I was a child. I cannot catalogue the great accomplishments of our world, since my life has been so limited to my own experience. If people are only worth protecting once they achieve great things, I am not among that worthy few! No, I wanted him to spare my world for the sake of its people, and all the creatures living alongside us, and the ocean. O, my ocean!

I could have told him this – I could have spoken my heart and explained that I selfishly wished to preserve the world so that I and everyone I love might continue inhabiting it, despite the dangers and dullnesses of existence.

What stopped me was that I suspected the Predator would not care.

335

This is not his fault; after all, his drive to survive is so consuming that he has become incapable of selflessness. It can be difficult to worry about others when you believe your own life is under constant threat. If I am honest, there was a time when I felt that way too – when I was so overwhelmed by my perilous Brain that I did not have the capacity to worry about anything other than enduring another day. Rather than pleading for what I wanted, I needed to appeal to his own desires.

"In fact," I said, assuming he could remember the thread of our conversation from before I went off into my thoughts, "it is because we are not singular that I hope you might be tempted to spare our world."

The Predator laughed – again, his mouth did not move, but I heard a kind of mirthful scream swirling around me.

I find myself eager to understand your logic. If you are not special, why do you deserve mercy?

"I am not saying we do." Suddenly, an idea popped into my mind, just as present and fully formed as any of my intrusive thoughts. "I just fear you might be acting a little pre-emptively."

Please elaborate.

"We have not reached our fullest potential," I said. "You told me of the marvellous knowledge you possess. Trust me when I say that nothing from our world can compete . . . at present. We are but a scattered group of shipwrecked Scholars, still struggling to learn our place in the universe. If you were to consume our world now, perhaps you would learn a few trivialities. But, say, in a thousand years—"

A blink of an eye to me.

"Precisely. Give us that amount of time, and our world's accomplishments will no doubt equal any of the wonders you have seen. If not exceed them."

The Predator tilted his tiny head at me.

You are captivating, E. You, too, are desperate to survive. Would you sacrifice the future of your world to preserve its present? Do you imagine that all the people who are not yet born will appreciate this exchange?

336

That thought did haunt me, but I did not have time to consider it further, because the Predator continued.

Your novel thinking intrigues me. I will accept your offer, with a condition. He leaned closer, and I looked into those pale, empty eyes. They were as pearls – curved and reflective, showing nothing but a warped vision of my own face.

You must give me some knowledge, he hissed. *To tide me over for a thousand years. Something I do not already know.*

"You would like me to teach you something?"

Nothing so complex, replied the creature. *I will consume the knowledge directly from your mind.*

"That sounds rather horrific. What exactly do you mean by consume—"

In a flash, the Predator loomed over me again, and I felt the unsettling sensation of my thoughts being spied upon.

If I imagine my Brain as a library – a visualisation strategy Dr Lyelle once urged me to try – then I felt as though I were wandering the stacks in darkness, flinching as footsteps followed me around the shelves and pages rustled under the rough touch of an unknown hand—

You hold largely uninteresting knowledge, noted the Predator. *But there is something I have never seen before.*

I wondered what that could possibly be. I do not think of myself as having an extraordinary number of skills. I can draw more than adequately, I am a moderately talented baker, and I have recently demonstrated a preternatural knack for winning boxed games that involve the omnipotent management of fictional tidepools.

You can make words out of pictures, he said. *Give that to me.*

"You mean my sketching?" (I suppose, after consuming thousands of worlds, he must have already learned how to bake.)

No, that is nothing special, the Predator replied. I tried not to take offence. *Let me show you.*

Again I found myself floating in an image – an image of myself, alone at night, in – this part almost broke my heart – in the dear, dear

Deep House, in my own little room, where I shall never write again. My hair reaches the floor again, and my fingers shake with that familiar tremor. This past version of me writes:

"Dear Scholar Clel,

Instead of reading further, I hope you will return this letter to its envelope . . ."

Perhaps, as I reviewed this memory, I ought to have thought something along the lines of "Back then, I would have never conceived of everything that would come to pass." But the woman who sat there, scribbling and sighing, could have conceived of any unbelievable future. I spent so much time absorbed in my obsessions, conjuring horrible fates that could never be real. While I would not have guessed that the world might end because of an enormous predatory fish, I constantly believed I was one step away from causing an unexpected apocalypse of my own. And I felt powerless to escape that impending doom, so I shut myself away to bear my thoughts alone and thwart the seemingly inescapable possibility of my actions creating calamities for others.

"You do not know how to write?" I asked. My question pulled me from the Deep House, away from my lovely and lonely past, and into the Predator's company once more.

Do you think you are the only world ever to develop a way of representing language? I can record information in signs stitched in tapestries, in series of numbers spat out by machines, in lines and strokes, in circles traced on the forest floor. I simply cannot do it exactly as you do. I must have it.

"Do you mean to say that I will not know how to write any longer?"

And you can never learn again. That is my price.

The thought terrified me. Or would have, under any other circumstances. Writing widened my world. Letters helped me connect with my sister even when she left, and led me to my superlative partner in life. At this point, however, I know I must let go of it. If I succeed with the Predator, I may yet be able to return home. I am not entirely sure I believe the process is as easy as the sea-woman suggested, but I remain

338

convinced that you – that is, the people whom I love – will figure out how to bring me back. When we are reunited, what need will I have for my words?

And if I am trapped here for eternity, I shall have no way to send letters anyway. (Though, as mentioned earlier, I do plan on dropping this letter into the sea once my conversation with the Predator concludes.)

I bit my lip and thought one last time of my correspondence. I remembered writing to Sophy during her expedition, telling her secrets in clipped postscripts and making wry comments about her instant love for the "friend" she described so glowingly. I even thought of writing to Arvist (and receiving no substantive replies), and to Seliara and Jeime.

Of course, though it pained and heartened me all at once, I recalled most fondly writing to you – to Henerey – finding myself completely at home with someone whom I had only known, at first, through words (and a particularly ostentatious author photograph). Undoubtedly, the time we've spent together since has been even more meaningful, but that is not to say that there was anything lacking in our letters. How I ache for you.

"Take it, then," I said to the Predator. "Must I do anything?"

The Predator almost salivated. He blinked within his bubble, and this very pen and paper appeared in my hand. They are shaky, flimsy things, and if you look too closely, you will notice immediately that something about them is simply not right. The paper is crumpled in the bottom right corner, yet that exact fold-mark repeats across the page like a pattern. The pen has the rough shape of a nib at the bottom, but it appears blurry no matter how closely I examine it. Despite these flaws, I recognised the pen as a replica of the one I used in the Deep House memory the Predator and I experienced together.

Write for me, he said. *Then I will consume it.*

"Is there anything in particular I should write?" I asked.

Whatever you like. Hurry, please. I am ravenous.

This letter – if it can be called a proper letter – is the result. He sits beside me now, watching with a primal hunger as my pen scratches. Sometimes he asks me to read out a phrase or sentence. Seeing these shapes shift into sounds is all new, and he starves for it.

I have not lost it yet, but I feel the words becoming harder to shape. At first, it was simply misspellings, which I was happy to fix. Now I find myself struggling with structure. That dash I used above. I know how I would articulate the pause when reading aloud but I do not know where to put one on the paper. It is a small loss in the scheme of things yet feels sharp all the same.

I should conclude before it is too late. These are indeed the last words I shall ever write and I can say with confidence that I do in fact hope you will read them.

Chapter 22

AUTOMATED POST MISSIVE FROM SOPHY CIDNORGHE TO E. CIDNOSIN, 1004

My beloved, brave sister,

I do not know when or how you will see this, but I desperately hope you shall. Your letter reached us. Tevn's friend . . . shall I call her Iridescence, as she requested? That certainly feels more suitable than "the Illogical One". At any rate, she alleged she "heard its journey" and managed to retrieve it from the cosmic sea. I am astonished by your courage and your compassion and your cleverness.

I am also furious. (To be clear – not at you!)

Despite the sea-woman's promises, it may be difficult for you to return immediately. I hate asking you to be patient when you have already endured so much, and I promise I will expend every effort to ensure you needn't wait long. You see, your letter made the return journey, but just barely. It looked like it was a thousand years old (and I say that as a cartographer who understands all too well what happens to paper over time).

Somehow, the temporally atypical existence of the island causes things to age when they depart. Iridescence certainly could bring you back right now, but she fears the journey would be as perilous for a person as for paper, and I cannot help but agree.

In the meantime, the sea-woman worked some magic with her

beloved "signals" that will allow us to write to you, even though you do not have an A.P. machine of your own. In what form will these words appear for you? Perhaps an unseen force will scratch them into the sand?

At any rate, you need not fear, because there are solutions in progress. Extraordinarily exciting ones! The Scholars hosted a meeting last night to discuss the issue of your (temporary!) displacement, and I was most eager to attend. I was delayed, however, when Tevn pulled me into a vestibule for a private conversation. (I say "pulled" metaphorically, because Tevn is so against unexpected physical contact himself that he would never subject someone else to it.) Shall I tell you about it to entertain you? (Just as I did during my Ridge expedition, I'd like to imagine my letters keeping you company when you are all alone.)

"Is everything all right, Tevn?" I asked at the time. "Should I find Niea? She's seeing off Vyerin's family."

"No, thank you," he responded, gazing intently at a point just to the left of my eyes. "I . . . I suppose I might as well say it. I would like your advice, Sophy."

"To what do I owe this pleasure?"

He sighed and stretched his neck backward in a gesture of dramatic despair. "I have a personal issue I need to solve. Niea is exceptionally kind and can say no wrong about anything. You, on the other hand—"

"Perhaps you oughtn't continue that sentence," I said. "What sort of straightforward, sceptical assistance can I offer you?"

Tevn did not correct me. "I just had a conversation with *her*," he said, emphasising the pronoun as always. "It appears she would like to enjoy my company on a more permanent basis."

"Is that not a positive development?"

"It is not so simple as renting a dormitory together. She wants me to – transform. Become one of them, like some of the Scholars did, years ago. When I imagine being able to speak with her, always, and becoming forever free of Society at large, it sounds sublime."

"And yet?"

342

"Well, the truth of the matter is that I am not sure I truly wish to become a cosmic sea-person," he said with a serious intensity that contrasted the content of his sentence. "Won't it feel awful to have a different set of sensations – different skin – a different shape completely, with extraordinary features I never possessed before?"

"You would also have many more teeth," I remarked gravely.

"Precisely!" Tevn exclaimed. "What's worse, if my thought processes somehow change as I become a different type of being ..."

"You would lose your sense of who you are," I said, but only after it was clear that he never intended to finish his sentence.

"I feel I have only recently come to terms with myself. After what happened on the first Ridge mission – after Rawsel manipulated me – I felt more out of sorts than ever before. I questioned whether anything was real, and I did not know how to handle myself or my interactions with others. I fear I could not endure such a shock to my system again. Is that selfish of me?"

"It is not selfish to take action that is necessary for your continued survival and wellbeing," I concluded. "Is that the advice you hoped I'd give?"

"It is, in fact," he said. "I assumed you might understand. You wouldn't exactly swallow that musical shell-potion to wait with your sister while we try to solve the island problem, would you? Because you know that would not be right for you?"

His words struck me, and I did consider leaving them out of this letter, but I suppose it's too late for that.

Now, this is all hypothetical, at any rate, because I have no reason to believe that there are more transporting goblets. Still, I cannot deny my own small, secret urge to flee to you – not only to comfort you, but to seek comfort from you, to hide in your arms as I did for that extremely brief time when I was very, very young.

Yet you said you made this decision for my sake, and I do not want to disrespect that. (If you needed me – truly *needed* me – I could come – and perhaps that is what a good sister ought to do – but I feel I would be more use to you on this side than the other – I do somewhat specialise in bringing you home from improbable locales, after all!)

Though I've attempted to discuss this matter in more detail here, I did not have time to answer Tevn himself. As it happened, a certain cosmic sea-person took that very moment to interrupt us.

We found ourselves in the water again, which glowed gold this time. Bubbles floated lazily about us in massive schools. When I examined them more closely, I noticed they were square instead of circular.

"You do not wish to join me, my friend?" asked Iridescence, who drifted nearer, sprawled atop an enormous square bubble as if it were perfectly solid. "Your words summoned me. Is it true?"

"Yes," Tevn said in his straightforward way. "I have come to understand that I do not especially wish to become something other than I am, even if that means accepting the limitations of my own form. I am sorry."

Iridescence nodded in what would have been a surprisingly serious fashion – except that a flock of octagonal bubbles took this moment to assemble into a crown on top of her head.

"You are like her, then," she intoned mournfully. "She did not want it either. Is it something the people of your planet have in common? My dear friends. I will be so lonely without you."

"You've had another friend from our world?" I said carefully. I gave Tevn a questioning glance, which went unanswered. Speaking personally, I might feel a little jealous if I learned that the mysterious being asking me to spend eternity with her had previously issued a similar invitation to someone else, but that is just me!

"Many friends, many years ago. But she haunts me most of all. She was not like this one," sang the sea-woman, gesturing at Tevn. "He asks beautiful questions, and she wrote beautiful poetry. When I gave her my dreams, she transformed what I said into pages of loveliness. Then when she died, as your kind do, I forgot every word of her language but one, and swore I must relearn it all if I were to speak with another from your world."

344

"That's why you spoke only Archaic Scholar when we first met," Tevn exclaimed. "I did wonder how you happened to have such vast knowledge of practically everything in the universe except for Academic Vernacular vocabulary."

"Her life was an isolated one," continued the Iridescence. "Perhaps I am to blame. I told her of the Predator and the Scholars and their creations. She thought her world must know, but none would believe her. I dread to think of what loneliness might have overcome her had we not remained friends until she grew too old."

"What was the word?" I asked. A funny sense of curiosity – and familiarity – had overtaken me. "The single word you allowed yourself to remember, in her memory."

Then Iridescence sang the word, letting each syllable swish in a pleasingly sibilant manner.

"Did you say – circumference?" asked Tevn. "As in, the perimeter of a circle? How curious."

"Her other friend was the poet!" I exclaimed. "The one who shared her poem with Darbeni, who shared it with the Fleet."

Tevn frowned most unhelpfully.

"'A Luminous Circumference', of course," I continued. "You know – the poem about the Entries that E. and Henerey found. They thought Darbeni wrote it, but their research uncovered that it had only been *published* by Darbeni, and penned by a mysterious woman . . ."

"I can't believe this," said Tevn, "but I fear I've been mistaken for Vyerin Clel *again*. Sophy, please do recall that not everybody in the world has read E. and Henerey's past correspondence: and we certainly don't need to hear it summarised, either."

Well, Tev's reaction matters little. I know you, E., will be most interested in this development. After all that you and Henerey did to sort out your many mysteries, is it not a wonder that I managed to contribute in some small way?

"The poet might not have succeeded in spreading your warning in her own time," I said to Iridescence, "but that poem brought E. to the

Darbeni archives, where she learned about the Fleet, which started the entire series of events that brought us here. I think your friend might have been pleased."

"But she is gone," said the sea-woman, atonally and dismally. "One day, you too will be gone, my friend. And what will I forget to pay tribute to you?"

"Is there not another way?" asked Tevn, as a flurry of triangular bubbles erupted from behind his shoulders. "I cannot become one of you. But I could, perhaps, extend my life to a length that you might find more reasonable. What if I remained in the city?"

"The Scholars are not overly fond of her," I cautioned. "Would they allow it?"

"If they are truly committed to rescuing people from the Predator, they will have to become more open to so-called illogical behaviour," he said firmly. "What other secrets will you share as the next thousand years pass, my friend? I could mediate for you – rather like an inter-campus ambassador of sorts. Didn't you want me to come to this city in the first place so I could change how the Scholars behave?"

Iridescence laughed, and all around us, the laughter took on shapes, becoming endless spirals of jewel-coloured sand. The grains made me sputter, yet Tevn did not falter as sound and sand spun around him.

"Your cleverness is resplendent!" she sang. "They will not appreciate you, not at first, but that is why you must stay. You are like no other, Tevn Mawr, and I shall delight to see how you manage them!"

"And perhaps, if I remain," Tevn said, more cautiously this time, "you might visit me more frequently?"

"As often as you like!" she trilled. "Your company enlivens me always, no matter what form you take. May I show you another form of mine?"

I didn't quite understand what she meant by this statement, but it set Tevn's eyes alight.

"That would be an honour," he said.

Iridescence shut her lips and hummed, as we do – completing a

346

surprisingly simple, minor scale. The notes floated from her mouth and onto her face and torso and tail, enveloping her in unbelievable euphony. When the song subsided, a tremendous fish, lithe like a strand of sea grass and scaled in the glossy purple of the evening tide, floated before us. In her true form, Tevn's friend possessed three eyes sparkling with countless speckles of vivid blue and no fewer than four rows of teeth set in jaws that protruded from her grinning maw.

Despite all the peculiar experiences I've endured lately, I did feel slightly startled by her sudden transformation. Tevn, however, swam forward and folded before the fish in an effortless underwater bow.

"You are unlike anything I have ever seen," Tevn murmured, breathlessly.

I know he can give no higher compliment.

"My dear, dear friend," Iridescence exclaimed in an eerily bubbling tone. "Shall I disappear and return so I may visit you now?"

"Only if you let me leave first," I said while I still had the chance. Though I know Tevn's interest in her is not romantic, I still felt rather like the odd one out!

Iridescence nodded, but before she sent me back, Tevn extended his hand to me. I did not reach out to take it, not exactly — but I extended mine in turn.

"I thank you, Sophy," he said. "I shall see you shortly."

To my relief, I was then returned quite expeditiously to the council room. For all I know, Tevn's friend might have kept us down there for a thousand years!

I soon sought out a seat next to my wife, in the second of the two chairs. Niea wove her arm around me and I leaned into her, enjoying the familiar stability of her shoulder (and the familiar scratchiness of the pink lace adorning today's frock).

"Where have you been?" she whispered as the Scholars entered.

"Why, enjoying a conversation with my dear friend Tev."

She raised an eyebrow at me. "Is that the most improbable thing to occur over the course of your journey?"

"I would say so," agreed Tevn, who appeared out of nowhere behind us. As I smirked back at him, I noticed Henerey standing silently to the side. I am looking out for him as best as I can, but I know he misses you desperately. (In fact, I imagine you will probably receive a message from him before I finish writing this one – if you haven't already!)

At any rate, Vyerin soon joined us (after seeing off his family in style, no doubt), and the planning commenced. With some trepidation, the First Scholars conceded that they cannot remain isolated if we are to prepare our world to survive the Predator before the next millennium passes. This concession, however, quickly devolved into a fractured debate between the First Scholars about what exactly those preparations might look like.

Considering that I had not, by this point, removed my head from Niea's shoulder, I suddenly felt her stir beneath me.

"I would like to take charge of operations in our world," she proclaimed.

It was a gorgeously clear and confident statement. I felt a profound thrill – and a sense of nostalgia. Why, E., I don't think I've heard Niea talk quite like that since she was leading us down at the Ridge!

"Somebody must," Niea added, as the Scholars gazed at her. "If our society has any hope of driving off the Predator, people need to know the truth about our cosmos. But we cannot simply return home and issue a grand cross-campus announcement about the universe's ocean and the beast within . . . and leave it at that. We must plan, carefully, and share information responsibly. These days, I am an educator by trade. I would be honoured to help your Scholars and mine learn together."

"And I," I murmured, standing beside her, "am honoured to be your wife."

What follows is a general summary of what we discussed next. Any attempt at cultivating collaboration between this world and ours must be long-term and sustainable. Because we cannot accomplish everything within our own limited lifetimes, we will document

348

everything as it happens. We will take what small actions we can, now, so that the next generation may continue our work.

But I don't know how much you really want to hear of the details, my dear sister – this letter is long enough already, and perhaps I should recount only that which is most relevant to us both?

After a rapid conversation with his friend, Tevn announced that the sea-people will work with the Scholars – "Firsts" and "Seconds" alike – to construct a kind of augmented Structure that we could use to have "visions", like you did long ago, of that island you now inhabit. We would not truly *be* there in the flesh, of course, but they say I would be able to see and speak with you once the device is operational. That shall be such a boon while we strive to get you home more permanently!

(This was the only part of the conversation during which Henerey paid close attention, but he drifted away once more after it became clear that this was a future project and not yet accessible. I do worry about him.)

While he had the floor, Tevn also informed the Scholars that he would serve as their ambassador to Iridescence and her siblings, and that they should approach him with any questions and disputes so he could provide logical solutions. This went over much more positively than imagined, thanks to the Fifteenth First Scholar! I think they are all a little overwhelmed by how frequently the sea-woman has been popping in and out of their city, and having communications filtered through someone as conscientious as Tevn Mawr must be a relief. Tev did make some concessions – he will have to become a full-fledged First Scholar and be trained in their record-keeping customs, for instance. I'm sure he could not be more thrilled.

Those are the most significant developments, but there is one other subject I ought to address before I finish. As I said, Henerey grieves your absence most deeply. He asked me, Niea, Vyerin, and the Fifteenth First Scholar to meet with him this evening. I do not know precisely what he will say, but I will update you when I can.

And I do mean that. I intend to update you all the time, E., so often that you may grow sick of it! I will write you a whole shipload of letters,

349

if that means you won't be lonely while you wait. I lost you once and I swore I would never do so again, but here we are. It has been but a tide since we reunited, and I barely managed to see you at all, thanks to the rather inconvenient matter of our world being under threat. I wanted to spend entire nights chatting and drinking tea and doing jigsaws with you, just like we used to, or simply staring out into the abyssal darkness on a depth-craft to see what unusual sea creatures we might spy. You told me that you had to leave because you would not destroy another home, but, my dearest sister, can't you see that you never destroyed our home in the first place?

The Deep House was a marvellous thing, to be true, and an utterly spectacular place for three odd children to enjoy an exceptionally odd childhood. But if you left and Arvist or I claimed it as our own, the house never would have been the same. It was our home because you made it that way, with your careful maintenance and eccentric decorations and ambitious spirulina pies. In time, I know you can make that perplexing little house on your island into a Deep House of your own, though it's stubbornly abovewater.

But I must sign off now before the hour grows too late (I am expected in this meeting with Henerey, as I mentioned).

In the meantime, if I may say it, I am tremendously proud to be your sister.

With love, always,

Sophy

AUTOMATED POST MISSIVE FROM VYERIN CLEL TO REIV CLEL, 1004

Dear Reiv,

I suppose you didn't expect to hear from me, did you? It's only been about an hour since you headed home with A. and O., but I thought I owed you some mail. With all the letter-writing and letter-reading

I've done over the past few years, can you believe I've only written to my own husband a handful of times? (I shouldn't count those secret postcards I sent you from the ship, as some might argue that flirtatious limericks are not exactly correspondence.)

I hope you'll take a moment to read so I can keep you company from afar until I return. It won't be much longer. I promise.

Tomorrow I will say goodbye to Henerey again.

I can't say I'm surprised. Surprised by the circumstances, maybe, but not the outcome. The poor fellow has despaired since E.'s been gone. I've never seen him so low, which is saying something, considering the melancholic tendencies my brother has always hidden beneath his friendly exterior. It reached the point where I would have done anything to lift his spirits. I'd commandeer the nearest available vessel, haul Henerey aboard, sail through the very universe in search of that blasted island, and fling him overboard, if that would help!

Seems he managed to find a more reasonable solution. A pity.

Henerey awaited us in this odd garden when Sophy, Niea, and I found him. To take my mind off things as we approached him, I was chatting with our favourite duo about various sundries. It seems they are interested in finding a new place to live when we are all back home, and I let them know they are welcome to stay with us in the interim. I'm sure you won't mind. I imagine Orey still asks after the lovely lady who tells stories about sea creatures.

(Between you and me, I am quite concerned about Sophy. I fear she may be somewhat in denial about how easy it will be to bring her sister back. I don't doubt that Sophy can do it, but I think it may require substantial time and effort. I would like to support her as much as I can – considering everything she's done for me!)

At any rate, the so-called Fifteenth First Scholar intercepted us about halfway there, and we all spotted my brother sitting on a bench.

To my surprise, Henerey was smiling. That's when I knew for sure what would happen. Honestly, Reiv, when I saw that look on his face again, I could hardly bring myself to be sad about it.

351

Now, unlike many people of my acquaintance, I rarely use my correspondence to record conversations. But this was an important one, so I'll do my best. For his sake.

"I spoke with Tevn," Henerey said. "He and his friend gave me hope, and I could not be happier." From behind his back, my brother carefully produced another shell-shaped goblet full of – something. Sound, I believe? I was with you during the relevant part of that fateful meeting and missed some key details. It matters not.

"There is more?" said Sophy. "How wonderful!"

Even I could discern that there were equal parts relief and envy in her voice.

"Not much more, it seems," he clarified, "but there is enough. While I know it's sudden, my mind is made up. I shall join her, just as soon as is reasonable." Then he turned to me, giving me the most earnestly regretful glance. "As long as that is all right with you, Vy?"

I took a deep breath. You'll be pleased to know that I didn't try to stop myself from tearing up.

"You don't need to ask me, you foolish fellow. I wouldn't be able to bear it if you didn't go."

Then we might have embraced. I know not.

"I am not leaving this very second, much as I would like to," Henerey said, once this sentimental interlude concluded. "I must pack and prepare so I may make things as comfortable as possible for me and E."

"Until we can bring you home, of course," said Sophy.

"Of course. I presume if I bring books and things in a bag, they will also be transported with me?"

"There are many practical considerations too," continued Sophy in her very Sophy way. "Books and things are lovely, I'm sure, but what will happen if one of you falls ill in the meantime?"

"That is unromantic but reasonable," said Henerey. He turned to the Fifteenth First Scholar. "How quickly could you train me in the basic principles and practices of Antepelagic medicine?"

"It would be a wasted effort," said the Fifteenth First Scholar.

"I assure you that I will dedicate myself to learning it, for her sake!"

"You needn't worry," said the Scholar with a funny smile. "It is – illogical – and rather difficult to explain, since it is beyond the scope of our understanding. You will not grow old there, nor fall ill. There is nothing on the island that could seriously injure you. Like us, you shall exist outside of time."

"Do you mean to say that they will be immortal if they never manage to leave?" asked Sophy. "Not that there is any possibility of that, of course."

"Of course," Henerey repeated, "but speaking hypothetically – goodness! If that came to pass, perhaps I would finally be able to learn even one-tenth of all the things I wish to discover!"

Speaking metaphorically, my brother's energy and passion already make him eternally youthful to me. Personally, the thought of living forever terrifies me. What a nightmare! (Though if I had my good health, I certainly wouldn't mind a few extra decades with you, dear fellow.) The notion of being trapped on an island for an entire eternity with only one other person for company is equally horrifying. I can say that because I know you'd feel the same. You and I are alike, aren't we – we need our people! But I cannot imagine anyone taking better advantage of such circumstances than my brother and his curious companion.

If they have no other choice, that is.

O, I've had enough of that dialogue transcription nonsense for now. In short, I will bid a final farewell to my brother in the morning. I must keep that between him and me, however, because if I tell you about it afterwards, Reiv, I may indeed start weeping again in a most unseemly fashion. I'm sure it will be as meaningful and memorable as any such goodbye ought to be, and that I will carry that experience with me for the rest of my days. (Before he departs, I also need him to help compose an informative letter to our parents, because there is no way I am going to explain all this to them by myself.)

353

So there you have it. The tale of two brothers – how we lost and found each other and then settled somewhere in between. I cannot truthfully say that I am heartbroken, though I will soon embrace my brother in person for what could be the last time. (Sophy assures me that it will not be.)

When I was completing my training as a captain, I learned of an antique sailors' superstition that dates back hundreds of years (if not to the dark time directly after the Dive itself). Legend says that when a captain breathes their last breath, their mind floats up on the breeze, catches a ship of spindrift waiting for them on the nearest wave, and sails far away until they reach a calm sea, full of friendly shallows that reflect only stars, never storms. Henerey is not dead, and I am sure he and E. will face some challenges as they adjust to their new situation. But because I am not the most fanciful person and cannot envision this alien sea that E. and Henerey will live beside, I imagine the bright ocean from that superstition instead – and will take comfort in knowing, for the time being, that my brother is safe, supported, and free of the cares and crises our world so often forced upon him.

And my wandering days are done for now, too. See you soon, chap. (Yes, before you ask, I did remember to bring back souvenirs for the children. They do like depth-craft instruction manuals, correct? I jest. You shall all have to wait and see.)

Vy

LETTER FROM HENEREY CLEL TO E. CIDNOSIN, 1004

Dear E.,

This is the second time I've written to you since your departure. You wouldn't know it, though, because there was no way that my previous letter (if the many fragmented drafts I wrote in my journal can be jointly counted as a single letter) could have been sent. It was a tragic, sentimental thing that probably would have increased your sorrow, so I am glad, in a way, that it will never reach you.

I have been most grateful to your sister over the past few days. Oddly – and perhaps fittingly, under the circumstances – it reminds me of the first time you visited the island, when you were hospitalised, and Sophy kept me updated on your condition. She loves you so strongly, E., and though it is not in the same way that I do, it gives us common ground.

Now that I am already a few paragraphs down the page, I must admit how silly it is that I wrote this letter in the first place. Not because you won't receive it – in fact, I can personally guarantee that it will arrive at your door! (By this point, as you read it, it already has). But I imagine that under ordinary circumstances, you would treat this letter as a precious piece of correspondence – just as I did, back in the day, with every letter you sent me.

Yet I promise you will forget about this letter very shortly.

Perhaps it was bold of me to assume, without asking first, that you might be open to the prospect of living with me on a cryptic island that we may examine and study as much as we wish. I apologise; I had no way of communicating with you before this decision was made. Even at this point, if you prefer your solitude, you are welcome to place within one of these most unusual windows a sign that says "HENEREY, NO", and I will desist, finding some other place upon the cosmic sea in which to shelter.

I very much hope, though, that my humble presence will be enough for you, for however long we remain here together. Sophy and Vyerin probably think it is a bit of a tragedy – a kind of noble sacrifice – that my devotion forced me to condemn myself to isolation. But I cannot stop thinking of the dreams we shared together – of a little place just for the two of us, apart from Society, where we can talk and explore and learn and love each other in our own quiet way. With that in mind, I am making no sacrifice whatsoever. I could not be happier that this is my fate, that I will be here with you, even if it is for always.

And I no longer need to use the future tense! I *am* here, anyway. Would you consider, if it suits you, putting down this letter and letting me in?

Chapter 23

AUTOMATED POST MISSIVE FROM THE THIRTIETH SECOND SCHOLAR TO LADY CORALEAN, 1005

Dear Lady,

I suppose our bargain is now complete, isn't it? I am grateful for your cooperation. In fact, yesterday I mentioned our correspondence in passing to the Fifteenth First Scholar, thinking she would be delighted by this example of intra-world collaboration. I'm afraid she did not find your crimes quite as charming as you do. Her loss, no doubt!

I know there is no need for us to continue writing to each other, but I did want to clarify one final point. I believe we might have miscommunicated previously, and, because of my Scholarly devotion to accuracy, I must endeavour to rectify any errors. Will you verify, for the record, that you remain in the employ of Chancellor Orelith Rawsel at present? You know, the one whom I termed "that awful man" previously.

O, on that note, would you like to hear a brief anecdote about him? Perhaps it will amuse you. When your Chancellor first arrived, I made an (understandable) error that rather displeased him.

"Might I clarify the spelling and meaning of your surname?" I said, once he had introduced himself – remember, Lady, my aforementioned devotion to accuracy, demanded by my Oaths!

When he rather crossly spelled it out for me, I then realised my mistake.

"Ah, that makes more sense! You see, from the way you overemphasised the R in 'Rawsel', I thought you had appended an A to the beginning, and unless your language has changed substantially over the past years, I consequently wondered if your surname was the same as a word referring to a heightened state of physical—"

At that moment, the Fifteenth First Scholar made the excellent decision of cutting short my linguistic revelations. (In fairness, that particular word appears frequently in some of the ancient romantic epics that *formerly* held me in thrall, so I might have been primed to think of it.) Yet, to my right, I noticed Scholar Clel scribble something in his journal, and then scrutinise it for a few moments while mouthing syllables to himself. As realisation dawned upon him, I suppose, he bit his lip and became exceedingly embarrassed.

"That certainly never would have occurred to *me*," I heard him whisper, as Scholar Cidnosin watched him with wry amusement. "Remarkable!"

That took rather longer to tell than I anticipated. I apologise! Let me return to the matter at hand. I had assumed you must still be working for this fellow, but I now realise that simply cannot be the case. After all, you mentioned your employer's devotion to his family. From what I've read, it seems nearly everyone *except* Chancellor Rawsel is motivated by their desire to preserve such bonds. If you'll please indulge me, then – who, exactly, bid you to gather these documents?

I understand if you prefer not to answer, but I do hope you will at least do me the courtesy of replying.

In eagerness,

30

AUTOMATED POST MISSIVE FROM LADY CORALEAN TO THE THIRTIETH SECOND SCHOLAR, 1005

Dear 30,

What an anecdote! Goodness, I never would have expected you, of all people, to confess to something of that nature. You may indeed be the most interesting person I have ever met. (Make of that what you will.)

Well, since my mission is complete – and I have already been handsomely rewarded, enough to buy me several fresh artificial whales – there is no reason why I cannot tell you.

After Chancellor Rawsel returned, he was a changed man. By his own report, that is. "Lady, I am a changed man!" were the very words with which he greeted me during what would become our last formal meeting. Though I imagine he expected these "changes" were for the better, I think your world unsettled him in a way he could not shake. He seemed just as grimly determined to rid the world of the Entries, but his attempts to do so were lacklustre. So lacklustre, in fact, that I had no choice but to increase my prices threefold if he wished to retain my services – which he rather foolishly declined. Chancellor Rawsel took to disseminating warnings around every Campus (quite efficiently, with my help, and then quite poorly afterwards), entreating everyone not to trust the disgruntled and disgraced Scholars who might spread lies simply to wreak havoc.

It was not an awful plan, all things considered. He might have even succeeded, if it weren't for Niea Cidnorghe's lecture.

"The Truth About The Ridge Expedition", read the posters. "A Most Thrilling Exposition Of Deep-Water Secrets, As Shared By Those Who Witnessed Them, And Illustrated With Wholly Original Photographic Images!" (Niea later told me, in confidence, that she was *not* the one who came up with the title.) The event was scheduled to take place in a tiny presenter's hall on Boundless, but the surge of attention they received from Scholars across the campuses resulted in a move to Intertidal's largest opera theatre. (My illicit review of the room reservation logs suggests that Scholar Irye Rux must have called in a favour with the Scholars of Sound.) As a result, everyone who's anyone is now fully aware of what truly occurred on the infamous Ridge expedition of 1002.

Niea has announced a follow-up – a symposium, open to Scholars and non-Scholars of every Campus – that will discuss the true history of the Dive. From what she's shared with me, she is planning it all most carefully. She wants to tell the truth about the Predator, but tell it thoughtfully. Some won't believe her, no doubt. Others (myself included, alas) may simply not care what happens to the world in a thousand years. I suspect, however, that Niea will cling to her hopeful belief that a sizeable number of people *will*.

But I also suspect I shall have to spend some more time investigating her to be sure. To that end, tomorrow I intend to help Niea and Sophy transport some unwieldy furniture into their new residence. As it happens, they have finally found their ideal home – on the Atoll, of all places. Two docks down from the Clel residence. "We're all essentially family now, aren't we? Vy and I could not be happier," Reiv Clel confided to me at one of his famous dinner parties. (Then he proceeded to ask who in the world I was and why I was attending his party without an invitation. I preserved my aura of beguiling mystery by departing immediately.) At any rate, Sophy and Niea are eager to settle in quickly, as they plan to depart on a much-belated nuptial voyage next tide, and I am ecstatic for them, because—

O, what am I saying?

Let us return to the event of most relevance – my parting from Rawsel. There I was, bereft of employment and rather miserable. I took up lodgings at Boundless Campus and tried offering my services to Apprentice Scholars. I did manage to retrieve an antique manuscript from a Scholar who previously hired me to steal it from his former

360

friend, but business proved scarce otherwise. One night, when faced with the difficult decision of whether I should stay awake another hour doing nothing or simply sleep, I heard my door chime. My calling-card collector produced a wordless triangular paper decorated with water-colours and three-dimensional embellishments.

The creator of this curious card, I surmised, must be affiliated with the School of Inspiration. What I did not guess was that this particular Scholar happened to be none other than Arvist Cidnan.

I had only met Cidnan briefly when the Chancellor and I joined the Entry project, but I remembered him well. His moustache had grown larger and more curvilinear, and his face was lined with weariness (or so I thought before realising that someone would probably describe my current countenance in the same way).

I invited Arvist into my parlour, where I bustled about, pretending to search for refreshments that I did not actually possess. Thankfully, he declined all sustenance, but I took that bustling time as an oppor-tunity to review everything I learned about the third Cidnosin sibling during my research for the Chancellor. He began his studies later in life, married the childhood neighbour who was a former flame of Sophy's, and is known for his experimental art practice that typically involves some combination of sculpture and live performance. (He is also right-handed, though he claims ambidexterity; strictly vegetarian, though he will eat fish in public because he is loath to be seen as "par-ticular" by his peers; and unshakably convinced that his artistic talent is exceptional (there is no "though" for that characteristic)).

"I plan to see my sister soon," he said, after I completed all the predictable prattle about how I could be of service, etc. "Not really see her, I mean, but – well, it's a fascinating technological experience. Truly sublime! We can interact with her and the phosphorescent place she calls home, as though we were sharing the same dream. My other sister, Sophy, does it all the time these days. The fact remains that I have not seen E. in years. I would like to truly apologise and prove my worth to her."

361

I understood none of this at the time – though our shared collection of documents certainly sheds some light on his statements!

"Emotional support is not among the many services I offer," I said in an appropriately chipper tone.

"No, that is not it at all!" he exclaimed. "Sophy and—"

"Ah, that explains it." I had to interrupt for efficiency's sake, of course. "Rawsel told me much about Sophy Cidnorghe. Nothing good, mind you, which always made me rather interested in befriending her – and that bafflingly good-hearted wife of hers. You are taking orders from your sister, then?"

"I am doing nothing of the sort!" Arvist cried again, in an exclamation even more dramatic than the first. Then, to my surprise, he paused for a moment, casting his eyes downwards as his lips formed a smile that was almost . . . humble?

"Sophy and I are working together," Arvist said, suddenly shy and sincere in a way that did not suit him whatsoever. "Since E. is gone, we are, well, trying new things. Meeting for meals. Playing games. Even weeping in each other's company, when circumstances demand."

"I certainly hope you do not intend to start weeping in my company." I eyed my inexpensive and undoubtedly non-waterproof carpet with dismay.

"It has taken me ages to work up the courage to speak with E., but Sophy and I concocted a plan," he continued. "I was a missing person for so much of my sister's story. I want to understand it all, and Sophy gave me an idea of something I might do to that end. You see, Sophy and Vyerin, who happens to be the brother of E.'s partner – the two of them once found E. and Henerey's letters, and—"

He summarised a fairly dull tale that mostly involved people reading letters and then discussing their feelings about said letters – I do not need to repeat it here! What matters is that Arvist Cidnan, in conjunction with Sophy Cidnorghe, wanted nothing more than to read everything else E. wrote that was not already part of Sophy and Vyerin's archive. He intended to hire me simply to organise all the

362

relevant documents Sophy and Vyerin already possessed, but I promised him we could do much better. I would not rest until I uncovered every last scrap of paper that could provide him with information about the parts of E.'s life he missed, especially during her time in your city. At present, I expect Cidnan has set himself to studying his copies of the very documents you and I have shared. I do not know when he will meet with his sister, nor how she will react – since she is one of the few people in this whole affair whom I never met – but I would like to think that his knowledge of her experiences will help them feel closer than ever.

Still, what do I care? I was paid, after all. (See previous note about great numbers of artificial whales and so forth.)

Does that answer your question? (There, see – since I have now written a question, you'll have to respond at least once more, won't you?)

L.

AUTOMATED POST MISSIVE FROM THE THIRTIETH SECOND SCHOLAR TO LADY CORALEAN, 1005

Dear L.,

Your letter makes something abundantly apparent to me – you've done a meaningful service for the Cidnosin and Clel families, even if you *were* compensated for your actions. I cannot help but admire that.

On that note, considering all you've said, I have something for you. Or, rather, a gift for your employer. Namely, a document relating to E. Cidnosin and Henerey Clel that I did not even keep in that box you purloined. (The document was one of the first written by Ambassador Mawr in his position, so new storage protocol had to be established.)

I could simply send this gift to you. I thought it would be far more interesting, however, if I visited you. It will be my first time travelling to your world, and I am nothing if not nervous. If you are not interested in hosting me, I am happy to pass you in the street, with the document tucked inside a small pocket on the underside of my cloak, and wait for you to seize it surreptitiously.

AUTOMATED POST MISSIVE FROM LADY CORALEAN TO THE THIRTIETH SECOND SCHOLAR, 1005

I accept! While it would be delightful to make such an exchange incognito, I think that is not necessary. Simply wear that cloak and pay attention to any distracting birds (for we do indeed have them *here*) as I make you supper (if you like), and you may find yourself relieved of your gift rather sooner than later. Nothing would make me more delighted than meeting you again.

That is, delighted for the sake of gaining closure for my employer, naturally! (Perhaps he shall throw in a bonus sum! And, if he does, I ought to expand my vessel investments and purchase something more sophisticated, like an artificial porpoise . . .)

Until soon,

L.

REPORT FROM THE VIEWING-POINT BY AMBASSADOR TEVN WINIVER MAWR, 1004

By my Oaths as a Scholar and as part of my duties as the Ambassador, I certify that the following report summarises that which I observed from what my friend calls her "Viewing-Point" of a most curious island.

The seas around this island are riotous. At the house, the wind persists in opening and shutting the oddly shaped windows. They rattle and dazzle, sending radiant reflections onto the path that leads through the land-bound kelp forest and down to the water.

The storm pauses as a figure drops into the ocean.

I could end my report here, concluding that the crossing proved successful, but something keeps me at my post. They say I must record everything, and I shall, to the best of my ability. This particular figure's life has been documented more than most – according to what I've heard, anyway – so I hope he will not mind.

The man swims a few hasty strokes before a wave flings him ashore like a seashell. He sits for a moment, gasping, his beard plastered against his cheeks and his hands shaking.

Then he delicately de-rumples his waterlogged cloak and collar, fishes his lost walking stick out of the receding tide, and smiles. It is an objectively remarkable smile.

He strides with purpose across the anomalous island. He does not stop for anything, though his eyes flicker here and there – taking notes, perhaps, of all the extraordinary things he wishes to examine further in the future. Nothing can frighten or frustrate him. When he makes a few false turns into impassable kelp thickets, he simply rotates and walks in a new direction.

It does not take him overlong to find the house. It appears shuttered and dark from the outside – the wind having decided at last that the windows should indeed be closed.

The island glows around the man, turning him alternately gold and pink and pale green. He identifies the entrance, slides a letter beneath the door, and leans against the wall with eyes alight to await a reply.

When the door opens, the response is not in the form of a letter – nor, I imagine, could it ever be adequately expressed in one.

Acknowledgements

Dear readers,

The main thing I ought to acknowledge is that I am indisputably *the worst* at acknowledgements. When I wrote my acknowledgements for *A Letter to the Luminous Deep*, I was intent upon perfection. I wanted to thank *everyone*, and thank them well, and, above all, avoid using the word "thank" too many times. (Seriously, go back and reread it, and observe the measures I took to avoid repetition and satisfy my brain!) Then I started panicking about accidentally excluding someone, and the panic turned into an obsession, and that obsession led to endless text-checking and research, and—

So, anyway, I'm going to try something different this time. Maybe I'll even allow myself to say the same words more than once. Will this be more heartfelt and less formal, or will I revert to my old ways in another sentence or two? I suppose you'll find out!

I would like to thank (thank!) the following people:

- Nadia Saward and Angelica Chong, who are the dream combination of editors
- Ellen Wright and Nazia Khatun, who are exceptionally accommodating of the challenges I face when participating in events
- Every member of the Orbit UK and US teams who has contributed to the publication of this series over the years!

- Raxenne Maniquiz, who illustrated the cover, and Charlotte Stroomer, who designed it: it's the perfect complement to the first book, and utterly fascinating in its own right
- Natasha Mihell, my agent, who continues to be immensely encouraging, unfailingly positive, and capable of doing all sorts of agent-y things that I find impossible myself
- My fellow authors, who have been very friendly and welcoming to me – whether we met at the rare event I've attended or exchanged letter-like correspondence over email
- The many independent booksellers around the U.S. who promoted *A Letter to the Luminous Deep* after it was selected as an Indies Introduce title!
- Emily Dickinson, in whose tribute I peppered Book 1 with one Dickinson family reference after another (perhaps, I think, to distract from the fact that the story was actually about my own mental illness), and who helped me better understand myself as a disabled person and a writer
- My long-standing friend N., who very kindly reviewed about half of this book before our writing calls were interrupted by my first year of parenthood (I'm glad we're back at it!)
- My toddler, who blinked knowingly as I read aloud early drafts during the newborn period
- My mother and father, who, respectively, nurtured my love of the ocean and sci-fi/fantasy
- My sister, who was the co-creator of many childhood games that shaped me as a storyteller
- (Hey, did you notice how many lines above begin with the word "my"? Progress!)
- The astronomer I saw at a shopping mall science presentation circa 2002, who inspired great childhood existential dread by first introducing the concept I would later come to know as the "Great Filter" (a major source of inspiration for the Predator)
- J., my beloved, to whom both books in the Sunken Archive are

dedicated and for whom I write all my stories (and fill them with occasional nods to certain lawyer video games)

- Everyone who has read the Sunken Archive, obviously! I find one-on-one conversation deeply perplexing (despite years of study and analysis), so let me thank you here instead

With more gratitude than I could hope to express in this ill-formed section,

Sylvie Cathrall

About the Author

Sylvie Cathrall is the author of the Sunken Archive duology and, now, a "duology" of questionable About the Author paragraphs. She lives in Wales with her spouse (formerly her pen pal) and their child (currently an inquisitive toddler).

Find out more about Sylvie Cathrall and other Orbit authors by registering for the free monthly newsletter at orbit-books.co.uk.